SUDS IN SPACE!

Herr Syrup gulped. The transition to weightlessness was an outrage, and the stars ramping around his field of view didn't help matters. His stomach lurched. Sarmishkidu groaned, hung onto the pretzel box with all six tentacles, and covered his eyes with his ears. Claus screamed, turning end for end in midair, and tried without success to fly. Herr Syrup reached for a control lever but didn't quite make it. Sarmishkidu uncovered one sick eye long enough to mumble: "Bloody blank blasted Coriolis force." Herr Syrup clenched his teeth, caught a mouthful of mustache, grimaced, spat it out, and tried again. This time he laid hands on the switch and pulled.

A cloud of beer gushed frostily from one of the transverse pipes. . . .

—from "A Bicycle Built for Brew"

Plus eight more classic tales by the bestselling author of *The Boat of a Million Years*.

"Vat kind of a landing do you call dat? I svear de beer is so shook up it explodes! By yumping Yudas—"

"Sacre bleu!" added Claus, fluttering about on ragged black wings. "*Teufelschwantzen und Schwefel!* Damn, blast, fap!"

"Now, now, Mr. Syrup," said Captain Radhakrishnan soothingly. "Now, now, now. After all, my dear fellow, I don't wish to make, ah, invidious comparisons, but the behavior of the internal field was scarcely what—what I would expect? Yes. What I would expect. In fact, the cook has just reported himself ill with, ah, what I believe is the first case of seasickness recorded in astronautical history."

Herr Syrup, who had dropped and broken a favorite pipe, was in no mood to accept criticism. He barked an order to Mr. Shubbish, to rip the guts out of the compensator in lieu of its manufacturer, and stormed up the companionway and along clangorous passages to the bridge, where he pushed open the door so it crashed and blew in like a profane whirlwind.

"My dear old chap!" exclaimed the captain. "I say! Please! What will they think?"

"Vat vill obscenity who blankety-blank t'ink?"

"The portmaster and, ah, the other gentleman—there." Radhakrishnan pointed at the main viewport and made agitated adjustments to his turban and jacket. "Most irregular. I don't understand it. But he insisted we remain inboard until— Dear, dear, *do* you think you could get some of the tarnish off this braid of mine before—"

Knud Axel Syrup stared at the outside view. Beyond the little spacefield was a charming vista of green meadows, orderly hedgerows, cottages and bowers, a white gravel road. Just below the near, sharply curving horizon stood Grendel's only town; from this height could be seen a few roofs and the twin spires of St. George's. The flag of the Kingdom, a Union Jack on a Royal Stuart field, fluttered there under a sky of darker blue than Earth's, a small remote sun, and a few of the brightest stars. Grendel was a typical right little, tight little Anglian asteroid, peacefully readying for the vacation-season influx of tourists from Briarton, York, Scotia, Holm, New Winchester, and other shires.

Or was it? For the flagstaff over the spaceport carried an alien banner, white, with a shamrock and harp in green. The two men striding over the concrete toward the ship wore clover-colored tunics and trousers, military boots, and side-arms. Similarly uniformed men paced along the wire fence or waited by machine gun nests. Not far away was berthed a space freighter, almost as old and battered as the *Girl* but considerably larger. And—and—

"Pest og forbandelse!" exclaimed Herr Syrup.

"What?" Captain Radhakrishnan swiveled worried eyes toward him.

"Plague and damnation," translated the engineer courteously.

"Eh? Where?"

"Over dere." Herr Syrup pointed. "Dat odder ship. Don't you see? Dere is a gun turret coupled onto her!"

"Well—I'll be—goodness gracious," murmured the captain.

Steps clanging on metal and a hearty roar drifted up to the bridge, together with a whiff of cool country air. In a few moments the large redhead entered the bridge. Behind him trailed a very tall, very thin, and very grim-looking middle-aged man.

"The top of the mornin' to yez," boomed the young one. He attempted a salute. "Major Rory McConnell of the Shamrock League Irredentist Expeditionary Force, *at* your ser-r-r-vice!"

"What?" exclaimed Radhakrishnan. He gaped and lifted his hands. "I mean—I mean to say, don't y' know, what? Has a war broken out? Or has it? Mean to say, y' know," he babbled, "we've had no such information, but then we've been en route for some weeks and—"

"Well, no." Major Rory McConnell shoved back his disreputable cap with a faint air of embarrassment. "No, your honor, 'tis not exactly a war we're havin'. More an act of justice."

The thin, razor-creased man shoved his long nose forward. "Perhaps I should explain," he clipped, "bein' as I am in command here. 'Tis indeed an act of necessary an' righteous justice we are performin', after what the spalpeens did to us forty years agone come St. Matthew's Day." His dark eyes glowed fanatically. "The fact is, in order to assert the rightful claims of the Erse nation ag'inst the unprovoked an' shameless aggression of the—pardon me language—English of the Anglian Kingdom—the fact is, this asteroid is now under military occupation." He clicked his heels and bowed. "Permit me to introduce meself. General Scourge-of-the-Sassenach O'Toole, of the Shamrock League Irredentist—"

"*Ja, ja,*" said Herr Syrup. He still carried a cargo of anger to unload on someone. "I heard all dat. I also heard dat de Shamrock League is only a political party in de Erse Cluster."

Scourge-of-the-Sassenach O'Toole winced. "Please. *Saorstat Erseann.*"

"So vat you ban doin' vit' a private filibustering expedition, ha? And vat has it got to do vit' us?"

"Well," said Major Rory McConnell, not quite at ease, "the fact is, your honors, I'm sorry to be sayin' it, but ye can't leave here just the now."

"What?" cried Captain Radhakrishnan. "Can't leave? What do you mean, sir?" He drew himself up to his full 1.6 meters. "This is a Venusian ship, may I remind you, of Terrestrial registry, and engaged on its—er, ahem—its lawful occasions. Yes, that's it, its lawful occasions. You can't detain us!"

McConnell slapped his sidearm with a meaty hand. "Can't we?" he asked, brightening.

"But—look here—see here, my dear chap, we're on schedule. We're expected at Alamo, don't y' know, and if we don't report in—"

"Yes. There is that. 'Tis been anticipated." General

O'Toole squinted at them. Suddenly he pointed a bony finger at the engineer. "Yez! What might your name be?"

"I ban Knud Axel Syrup of Simmerboelle, Langeland," said the engineer indignantly, "and I am going to get in touch vit' de Danish consul at—"

"Mister *who*?" interrupted McConnell.

"Syrup!" It is a perfectly good Danish name, though like Middelfart it is liable to misinterpretation by foreigners. "I vill call my consulate on New Vinshester, *ja*, by Yudas, I vill even call de vun on Tara in Erse—"

"Teamhair," corrected O'Toole, wincing again.

"You see," said Radhakrishnan, anxiously fingering his monocle, "our cargo to Alamo carries a stiff penalty clause, and if we're held up here any length of time, then—"

"Quiet!" barked O'Toole. His finger stabbed toward the Earthmen. "So 'twas Venus ye were on last, eh? Well, as military commandant of this occupied asteroid, I hereby appoints meself medical officer an' I suspect ye of carryin' Polka Dot Plague."

"Polka Dot!" bellowed Herr Syrup. A red flush went up from his hairy chest till his scalp gleamed like a landing light. "Vy, you spoutnosed son of a Svedish politician, dere hasn't been a case of Polka Dot in all de Imperium for tventy-five Eart' years!"

"Possibly," snapped O'Toole. "However, under international law the medical officer of any port has a right an' duty to hold any vessel in quarantine whin he suspects a dangerous disease aboard. I suspects Polka Dot Plague, an' this whole asteroid is hereby officially quarantined."

"But!" wailed Radhakrishnan.

"I think six weeks will be long enough," said O'Toole more gently. "Meanwhile ye'll be free to move about an'—"

"Six weeks here will ruin us!"

"Sorry, sir," answered McConnell. He beamed. "But take heart, ye're bein' ruined in a good cause: redressin' the wrongs of the Gaelic race!"

Chapter 2

Fuming away on a pipe which would have been banned under any smog-control ordinance, Knud Axel Syrup bicycled into Grendel Town. He ignored the charm of thatch and tile roofs, half-timbered Tudor facades, and swinging signboards. Those were for tourists, anyway; Grendel lived mostly off the vacation trade. But it did not escape him how quiet the place was, its usual cheerful pre-season bustle dwindled to a tight-lipped housewife at the greengrocer's and a bitterly silent dart game in the Crown & Castle.

Occasionally a party of armed Erse, or a truck bearing the shamrock sign, went down the street. The occupying force seemed composed largely of very young men, and it was not professional. The uniforms were homemade, the arms a wild assortment from grouse guns up through stolen rocket launchers, the officers were saluted when a man happened to feel like saluting, and the idea that it might be a nice gesture to march in step had never occurred to anyone.

Nevertheless, there were something like a thousand invaders on Grendel, and their noisy, grinning, well-meaning sloppiness did not hide the fact that they could be tough to fight.

Herr Syrup stopped at the official bulletin board in the market square. Brushing aside ivy leaves, the announcement of a garden party at the vicarage three months ago, and a yellowing placard wherein the Lord Mayor of Grendel invited bids for the construction of a fen country near the Heorot Hills, he found the notice he was looking for. It was gaudily hand-lettered in blue and green poster paints and said:

> Know all men by these presents, that forty Earth-years ago, when the planetoid clusters of Saorstat Erseann and the Anglian Kingdom were last approaching conjunction, the asteroid called Lois by the Anglians but rightfully known to its Erse discoverer Michael Boyne as Laoighise (pronounced Lois) chanced to drift between the two nations on its own skewed orbit. An

Anglian prospecting expedition landed, discovered rich beds of praseodymium, and claimed the asteroid in the name of King James IV. The Erse Republic protested this illegal seizure and sent a warship to remove the Anglian squatters, only to find that King James IV had caused two warships to be sent; accordingly, despite this severe provocation, the peace-loving Erse Republic withdrew its vessel. The aforesaid squatters installed a powerful gyrogravitic unit on Laoighise and diverted its orbit into union with the other planetoids of the Anglian Cluster. Since then Anglia has remained in occupation and exploitation.

The Erse Republic has formally protested to the World Court, on the clear grounds that Michael Boyne, an Erse citizen, was the first man to land on this body. The feeble Anglian argument that Boyne did not actually claim it for his nation and made no effort to ascertain its possible value, cannot be admissible to any right-thinking man; but for forty Earth-years the World Court, obviously corrupted by Stuart gold, has upheld this specious contention.

Now that the Erse and Anglian nations are again orbiting close toward each other, the Shamrock League Irredentist Expeditionary Force has set about rectifying the situation. This is a patriotic organization which, though it does not have the backing of its own government at the moment, expects that this approval will be forthcoming and retroactive as soon as our sacred mission has succeeded. Therefore, the Shamrock League Irredentist Expeditionary Force is not piratical, but operating under international laws of war, and the Geneva Convention applies. As a first step in the recovery of Laoighise, the Shamrock League Irredentist Expeditionary Force finds it necessary to occupy the asteroid Grendel.

All citizens are therefore enjoined to cooperate with the occupying authorities. The personal and property rights of civilians will be respected provided they refrain from interference with the lawfully constituted authorities, namely ourselves. All arms and communications equipment must be surrendered for sequestration. Any attempt to leave Grendel or communicate beyond its atmosphere is forbidden and punishable under the rules of war. All citizens are reminded again that the Shamrock League Irredentist Expeditionary Force is here for a legitimate purpose which is to be respected.

Erin go bragh!

General Scourge-of-the-Sassenach O'Toole
Commanding Officer, S.L.I.E.F.
per: Sgt. 1/cl Daniel O'Flaherty
(New Connaught O'Flahertys)

"Ah," said Herr Syrup. "So."

He pedaled glumly on his way. These people seemed to mean business.

Though he sometimes lost his temper, Knud Axel Syrup was not a violent man. He had seen his share of broken knuckles, from St. Pauli to Hellport to Jove Dock; he much preferred a mug of beer and a friendly round of pinochle. The harbor girls could expect no more from him than a fatherly smile and a not quite fatherly pat; he had his Inga back in Simmerboelle. She was a good wife, aside from her curious idea that he would instantly fall a prey to pneumonia without an itchy scarf around his neck. Her disapproval of the myriad little nations which had sprung up throughout the Solar System since gyrogravitics made terraforming possible was more vocal than his; but, in a mild and tolerant way, he shared it. Home's best.

Nevertheless, a man had some right to be angry. For instance, when a peso-pinching flock of Venusian owners, undoubtedly with more scales on their hearts than even their backs, made him struggle along with a spinor that should have been scrapped five years ago. But what, he asked himself, is a man to do? There were few berths available for the aging crew of an aging ship, without experience in the latest and sleekest apparatus. If the *Mercury Girl* went on the beach, so, mostly likely, did Knud Axel Syrup. Of course, there would be a nice social worker knocking at his home to offer a nice Earthside job—say, the one who had already mentioned a third assistantship in a food-yeast factory—and Inga would make sure he wore his nice scarf every day. Herr Syrup shuddered and pushed his bicycle harder.

At the end of Flodden Field Street he found the tavern he was looking for. Grendel did not try exclusively for an Old Tea Shoppe atmosphere. The Alt Heidelberg Rathskeller stood between the Osmanli Pilaff and Pizen Pete's Last Chance Saloon. Herr Syrup leaned his bicycle against the wall and pushed through an oak door carved with the image of legendary Gambrinus.

The room downstairs was appropriately long, low, and smoky-raftered. Rough-hewn tables and benches filled a candle-lit gloom; great beer barrels lined the walls; sabers hung crossed above rows of steins which informed the world that *Gutes Bier und junge Weiber sind die besten Zeitvertreiber*. But it was empty. Even for midafternoon, there was something ominous about the silence. The Stuart legitimists who settled the Anglian Cluster had never adopted the closing laws of the mother country.

Herr Syrup planted his stocky legs and stared around. "Hallo!" he called. "Hallo, dere! Is you home, Herr Bachmann?"

It slithered in the darkness behind the counter. A Martian came out. He stood fairly tall for a Martian, his hairless gray cupola of a head-cum-torso reaching past the Earthman's waist, and his four thick walking tentacles carried him across the floor with a speed unusual for his race in Terrestrial gravity. His two arm-tentacles writhed incoherently, his flat nose twitched under the immense brow, his wide lipless mouth made bubbling sounds, his bulging eyes rolled in distress of soul. As he came near, Herr Syrup saw that he had somehow poured himself into an embroidered blouse and *Lederhosen.* A Tyrolean hat perched precariously on top of him.

"Ach!" he piped. *"Wer da? Wilkommen, mein* dear friend, *sitzen* here and—"

"Gud bevare's," said the engineer, catching his pipe as it fell from his jaws, "vat's going on here? Vere is old Hans Bachmann?"

"*Ach,* he has retired," said the Martian. "I have taken over der business. Pardon me, I mean I have der business overgetaken." He stopped in front of his guest, extending three boneless fingers. "My name is Sarmishkidu. I mean, Sarmishkidu von Himmelschmidt. Sit down, make yourself *gemütlich.*"

"Vell, I am Knud Axel Syrup of de *Mercury Girl.*"

"Ah, the ship what is bringing me mine beer? Or was? Well, have a drink." The Martian scuttled off, drew two steinsful, came back and writhed himself onto the bench across the table at which the Earthman had sat down. *"Prosit."*

A Martian standing anyone a beer was about the most astonishing event of this day. But it was plain to see that Sarmishkidu von Himmelschmidt was not himself. His skin twitched as he filled a Tyrolean pipe, and he fanned himself with his elephantine ears.

"How did you happen to enter dis business?" asked Herr Syrup, trying to put him more at ease.

"Ach! I came here last Uttu-year—Mars-year—on sabbatical. I am a professor of mathematics at Enliluraluma University." Since every citizen of Enliluraluma has some kind of position at the University, usually in the math department, Herr Syrup was not much impressed. "At that time this enterprise was most lucrative. Extrapolating probabilistically, I induced myself to accept Herr Bachmann's offer of a transfer of title. I invested all my own savings and obtained a mortgage on Uttu for the balance—"

"Oh, oh," said Herr Syrup, sympathetically, for not even the owners of the Black Sphere Line could be as ruthless as any and all Martian bankers. They positively enjoyed foreclosing. They made a ceremony of it, at which dancing clerks strewed cancelled checks while a chorus of vice presidents sang a litany. "And now business is not so good, vat?"

"Business is virtually at asymptotic zero," mourned Sarmishkidu. "The occupation, you know. We are cut off from the rest of the universe. And vacation season coming in two weeks! The Erse do not plan to leave for six weeks yet, at a minimum—and meanwhile this entire planetoid will have been diverted into a new orbit off the regular trade lanes—possibly ruined in the fighting around Lois. In view of all this uncertainty, even local trade has slacked off to negligibility. *Ach, es ist ganz schrecklich!* I am ruined!"

"But if I remember right," said Herr Syrup, bewildered, "New Vinshester, de Anglian capital, is only about ten t'ousand kilometers from here. Vy do dey not send a varship?"

"They are not aware of it," said Sarmishkidu, burying his flat face in the tankard. "Excuse me, I mean they do not know what fumblydiddles is here going on. Before vacation time, we never get many ships here. Der Erses landed just four days ago. They took ofer *der Rundfunk*, the radio, and handled routine messages as if nothing had happened. Your ship was the first since der invasion."

"And may be de last," gloomed Herr Syrup. "Dey made some qvack-qvack about plague and qvarantined us."

"Ach, so!" Sarmishkidu passed a dramatic hand over his eyeballs. "Den ve iss ruined for certain. Dot iss just the excuse the Erses have been wanting. Now they can call New Winchester, making like they was der real medical officer, and say the whole place is quarantined on suspicion of plague. So natural, no one else vill land for six weeks, so they not be quarantined too and maybe even get sick. Your owners is also notified and does not try to investigate what has to you happened. So for six weeks the Erses has a free hand here to do what they want. Und what they want to do means the ruin of all Grendel!"

"My captain is still arguing vit' de Erse general," said

Herr Syrup. "I am yust de engineer. But I come down to see if I could save us anyt'ing. Even if ve lose money because of not delivering our cargo to Alamo, maybe at least ve get paid for de beer ve bring you. No?"

"*Gott in Himmel!* Without vacation season business like I was counting on, where vould I find the moneys to pay you?"

"I vas afraid of dat," said Herr Syrup.

He sat drinking and smoking and trying to persuade himself that an Earthside job as assistant in a yeast factory wasn't really so bad. Himself told him what a liar he was.

The door opened, letting in a shaft of sun, and light quick steps were heard. A feminine voice cried: "Rejoice!"

Herr Syrup rose clumsily. The girl coming down the stairs was worth rising for, being young and slim, with a shining helmet of golden hair, large blue eyes, pert nose, long legs, and other well-formed accessories. Her looks were done no harm by the fact that—while she avoided cosmetics—she wore a short white tunic, sandals, a laurel wreath on her head, and nothing else.

"Rejoice!" she cried again, and burst into tears.

"Now, now," said Herr Syrup anxiously. "Now, now, *Froeken* . . . er, Miss—now, now, now, yust a minute."

The Martian had already gone over to her. "That is *nicht* so bad, Emily," he whistled, standing on tiptentacle to pat her shoulder. "There, there. Remember Epicurus."

"I don't care about Epicurus!" sobbed the girl, burying her face in her hands.

"Outis epoisei soi bareias cheiras," said Sarmishkidu bravely.

"Well," wept the girl, "w-well, of course. At least, I hope so." She dabbed at her eyes with a laurel leaf. "I'm sorry. It's just that—that—oh, everything."

"Yes," said the Martian, "the situation indubitably falls within the Aristotelian definition of tragedy. I have calculated my losses so far at a net fifty pounds sterling, four shillings and thruppence ha'penny per diem."

Wet, but beautiful, the girl blinked at Herr Syrup. "Pardon

me, sir,'' she said tremulously. ''This situation on Grendel, you know. It's so overwreaking.'' She put her finger to her lips and frowned. ''Is that the word? These barbarian languages! I mean, the situation has us all overwrought.''

''Ahem!'' said Sarmishkidu. ''Miss Emily Croft, may I present Mister, er—''

''Syrup,'' said Herr Syrup, and extended a somewhat engine-grimy hand.

''Rejoice,'' said the girl politely. *''Hellenicheis?''*

''Gesundheit,'' said Herr Syrup.

Miss Emily Croft stared, then sighed. ''I asked if you spoke Attic Greek,'' she said.

''No, I'm sorry, I do not even speak basement Greek,'' floundered Herr Syrup.

''You see,'' said Miss Croft, ''I am a Duncanite—even if it does make Father furious. He's the vicar, you know—and I'm the only Duncanite on Grendel. Mr. Sarmishkidu—I'm sorry, I mean Herr von Himmelschmidt—speaks Greek with me, which does help, even though I cannot always approve his choice of passages for quotation.'' She blushed.

''Since ven has a Martian been talking Greek?'' asked the engineer, trying to get some toehold on reality.

''I found a knowledge of the Greek alphabet essential to my study of Terrestrial mathematical treatises,'' explained Sarmishkidu, ''and having gone so far, I proceeded to learn the vocabulary and grammar as well. After all, time is money, I estimate my time as being conservatively worth five pounds an hour, and so by using knowledge already acquired for one purpose as the first step in gaining knowledge of another field, I saved study time worth almost—''

''But I'm afraid Herr von Himmelschmidt is not a follower of the doctrines of the Neo-Classical Enlightenment,'' interrupted Emily Croft. ''I mean, as first expounded by Isadora and Raymond Duncan. I regret to say that Herr von Himmelschmidt is only interested in the, er,'' she blushed again, charmingly, ''less laudable passages out of Aristophanes.''

"They are *filthy*," murmured Sarmishkidu with a reminiscent leer.

"And, I mean, please don't think I have any race prejudices or anything," went on the girl, "but it's just undeniable that Herr von Himmelschmidt isn't, well, isn't meant for classical dancing."

"No," agreed Herr Syrup after a careful study. "No, he is not."

Emily cocked her head at him. "I don't suppose you would be interested?" Her tone was wistful.

Herr Syrup rubbed his bald pate, blew out his drooping mustache, and looked down past his paunch at his Number Twelve boots. "Is classical dancing done barefoot?" he asked.

"Yes! And vine crowned, in the dew at dawn!"

"I vas afraid of dat," sighed Herr Syrup. "No, t'anks."

"Well," said the girl. Her head bent a little.

"But I am not so bad at de hambo," offered Herr Syrup.

"No, thank you," said Miss Croft.

"Vill you not sit down and have a beer vit' us?"

"Zeus, no!" She grimaced. "How could you? I mean, that awful stuff just calcifies the liver."

"Miss Croft drinken only der pure spring vater und eaten der fruits," said Sarmishkidu von Himmelschmidt rather grimly.

"Well, but really, Mister Syrup," said the girl, "it's ever so much more natural than, oh, all this raw meat and—well, I mean if we had no other reason to know it, couldn't you just tell the Erse are barbarians from that dreadful stuff they drink, and all the bacon and floury potatoes and— Well, I mean to say, really."

Herr Syrup sat down by his stein, unconvinced. Emily perched herself on the table top and accepted a few grapes from a bowl of same which Sarmishkidu handed her in a gingerly fashion. The Martian then scuttled back to his own beer and pipe and a dish of pretzels.

"Do you know yust vat dese crazy Ersers is intending to do, anyhow?" asked Herr Syrup.

The girl clouded up again. "That's what I came to see you about, Mr. Sarmishkidu," she said. Her pleasant lower lip quivered. "That terrible Major McConnell! The big noisy red one. I mean, he keeps speaking to me!"

"I am afraid," began the Martian, "that it is not in my province to—"

"Oh, but I mean, he stopped me in the street just now! He, he bowed and—and asked me to—Oh, no!" Emily buried her face in her hands trembling.

"To vat?" barked Herr Syrup, full of chivalrous indignation.

"He asked me . . . if . . . I would . . . oh . . . would *go to the cinema* with him!"

"Vy, vat is playing?" asked Herr Syrup, interested.

"How should I know? It certainly isn't Aeschylus. It isn't even Euripides!" Emily raised a flushed small countenance and shifted gears to wrath. "I thought, Mr. Sarmishkidu, I mean, we've been friends for a while now and we Greeks have to stick together and all that sort of thing, couldn't you just refuse to sell him whisky? I mean, it would teach those barbarians a lesson, and it might even make them go home again, if they couldn't buy whisky, and Major McConnell wouldn't get a calcified liver."

"Speak of the divvil!" bawled a hearty voice. Huge military boots crashed on the stairs and Major Rory McConnell, all 200 redhaired centimeters of him, stalked down into the rathskeller. "Pour me a drop of cheer, boy. No, set out the bottle an' we'll figure the score whin I'm done. For 'tis happy this day has become!"

"Don't!" blazed Emily, leaping to her feet.

"*Aber, aber* that whisky I sell at four bob the shot," said Sarmishkidu, slithering hastily off his bench.

Major McConnell made a gallant flourish toward the girl. "To be sure," he roared, "there's no such thing as an unhappy day wi' this colleen about. Surely the good God was in a rare mood whin she was borned, perhaps His favorite littlest angel had just won the spellin' prize, for faith an' I nivver seen a sweeter bundle of charms, not even on the Auld Sod herself whin I made me pilgrimage."

"Do you see what happens to people who, who eat meat and drink distilled beverages?" said Emily to Herr Syrup. "They just turn into absolute oafs. I mean to say, you can hear their great feet stamping two kilometers off."

McConnell sprawled onto a bench, leaning against the table and resting his great feet on the floor at the end of prodigious legs. He winked at the Earthman. "She's the light darlin' on her toes," he agreed, "but then she's not just overburdened wi' clothing. Whin I make her me missus, that'll have to be changed a bit, but for now 'tis pleasant the sight is."

"Your wife?" screamed Emily. "Why—why—" She fought valiantly with herself. At last, in a prim tone: "I won't say anything, Major McConnell, but you will find my reply in Aristophanes, *The Frogs*, lines—"

"Here the bottle is," said Sarmishkidu, returning with a flask labelled *Callahan's Rose of Tralee* 125 *Proof*. "Und mind you," he added, rolling a suspicious doorknob eye at the Erseman, "when it comes to paying the score, we will make with the analytical balances to show how much you have getaken."

"So be it." McConnell yanked out the stopper and raised the bottle. "To the Glory of God and the Honor of Ireland!" He caught Herr Syrup's eye and added politely: *"Skaal."*

The Dane lifted a grudging stein to him.

" 'Tis the fine day for celebratin'," burbled McConnell. "I've had the word from the engineering corps; our new droive unit tests out one hundred percent. They'll have it ready to go in three weeks."

"Oh!" gasped Emily. She retreated into a dark corner behind a beer keg. Even Sarmishkidu began to look seriously worried.

"Vat ban all dis monkeyshining anyvay?" demanded Herr Syrup.

"Why, 'tis simple enough, 'tis," said the major. "Ye're well aware the rare earth praseodymium has high value, since 'tis of critical importance to a geegee engine. Now the asteroid—"

"*Ja*, I have read de proclamation. But vy did you have to land here at all? If Erse vants Lois, vy not attack Lois like honest men and not bodder my poor spaceship?"

McConnell frowned. " 'Tis that would be the manly deed," he admitted. "Yit the opposition party, the Gaelic Socialists, may their cowardly souls fry in hell, happen to be in power at home, an' they won't sind the fleet ag'inst Laoighise; for the Anglians have placed heavy guard on it, in case of just such a frontal assault, an' that base act of aggression holds our Republic in check, for it shall never be said we were the first to start a war."

He tilted the flask to his lips again and embarked on a lengthy harangue. Herr Syrup extracted from this that the Shamrock League, the other important political party in the Erse Cluster, favored a more vigorous foreign policy: though its chiefs would not also have agreed to an open battle with the Anglian Navy. However, Scourge-of-the-Sassenach O'Toole was an extremist politician even for the League. He gathered men, weapons, and equipment, and set out unbeknownst to all on his own venture. His idea was first to occupy Grendel. This had been done without opposition; armed authority here consisted of one elderly constable with a truncheon. Of course, it was vital to keep the occupation unknown to the rest of the universe, since the Shamrock League Irredentist Expeditionary Force could not hope to fight off even a single gunboat sent from any regular fleet. The arrival of the *Mercury Girl*, and the chance thus presented to announce a quarantine, was being celebrated up and down the inns of Grendel as unquestionably due to the personal intervention of good St. Patrick.

As for the longer-range scheme—oh, yes, the plan. Well,

like most terraformed asteroids, Grendel had only a minimal gyrogravitic unit, powerful enough to give it a 24-hour rotational period (originally the little world had spun around once in three hours, which played the very devil with tea time) and an atmosphere-retaining surface field of 980 cm./sec.^{2}. Maintaining that much attraction, warming up the iron mass enough to compensate for the sun's remoteness, and supplying electricity to the colonists, was as much as the Grendelian atomic-energy plant could do.

O'Toole's boys had brought along a geegee of awesome dimensions. Installed at the center of mass and set to repulsor-beam, this one would be able to move the entire planetoid from its orbit.

"Move it ag'inst Laoighise!" cried McConnell. "An' we've heavy artillery mounted, too. Ah, what think ye of that, me boy? How long do ye think the Anglian Navy will stand up ag'inst a warcraft of this size? Eh? Ha, ha! Drink to the successful defense of Gaelic rights ag'inst wanton an' unprovoked aggression!"

"I t'ink maybe de Anglian Navy vait yust long enough to shoot two, t'ree atomic shells at you and den land de marines," said Herr Syrup dubiously.

"Shell their own people livin' here?" answered McConnell. "No, even the Sassenach are not that grisly. There'll not be a thing they can do but retire from the scene in all their ignominy. An' faith, whin we return home wi' poor auld lost Laoighise an' put her into her rightful orbit with the ither Erse Cluster worlds—"

"I t'ought her orbit vas orig'inally not de same as eider vun of your nations."

"Exactly, sir. For the first time since the Creation, Laoighise will be sailin' where the Creator intended. Well, then, all Erse will rise to support us, the craven Gaelic Socialist cabinet will fall an' the tide of victory sweep the Shamrock League to its proper place of government an' your humble servant to the Ministry of Astronautics, which same portfolio Premier-to-be O'Toole has promised me for me help. An' then ye'll see Erse argosies plyin' the deeps of space as never before in history—an' me the skipper of the half of 'em!"

"Gud bevare's," said Herr Syrup.

McConnell rose with a bearlike bow at Emily, who had recovered enough composure to return into sight. "Of course, Grendel will thin be returned to Anglia," he said. "But her one finest treasure she'll not bring home, a Stuart rose plucked to brighten a field of shamrocks."

The girl lifted a brow and said coldly: "Do I understand, Major, that you wish to keep me forever as a shield against the Anglian Navy?"

McConnell flushed. " 'Tis the necessity of so usin' your people that hurts every true Erse soul," he said, "an' be sure if it were not certain that no harm could come to the civilians here, we'd never have embarked on the adventure." He brightened. "An' faith, is it not well we did, since it has given me the sight of your sweet face?"

Emily turned her back and stamped one little foot.

"Also your sweet legs," continued McConnell blandly, "an' your sweet—er—Drink, Mister Syrup, drink up wi' me to the rightin' of wrongs an' the succorin' of the distressed!"

"Like me," mumbled the engineer.

The girl whirled about. "But people will be hurt!" she cried. "Don't you understand? I've tried and tried to explain to you, my father's tried, everyone on Grendel has and none of you will listen! It's been forty years since our nations were last close enough together to have much contact. I mean, you just don't know how the situation has changed in Anglia. You think you can steal Lois, and our government will swallow a *fait accompli* rather than start a war—the way yours did when we first took it. But ours won't! Old King James died ten years ago. King Charles is a young man—a fire-eater—and the P.M. claims descent from Sir Winston Churchill—they won't accept it! I mean to say, your government will either have to repudiate you and give Lois back, or there'll be an interplanetary war!"

"I think not, *acushla*, I think not," said McConnell. "Ye mustn't trouble your pretty head about these things."

"I t'ink maybe she ban right," said Herr Syrup. "I ban in Anglia often times."

"Well, if the Sassenach want a fight," said McConnell merrily, "a fight we'll give them!"

"But you'll kill so many innocent people," protested Emily. "Why, a bomb could destroy the Greek theater on Scotia! And all for what? A little money and a mountain of pride!"

"*Ja*, you ruin my business,' croaked Sarmishkidu.

"And mine. My whole ship," said Herr Syrup, almost tearfully.

"Oh, now, now, now, man, ye at least should not be tryin' to blarney me," said McConnell. "What harm can a six or seven weeks holiday here do to yez?"

"Ve ban carrying a load of Brahma bull embryos in exogenetic tanks," said Herr Syrup. "All de time, dose embryos is growing." He banged his mug on the table. "Dey is soon fetuses, by Yudas! Ve have only so much room aboard ship; and it takes time to reach Alamo from here. If ve are held up more dan two, t'ree veeks—"

"Oh, no!" whispered McConnell.

"*Ja,*" said Herr Syrup. "Brahma bull calves all over de place. Ve cannot possibly carry dem, and dere is a stiff penalty in our contract."

"Well, now." McConnell looked uneasy. "Sure, an' 'tis sorry I am, an' after this affair has all been settled, if yez wish to file a claim for damages at Teamhair I am sure the O'Toole government will— Oh, oh." He stopped. "Where did ye say your owners are?"

"Anguklukkakok City, Venus."

"Well—" Major McConnell stared at his toes, rather like a schoolboy caught in the cookie jar. "Well, now, I meself think 'twas a good thing the Anguklukkakok Venusians were all converted last century, but truth 'tis, Jiniral O'Toole is pretty strict an'—"

"I say," broke in Emily, "what's the matter? I mean, if your owners are—"

"Baptists," said Rory McConnell.

"Oh," said Emily in a small voice.

McConnell leaped to his feet. One huge fist crashed on the table so the beer steins leaped. "Well, 'tis sorry I am!" he shouted. Sarmishkidu flinched from the noise and folded up his ears. "I've no ill will to anyone, meself, 'tis a dayd done for me country, an'—an'—an' why must all of yez be turnin' a skylarkin' merry-go into hurt an' harm an' sorrow?"

He stormed toward the exit.

"The score!" thundered Sarmishkidu in his thin, reedy voice. "The score, you unevaluated partial derivative!"

McConnell ripped out his wallet, flung a five-pound note blindly on the floor, and went up the stairs three at a time. The door banged in his wake.

CHAPTER 3

The sun was low when Knud Axel Syrup pedaled a slightly erratic course over the spaceport concrete. He had given the Alt Heidelberg several hours' worth of his business: partly because there was nothing else to do but work his way down the beer list, and partly because Miss Emily Croft—once her tears were dried—was pleasant company, even for a staid old married man from Simmerboelle. Not that he cared to listen to her exposition of Duncanite principles, but he had prevailed on her to demonstrate some classical dances. And she had been a sight worth watching, once he overcame his natural disappointment at learning that classical dance included neither bumps nor grinds, and found how to ignore Sarmishkidu's lyre and syrinx accompaniment.

"Du skal faa min sofacykel naar jeg doer—" sang Herr Syrup mournfully.

"An' what might that mean?" asked the green-clad guard posted beneath the *Mercury Girl.*

"You shall have my old bicycle ven I die," translated Herr Syrup, always willing to oblige.

"You shall have my old bicycle ven I die,
For de final kilometer
Goes on tandem vit' St. Peter.
You shall have my old bicycle ven I die."

"Oh," said the guard rather coldly.

Herr Syrup leaned his vehicle against the berth. "Dat is a more modern verse," he explained. "De orig'inal song goes back to de T'irty Years' Var."

"Oh."

"Gustavus Adolphus' troops ban singing it as—" Something told Herr Syrup that his little venture into historical scholarship was not finding a very appreciative audience. He focused, with some slight difficulty, on the battered hull looming above him. "Vy is dere no lights?" he asked. "Is all de crew still in town?"

"I don't know what," confessed the guard. His manner thawed; he brought up his rifle and began picking his teeth with the bayonet. " 'Twas a quare thing, begorra. Your skipper, the small wan in the dishcloth hat, was argyfyin' half the day wi' General O'Toole. At last he was all but thrown out of headquarters an' came back here. He found our boys just at the point of removin' the ship's radio. Well, now, sir, ye can see how we could not let ye live aboard your ship an' not see-questrate the apparatus by which ye might call New Winchester an' bring the King's bloody soldiers down on our heads. But no, that poor little dark sad man could not be reas'nable, he began whoopin' and screamin' for all his crew, an' off he rushed at the head of 'em. Now I ask ye, sir, is that any way to—"

Knud Axel Syrup scowled, fished out his pipe, and tamped it full with a calloused thumb. One could not deny, he thought, Captain Radhakrishnan was normally the mildest of human creatures; but he had his moments. He superheated, yes, that was what he did, he superheated without showing a sign, and then all at once some crucial thing happened and he flashed off in live steam and what resulted thereafter, that was only known to God and also the Lord.

"Heigh-ho," sighed the engineer. "Maybe someone like me vat is not so excited should go see if dere is any trouble."

He lit his pipe, stuck it under his mustache, and climbed back onto his bicycle. Four roads led out of the spaceport, but one was toward town—so, which of three?—wait a minute. The crew would presumably not have stampeded quite at random. They would have intended to do something. What? Well, what would send the whole Shamrock League adventure downward and home? Sabotage of their new drive unit. And the asteroid's geegee installations lay down *that* road.

Herr Syrup pedaled quickly off. Twilight fell as he crossed the Cotswold Mountains, all of 500 meters high, and the gloom in Sherwood Forest was lightened only by his front-wheel lamp. But beyond lay open fields where a smoky blue dusk lingered, enough light to show him farmers' cottages and hayricks and—and— He put on a burst of speed.

The *Girl*'s crew were on the road, brandishing as wild an assortment of wrenches, mauls, and crowbars as Herr Syrup had ever seen. Half a dozen young Grendelian rustics milled about among them, armed with scythes and pitchforks. The whole band had stopped while Captain Radhakrishnan exhorted a pair of yeomen who had been hoeing a wayside cabbage patch and now leaned stolidly on their tools. As he panted closer, Herr Syrup heard one of them:

"Nay, lad, tha'll no get me to coom."

"But, that is to say, but!" squeaked Captain Radhakrishnan. He jumped up and down, windmilling his arms. The last dayglow flashed off his monocle; it fell from his eye and he popped it back and cried: "Well, but haven't you any courage? All we need to do, don't y' know, is destroy their geegee and they'll jolly well have to go home. I mean to say, we can do it ten minutes, once we've overcome whatever guards they have posted."

"Posted wi' machine guns," said the farmer.

"Aye," nodded his mate. "An' brass knuckles, Ah'll be bound."

"But where's your patriotism?" shouted Captain Radhakrishnan. "Imitate the action of the tiger! Stiffen the sinews, summon up the blood, disguise fair nature with hard-favour'd rage, and all that sort of thing."

At this point Herr Syrup joined them. "You ban crazy?" he demanded.

"Ah." Captain Radhakrishnan turned to him and beamed. "The very man. Come, let's leave these bally caitiffs and proceed."

"But!" wailed Herr Syrup.

His assistant, Mr. Shubbish, nudged him with a tentacle and leered: "I fixed up a Molotov cocktail, chief. Don't worry. We got it made."

There was something in the air, a smell which—Herr Syrup's bulbous nose drank deep. Yes. Irish whisky. The crew must have spent a convivial afternoon with the spaceport sentries. So that explained why they were so eager!

"Miss Croft is right," he muttered. "About whisky, anyhow. It calcifies de liver."

He pushed his bicycle along the road, beside Radhakrishnan's babbling commando, and tried to think of something which would turn them back. Eloquence was never his strong point. Could he borrow some telling phrase from the great poets of the past, to recall them to reason? But all that rose into his churning brain was the Death Song of Ragnar Lodhbrok, which consists of phrases like *"Where the swords were whining while they sundered helmets"*—and did not seem to fit his present needs.

Vaguely through dusk and a grove of trees, he saw the terraforming plant. And then the air whirred and a small flyer slipped above him. It hung for an instant, then pounced low and fired a machine-gun burst. The racket was unholily loud, and the tracer stream burned like meteorites.

"Oh, my goodness!" exclaimed Captain Radhakrishnan.

"Wait there!" bawled an amplified voice. "Wait there an' we'll see what tricks ye're up to, ye Sassenach *omadhauns!*"

"Eek," said Mr. Shubbish.

Herr Syrup ascertained that no one had been hit. As the flyer landed and disgorged more large Celts than he had thought even a spaceship could hold, he switched off his bicycle lamp and wheeled softly back out of the suddenly quiet and huddled rebel band. Crouched beneath a hedgerow, he heard a lusty bellow:

"An' what wad ye be a-doin' here, where 'tis forbidden to venture by order of the General?"

"We were just out for a walk," said Captain Radhakrishnan, much subdued.

"Sure, sure. With weapons to catch the fresh air, no doubt."

Herr Syrup stole from the shadows and began to pedal back the way he came. Words drifted after him: "We'll jist see what himself has to say about this donnybrookin', me lads. Throw down your gear! 'Bout face! March!"

Herr Syrup pedaled a little faster. He would do no one any good languishing in the Grendel calaboose and living off mulligan stew.

Not, he thought gloomily, that he was accomplishing much so far.

The asteroid night deepened around him. In this shallow atmosphere the stars burned with wintry brilliance. Jupiter was not many millions of kilometers away, so whitely bright that Grendel's trees cast shadows; you could see the Galilean satellites with the naked eye. A quick green moon stood up over the topplingly close horizon and swung toward Aries—one of the other Anglian asteroids, spinning with its cluster mates around a common center of gravity, along a common resultant orbit. Probably New Winchester itself, maddeningly near. When you looked carefully at the sky, you could identify other little worlds among the constellations. The Erse Republic was still too remote to see without a telescope, but it was steadily sweeping closer; conjunction, two months hence, would bring it within a million kilometers of Anglia.

Herr Syrup, who was a bit of a bookworm, wondered in a wry way what Clausewitz or Halford Mackinder would think of modern astropolitics. Solemn covenants were all very well for countries which stayed put; but if you made a treaty with someone who would be on the other side of the sun next year, you must allow for the fact. There were alliances contingent on the phase of a moon and customs unions which existed only on alternate Augusts and—

And none of this was solving a problem which, if unsolved, risked a small but vicious interplanetary war and would most certainly put the *Mercury Girl* and the Alt Heidelberg Rathskeller out of business.

When he re-entered the spaceport, Herr Syrup met a blaze of lights and a bustle of men. Trucks rumbled back and forth, loaded with castings and fittings, sacks of cement and gangs of laborers. The Erse were working around the clock to make Grendel mobile. He dismounted and walked past a sentry, who gave him a suspicious glare, to the berth ladder, and so up to the airlock. He whistled a little tune as he climbed, trying to assure himself that no one could prove he had not merely been out on a spin for his health.

The ship was depressingly large and empty. His footsteps clanged so loud that he jumped, which only made matters worse, and peered nervously into shadowed corners. There was no good reason to stay aboard, he thought; an inn would be more cheerful and he could doubtless get off-season rates; but no, he had been a spaceman too long, one did not leave a ship completely unwatched. He contented himself with appropriating a case of Nashornbräu from the cargo—since the consignee had, after all, refused acceptance—and carried it back to his personal cubbyhole off the engine room.

Claus the crow blinked wicked black eyes at him from the bunk. *"Goddag,"* he said.

"Goddag," said Herr Syrup, startled. To be courteously greeted by Claus was so rare that it was downright ominous.

"Fanden hade dig!" yelled the bird. *"Chameau!* Go stuff yourself, you scut! *Vaya al Diablo!"*

"Ah," said Herr Syrup, relieved. "Dat's more like it."

He sat down on the bunk and pried the cap off a bottle and tilted it to his mouth. Claus hopped down and poked a beak in his coat pocket, looking for pretzels. Herr Syrup stroked the crow in an absentminded way.

He wondered if Claus really was a mutant. Quite possibly. All ships carried a pet or two, cat or parrot or lizard or uglopender, to deal with insects and other small vermin, to test dubious air, and to keep the men company. Claus was the fourth of his spacefaring line; there had been radiation, both cosmic and atomic, in his ancestral history. To be sure, Earthside crows had always had a certain ability to talk, but Claus' vocabulary was fantastic and he was constantly adding to it. Also, could chance account for the selectivity which made most of his phrases pure billingsgate?

Well, there was a more urgent question. How to get a message to New Winchester? The *Girl*'s radio was carefully gutted. How about making a substitute on the sly, out of spare parts? No, O'Toole was not that kind of a dolt; he would have confiscated the spare parts as well, including even the radar.

But let's see. New Winchester was only some thousands of kilometers off. A spark-gap oscillator, powered by the ship's plant, could send an S.O.S. that far, even allowing for the inverse-square enfeeblement of an unbeamed broadcast. It would not be too hard to construct such an oscillator out of ordinary electrical stuff lying around the engine room. But it would take a while. Would O'Toole let Knud Axel Syrup tinker freely, day after day, in the captive ship? He would not.

Unless, of course, there was a legitimate reason to tinker. If there was some *other* job to be done, which Knud Axel Syrup could pretend to be doing while actually making a

Marconi broadcaster. Only, there were competent engineers among the Erse. It would be strange if one of them, at least, did not inspect the work aboard the *Girl* from time to time. And such a man could not be told that an oscillator was a dreelsprail for the hypewangle camit.

So. Herr Syrup opened another bottle and recharged his pipe. One thing you must say for the Erse: given a trail of logic to follow, they follow it till the sun freezes over. Having mulled the question in his mind for an hour or two, Herr Syrup concluded that he could only get away with building an oscillator if he was in some place where no Erse engineer would come poking an unwelcome nose. So what was needed was an excuse to—

Along about midnight, Herr Syrup left his cabin and went into the engine room. Happily humming, he opened up the internal-field compensator which had so badly misbehaved on the trip down. Hm, hm, hm, let us see . . . yes, the trouble was there, a burned-out field coil, easily replaced . . . tum-te-tum-te-tum. Herr Syrup installed a coil of impedance calculated to unbalance the circuits. He shorted out two more coils, sprayed a variable condenser lightly with clear plastic, removed a handful of wiring and flushed it down the toilet, and spent an hour opening two big gas-filled rectifier tubes, injecting them with tobacco-juice vapor, and resealing them. Having done which, he returned to his bunk, changed into night clothes, and took a copy of Kant's *Critique* off the shelf to read himself to sleep.

"Kraa, kraa, kraa," grumbled Claus. "Bloody foolishness, damme. *Pokker! Ungah, ungah!*"

Chapter 4

Inquiry in the morning established that the office of the Erse military commander had been set up in a requisitioned loft room downtown, above Miss Thirkell's Olde Giftie Shoppe. Shuddering his way past a shelf of particularly malignant-looking china dogs, Herr Syrup climbed a circular stair so quaint that he could barely squeeze his way along it. Halfway up, a small round man coming hastily down caromed off his paunch.

"I say!" exclaimed the small man, adjusting his pince-nez indignantly. He picked up his briefcase. "*Would* you mind backing down again and letting me past?"

"Vy don't you back up?" asked Herr Syrup in a harsh mood.

"My dear fellow," said the small man, "the right-of-way in a situation like this has been clearly established by Gooch vs. Torpenhow, Holm Assizes 2098, not to mention—"

Herr Syrup gave up and retreated. "You is a lawyer?" he asked.

"A solicitor? Yes, I have the honor to be Thwickhammer of Stonefriend, Stonefriend, Thwickhammer, Thwickhammer, Thwickhammer, Thwickhammer, and Stonefriend, of Lincoln's Inn. My card, sir." The little man cocked his head. "I say, aren't you one of the spacemen who arrived yesterday?"

"*Ja.* I vas yust going to see about—"

"Don't bother, sir, don't bother. Beasts, that's all these invaders are, beasts with green tunics. When I heard of your crew's arrest, I resolved at once that they should not lack for legal representation, and went to see this O'Toole person. 'Release them, sir,' I demanded, 'release them this instant on reasonable bail or I shall be forced to obtain a writ of habeas corpus.' " Mr. Thwickhammer turned purple. "Do you know what O'Toole told me I could do with such a writ? No, you cannot imagine what he said. He said—"

"I can imagine, *ja*," interrupted Herr Syrup. Since they were now back in earshot of Miss Thirkell and the china dogs, he was spared explicit details.

"I am afraid your friends will be held in gaol until the end of the occupation," said Mr. Thwickhammer. "Beastly, sir.

I have assured myself that the conditions of detention are not unduly uncomfortable, but really—I must say—!'' He bowed. ''Good day, sir.''

Miss Thirkell looked wistfully at Herr Syrup, across the length of her deserted shoppe, and said: ''If you don't care for one of the little dogs, sir, I have some nice lampshades with 'Souvenir of Grendel' and a copy of *Trees* printed on them.''

''No, t'ank you yust the same,'' said Herr Syrup, and went quickly back upstairs. The thought of what an ax could do among all those Dresden shepherdesses and clock-bellied Venuses made him sympathize with his remote ancestors' practice of going berserk.

A sentry outside the office was leaning out the window, admiring Grendel's young ladies as they tripped by in their brief light dresses under a fresh morning breeze. Herr Syrup did not wish to interrupt him, but went quickly through the anteroom and the door beyond.

General Scourge-of-the-Sassenach O'Toole looked up from a heap of papers on his desk. The long face tightened. Finally he clipped: ''So there ye are. An' who might have given ye an appointment?''

''*Ja,*'' agreed Herr Syrup, sitting down.

''If 'tis about your spalpeen friends ye've come, waste no time. Ye'll not see thim released before Laoighise shall be free.''

''From de Shannon to de sea?''

''Says the Shan Van Vaught!'' roared O'Toole automatically. He caught himself, snapped his mousetrap mouth shut, and glared.

''Er—'' Herr Syrup gathered courage and rushed in. ''Ve have trouble on our ship. De internal compensator has developed enough bugs to valk avay vit' it. As long as ve is stranded here anyhow, you must let us make repairs.''

''Oh, must I?'' murmured O'Toole, the glint of power in his eye.

''*Ja*, any distressed ship has got to be let fixed, according to de Convention of Luna. You vould not vant it said dat you vas a barbarian violating international law, vould you?''

General O'Toole snarled wordlessly. At last he flung back: ''But your crew broke the law first, actin' as belligerents when they was supposed to be neutrals. I've every right to hold them, accident to their ship or not, while the state of emergency obtains.''

Herr Syrup sighed. He had expected no more. ''At least you have no charge against me,'' he said. ''I vas not any place near de trouble last night. So you got to let me repair de damage, no?''

O'Toole thrust a bony jaw at him. ''I've only your word there's any damage at all.''

''I knew you vould t'ink dat, so before I come here I asked your shief gyronics enshineer vould he please to look at our compensator and check it himself.'' Herr Syrup unfolded a sheet of S.L.I.E.F. letterhead from his pocket. ''He gave me dis.''

O'Toole squinted at the green paper and read:

> TO WHOM IT MAY CONCERN:
>
> This is to say that I have personal inspected the internal field compensator of I/S *Mercury Girl* and made every test known to man. I certify that I have never seen any piece of apparatus so deranged. I further certify as my considered opinion that the devil has got into it and only Father Kelly can make the necessary repairs.
>
> Shamus O'Banion
> Col., Eng., S.L.I.E.F.

''Hm,'' said O'Toole. ''Well, yes.''

''You realize I must take de ship up and put her in orbit outside Grendel's geegee field,'' said Herr Syrup. ''I vill need freefall conditions to test and calibrate my repairs.''

''Yes!'' O'Toole's arm shot out till his accusing finger was almost in the Dane's mustache. "Let ye take the ship aloft so ye can sail it clear to New Winchester!"

Herr Syrup suppressed an impulse to bite. "I expect you vill put a guard aboard," he said. "Yust some dumb soldier vat does not know enough about technics to be of any use to you down here."

"Hm," said O'Toole. "Hm, hm, hm." He gave the other man a malevolent glance. " 'Tis nothin' but trouble I've had wi' the lot of yez," he complained, "an' sure I am in me heart ye're plottin' to make more. No, I'll not let ye do it. By the brogansiv Brian Boru, here on the ground ye stay!"

Herr Syrup shrugged. "Vell," he said, "if you vant all de Solar System to know later on how you vas breaking de Lunar Convention and not letting a poor old spaceman fix his ship like de law says he is entitled to—*ja*, I guess maybe de Erse Republic does not care vat odder countries t'ink about its civilization."

"The devil take ye for a hairsplittin' wretch!" howled O'Toole. "Sit there. Wait right there, me fine lad, an' if 'tis space law ye want, then space law ye'll get!"

His finger stabbed the desk communicator buttons. "I want Captain Flanahan . . . No, no, no, ye leatherhead, I mean *Captain* Flanahan, the captain of the Shamrock League Irredentist Expeditionary Force's ship *Dies I.R.A.!*"

After an interchange of Gaelic, O'Toole snapped off the communicator and gave Herr Syrup a triumphant look. "I've checked the space law," he growled. " 'Tis true ye're entitled to put your vessel in orbit if that's needful for your repairs. But I'm allowed to place a guard aboard her to protect our own legitimate interests; an' the guard is entitled not to hazard his life in an undermanned ship. Especially whin I legally can an' will take the precaution of impoundin' all the lifeboats an' propulsive units an' radios off the spacesuits, as well as the ship's radio an' radar which I have already got. So by the law, I cannot allow ye to lift with me guardsman aboard unliss ye've a crew iv at least three. An' your own crew is all in pokey, where I'm entitled to keep them till the conclusion of hostilities! Ha, ha, Mister Space Lawyer, an' how do ye like that?''

CHAPTER 5

Herr Syrup leaned his bicycle against the wall of the Alt Heidelberg and clumped downstairs. Sarmishkidu von Himmelschmidt hitched up his leather shorts and undulated to meet the guest. *''Grüss Gott,''* he piped. ''And what will we have to drink today?''

''Potassium-40 cyanide on de rocks,'' said the engineer moodily, lowering himself to a bench. ''Unless you can find me a pair of spacemen.''

''What for?'' asked the Martian, drawing two mugs and sitting down.

Herr Syrup explained. Since he had to trust somebody somewhere along the line, he assumed Sarmishkidu would not blab what the real plan was, to construct a spark-gap transmitter and signal King Charles.

''Ach!'' whistled the innkeeper. ''So! So you are actual trying to do somet'ings about dis situation what is mine business about to ruin.'' In a burst of sentiment, he cried out: ''I salute you, Herr Syrup! You are such a hero, I do not charge you for dis vun beer!''

''T'anks,'' snapped the Dane. ''And now tell me vere to find two men I can use.''

''Hmmm. Now that is somewhat less susceptible to logical analysis.'' Sarmishkidu rubbed his nose with an odd tentacle. ''It is truistic that we must axiomatize the problem. So, imprimis, there are no qualified Anglian spacemen on Grendel at the moment. The interasteroid lines all maintain their headquarters elsewhere. Secundus, while there are no active collaborationist elements in the population, the nature of its distribution in n-dimensional psychomathematical phase space implies that there would be considerable difficulty in finding suitable units of humanity, dH. The people of Grendel tend to be either stolid farmers, mechanics, *und so weiter*, brave enough but too unimaginative to see the opportunities in your scheme, or else tourist-facility keepers whose lives have hardly qualified them to take risks. Those persons with enough fire and flexibility to be of use to you would probably lack discretion and might blurt out—"

"Ja, ja, ja," said Herr Syrup. "But dere are still several t'ousand people on dis asteroid. Among dem all dere must be some ready and able to, uh, strike a blow for freedom."

"I am!" cried a clear young voice at the door, and Emily Croft tripped down the stairs trailing vine leaves.

Herr Syrup started. "Vat are you doing here?" he asked.

"I saw your bicycle outside," said the girl, "and, well, you were so sympathetic yesterday that I wanted to—" She hesitated, looking down at her small sandaled feet and biting a piquantly curved lip. "I mean, maybe you were spreading pumpernickel with that awful Limburger cheese instead of achieving glowing health with dried prunes and other natural foods, but you were so nice about encouraging me to show you classical dance that I thought—"

Herr Syrup's pale eyes traveled up and down an assemblage of second through fifth order curves which, while a bit on the slender side of his own preferences, was far and away the most attractive sight he had encountered for a good many millions of kilometers. *"Ja,"* he said kindly. "I am interested in such t'ings and I hope you vill show me more—Ahem!" He blushed. Emily blushed. "I mean to say, Miss Croft, I have seldom seen so much— Vell, anyhow, later on, sure. But now please to run along. I have got to talk secrets vit' Herr von Himmelschmidt."

Emily quivered. "I heard what you said," she whispered, large-eyed.

"You mean about making Grendel free?" asked Herr Syrup hopefully.

His hopes were fulfilled. She quivered again. "Yes! Oh, but do you think, do you really think you can?"

He puffed himself and blew out his mustache. "*Ja*, I t'ink dere is a chance." He buffed his nails, looked at them critically, and buffed them some more. "I have my met'ods," he said in his most mysterious accent.

"Oh, but that's wonderful!" caroled Emily, dancing over to take his arm. She put her face to his ear. "What can I do?" she breathed.

"Vat? You? Vy, you yust vait and—"

"Oh, no! Honestly! I mean to say, Mr. Syrup, I know all about spies and, and revolutions and interplanetary conspiracies and everything. Why, I found a technical error in *The Bride of the Spider* and wrote to the author about it and he wrote back the nicest letter admitting I was right and he hadn't read the book I cited. There was this old chap, you see, and this young chap, and the old chap had invented a death ray—"

"Look," said Herr Syrup, "ve is not got any deat' rays to vorry about. Ve have yust got somet'ing to do vat should not be known to very many folks before ve do it. Now you run on home and vait till it is all over vit'."

Emily clouded up. She sniffed a tiny sniff. "You don't think I can be trusted," she accused.

"Vy, I never said dat, I only said—"

"You're just like all the rest." She bent her golden head and dabbed at her eyes. "All of you. You either call me crazy, and believe those horrible lies about Miss Duncan's private life, and try to force things on me to calcify my liver, or you—you let me go on, I mean making a perfect ass of myself—"

"I never said you vas a perfect ass!" shouted Herr Syrup. He paused and reflected a moment. "Aldough," he murmured, "you do have—"

"—and laugh at me behind my back, and, and, and, uh-h-h-h!" Emily took her face out of her hands, swallowed, sniffled, and turned drooping toward the stairs. "Never mind," she said disconsolately. "I'll go. I know I bother you, I mean to say I'm sorry I do."

"But—*pokker*, Miss Croft, I vas only—"

"One moment," squeaked Sarmishkidu. "Please! Wait a short interval of time dT, please. I have an idea."

"Yes?" Emily pirouetted, smiling like sunshine through rain.

"I think," said Sarmishkidu, "we will do well to take the young lady into our confidence. Her discretion may not be infinite but her patriotism will superimpose caution. And, while she has not unduly encouraged any young men of Grendel during the period of my residence here, I am sure she must be far better acquainted with a far larger circle thereof than foreigners like you and me could ever hope to become. She can recommend whom you should approach with your plan. Is that not good?"

"By Yudas, *ja!*" exclaimed Herr Syrup. "I am sorry, Miss Croft. You really can help us. Sit down and have a glass of pure spring vater on me."

Emily listened raptly as he unfolded his scheme. At the end, she sprang to her feet, threw herself onto Herr Syrup's lap, and embraced him heartily.

"Hoy!" he said, grabbing his pipe as it fell and brushing hot coals off his jacket. "Hoy, dis is lots of fun, but—"

"You have your crew right here already, you old silly," the girl told him. "Me."

"You?"

"And Herr von Himmelschmidt, of course." Emily beamed at the Martian.

"Eep!" said Sarmishkidu in horror.

Emily bounced back to her feet. "But of course!" she warbled. "Of course! Don't you see it? You can't get really-truly spacemen anyway, I mean a garageman or a chef couldn't help you in your real work, so why let the secret go further than it has already? I mean, dear old Sarmishkidu and I could hand you your spanner and your ape wrench and your abacus or whatever that long thin calculating thing is called, just as well as Mr. Groggins down at the sweet shop, and if there are any secret messages, why, we can talk to each other in Attic Greek. And I do make tea competently, Mum admits it, even though I never drink tea myself because it tans the kidneys or something, and I can take along some dried apricots and bananas and apples for myself and won't that terrible Major McConnell be just furious when he sees how we outsmarted him! Maybe then he will understand what all that whisky and bacon is doing to his brain, and will stop doing it and exercise himself in classical dance, because he really is quite graceful, don't you know—"

"Ooooh!" said Sarmishkidu. "No, wait, wait, wait, *ach*, wait just one moment! We are not qualified spacemen anyhow, so O'Toole does not accept us for a crew."

"I t'ought dat over," said Herr Syrup, "and checked in de law books to make sure. In an emergency like dis, de highest ranking officer available, me, can deputize noncertified personnel, and dey vill have regular spacemen's standing vile de situation lasts. O'Toole vill eider have to let me raise ship vit' you two or else release two of my shipmates."

"Then you will take us along?" pounced Emily.

Herr Syrup shrugged. He might as well have a crew worth looking at. "Sure," he said. "You is velcome."

Sarmishkidu rolled his eyes uneasily. "Better I stay on de ground. I got mine business to look after."

"Oh, nonsense!" said Emily. "If I go, we just about have to have a Martian for a chaperone, not that I don't trust Mr. Syrup because he really is a sweet old gentleman—oh, I'm sorry, Mr. Syrup, I didn't mean to make you wince—well, I mean to say, of course I'll have to go aboard without letting Father know or he would forbid me, but why distress the old dear afterward with the thought that even if I liberated Grendel I compromised my reputation? I mean, he is the vicar, you know, and it's been hard enough for him, my bringing home Duncanite teachings from Miss Carruthers' Select School for Young Ladies on Wilberforce. Though I didn't learn about it in class but from a lecture in the town hall which I happened to attend, and— And your tavern business, Mr. Sarmishkidu, isn't worth tuppence if we don't get rid of the Erse before vacation season begins, so won't you please come, there's a dear, or else I'll ask all my young men friends never to come in here again.''

Sarmishkidu groaned.

Chapter 6

Herr Syrup halted his bicycle and Herr von Himmelschmidt untied his tentacles from around the baggage rack. A small bright sun shone through small bright clouds on Grendel's spaceport, the air blew soft and sweet, and even the old *Mercury Girl* looked a trifle less discouraged than usual. Not far away a truckload of Erse soldiers was bowling toward the geegee site to work, and however much one desired to throw them off his planetoid, one had to admit their young voices soared meticulously sweet.

''—Ochone! Ochone! the men of Ulster cry.
Ochone! Ochone! The lords an' ladies weepin'!
Dear, dear the man that nivver, nivver more shall be.
Hoy, there, Paddy, see the colleen, ah, the brave broight soight iv her, whee-ee-whee-ew!''

The sentry at the ship berth slanted his rifle across Herr Syrup's path. ''Halt,'' he said.

''Vat?'' asked the engineer.

''Or I shoot,'' explained the guard earnestly.

''Vat is dis?'' protested Herr Syrup. ''I got a right on my own ship. I got de General's written permission, by yiminy, to take her up.''

''That's as may be,'' said the guard, hefting his weapon, ''but I've me orders too, which is that ye're not trusted an' ye don't go aboard till your full crew *an'* the riprysintative of the Shamrock League is here.''

"Oh, vell, if dat is all," said Herr Syrup, relieved, "den here comes Miss Croft now, and I see a Erser beside her too."

Still trailed by a receding tide of whistles, Emily came with long indignant strides across the concrete. She bore an outsize picnic basket which her green-clad escort kept trying to take for her. She would snatch it from him, stamp her foot, and try to leave him behind. Unfortunately, he was so big that her half-running pace was an easy amble for him.

Sarmishkidu squinted. "By all warped Riemannian space," he said at last, "is that not Major McConnell?"'

Herr Syrup's heart hit the ground with a dull thud.

"Ah, there, greetin's an' salutations!" boomed the large young man. "An' accept me congratulations, sir, on choosin' the loveliest crew which ivver put to sky! Though truth 'tis, she might be just a trifle friendlier. Ah, but once up among the stars, who knows what may develop?"

"You don't mean you ban our guard?" choked Herr Syrup.

"Yes. An' 'tis guardsmanlike I look, eh, what?" beamed Rory McConnell, slapping the machine pistol and trench knife holstered at his belt, the tommy gun at his shoulder, and the rifle across his fifty-kilo field pack.

"But you ban needed down here!"

"Not so much, now that we're organized an' work is proceedin' on schedule." McConnell winked. "An' faith, when I heard what crew yez would have, sir, why, I knew at once where me real obligations lay. For 'tis five years an' more that me aged mither on Caer Dubh has plagued me to marry, that she may have grandchilder to brighten her auld age; so I am but doin' me filial duty." He nudged Herr Syrup with a confidential thumb.

When the engineer had been picked up, dusted off, and apologized to, he objected: "But does your chief, O'Toole, know you ban doing dis? I t'ought he would not like you associating vit' us."

"O'Toole is somewhat of a fanatic," admitted McConnell, "but he gave me this assignment whin I asked for it. For ye understand, sir, he is not easy in the heart of him, as long as ye are in orbit with any chance whatsoever to quare his plans. So 'tis happiest he'll be, the soonest ye've finished your repairs an' returned here. Now I am certificated more as a pilot an' navigator than an injineer, but ye well know each department must be able to handle the work of t'other in emergency, so I will be able to give yez skilled assistance in your task. I've enough experience in geegees to know exactly what ye're doin'."

"Guk," said Sarmishkidu.

"What?" asked McConnell.

"I said, 'Guk,' " answered Sarmishkidu in a chill voice, "which was precisely my meaning."

"All aboard!" bawled the Erseman, and went up the berth ladder two rungs at a time.

Emily hung back. "I couldn't *do* anything about it," she whispered, white-faced. "He just insisted. I mean, I even hit him on the chest as hard as I could, and he grinned, you have to admit he's as strong as Herakles and if he would only study classical dance to improve his gait he would be nearly perfect." She flushed. "Physically, I mean, of course! But what I wanted to say is, shall we give up our plan?"

"No," said Herr Syrup glumly, "ve ban committed now. And maybe a chance comes to carry it out. Let's go." He took his bicycle by the seat bar and dragged it up into the ship. No Dane is ever quite himself without a bicycle, though it is not true that all of them sleep with their machines. Fewer than ten percent do this.

He had been prepared to pilot the *Girl* into orbit himself, which was not beyond his training; but McConnell did it with so expert a touch that even the transition from geegee field to free fall was smooth. Once established in path, Herr Syrup jury-rigged a polarity reverser in the ship's propulsive circuits, to furnish weight again inside the hull. It was against regulations, since it immobilized the drive; and, of course, it lacked the self-adjustment of a true compensator. But this was a meteor-swept region, so there was no danger in floating inert; and, though neither spacemen nor asterites mind weightlessness *per se*, an attractive field always simplifies work. No one who has not toiled in free fall, swatting gobs of molten solder from his face while a mislaid screwdriver bobs off on its own merry way, has experienced the full perversity of matter.

"Ve can turn off de pull ven ve vish to test repairs," said Herr Syrup.

Rory McConnell looked around the crowded engine room and the adjacent workshop. "I envy yez this," he said, with a bare touch of wistfulness. " 'Tis spaceships are me proper place, an' not all this hellin' about wi' guns an' drums."

"Er—*ja.*" Herr Syrup hesitated. "Vell, you know, dere is really no reason to bodder you vit' de yob in here. Yust leave me do it alone and—hm—*ja,*" he finished in a blaze of genius, "go talk at Miss Croft."

"Oh, I'll be doin' that, all right," grinned McConnell, "but I'd not be dallyin' about all the time whin another man was laborin'. No, I'll sweat over that slut of a machine right along wi' yez, Pop." He raised one ruddy eyebrow above a wickedly blue sidelong glance. "Also, I'll not be makin' of unsubstantiated accusations, but 'tis conceivable ye might not work on it yourself at all, at all, if left alone. Some might even imagine ye—oh—makin' a radio to call his bloody majesty. So, just to keep evil tongues from waggin', we'll retain all electrical equipment in here, an' here I meself will work an' sleep. Eh?" He gave Herr Syrup a comradely slap on the back.

"Gott in Himmel!" yelped Sarmishkidu from the passageway outside. "What exploded in there?"

An arbitrary pattern of watches had been established to give the *Mercury Girl* some equivalent of night and day. After supper, which she had cooked, Emily Croft wandered up to the bridge while Sarmishkidu was simultaneously washing the dishes and mopping the galley floor. She stood gazing out the viewports for a long time.

Only feebly accelerated by Grendel's weak natural gravity, the ship would take more than a hundred hours to complete one orbit. At this distance, the asteroid filled seven degrees of sky, a clear and lovely half-moon, though only approximately spherical. On the dark part lay tiny twinkles of light, scattered farms and hamlets, the starlit sheen of Lake Alfred the Great. The town, its church on the doll-like edge of naked-eye visibility, its roofs making a ruddy blur, lay serene a bit west of the sunset line: tea time, she thought sentimentally, scones and marmalade before a crackling fire, and Dad and Mum trying not to show their worry about her. Then, dayward, marched the wide sweep of fields and woods under shifting cloud bands, the intense green of the fens, the Cotswolds and rustling Sherwood beyond. Grendel turned slowly against a crystal blackness set with stars, so many and so icily beautiful that she wanted to cry.

When she actually felt tears and saw the vision blur, she bit her lip. Crying wouldn't be British. It wouldn't even be Duncanite. Then she realized that the tears were due to a whiff from Herr Syrup's pipe.

The engineer slipped through the door and closed it behind him. "Hist!" he warned hoarsely.

"Oh, go hist yourself!" snapped the girl. And then, in contrition: "No, I'm sorry. A bad mood. I just don't know what to think."

"*Ja.* I feel I am up in an alley myself."

"Maybe it's the water aboard ship. It's tanked, isn't it? I mean, it doesn't come bubbling up from some mossy spring, does it?"

"No."

"I thought not. I guess that's it. I mean, why I feel so mixed up inside, all sad and yet not really sad. Do you know what I mean? I'm afraid I don't myself."

"Miss Croft," said Herr Syrup, "ve is in trouble."

"Oh. You mean about Ro—about Major McConnell?"

"*Ja.* He has taken inventory of everyt'ing aboard. He has stowed all de electric stuffs in a cabinet vich he has locked, and he has de key, himself. How are ve going to make a broadcaster now?''

''Oh, damn Major McConnell!'' cried Emily. ''I mean, damn him, actually!''

''Dere is a hope I can see,'' said Herr Syrup. ''It vill depend on you.'

''Oh!'' Emily brightened. ''Why, how wonderful! I mean, I was afraid it would be so dull, just waiting for you to— And I'm sorry to say it, but the ship is not very esthetic, I mean there's just white paint and all those clocks and dials and thingummies and really, I haven't found any books except things like *The Jovian Intersatellite Pilot With Ephemerides* or something else called *Pictures For Men*, where the women aren't in classical poses at all, I mean it's—'' She broke off, confused. ''Where was I? Oh, yes, you wanted me to— But that's terrif! I mean, whee!'' She jumped up and down, twirled till her tunic stood out horizontally and her wreath tilted askew, and grabbed Herr Syrup's hands. ''What can I do? Do you want any secret messages translated into Greek?''

''No,'' said the engineer. ''Not yust now. Uh . . . er—'' He stared down, blushing, and dug at the carpet with one square-toed boot. ''Vell, you see, Miss Croft, if McConnell got distracted from vorking on de compensator . . . if he vas not in de machine shop vit' me very often, and den had his mind on somet'ing else . . . I could pick de lock on de electrics box and sneak out de parts I need and carry on vit' our plan. But, vell, first he must be given some odder interest dat vill hold all his attention for several days.''

''Oh, dear,'' said Emily. She laid a finger to her cheek. ''Let me think. What is he interested in? Well, he talks a lot about spaceships, he wants to be an interplanetary explorer when this trouble is over, and, you know, he really is enthusiastic about that, why, he's so much like a little boy I want to rumple his hair—'' She stopped, gulping. ''No. That won't do. I mean, the only person here who can talk to him about spaceships is yourself.''

"I am afraid I am not yust exactly his type," said Herr Syrup in an elaborate tone.

"I mean, *you* can't keep him distracted, because you're the one we want to have working behind his back," said Emily. "Let me see, what else? Yes, I believe Major McConnell mentioned being fond of poker. It's a card game, you know. And Mr. Sarmishkidu is very interested in, uh, permutations. So maybe they could—"

"I am afraid Sarmishkidu is not yust exactly his type eider." Herr Syrup frowned. "For a young lady vat is so mad vit' dat crazy Erser, you ban spending a lot of time vit' him to know his tastes so vell."

Emily's face heated up. "Don't you call me a collaborationist!" she shouted. "Why, when the invaders first landed I put on a Phrygian liberty cap and went around with a flag calling on all our men to follow me and drive them off. And nobody did. They said they had nothing more powerful than a few shotguns. As if that made any difference!"

"It does make some difference," said Herr Syrup placatingly.

"But as for seeing Major McConnell since, why, how could I help it? I mean, O'Toole made him the liaison officer for us Grendelians, because even O'Toole must admit that Rory has more charm. And naturally he had to discuss many things with my father, who's one of Grendel's leading citizens, the vicar, you know. And while he was in our house, well, he's a guest even if he is an enemy, and no Croft has been impolite to a guest since Sir Hardman Croft showed a Puritan constable the door in 1657. I mean, it just isn't done. Of course I had to be nice to him. And he does have a lovely soft voice, and any Duncanite appreciates musical qualities, and that doesn't make me a collaborator, because I'd lead an attack on their spaceship this very day if somebody would only help me. And if I don't want any of them to get hurt, why, I'm only thinking about their innocent parents and, and sweethearts, and so there!"

"Oh," said Herr Syrup.

His pipe had gone out. He became very busy rekindling it. "Vell, Miss," he said, "in dat case you vill help us out and try to distract de mayor's mind off his vork, vill you not? It ban your patriotic duty. Yust-encourashe-him-in-a-nice-vay-because-he-is-really-in-love-vit'-you-okay? Good night." And hiding his beet-colored face in a cloud of smoke, Herr Syrup bolted.

Emily stared at him. "Why, good heavens," she whispered. "I mean, actually!"

Her eyes traveled back to Grendel and the stars. "But that isn't so," she protested. "It's just what they call blarney. *Makros logos* to be exact."

No one answered her for a moment, then feet resounded in the companionway and a hearty voice boomed: "Emily, are ye up there?"

"Oh, dear!" exclaimed the girl. She looked around for a mirror, made do with a polished chrome surface, and adjusted her wreath and the yellow hair below it. She must not let a foreigner see an Anglian lady disarrayed, and really, she regretted not having any lipstick and felt sure that abstention from such materials didn't represent the true Duncanism.

Rory McConnell clumped in, his shoulders brushing the door jambs and his head stooped under the lintel. "Ah, macushla, I found ye," he said. "Will ye not speak for a bit to a weary man, so he can sleep content? For even the hour or two of testin' I've been able to do today on that devil's machine has revealed nothin' to me but me own bafflement, an' 'tis consolation I need."

Emily found herself breathing as hard as if she had run a long distance. *Oh, stop it!* she scolded. *Hyperventilating! No wonder you feel so weak and dizzy.*

The Erseman leaned close. For once he did not grin, he smiled, and it was not fair that a barbarian could have so tender a smile. "Sure an' I never knew a pulse in any throat could be that adorable," he murmured.

"Nice weather we're having, isn't it?" said Emily, since nothing else came to mind.

"The wither in space is always noice, though perhaps just a trifle monotonous," quirked McConnell. He came around the pilot chair and stood beside her. The red hairs on the back of one hand brushed her bare thigh; she gulped and clung to the chair for support.

After all, her duty was to distract him. She was certain that even Isadora Duncan, the pure and serene, would have approved.

McConnell reached out a long arm and switched off the bridge lights, so that they stood in the soft, drenching radiance of Grendel, among a million stars. " 'Tis enough to make a man believe in destiny," he said.

"It is?" asked Emily. Her voice wobbled, and she berated herself. "I mean, what is?"

"Crossin' space on this mission an' findin' ye waitin' at the yonder end. For I'll admit to yez what I've dared say to no one else, 'tis not important to me who owns that silly piece of ore Laoighise. I went with O'Toole because a McConnell has never hung back from any brave venture, arragh, how ye wring truth from me which I had not ayven admitted to meself! Oh, to be sure, I'm proud to do me country a service, but I cannot think 'tis so great an' holy a deed as O'Toole prates of. So I came more on impulse than plan, me darlin', an' yet I found me destiny. The which is your own sweet self."

Emily's heart thumped with unreasonable violence. She clasped her hands tightly to her breast, because one of them had been sneaking toward McConnell's broad paw. "Oh?" she said out of dry lips. "I mean, really?"

"Yes. An' sorry I am that our work distresses yez. I can only hope to make amends later. But I trust we'll have fifty or sixty years for that!"

"Er, yes," said Emily.

"What?" roared McConnell. He spun on his heel, laid his hands about her waist, and stared wildly down into her eyes. "Did I hear ye say yes?"

"I . . . I . . . I—No, please listen to me!" wailed Emily,

pushing against his chest. "Let go! I mean, all I wanted to say was, if you don't really care how this business comes out, if you really don't think Lois is worth risking a war over and—" She drew a deep breath and tacked a smile on her face. Now was the time to distract him, as Mr. Syrup had requested. "And if you really want to please me, R-r-r-ro— Major McConnell, then why don't you help us right now? Just let us make that sparky osculator or whatever it is to call New Winchester for help, and everything will be so nice and—I mean—"

His hands fell to his sides and his mouth stretched tight. He turned from her, leaned on the instrument board and stared out at the constellations.

"No," he said. "I've given me oath to support the Force to the best of me ability. Did I turn on me comrades, there'd be worse than hellfire waitin' for me, there'd be the knowin' of meself for less than a man."

Emily moistened her lips. There must be some way to distract him, she thought frantically. That beautiful lady agent in *The Son of the Spider*, the one who lured Sir Frederic Banton up to her apartment while the Octopus stole the secret papers from his office— She stood frozen among thunders, unable to bring herself to it, until another memory came, some pictures of an accidental atomic explosion on Callisto and its aftermath. That sort of thing might be done to little children, deliberately, if there was a war.

She stole up behind McConnell, laid her cheek against his back and her arms around his waist. "Oh, Rory," she said.

"What?" He spun around again. He was so quick on his feet she didn't have time to let go and was whipped around with him. "Where are ye?" he called.

"Here," she said, picking herself up.

She leaned on his arm—she had never before known a man who could take her whole weight thus without even stirring— and forced her eyes toward his. "Oh, Rory," she tried again.

"What do ye mean?" It was a disquieting surprise that he

did not sweep her into his embrace, but stood rigidly and stared.

"Rory," she said. Then, feeling that her conversation was too limited, she got out in a rush of words: "Let's just forget all these awful things. I mean, let's just stay up here and, and, and I'll explain about Duncanism to you and, well, I mean don't go back to the engine room, please!"

He said in a rasp: "So 'tis me ye'd be keepin' up here whilst auld Syrup does what he will in the stern? An' what do ye offer me besides conversation?"

"Everything!" said Emily, taking an automatic cue from the beautiful lady agent vs. Sir Frederic; because her own mind felt full of glue and hammers.

"Everything, eh?"

Suddenly his arm jerked from beneath her. She fell in a heap. The green-clad body towered above, up and up and *up*, and a voice like gunfire crashed:

"So that's the game, is it? So ye think I'd sell the honor of the McConnells for—for— Why, had I known yez for what ye are, I'd not have given yez a second look the third time we met. An' to think I wanted yez for the mother of me sons!"

"No," cried Emily. She sat up, hearing herself call like a stranger across light-years. "No, Rory, when I said everything I didn't mean everything! I just—"

"Never mind," he snarled, and went from the bridge. The door cracked shut behind him.

Chapter 7

Knud Axel Syrup paused a moment in the after transverse corridor. The bulkhead which faced him bore a stencilled KEEP OUT and three doors: the middle one directly to the engine room, the right-hand one to the machine shop, and the left to his small private cabin. These two side chambers also had doors opening directly on the engine room. It made for a lack of privacy distressing in the present cloak-and-dagger situation.

However, the wild Erseman would no doubt be up on the bridge for hours. Herr Syrup sighed, a little enviously, and went through the central door.

"Awwrk," said Claus, flapping in from the cabin. *"Nom d'un nom d'une vache! Schweinhund! Sanamabiche!"*

"Exactly," said Herr Syrup. He entered the little bathroom behind the main energy converter and extracted a bottle of beer from a cooler which he had installed himself. Claus paced impatiently along a rheostat. Herr Syrup crumbled a pretzel for him and poured a little beer into a saucer. The crow jabbed his beak into the liquid, tilted back his black head, shook out his feathers, and croaked: *"Gaudeamus igitur!"*

"You're velcome," said Herr Syrup. He inspected the locked electrical cabinet. Duplicating a Yale key would call for delicate instruments and skilled labor. After latching all doors to the outside, he went into the machine shop, selected various items, and returned. First, perhaps, a wire into the slot. . . .

The main door shivered under a mule kick. Faintly through its insulated metal thickness came a harsh roar: "Open up, ye auld scut, or I'll crack the outer hatches an' let ye choke!"

"Yumping Yupiter," said Herr Syrup.

He pattered across the room and admitted Rory McConnell, who glared down upon him and snarled: "So 'tis up to your sneakin' tricks ye are again, eh? Throw a pretty face an' long legs at me an'—Aargh! Be off wi' yez!"

"But," bleated Herr Syrup. "But vas you not talkin' vit' Miss Croft?"

"I was," said McConnell. " 'Tis not a mistake I'll make ag'in. Go tell her to save her charms for bigger fools than me. I'm goin' to sleep now." He tore off his various weapons, laid them beside his pack, and sat down on the floor.

"Git out!" he rapped, fumbling at a boot zipper. His face was like fire. "Tomorry perhaps I can look at ye wi'out bokin'!"

"Oh, dear," said Herr Syrup.

"Oh, shucks," said Claus, though not in just those words.

Herr Syrup picked up his miscellaneous tools and stole back into the workshop. A moment afterward he remembered his bottle of beer and stuck his head back through the communicating door. McConnell threw a boot at him. Herr Syrup closed the door and toddled out to make another requisition on the cargo.

Having done so, he stopped by the saloon. Emily was there, her face in her arms, her body slumped over the table and shuddering with sobs. At the far end sat Sarmishkidu, puffing his Tyrolean pipe and making calculations.

"Oh, dear," said Herr Syrup again, helplessly.

"Can you console her?" asked Sarmishkidu, rolling an eye in his direction. "I have endeavored to do so, and am sorry to report absolute failure."

Herr Syrup took a strengthening pull from his bottle.

"You see," explained the Martian, "her noise distracts me."

He fumed smoke for a dour moment. "I should at least think," he whined, "that having dragged me here, away from my livelihood and all the small comforts which mean so much to a poor lonely exile among aliens like myself—sustaining, heartening consolations which already I find myself in sore need of—namely a table of elliptic integrals—having so ruthlessly forced me into the trackless depths of outer space, and apparently not even to any good purpose, she would have the consideration not to sit there and weep at me."

"Dere, dere," said Herr Syrup, patting the girl's shoulder.

"Uhhhhh," said Emily.

"Dere, dere, dere," continued Herr Syrup.

The girl raised streaming eyes and sobbed pathetically: "Oh, go to hell."

"Vat happened vit' you and de mayor?"

A bit startled, Emily sniffed out: "Why, nothing, unless you mean that time last year when he asked me to preside at the Ladies' Potato Race, during the harvest festi— Oh! The major!" She returned her face to her arm. "Uhhhh-hoo-hoo-hoo!"

"I gather she tried to seduce him and failed," said Sarmishkidu. "Naturally, her professional pride is injured."

Emily leaped to her feet. "What do you mean, professional?" she screeched.

"*Warum*, nothing," stammered Sarmishkidu, retreating into a different character. "I just meant your female prides. All women are females by profession, *nicht war*? That is a joke. Ha, ha," he added, to make certain he would be understood.

"And I *didn't* try to—to—Oh!" Emily stormed out of the saloon. A string of firecracker Greek trailed after her.

"Vat is she saying?" gaped Herr Syrup.

Herr von Himmelschmidt turned pale. "Please don't to ask," he said. "I did not know she was familiar with that edition of Aristophanes."

"Helledusse!" said the engineer moodily. "Ve ban hashed now."

"Hmmm," muttered Sarmishkidu. "It is correct that the enemy is armed and we are not. Nevertheless, it is an observational datum that there are three of us and only one of him, and so if we could separate him from his weapons, even briefly, and—"

"And?"

"Oh. Well, nothing, I suppose." Sarmishkidu brooded. "True," he said at last, "one of him would still be equivalent to four or five of us." He pounded the table with an indignant hand. Since the hand, being boneless, merely flopped when it struck, this was not very dramatic. "It is most unfair of him," he squeaked. "Ganging up on us like that."

Herr Syrup stiffened with thought.

"Unlautere Wettbewerb," amplified the Martian.

"Do you know—" whispered the Dane.

"What?"

"I hate to do dis. It does not seem right. I know it is not right. But by Yoe, maybe he ban asleep now!"

The idea dawned on Sarmishkidu. "Well, I'll be an unelegantly proven lemma," he breathed. "So he doubtless is."

"And for veapons, in de machine shop is all de tools. Like wrenches, hammers, vire cable—"

"Blowtorches," added Sarmishkidu eagerly. "Hacksaws, sulfuric acid—"

"No, hoy, vait dere! Just a minute! I don't vant to hurt him. Yust a little bonk on de head to make him sleep sounder, vile ve tie him up, dat's all." Herr Syrup leaped erect. "Let's go!"

"Good luck," said Sarmishkidu, returning to his calculations.

"Vat? But hey! Is you leaving me to do dis all alone?"

Sarmishkidu looked up. "Go!" he said in a ringing croak. "Remember the Vikings! Remember Gustavus Adolphus! Remember King Christian standing by the high mast in smoke and steam! The blood of heroes is in your veins. Go, go to glory!"

Fired, Herr Syrup started for the door. He stopped there and asked wistfully, "Don't you vant a little glory too?"

Sarmishkidu blew a smoke ring and scribbled an equation. "I am more the intellectual type," he said.

"Oh." Herr Syrup sighed and went down the corridors. His resolution endured till he actually stood in the workshop, by the glow of a dim night light, hefting a pipe wrench. Then he wavered.

The sound of deep, regular breathing assured him that Major McConnell slept in the adjoining bedchamber. But—"I don't vant to hurt him," repeated Herr Syrup. "I could so easy clop him too hard." He shuddered. "Or not hard enough. I better make another requisition on de cargo first. . . . No. Here ve go." Puffing out his mustache and mopping the sweat off his pate, the descendant of Vikings tiptoed into the engine room.

Rory McConnell would scarcely have been visible at all, had his taste in pajamas not run to iridescent synthesilc embroidered with tiny shamrocks. As it was, his body, sprawled on a military bedroll, seemed in the murk to stretch on and on, interminably, besides having more breadth and thickness than was fair in anything but a gorilla. Herr Syrup hunkered shakily down by the massive red head, squinted till he had a spot, just behind one ear identified, and raised his weapon.

There was a snick of metal. The wan light glimmered along a pistol barrel. It prodded Herr Syrup's nose. He let out a yelp and broke all Olympic records for the squatting high jump.

Rory McConnell chuckled. "I'm a sound sleeper when no one else comes sneakin' close to me," he said, "but I've hunted in too many forests not to awaken thin. Goodnight, Mister Syrup."

"Goodnight," said Knud Axel Syrup in a low voice.

Blushing, he went back to the machine room. He waited there a moment, ashamed to return to his cabin past McConnell and yet angry that he must detour. Oh, the devil with it! He heard the slow breath of slumber resume. Viciously, he slammed his tool back into the rack loudly enough to wake an estivating Venusian. The sleeper did not even stir. And that was the unkindest cut of all.

Stamping his feet, slamming doors, and kicking panels as he went by—all without so much as breaking the calm rhythm of Rory McConnell's lungs—Herr Syrup took the roundabout way to his cabin. He switched on the light and pointed a finger at Claus. The crow hopped off the Selected Works of Oehlenschläger and perched on the finger.

"Claus," said Herr Syrup, not quite bellowing, "repeat after me: McConnell is a louse. McConnell is no good. McConnell eats vorms. On Friday. McConnell—"

—slept on.

Herr Syrup decided at last to retire himself. With a final sentence for Claus to memorize, an opinion in crude language of Major McConnell's pajamas, he took off his own clothes and slipped a candy-striped nightshirt over his head. Stretched out in his bunk, he counted herrings for a full half hour before realizing that he was more awake than ever.

''Satans ogsaa,'' he mumbled, and switched on the light and reached at random for a book. It turned out to be a poetry anthology. He opened it and read:

''—The secret workings of the yeast of life.''

''Yudas,'' he groaned. ''Yeast.''

For a moment Herr Syrup, though ordinarily the gentlest of men, entertained bloodshot fantasies of turning the ship's atomic-hydrogen torch into a sort of science fiction blaster and burning Major McConnell down. Then he decided that it was impractical and that all he could do was requisition a case of lager and thus get to sleep. Or at least pass the night watch more agreeably. He decorated his feet with outsize slippers and padded into the corridor.

Emily Croft jumped. ''Oh!'' she squeaked, whipping her robe about her. The engineer brightened a little, having glimpsed that her own taste in sleeping apparel ran merely to what nature had provided.

''Vich is sure better dan little green clovers,'' he muttered.

''Oh . . . you startled me.'' The girl blinked. ''What did you say?''

''Dat crook in dere.'' Herr Syrup jerked a splay thumb at the engine room door. ''He goes to bed in shiny payamas vit' shamrocks measled all over.''

''Oh, dear,'' said Emily. ''I hope his wife can teach him—'' She skidded to a halt and blushed. ''I mean, if any woman would be so foolish as to have such a big oaf.''

''I doubt it,'' snarled the Dane. ''I bet he snores.''

''He does not!'' Emily stamped her foot.

''Oh-ho,'' said Herr Syrup. ''You ban listening?''

''I was only out for a constitutional in the hope of overcoming an unfortunate insomnia,'' said Miss Croft primly. ''It was sheer chance which took me past here. I mean, nobody who can lie there like a pig and, and sleep when—'' She clouded up for a rainstorm. ''I mean, how *could* he?''

"Vell, but you don't care about him anyvay, do you?"

"Of course not! I hope he rots, I mean decays. No, I don't actually mean that, you know, because even if he is an awful lout he is still a human being and, well, I would just like to teach him a lesson. I mean, teach him to have more consideration for others and not go right to sleep as if nothing at all had happened, because I could see that he was hurt and if he had only given me a chance to explain, I— Oh, never mind!" Emily clenched her fists and stamped her foot again. "I'd just like to lock him up in there, since he's sleeping so soundly. That would teach him that other people have feelings even if he doesn't!"

Herr Syrup's jaw dropped with an audible clank.

Emily's eyes widened. One small hand stole to her mouth. "Oh," she said, "is anything wrong?"

"By yiminy," whispered Herr Syrup. "By jumping yiminy."

"Oh, really now, it isn't that bad. I mean, I know we're in an awful pickle and all that sort of thing, but really—"

"No. I got it figured. I got a vay to get de Erser off of our necks!"

"What?"

"*Ja, ja, ja*, it is so simple I could beat my old knucklebone brains dat I don't t'ink of it right avay. Look, so long as ve stay out of de engine room he sleeps yust like de dummy in a bridge game vaiting for de last trump. No? Okay, so I close all de doors to him, dere is only t'ree, dis main vun and vun to my cabin and vun to de vorkshop. I close dem and veld dem shut and dere he is!"

Emily gasped.

She leaned forward and kissed him.

"Yudas priest," murmured Herr Syrup faintly. His revolving eyeballs slowed and he licked his lips. "T'ank you very kind," he said.

"You're wonderful!" glowed Emily, brushing mustache hairs off her nose.

And then, suddenly: "No. No, we can't. I mean, he'll be right in there with the machinery and if he turns it off—"

"Dat's okay. All de generators and t'ings is locked in deir shieldings, and dose keys I have got." Herr Syrup stumped quickly down the hall and into the machine shop. "His gun does him no good behind velded alloy plating." He selected a torch, plugged it in, and checked the current. "So. Please to hand me dat helmet and apron and dose gloves. Don't look bare-eyed at de flame."

Gently, he closed the side door. Momentarily he was terrified that McConnell would awaken: not that the Erseman would do him any harm, but the scoundrel was so unfairly large. However, even the reek of burning paint, which sent Emily gagging back into the corridor, failed to stir him.

Herr Syrup plugged his torch to a drum of extension cord and trailed after her. "Tum-te-tum-te-tum," he warbled, attacking the main door. "How does dat old American vork song go? Yohn Henry said to de captain, Vell, a man ain't not'ing but a man, but before I umpty-tumty-somet'ing-somet'ing, I'll die vit' a somet'ing-umpty-tum, Lord, Lord, I'll die vit' a tiddly-tiddly-pom!" He finished the job. "And now to my cabin, and ve is t'rough."

Emily's mouth quivered. "I do hate to do this," she said. "I mean, he is such a darling. No, of course he isn't, I mean he's an oaf, but—not really an oaf either, he just has never had a chance to—Oh, you know what I mean! And now he'll be shut away in there, all alone, for days and days and days."

Herr Syrup paused. "You can talk to him on de intercom," he suggested.

"What?" She elevated her nose. "That big lout? *Let* him sit all alone! Maybe then he can see there are other people in the universe besides himself!"

Herr Syrup entered his cabin and began to close the inner door.

"McConnell is a four-lettering love child!" screamed Claus.

"He is not either!" yelled Emily, turning red.

There was a stir in the engine-room darkness. "What's all that racket out there?" complained a lilting basso. "Is it not enough to break me heart, ye must keep me from the sleep which is me one remainin' comfort?"

"Sorry," said Herr Syrup, and closed the door.

"Hey, there!" bawled McConnell. He bounced off his bedroll. The vibration of it shivered in the metal. "What's going on?"

"Yust lie down," babbled Herr Syrup. "Go back to sleep." His cracked baritone soared as he switched on the torch. Sparks showered about him. *"Lullaby-y-y and good night, dy-y-y mo-o-o-der's deli-ight—"*

"Ah, ha!" McConnell thundered toward the door. "So 'tis cannin' me ye are, ye treacherous Black-an'-Tanners! We'll see about that!"

"Look out!" screamed Emily. "Look out, Rory! It's hot!"

A torrent of Gaelic oaths, which made Claus gape in awe, informed her that McConnell had discovered this for himself. Herr Syrup played the flame up and down and crossways. A tommy gun rattled on the other side, but the *Girl*, though old, was of good solid construction, and nothing happened but a nasty spang of ricochet.

"Don't!" pleaded Emily. "Don't, Rory! You'll kill yourself! Oh, Rory, be careful!"

Herr Syrup cut off his torch, slapped back his helmet, and looked with enormous self-congratulation at the slowly cooling seams. "Dere, now," he said. "Dat's dat!"

Claus squawked. The engineer turned around just in time to see his bunk blankets spring up in flame.

Emily leaned against the wall and cried through smoke and fire extinguisher fumes: "Rory, Rory! Are you all right, Rory?"

"Oh, yes, I'm alive," growled the voice behind the panels. "It pleases ye better to let me thirst an' starve to death in here than kill me honestly, eh?"

"Ou ma Dia!" gasped the girl. "I didn't think of that!"

"Yes, yes. Tell it to the King's marines."

"Just a minute!" she begged, frantic. "Just a minute and I'll get you out! Rory, I swear I never— Look out, I'll have to cut the door open—"

Herr Syrup dropped the plastifoam extinguisher and clapped a hand on her wrist as she picked up the torch. "Vat you ban doing?" he yelped.

"I've got to release him!" cried Emily. "We've got to! He hasn't anything in there to keep him alive!"

Herr Syrup gave her a long stare. "So you t'ink his life is vort' more dan all de folk vat maybe get killed if dere is a var, huh?" he asked slowly.

"Yes . . . no . . . oh, I don't know!" sobbed the girl, struggling in his grasp and kicking at his ankles. "We've got to let him out, that's all!"

"Now vait, vait yust a minute. I t'ought of dis problem right avay. It is not so hard. Dere is ventilator shafts running all t'rough de ship, maybe ten centimeters diameter. Ve yust unscrew a fan in vun and drop down cans of space rations to him. And a can opener, natural. It vill not hurt him to eat cold beans and drink beer for a vile. He has also got a bat'-room in dere, and I t'ink a pack of cards. He vill be okay."

"Oh, thank God!" whispered Emily.

She put her lips close to the door and called: "Did you hear that, Rory? We'll send you food through the ventilator. And don't worry about it being just cold beans. I mean, I'll make you nice hot lunches and wrap them well so you can get them intact. I'm not a bad cook, Rory, honestly, I'll prove it to you. Oh, and do you have a razor? Otherwise I'll find one for you. I mean, you don't want to come out all bristly— I mean—oh, never mind!"

"So," rumbled the prisoner. "Yes, I heard." Suddenly he shouted with laughter. "Ah, 'tis sweet of yez, darlin', but it won't be needful. Ye'll be releasin' me in a day or two at the most."

Herr Syrup started and glared at the door. "Vat's dat?" he snapped.

"Why, 'tis simple 'tis. For the lifeboats are down on Grendel, an' even the propulsive units of every spacesuit aboard, not to speak of the radio an' radar, an' the spare electrical parts is all in here with me. An' so, for the matter of it, is the engines. Ye can't get the King's help, ye can't even get back to ground, without a by-your-leave from me. So I'll expect ye to open the door in as few hours as it takes for that fact to sink home into the square head of yez. Haw, haw, haw!"

"Det var som fanden," said the engineer.

"What?"

"De hell you say. I got to look into dis." Herr Syrup scurried from the cabin, his nightgown flapping about his hairy shanks and the forgotten fire extinguisher still jetting plastifoam on the floor behind him.

"Oh, dear." Emily wrung her hands. "We just don't have any luck."

McConnell's voice came back: "Never mind, macushla, for I heard how ye feared for me life, an' that at a moment whin ye thought ye'd the upper hand. So 'tis humbly I ask your pardon for all I said earlier this night. 'Twas a good trick ye've played on me now, even if it did not work, an' many a long winter evenin' we'll while away in after years a-laughin' at it."

"Oh, Rory!" breathed Emily, leaning against the door.

"Oh, Emily!" breathed McConnell on his side.

"Rory!" whispered the girl, closing her eyes.

The unnoticed plastifoam crept up toward her ears.

CHAPTER 8

Sarmishkidu slithered into the Number Three hold and found Herr Syrup huddled gloomily beneath one of the enormous beer casks. He had a mug in one hand and the tap of the keg in the other. Claus perched on a rack muttering: "Damn

Rory McConnell. Damn anybody who von't damn Rory McConnell. Damn anybody who von't sit up all night damning Rory McConnell."

"Oh, there you are," said the Martian. "Your breakfast has gotten cold."

"I don't vant no breakfast," said Herr Syrup. He tossed off his mug and tapped it full again.

"Not even after your triumph last watch?"

"Vat good is a triumph ven I ain't triumphant? I have sealed him into de engine room, *ja*, vich is to say ve can't move de ship from dis orbit. You see, de polarity reverser vich I installed on de geegee lines, to give us veight, is in dere vit' him, and ve can't travel till it has been taken out again. So ve can't go direct to New Vinshester ourselves. And he has also de electrical parts locked up vit' him."

"I have never sullied my mathematics with any attempt at a merely practical application," said Sarmishkidu piously, "but I have studied electromagnetic theory and it would appear upon integration of the Maxwell equations that you could rip out wires here and there, machine the bar and plate metal stored for repair work in the shop, and thus improvise an oscillator."

"Sure," said Herr Syrup. "Dat is easy. But remember, New Vinshester is about ten t'ousand kilometers avay. Any little laboratory model powered yust off a 220-volt line to some cabin, is not going to carry a broadcast dat far. At least, not vun vich has a reasonable shance of being noticed dere in all de cosmic noise. I do have access to some powerful batteries. By discharging dem very quick, ve can send a strong signal: but short-lived, so it is not likely in so little a time dat anyvun on de capital asteroid is listening in on dat particular vavelengt'. For you see, vit'out de calibrated standards and meters vich McConnell has, I cannot control de freqvency vich no vun of New Vinshester's small population uses or is tuned in on."

He sighed. "No, I have spent de night trying to figure out somet'ing, and all I get is de answer I had before. To make an S.O.S. dat vill have any measurable shance of being heard, ve shall have to have good cable, good impedances, meters and so on—vich McConnell is now sitting on. Or else ve shall have to run for a long time t'rough many unknown freqvencies, to be sure of getting at least vun vich will be heard; and for dat ve shall have to use de enshine room g'enerator, vich McConnell is also sitting on."

"He is?" Sarmishkidu brightened. "But it puts out a good many thousands of volts, doesn't it?"

"I vas speaking figurative, damn de luck." Herr Syrup put the beer mug to his lips, lifted his mustache out of the way with a practiced forefinger, and bobbed his Adam's apple for a while.

Sarmishkidu folded his walking tentacles and let down his bulbous body. He waggled his ears, rolled his eyeballs, and protested: "But we can't give up yet! We just can't. Here iss all dis beautiful beer that I could sell at fifty percent profit, even if I have the pretzels and popcorn free. And what good is it doing? None!"

"Oh, I vouldn't say dat," answered Herr Syrup, a trifle blearily, and drew another mugful.

"Dis lot has too much carbonation for my taste," he complained. "You t'ink I ban an American? It makes too much head."

"That's on special order from me," confided the Martian. "In the head is the profit, if one is not too generous in scrapping it off."

"You is got too many arms and not enough soul," said Herr Syrup. "I t'ink for dat I let you clean out my cabin. It is got full vit' congealed plastifoam. And to make a new fire extingvisher for it, vy, I take a bottle of your too carbonated beer and if dere is a fire I shake it and take my t'umb off de mout' and— Of course," mused Herr Syrup, "could be you got so much CO_2 coming out, I get t'rown backwards."

"If you don't like my beer," said Sarmishkidu, half closing his eyes, "you can just let me have the stein you got."

"Action and reaction," said Herr Syrup.

"Hm?"

"Newton's t'ird law."

"Yes, yes, yes, but what relevance does that have to—"

"Beer. I shoot beer out de front end of de bottle, I get tossed on my can."

"But you said it was a bottle."

"Ja, ja, ja, ja—"

"Weiss' nicht wie gut ich dir bin?" sang the Martian.

"I mean," said Herr Syrup, wagging a solemn finger, "de bottle is a kind of rocket. Vy, it could even—it could even—"

His voice ground to a halt. The mug dropped from his hand and splashed on the floor.

"Beerslayer!" screamed Claus.

"But darlin'," said Rory McConnell into the intercom, "I don't like dried apricots."

"Oh, hush," said Emily Croft from the galley. "You've never been healthier in your life."

"I feel like I'm rottin' away. Not through the monotony so much, me sweet, whilst I can be hearin' the soft voice of yez, but the only exercise I can get is calisthinics, which has always bored me grievous."

"True," said Emily, "all those fuel pipes and things don't leave much room for classical dancing, do they? Poor dear!"

"I'd trade me mother's brown pig for a walk in the rain wi' yez, macushla."

"Well, if you'd only give us your parole not to make trouble, dear, we could let you out this minute."

"No, ye well know the Force has me prior oath an' the Force I'll fight for till 'tis disbanded either through victory or defeat. An' how long will it take the auld *omadhaun* Syrup to realize 'tis him has been defayted? I've lain in here almost a week be the clock. I hear noises day an' night from the machine room, an' devil a word I can get of what's goin' on. Let me out, swateheart! I bear no ill will. I'll kiss the pretty lips of ye an' we'll all go down to Grendel an' say nothin' about what's happened. Save of course that I've won the loveliest girl in the galaxy for me own."

"I wish I could," sighed Emily. "How I wish it! *'O Dion who sent my heart mad with love!'* "

"Who's this Dion?" bristled Major McConnell.

"Nobody you need worry about, dear. It's only a quotation. Translated, naturally. But what I mean to say is, Mr. Syrup and Mr. Sarmishkidu have so much to take care of and it won't be long now, I swear it won't, just another day or two, they say, and then their project will be over and they can— Oh! I promised not to tell! But what I mean, dear, is that I'll stay behind and I'm not supposed to let you out immediately, maybe not for still another day, but I'll look after you and make you nice lunches and—Yes," said Emily with a slight shudder, "there won't even be any more dried fruit in your meals, because I've run out of what there was; in fact, for days now I've been giving it all to you and eating corned beef and drinking beer myself, and I must admit it tastes better than I remembered, so if you insist on calcifying your liver after we're married, why, I suppose I'll have to also, and actually, darling, I don't know anyone who I'd rather calcify my liver with. Really."

"What is all this?" Rory McConnell stepped back, his big frame tensing. "Ye mean they've not just been putterin' about, but have some plan?"

"I mustn't tell! Please, beloved, honestly, I've been sworn to absolute secrecy, and now I must go. They need me to help too. I have been installing pipe lines and things and actually, dear, it's very exciting. I mean, when I use a welding torch I have to wear a helmet very much like a classical dramatic mask, so I stand there reciting from the *Agamemnon* as if I were on a real Athenian stage, and do you know, I think when this is all over and we're married and have our own Greek theater in the garden I'll organize a presentation of the whole *Orestes* trilogy—in the original, of course—with welding outfits. 'Bye now!" Emily blew a kiss down the intercom and pattered off.

Rory McConnell sat down on a generator shield and began most furiously to think.

CHAPTER 9

The first beer-powered spaceship in history rested beneath a derrick by the main cargo hatch.

It was not as impressive as Herr Syrup could have wished. Using a small traveling lift for the heavy work, he had joined four ten-ton casks of Nashornbräu end to end with a light framework. The taps had been removed from the kegs and their bungholes plugged, simple electrically-controlled Venturi valves in the plumb center being substituted. Jutting on orthogonal axes from each barrel there were also L-shaped exhaust pipes, by which it was hoped to control rotation and sideways motion. Various wires and shafts, their points of entry sealed with gunk, plunged into the barrels, ending in electric beaters. A set of relays was intended to release each container as it was exhausted. The power for all this—it did not amount to much—came from a system of heavy-duty EXW batteries at the front end.

Ahead of those batteries was fastened a box, some two meters square and three meters long. Sheets of plastic were set in its black-painted sides by way of windows. The torso and helmet of a spacesuit jutted from the roof, removably fastened in a screwthreaded hatch cover which could be turned around. Beside it was a small stovepipe valve holding two self-closing elastic diaphragms through which tools could be pushed without undue air loss. The box had been put together out of cardboard beer cases, bolted to a light metal frame and carefully sized and gunked.

''You see,'' Herr Syrup had explained grandly, ''in dis situation, vat do ve need to go to New Vinshester? Not an atomic motor, for sure, because dere is almost negligible gravity to overcome. Not a nice streamlined shape, because ve have no air hereabouts. Not great structural strengt', for dere is no strain odder dan a very easy acceleration; so beer cardboard is strong enough for two, t'ree men to sit on a box of it under Eart' gravity. Not a fancy t'ermostatic system for so short a hop, for de sun is far avay, our own bodies make heat and losing dat heat by radiation is a slow process. If it does get too hot inside, ve can let a little vater evaporate into space t'rough de stovepipe to cool us; if ve get chilly, ve can tap a little heat t'rough a coil off de batteries.

"All ve need is air. Not even much air, since I is sitting most of de time and you ban a Martian. A pair of oxygen cylinders should make more dan enough; *ja*, and ve vill need a chemical carbon-dioxide absorber, and some desiccating stuffs so you do not get a vater vapor drunk. For comfort ve vill take along a few bottles beer and some pretzels to nibble on.

"As for de minimal boat itself, I have tested de exhaust velocity of hot, agitated beer against vacuum, and it is enough to accelerate us to a few hundred kilometers per hour, maybe t'ree hundred, if ve use a high enough mass ratio. And ve vill need a few simple navigating instruments, an ephemeris, slide rule, and so on. As a precaution, I install my bicycle in de cabin, hooked to a simple homemade generator, yust a little electric motor yuggled around to be run in reverse, vit' a rectifier. Dat vay, if de batteries get too veak ve can recharge dem. And also a small, primitive oscillator ve can make, short range, *ja*, but able to run a gamut of freqvencies vit'out exhausting de batteries, so ve can send an S.O.S. ven ve ban qvite close to New Vinshester. Dey hear it and send a spaceship out to pick us up, and dat is dat."

The execution of this theory had been somewhat more difficult, but Herr Syrup's years aboard the *Mercury Girl* had made him a highly skilled improviser and jackleg inventor. Now, tired, greasy, and content, he smoked a well-earned pipe as he stood admiring his creation. Partly, he waited for the electric coils which surrounded the boat and tapped the ship's power lines, to heat the beer sufficiently; but that was very nearly complete, to the point of unsafeness. And partly he waited for the ship to reach that orbital point which would give his boat full tangential velocity toward the goal; that would be in a couple of hours.

"Er . . . are you sure we had better not test it first?" asked Sarmishkidu uneasily.

"No, I t'ink not," said Herr Syrup. "First, it vould take too long to fix up an extra barrel. Ve been up here a veek or more vit'out a vord to Grendel. If O'Toole gets suspicious and looks t'rough a telescope and sees us scooting around, right avay he sends up a lifeboat full of soldiers; vich is a second reason for not making a test flight."

"But, well, that is, suppose something goes wrong?"

"Den de spacesuit keeps me alive for several hours and you can stand vacuum about de same lengt' of time. Emily vill be vatching us t'rough de ship's telescope, so she can let McConnell out and he can come rescue us."

"And what if he can't find us? Or if we have an accident out of telescopic range from here? Space is a large volume."

"I prefer you vould not mention dat possibility," said Herr Syrup with a touch of hauteur.

Sarmishkidu shuddered. "The things that an honest businessman has got to— *Donnerwetter! Was ist das?*"

The sharp crack was followed by an earthquake tremble through girders and plates. Herr Syrup sat down, hard. The deck twitched beneath him. He bounced up and pelted toward the exit. "Dat vas from de stern!" he shouted.

He whipped through the bulkhead door, Sarmishkidu toiling in his wake, and up an interhold ladder to the axial passageway. Emily Croft had just emerged from the galley, a frying pan in one hand and an apron tied around her classic peplum. "Oh, dear," she cried, "I'm sure Rory's cake has fallen. What was that noise?"

"Yust vat I vould like to know." The engineer flung himself down the corridor. As he neared the stern, a faint acrid whiff touched his nose. "In de engine room, I am afraid," he panted.

"The engine—*Rory!*" shrieked the girl.

"Comin', macushla," said a cheerful voice, and the gigantic red-thatched shape swung itself up from the after companionway.

Rory McConnell hooked thumbs in his belt, planted his booted feet wide, and grinned all over his smoke-blackened snub face. Herr Syrup crashed to a halt and stared frog-eyed. The Erseman's green tunic hung in rags and blood trickled from his nose. But the soot only made his teeth the more wolfishly white and his eyes the more high-voltage blue, while his bare torso turned out to carry even thicker muscles than expected.

"Well, well, well," he beamed. "An' so here we all are ag'in. Emily, me love, I ask your humble pardon for inny damage, but I couldn't wait longer for the sight of yez."

"Vat have you done?" wailed Herr Syrup.

"Oh, well, sir, 'twas nothin'. I had me cartridges, an' a can opener an' me teeth an' other such tools. So I extracted the powder, tamped it in an auld beer bottle, lay a fuse, fired me last shot to light same, an' blew out one of them doors. An' now, sir, let's have a look at what ye been doin' this past week, an' then I think it best we return to the cool green hills of Grendel."

"Ooooh," said Herr Syrup.

McConnell laughed so that the hall rang with his joy, looked into the stricken wide gaze of his beloved, and opened his arms. "No so much as a kiss to seal the betrothal?" he said.

"Oh . . . yes . . . I'm sorry, darling." Emily ran toward him.

"I *am* sorry," she choked, burst into tears, and clanged the frying pan down on his head.

McConnell staggered, tripped on his boots, recovered, and waltzed in a circle. "Get away!" screamed Emily. "Get away!"

Herr Syrup paused for one frozen instant. Then he flung out a curse, whirled, and pounded back along the corridor. At the interhold ladderhead he found Sarmishkidu, puffing along at the slow pace of a Martian under Terrestrial gee. "What has transpired?" asked Sarmishkidu.

Herr Syrup scooped him up under one arm and bounded down the ladder. "Hey!" squealed the Martian. "Let me go! *Bist du ganz geistegestört?* What do you mean, sir? *Urush nergatar shalmu ishkadam!* This instant! *Versteh'st du?*"

Rory McConnell staggered to the nearest wall and leaned on it for a few seconds. His eyes cleared. With a hoarse growl, he sprang after the engineer. Emily stuck a shapely leg in his path. Down he went.

"Please!" she wept. "Please, darling, don't make me do this!"

"They're gettin' away!" bawled McConnell. He got to his feet. Emily hit him with the frying pan. He sagged back to hands and knees. She stooped over him, frantically, and kissed the battered side of his head. He lurched erect. Emily slugged him again.

"You're being cruel!" she sobbed.

The bulkhead door closed behind Herr Syrup. He set the unloading controls. "Ve ban getting out of here," he panted. "Before de Erser gets to de master svitch and stops everyt'ing cold."

"What Erser?" sputtered Sarmishkidu indignantly.

"Ours." Herr Syrup trotted toward the beer boat.

"Oh, that one!" Sarmishkidu hurried after him.

Herr Syrup climbed to the top of his boat's hull and lifted the space armor torso. Sarmishkidu swarmed after him like a herpetarium gone mad. The Dane dropped the Martian inside, took a final checkaround, and lowered himself. He screwed the spacesuit into place and hunched, breathing heavily. His bicycle headlamp was the only illumination in the box. It showed him the bicycle itself, braced upright with the little generator hitched to its rear wheel; the pants of his space armor, seated on a case of beer; a bundle of navigation instruments, tables, pencils, slide rule, and note pad; a tool box; two oxygen cylinders and a CO_2–H_2O absorber unit with an electric blower, which would also circulate the air as needed during free fall; the haywired control levers which were supposed to steer the boat; Sarmishkidu, draped on a box of pretzels; and Claus, disdainfully stealing from a box of popcorn which Herr Syrup suddenly realized he had no way of popping. And then, of course, himself.

It was rather cramped quarters.

The air pump roared, evacuating the chamber. Herr Syrup saw darkness thicken outside the boat windows, as the fluoro light ceased to be diffused. And then the great hatch swung ponderously open, and steel framed a blinding circle of stars.

"Hang on!" he yelled. "Here ve go!"

The derrick scanned the little boat with beady photoelectric eyes, seized it in four claws, lifted it, and pitched it delicately through the hatch, which thereupon closed with an air of good riddance to bad rubbish. Since there was no machine outside to receive the boat, it turned end for end, spun a few meters from the *Mercury Girl*, and drifted along in much the same orbit, still trying to rotate on three simultaneous axes.

Herr Syrup gulped. The transition to weightlessness was an outrage, and the stars ramping around his field of view didn't help matters. His stomach lurched. Sarmishkidu groaned, hung onto the pretzel box with all six tentacles, and covered his eyes with his ears. Claus screamed, turning end for end in midair, and tried without success to fly. Herr Syrup reached for a control lever but didn't quite make it. Sarmishkidu uncovered one sick eye long enough to mumble: "Bloody blank blasted Coriolis force." Herr Syrup clenched his teeth, caught a mouthful of mustache, grimaced, spat it out, and tried again. This time he laid hands on the switch and pulled.

A cloud of beer gushed frostily from one of the transverse pipes. After several rather unfortunate attempts, Herr Syrup managed to stop the boat's rotation. He looked around him. He hung in darkness, among blazing stars. Grendel was a huge gibbous green moon to starboard. The *Mercury Girl* was a long rusty spindle to port. The asteroid sun, small and weak but perceived by the adaptable human eye as quite bright enough, poured in through the spacesuit helmet in the roof and bounced dazzlingly off his bare scalp.

He swallowed sternly, to remind his stomach who was boss, and began taking navigational sights. Sarmishkidu rolled a red look "upward" at Claus, who clung miserably to the Martian's head with eyes tightly shut.

Herr Syrup completed his figuring. It would have been best to wait a while yet, to get the maximum benefit of orbital velocity toward New Winchester; but McConnell was not going to wait. Anyhow, this was such a slow orbit that it didn't make much difference. Most likely the factor would be quite lost among the fantastically uncertain quantities of the boat itself. One would have to take what the good Lord sent. He gripped the control levers.

A low murmur filled the cabin as the rearmost beer barrel snorted its vapors into space. There was a faint backward tug of acceleration pressure, which mounted very gradually as mass decreased. The thrust was not centered with absolute precision, and of course the distribution of mass throughout the whole structure was hit-or-miss, so the boat began to pick up a spin again. Steering by the seat of his pants and a few primitive meters, Herr Syrup corrected that tendency with side jets.

Blowing white beer fumes in all directions, the messenger boat moved slowly along a wobbling spiral toward New Winchester.

CHAPTER 10

"Oh, darling, dearest, beloved," wept Emily, dabbing at Rory McConnell's head, "forgive me!"

"I love yez too," said the Erseman, sitting up, "but unliss

ye'll stop poundin' in me skull I'll have to lock yez up for the duration."

"I promise . . . I promise . . . oh, I couldn't bear it! Sweetheart—" Emily clutched his arm as he rose—"can't you let them go now? I mean, they've gotten clean away, you've lost, so why don't we wait here and, well, I mean to say, really."

"What do you mean to say?"

Emily blushed and lowered her eyes. "If you don't know," she said in a prim voice, "I shall certainly not tell you."

McConnell blushed too.

Then, resolutely, he started toward the bridge. The girl hurried after him. He flung back: "Tell me what it is they're escapin' in, an' maybe I'll be ready to concede hon'rable defeat." But having been informed, he only barked a laugh and said, "Well, an' tis a gallant try, 'tis, but me with a regular spaceship at me beck can't admit the end of the game. In fact, me dear, I'm sorry to say they haven't a Plutonian's chance in hell."

By that time he was in the turret, sweeping the skies with its telescope. It took him a while to find the boat; already it was a mere speck in the gleaming dark. He scowled, chewed his lip, and muttered half to himself:

" 'Twill take time to extract the polarity reverser, an' me not a trained engineer. By then the craft will be indeed hard to locate. If I went on down to Grendel to get help, 'twould take hours to reach the ear of himself an' assimble a crew, if I know me Erse lads. An' hours is too long. So—I'll have to go after our friends there alone. Acushla, I don't think ye'll betray their cause if ye fix me a sandwich or six an' open me a bottle of beer whilst I work."

McConnell did, in fact, require almost an hour to get the geegee repulsors to repulsing again. With the compensator still on the fritz, that put the ship's interior back in free fall state. He floated, dashing the sweat from his brow, and smiled at Emily. "Go strap yourself in, me rose of Grendel, for I may well have to make some sharp maneuvers an' I wouldn't be bruisin' of that fair skin— Damn! Git away!'' That was addressed to the sweat he had just dashed from his brow. Swatting blindly at the fog of tiny globules, he pushed one leg against a wall and arrowed out the door.

Up in the turret again, harnessed in his seat before the pilot console, he tickled its controls and heard the engines purr. ''Are ye ready, darlin'?'' he called into the intercom.

''Not yet, sweetheart,'' Emily's voice floated back. ''One moment, please.''

''A moment only,'' warned McConnell, squinting into the telescope. He could not have found the fleeting boat at all were it not for the temporary condensation of beer vapor into a cloud as expansion chilled it. And all he saw was a tiny, ghostly nebula on the very edge of vision. To be sure, knowing approximately what path the fugitives must follow gave him a track; he could doubtless always come within a hundred kilometers of them that way; but—

''Are ye ready, me sugar?''

''Not yet, love. I'll be with you in a jiffy.''

McConnell drummed impatient fingers on the console. The *Mercury Girl* swung gently around Grendel. His head still throbbed.

''Da-a-a-arlin'! Time's a-wastin'! We'll be late!''

''Oh, give me just a sec. Really, dearest, you might remember when we're married and have to go out someplace, a girl wants to look her best, and that takes time, I mean dresses and cosmetics and so on aren't classical but I guess if I can give up my principles for you so you can be proud of me and if I can eat the things you like even if they aren't natural, well, then you can wait a little while for me to make myself presentable and—''

''A man has two choices in this universe,'' said McConnell grimly to himself, ''he can remain celibate or he can resign himself to spendin' ten per cent of his life waitin' for women.''

He glared at the chronometer. ''We're late already!'' he

snapped. "I'll have to run off a different approach curve to our orbit an'—"

"Well, you can be doing it, can't you? I mean, instead of just sitting there grumbling at me, why don't you do something constructive like punching that old computer or whatever it is?"

McConnell stiffened. "Emily," he said through thinned lips, "are ye by any chance stallin' me?"

"Why, Rory, how could you? Merely because a girl has to—"

He calculated the required locus and said, "Ye've got just sixty seconds to prepare for acceleration."

"But Rory!"

"Fifty seconds."

"But I mean to say, actually—"

"Forty seconds."

"Oh, right-o, then. And I'm not angry with you, love, really I'm not. I mean, I want you to know a girl admires a man like you who actually is a man. Why, what would I do with one of those awful 'Yes, dear' types, they're positively Roman! Imperial Roman, I mean. The Republican Romans were at least virile, though of course they were barbarians and rather hairy. But what I meant to say, Rory, is that one reason I love you so much—"

After about five minutes of this, Major McConnell realized what was going on. With an inarticulate snarl he stabbed the computer, corrected his curve for time lost, punched it into the autopilot, and slapped down the main drive switch.

First the ship turned, seeking her direction, and then a Terrestrial gravity of acceleration pushed him back into the chair. No reason to apply more; he felt sure that leprechaun job he was chasing could scarcely pick up one meter per second squared, and matching velocities would be a tricky enough business for one man alone. He saw Grendel swing past the starboard viewport and drop behind. He applied a repulsor field forward to kill some of his present speed, simultaneously giving the ship an impulse toward ten-thirty o'clock, twenty-three degrees "high." In a smooth arc, the *Mercury Girl* picked up the trail of Herr Syrup and began to close the gap.

"Ah, now we'll end this tale," murmured Rory McConnell, "an' faith, ye've been a worthy foeman an 'tis not I that will stint ye when we meet ag'in in some friendly pub after the glorious redemption of Gaelic La— Oops!"

For a horrible moment, he thought that some practical joker had pulled the seat out from under him. He fell toward the floor, tensing his gluteal muscles for the crash . . . and fell, and fell, and after a few seconds realized he was in free fall.

"What the jumpin' blue hell?" he roared and glared at the control board meters, just as the lights went out.

A thousand stars leered through the viewport. McConnell clawed blindly at his harness. He heard the ventilator fans sigh to a halt. The stillness became frightful. "Emily!" he shouted, "Emily, where are ye?" There was no reply. Somehow he found the intercom switch and jiggled it. Only a mechanical clicking answered; that circuit was also dead.

Groping and flailing his way aft, he needed black minutes to reach the engine room. It was like a cave. He entered, blind, drifting free, fanning the air with one invisible hand to keep from smothering in his own unventilated exhalations, his heartbeat thick and horrible in his ears. There should be a flashlight clipped somewhere near the door—but where? "Mother of God!" he groaned. "Are we fallen into the devil's fingers?"

A small sound came from somewhere in the gloom. "What's that?" he bawled. "Who's there? Where are ye? Speak up before I beat the bejasus out of yez, ye—" and he went on with a richness of description to be expected when Gaelic blood has had a checkered career.

"Rory!" said an offended feminine voice out of the abyss. "If you are going to use that kind of language before me, you can just wipe your mouth out and not come back until you are prepared to say it in Greek like a gentleman! I mean, really!"

"Are ye here? Darlin', are ye here? I thought—"

"Well," said the girl, "I know I promised not to hit you anymore, and I wouldn't, not for all the world, but I still have to do what I can, don't I, dear? I mean, if I gave up you'd just despise me. It wouldn't be British."

"What have ye done?"

After a long pause, Emily said in a small voice: "I don't know."

"How's that?" snapped McConnell.

"I just went over to that control panel or whatever it is and started pulling switches. I mean to say, you don't expect me to know what all those things are for, do you? Because I don't. However," said Emily brightly, "I can parse Greek verbs."

"Oh . . . no!" groaned McConnell. He began fumbling his way toward the invisible board. Where was it, anyhow?

"I can cook too," said Emily. "And sew. And I'm awfully fond of children."

Herr Syrup noted on his crude meters that the first-stage beer barrel was now exhausted. He pulled the switch that dropped it and pushed himself up into the spacesuit to make sure that that had actually been done. Peering through the helmet globe, he saw that one relay had stuck and the keg still clung. He popped back inside and told Sarmishkidu to hand him some sections of iron pipe through the stovepipe valve; this emergency was not unanticipated. Clumsy in gauntlets, his fingers screwed the pieces together to make a prod which could reach far aft and crack the empty cask loose.

It occurred to him how much simpler it would have been to keep his tools in a box fastened to the outer hull. But of course such things only come to mind when a model is being tested.

He stared aft. The *Mercury Girl* was visible to the unaided eye, though dwindling perceptibly. She still floated inert, but he could not expect that condition to prevail for long. Well, a man can but try. Herr Syrup wriggled out of the armor torso and back into the cabin. Claus was practicing free-fall flight technique and nipping stray droplets of beer out of the air; sometimes he collided with a drifting empty bottle, but he seemed to enjoy himself.

"Resuming acceleration," said Herr Syrup. "Give me a pretzel."

Suds gushed from the second barrel. The boat wobbled crazily. Of course the loss of the first one had changed its spin characteristics. Herr Syrup compensated and plowed doggedly on. The second cask emptied and was discharged without trouble. He cut in the third one.

Presently Sarmishkidu crawled "up" into the spacesuit. A whistle escaped him.

"Vat?" asked Herr Syrup.

"There—behind us—your spaceship—und it is coming *verdammten* fast!"

Having strapped his fiancée carefully into the acceleration chair beside his own, Rory McConnell resumed pursuit. He had lost a couple of hours by now, between one thing and another. And while she drifted free, the *Girl* had of course orbited well off the correct track. He had to get back on it and then start casting about. For a half hour of strained silence, he maneuvered.

"There!" he said at last.

"Where?" asked Emily.

"In the scope," said McConnell. His ill humor let up and he squeezed her hand. "Hang on, here we go. I'll have thim back aboard in ten minutes."

The hazy cloud waxed so fast that he revised his estimate upward. He had too much velocity; it would be necessary to overshoot, brake, and come back—

Then *crash! clang-ng-ng!* His teeth jarred together. For a moment, his heart paused and he knew naked fear.

"What was that?" asked Emily.

He hated to frighten her, but he forced out of suddenly stiff and sandy lips: "A meteor, I'm sure. An' judgin' from the sound of it, 'twas big an' fast enough to stave in a whole compartment.'' You could not exactly roll your eyes heavenward in free space, but he tried manfully. ''Holy St. Patrick, is this any way to treat your loyal son?''

He shot past the wallowing beer boat at kilometers per second, falling free while he ripped off his harness. ''The instruments aren't showin' damage, but belike the crucial one is been knocked out,'' he muttered. ''An' us with no engine crew an' no deckhands. I'll have to go out there meself to check. At least this section is unharmed.'' He nodded at the handkerchief he had thrown into the air; when the ventilators were briefly turned off, it simply hung, borne on no current of leakage. ''If we begin to lose air elsewhere, sweetheart, there'll be automatic ports to seal yez off, so ye're all right for the next few hours.''

''But what about you?'' she cried, white-faced now that she understood. ''What about you?''

''I'll be in a spacesuit.'' He leaned over and kissed her. '' 'Tis not the danger that's so great as the delay. For somethin' I'll have to do, jist so acceleration strain don't pull the damaged hull apart. I'll be back when I can, darlin'.''

And yet, as he went aft, there was no sealing bulwark in his way, nowhere a wind whistling toward the dread emptiness outside. Puzzled and more than a little daunted, Rory McConnell completed his interior inspection in the engine room, broke out his own outsize space armor from his pack, and donned it: a slow, awkward task for one man alone. He floated to the nearest airlock and let himself out.

It was eerie on the hull, where only his clinging bootsoles held him fast among streaming cold constellations. The harshness of undiffused sunlight and the absolute blackness of shadow made it hard to recognize anything for what it was. He saw a goblin and crossed himself violently before realizing it was only a lifeboat tank; and he was an experienced spaceman.

An hour's search revealed no leak. There was a dent in the bow which might or might not be freshly made, nothing else. And yet that meteor had struck with such a doomsday clang that he had thought the hull might be torn in two. Well, evidently St. Patrick had been on the job. McConnell returned inside, disencumbered himself, went forward, reassured Emily, and began to kill his unwanted velocity.

Almost two hours had passed before he was back in the vicinity of the accident, and then he could not locate the fugitive boat. By now it would have ceased blasting; darkly painted, it would be close to invisible in this black sky. He would have to set up a search pattern and—He groaned.

Something drifted across his telescopic field of view. What the deuce? He nudged the spaceship closer, and gasped.

"Son of a—" Hastily, he switched to Gaelic.

"What is it, light of both my eyes?" asked Emily.

McConnell beat his head against the console. "A couple of hoops an' some broken staves," he whimpered. "Oh, no, no, no!"

"But what of it? I mean, after all, when you consider how Mr. Syrup put that boat together, well, actually."

"That's just it!" howled McConnell. "That's what's cost me near heart failure, plus two priceless hours or more an'—That was our meteor! An empty beer barrel! Oh, the ignominy of it!"

Chapter 11

Herr Syrup stopped the exhaust of his fourth-stage keg and leaned back into weightlessness with a sigh. "Ve better not accelerate any more," he said. "Not yust now. Ve vill need a little reserve to maneuver later on."

"Vot later on?" asked Herr von Himmelschmidt sourly. "I don't know vy der ship shot on past us, but soon it comes back und den ve iss maneuvered into chail."

"Vell, meanvile shall ve pass de time?" Herr Syrup took a greasy pack of cards from his jacket and riffled them suggestively.

"Stop riffling them suggestively!" squealed Sarmishkidu. "This is no time for idle amusements."

"Vat else is it a time for?"

"Well . . . hmmm . . . no, not that . . . Perhaps . . . no . . . Shilling ante?"

At the end of some four hours, when he was ahead by several pounds sterling in I.O.U.'s and Sarmishkidu was whistling like an indignant bagpipe, Herr Syrup noticed how dim the light was getting. The gauge showed him that the outside batteries were rather run down also. Everything would have to be charged up again. He explained the situation. "Do you vant first turn on de bicycle or shall I?" he asked.

"Who, me?" Sarmishkidu wagged a languid ear. "Whatever gave you the idea that evolution has prepared my race for bicycle riding?"

"Vell . . . I mean . . . dat is—"

"You are letting your Danishness run away with you."

"Satan i helvede!" muttered Herr Syrup. He floated himself into the saddle, put feet to pedals, and began working.

"And de vorst of it is," he grumbled, "who is ever going to believe I crossed from Grendel to New Vinshester on a bicycle?"

Slowly, majestically, and off-center, the boat picked up an opposite rotation.

"There they be!" cried Rory McConnell.

"Oh dear," said Emily Croft.

The beer boat swelled rapidly in the forward viewport. The weariness of hour upon hour, searching, dropped from the Erseman. "Here we go!" he cried exultantly. *"Tantivy, tantivy, tantivy!"*

Then, lacking radar, he found that the human eye is a poor judge of free-space relationships. He buckled down to the awkward task of matching speeds.

"Whoops!" he said. "Overshot!" Ten kilometers beyond, he came to a relative halt, twisted the cumbersome mass of the ship around, and approached slowly. He saw a head pop up into the spacesuit helmet, glare at him, and pop back again. Foam spouted; the boat slipped out of his view.

McConnell readjusted and came alongside, so that he looked directly from the turret at his prey. "He hasn't the acceleration to escape us," he gloated. "I'll folly each twist an' turn he cares to make, from now until—" He stopped.

"Until we get to New Winchester?" asked Emily in a demure tone.

"But—I mean to say—but!" Major McConnell bugged tired eyes at the keg-and-box bobbing across the stars.

"But I've overhauled them!" he shouted, pounding the console. "I've a regular ship with hundreds of times their mass an' . . . an' . . . they've got to come aboard! It isn't fair!"

"Since we have no wireless, how can you inform them of that?" purred the girl. She leaned over close and patted his cheek. Her gaze softened. "There, there. I'm sorry. I do love you, and I don't want to tease you or anything, but honestly, don't you think you're becoming a bit of a bore on this subject? I mean, enough's enough, don't you know."

"Not if ye're of Erse blood, it isn't." McConnell set his jaw till it ached. "I'll scoop 'em up, that's what I will!"

There was a master control for the cargo machinery in the engine room, but none on the bridge. McConnell unstrapped himself, shoved grimly "down" to the hold section, pumped out the main hatch chamber and opened the lock. Now he had it gaping wide enough to swallow the boat whole, and—

Weight came back. He crashed into the deck. "Emily!" he bellowed, picking himself up with a bloody nose. "Emily, git away from them controls!"

Three Terrestrial gravities of acceleration were a monstrous load on any man. He took minutes to regain the bridge, drag himself to the main console, and slap down the main drive switch. Meanwhile Emily, sagging in her chair and gasping for breath, managed a tolerant smile.

When they again floated free, McConnell bawled at her: "I love yez more than I do me own soul, an' ye're the most beautiful creature the cosmos will ever see, an' I've half a mind to turn yez over me knee an' paddle ye raw!''

''Watch your language, Rory,'' the vicar's daughter reproved. ''Paddle me black and blue, *if* you please. I mean, I don't like double entendres.''

''Ah, be still, ye blitherin' angel,'' he snarled. He swept the sky with a bloodshot telescope. The boat was out of sight again. Of course.

It took him half an hour to relocate it, still orbiting stubbornly on toward New Winchester. And New Winchester had grown noticeably more bright.

''Now we'll see what we'll see,'' grated Major McConnell.

He accelerated till he was dead ahead of the boat, matched speeds—except for a few K.P.H. net toward him which he left for his quarry—and spun broadside to. As nearly as he could gauge it, the boat was aimed directly into his open cargo hatch.

Herr Syrup applied a quick side jet, slipped ''beneath'' the larger hull, and continued on his way.

''Aaaargh!'' Tiny flecks of foam touched McConnell's lips. He tried again.

And again.

And again.

''It's no use,'' he choked at last. ''He can slide past me too easy. The wan thing I could do would be to ram him an' be done— Arragh, hell have him, he knows I'm not a murderer.''

''Really, dear,'' said Emily, ''it would all be so simple if you would just give up and admit he's won.''

''Small chance of that!'' McConnell brooded for a long minute. And slowly a luster returned to his eyes. ''Yes. I have it. The loadin' crane. I'll have to jury-rig a control to the bridge, as well as a visio screen so I can see what I'm doin'. But havin' given meself that much, why, I'll approach ag'in with the crane grapple projectin' from the hatch, reach out, an' grab hold!''

"Rory," said Emily, "you're being tiresome."

"I'm bein' Erse, by all the saints!" McConnell rubbed a bristly red jaw. " 'Tis hours 'twill take me, an' him fleein' the while. Could ye hold us alongside, me only one?"

"Me?" The girl opened wide blue eyes and protested innocently. "But darling, you told me after that last time to leave the controls alone, and I admit I don't know a thing about it. I mean, it would be unlawful for me to try piloting, wouldn't it, and positively dangerous. I mean to say, *medén pratto*."

"Ah, well, I might have known how the good loyal heart of yez would make ye a bloody nuisance. But either give me your word of honor not to touch the pilot board ag'in, or I must break me own heart by tyin' yez into that chair."

"Oh, I promise, dear. I'll promise you anything within reason."

"An' whatsoever ye don't happen to want is unreasonable. Yes." Rory McConnell sighed, kissed his lady love, and went off to work. The escape boat blasted feebly but steadily into a new orbit—not very different, but time and the pull of the remote sun on an inert ship would show their work later on.

General Scourge-of-the-Sassenach O'Toole lifted a gaunt face and glared somberly at the young guardsman who had finally won through to his office. "Well?" he clipped.

"Beggin' your pardon, sir, but—"

"Salute me, ye good-for-nothin' scut!" growled O'Toole. "What kind of an army is it we've got here, where a private soldier passin' the captain in the street slaps his back an' says, 'Paddy, ye auld pig, the top of the mornin' to yez an' if ye've a moment to spare, why 'tis proud I'll be to stand yez a mug of dark in yon tavern'—eh?"

"Well, sir," said the guardsman, his Celtic love of disputation coming to the fore, "I say 'twas a fine well-run army of outstandingly high morale. Though truth to speak, the captain I've been saddled with is a pickle-faced son of a landlord who would not lift his hat to St. Bridget herself, did the dear holy colleen come walkin' in his door."

"Morale, ye say?" shouted O'Toole, springing from his chair. "Morale cuts both ways, ye idiot! How much morale do ye think the officer's corps has got, or I meself, when me own men name me Auld S.O.T.S. to me face, not even bothérin' to sound the initials sep'rit, an' me havin' not touched a drop in all me life? I'll have some respect hereabouts, begorra, or know the reason why!"

"If ye want to know the reason I can give it to ye, General, sir, ye auld maid in britches!" cried the guardsman. His fist smote the desk. " 'Tis just the sour face of yez, that's the rayson, an' if ye drink no drop 'tis because wan look at yez would curdle the poteen in the jug! Now if ye want some constructive suggistions for improvin' the management of this army—"

They passed an enjoyable half hour. At last, having grown hoarse, the guardsman bade the general a friendly good day and departed.

Five minutes later there was a scuffle in the anteroom. A sentry's voice yelped, "Ye can't go in there to himself without an appointment!" and the guardsman answered, "An appointment I've had, since the hour before dawn whin I first came an' tried to get by the bureaucratic lot of yez!" and the scuffle got noisier and at last the office door went off its hinges as the guardsman tossed the sentry through it.

"Beggin' your pardon, sir," he panted, dabbing at a bruised cheek and judiciously holding the sentry down with one booted foot, "but I just remembered why I had to see yez."

"Ye'll go to the brig for this, ye riotous scum!" roared O'Toole. "Corp'ril of the guard! Arrest this man!"

"That attitude is precisely what I was criticizin' earlier," pointed out the soldier. " 'Tis officers like yez what takes all the fun out of war. Why, ye walleyed auld Fomorian, if ye'd been in charge of the Cattle Raid of Cooley, the Brown Bull would still be chewin' cud in his meaddy! Now ye listen to me—''

As four freshly arrived sentries dragged him off, he shouted back: ''All right, then! If ye're going' to be that way about it, all right an' be damned to yez! I won't tell ye my news! I won't speak a word of what I saw through the tellyscope just before sunrise—or failed to see—ye can sit there in blithe ignorance of the Venusian ship havin' vanished from her orbit, till she calls down the Anglian Navy upon yez! See if I care!''

For a long, long moment, General Scourge-of-the-Sassenach O'Toole gaped out at Grendel's blue sky.

CHAPTER 12

Spent, shaking with lack of sleep and sheer muscular weariness, Rory McConnell weaved through free fall toward the bridge. As he passed the galley, Emily stopped him. Having had a night watch of rest, she looked almost irritatingly calm and beautiful. ''There, there, love,'' she said. ''Is it all over with? Come, I've fixed a nice cup of tea.''

''Don't want any tea,'' he growled.

''Oh, but darling, you must! Why, you'll waste away. I swear you're already just skin and bones . . . oh, and your poor dear hands, the knuckles are all rubbed raw. Come on, there's a sweetheart, sit down and have a cup of tea. I mean, actually you'll have to float, and drink it out of one of those silly suction bottles, but the principle is the same. That old boat will keep.''

''Not much longer,'' said McConnell. ''By now, she's far closer to the King than she is to Grendel.''

"But you can wait ten minutes, can't you?" Emily pouted. "You're not only neglecting your health, but me. You've hardly remembered I exist. All those hours, the only thing I heard on the intercom was swearing. I mean, I imagine from the tone it was swearing, though of course I don't speak Gaelic. You will have to teach me after we're married. And I'll teach you Greek. I understand there is a certain affinity between the languages." She rubbed her cheek against his bare chest. "Just as there is between you and me . . . Oh, dear!" She retired to try getting some of the engine grease off her face.

In the end, Rory McConnell did allow himself to be prevailed upon. For ten minutes only. Half an hour later, much refreshed, he mounted to the bridge and resumed acceleration.

Grendel was little more than a tarnished farthing among the stars. New Winchester had swelled until it was a great green and gold moon. There would be warships in orbit around it, patrolling—McConnell dismissed the thought and gave himself to his search.

After all this time, it was not easy. Space is big and even the largest beer keg is comparatively small. Since Herr Syrup had shifted the plane of his boat's orbit by a trifle—an hour's questing confirmed that this must be the case—the volume in which he might be was fantastically huge. Furthermore, drifting free, his vessel painted black, he would be hard to spot, even when you were almost on top of him.

Another hour passed.

"Poor darling," said Emily, reaching from her chair to rumple the major's red locks. "You've tried so hard."

New Winchester continued to grow. Its towns were visible now, as blurred specks on a subtle tapestry of wood and field and ripening grain; the Royal Highroad was a thin streak across a cloud-softened dayface.

"He'll have to reveal himself soon," muttered McConnell from his telescope. "That beer blast is so weak—"

"Dear me, I understood Mr. Sarmishkidu's beer was rather strong," said Emily.

McConnell chuckled. "Ah, they should have used Irish whisky in their jet. But what I meant, me beloved, was that in so cranky a boat, they could not hope to hit their target on the nose, so they must make course corrections as they approach it. And with so low an exhaust velocity, they'll need a long time of blastin' to— *Hoy! I've got him!"*

The misty trail expanded in the viewfield, far and far away. McConnell's hands danced on the control board. The spaceship turned about and leaped ahead. The crane, projecting out of the cargo hatch, flexed its talons hungrily.

Fire burst!

After a time of strangling on his own breath, McConnell saw the brightness break into rags before his dazzled eyes. He stared into night and constellations. "What the devil?" he gasped. "Is there a Sassenach ship nearby? Has the auld squarehead a gun? That was a shot across our bows!"

He zipped past the boat at a few kilometers' distance while frantically scouring the sky. A massive shape crossed his telescopic field. It grew before his eyes as he stared—it couldn't be— "Our own ship!" choked McConnell. "Our own Erse ship."

The converted freighter did not shoot again, for fear of attracting Anglian attention. It edged nearer, awkwardly, seeking to match velocities and close in on the *Mercury Girl.* "Get away!" shouted McConnell. "Get out of the way, ye idiots! 'Tis not meself ye want, 'tis auld Syrup, over there. Git out of me way!" He avoided imminent collision by a wild backward spurt.

The realization broke on him. "But how do they know 'tis me on board here?" he asked aloud.

"Telepathy?" suggested the girl, fluttering her lashes at him.

"They don't know. They can't even have noticed the keg

boat, I'll swear. So 'tis us they wish to board an'— Get out of the way, ye son of a Scotchman!''

The Erse ship rushed in, shark-like. Again McConnell had to accelerate backward to avoid being stove. New Winchester dwindled in his viewports.

He slapped the console with a furious hand. ''An' me lackin' a radio to tell 'em the truth,'' he groaned. ''I'll jist have to orbit free, an' let 'em lay alongside an' board, an' explain the situation.'' His teeth grated together. ''All of which, if I know any one thing about the Force's high command, will cost us easy another hour.''

Emily smiled. The *Mercury Girl* continued to recede from the goal.

''I t'ink ve is in good broadcast range now,'' said Herr Syrup.

His boat was again inert, having exhausted nearly all its final cask. New Winchester waxed, already spreading across several degrees of arc. If only some circling Navy ship would happen to see the vessel; but no, the odds were all against that. Ah, well. Weary, bleary, but justifiably triumphant, Herr Syrup tapped the oscillator key.

Nothing happened.

''Vere's de spark?'' he complained.

''I don't know,'' said Sarmishkidu. ''I thought you would.''

''Bloody hell!'' screamed Claus.

Herr Syrup snarled inarticulately and tapped some more. There was still no result. ''It vas okay ven I tested back at de ship,'' he pleaded. ''Of course, I did not dare test much or de Ersers might overhear, but it did vork. Vat's gone crazy since?''

''I vould suggest that since most of the transmission apparatus is outside by the batteries, something has worked loose,'' answered Sarmishkidu. ''We could easily have jarred a wire off its terminal or some such thing.''

Herr Syrup swore and stuffed himself up into the spacesuit and tried to see what was wrong. But the oscillator parts were not accessible, or even visible, from this position: another point overlooked in the haste of constructing the boat. So he would have to put on the complete suit and crawl back to attempt repairs; and that would expose the interior of the cabin, including poor old Claus, to raw space—"Oh, Yudas," he said.

There was no possibility of landing on New Winchester; there never had been, in fact. Now the barrel didn't even hold enough reaction mass to establish an orbit. The boat would drift by, the oxygen would be exhausted, unless first the enemy picked him up. Staring aft, Herr Syrup gulped. The enemy was about to do so.

He had grinned when he saw the two Erse-controlled ships nudge each other out of sight. But now one of them, yes, the *Girl* herself, with a grapnel out at the side, came back into view.

His heart sagged. Well, he had striven. He might as well give up. Life in a yeast factory was at least life.

No, by heaven!

Herr Syrup struggled back into the box. "Qvick!" he yelled. "Give me de popcorn!"

"What?" gaped Sarmishkidu.

"Hand me up de carton vit' popcorn t'rough the valve, an' den give me about a minute of full acceleration forvard."

Sarmishkidu shrugged with all his tentacles, but obeyed. A quick pair of blasts faced the boat away from the approaching ship. Herr Syrup's space-gauntleted hand closed on the small box as it was shoved up through the stovepipe diaphragm, and he hurled it from him as his vessel leaped ahead.

The popcorn departed with a speed which, relative to the *Girl*, was not inconsiderable. Exposed to vacuum, it exploded from its pasteboard container as it gained full, puffy dimensions.

Now one of the oldest space war tactics is to drop a mass of hard objects, such as ball bearings, in the path of a pursuing enemy. And then there are natural meteors. In either case, the speeds involved are often such as to wreak fearful damage on the craft. Rory McConnell saw a sudden ghastly vision of white spheroids hurtling toward him. Instinctively, he stopped forward acceleration and crammed on full thrust sideways.

Almost, he dodged the swarm. A few pieces did strike the viewport. But they did not punch through, they did not even crater the tough plastic. They spattered. It took him several disgusted minutes to realize what they had been. By that time, the Erse ship had come into view with the plain intention of stopping him, laying alongside, and finding out what the devil was wrong now. When everything had been straightened out, a good half hour had passed.

"Dere is for damn sure no time to fix de oscillator," said Herr Syrup. "Ve must do vat ve can."

Sarmishkidu worked busily, painting the large pretzel box with air-sealing gunk. "I trust the bird will survive," he said.

"I t'ink so," said Herr Syrup. "I t'row him and de apparatus avay as hard as I can. Ve vill pass qvite close to de fringes of de asteroid's atmosphere. He has not many minutes to fall, and de oxygen keeps him breat'ing all dat vile. Ven de whole t'ing hits de air envelope, dere vill be enough impact to tear open de pretzel box and Claus can fly out."

The boat rumbled softly, blasting as straight toward New Winchester as its crew had been able to aim. It gave a feeble but most useful weight to objects within. Sarmishkidu finished painting the box and attached a tube connecting it with one of the oxygen flasks.

"Now, den, Claus," said Herr Syrup, "I have tied a written message to your leg, but if I know you, you vill rip it off and eat it as soon as you are free. However, if I also know you, you vill fly straight for de nearest pub and try to bum a beer. So, repeat after me: 'Help! Help! Invaders on Grendel.' Dat's all. 'Help! Help! Invaders on Grendel.' "

"McConnell is a skunk," said Claus.

"No, no! 'Help! Invaders on Grendel.' "

"McConnell cheats at cards," said Claus. "McConnell is a teetotaller. McConnell is a barnacle on de nose of society. McConnell—"

"No, no, no!"

"No, no, no!" echoed Claus agreeably.

"Listen," said Herr Syrup after a deep breath. "Listen, Claus. Please say it. Yust say, 'Help! Help! Invaders on Grendel.' "

"Nevermore," said Claus.

"We had best proceed," said Sarmishkidu.

He stuffed the indignant crow into the box and sealed it shut while Herr Syrup got back in the spacesuit: including, this time, its pants. And then, having aerated himself enough to stand vacuum for a while, Sarmishkidu unfastened the armor from the hatch cover. Herr Syrup popped inboard. Air rushed out. Herr Syrup pushed the oxygen cylinder, with Claus' box, through the hole.

New Winchester was so close it filled nearly half the sky. Herr Syrup made out towns and farms and orchards, through fleecy clouds. He sighed wistfully, shoved the tank from him as hard as he could, and watched it dwindle. A moment afterward, the asteroid itself began to recede; he had passed peri-New Winchester and was outward bound on a long cold orbit.

"So," said Herr Syrup, "let de Erse come pick us up." He realized he was talking to himself: no radio, and anyhow Sarmishkidu had curled into a ball. There was no point in resealing the cabin—the other oxygen bottle was long exhausted.

"I never t'ought de future of two nations could depend on vun old crow," sighed Herr Syrup.

CHAPTER 13

"Tsk-tsk-tsk," said Rory McConnell. "An' your radio didn't work after all?"

"No," wheezed Herr Syrup. He was still a little blue around the nose. It had been a grim wait of many hours, crouched in the spinning wreckage of his boat; his suit's air supply had been low indeed when the *Mercury Girl* finally came to him.

"An' ye say your poor auld bird was lost as well?"

"Blown out ven de gasket blew out dat I told you of." Herr Syrup accepted a cigar and leaned his weary frame gratefully back against the gymbal-swung acceleration bench in the saloon. There was still no functioning compensator and the *Mercury Girl*, with an Erse crew aboard, was pacing back to Grendel at a quarter gee.

"Then all your trouble was for nothin'?" McConnell did not gloat; if anything, he was too sympathetic.

"I guess so," Herr Syrup answered rather bleakly, thinking of Claus. No doubt the crow would look at once for human society; but what was he likely to convey except a string of oaths? Too late, the engineer saw that he should have put some profanity into his message.

"Well, ye were a brave foe, an' 'tis daily I'll come by Grendel gaol to cheer yez," said McConnell, clapping his shoulder. "For I fear the General will insist on lockin' yez up for the duration. He was more than a little annoyed, I can tell yez; he was spittin' rivets. He wanted for to leave you drift off to your fate, an' we had quite an argument about it, wherefore I am now just another private soldier in the ranks." McConnell rubbed his large knuckles reminiscently. "However, I won me point. Himself went back hours ago in t'other ship, but he let me stay wi' this one and pick yez up. But I dared not go close to the Anglian capital, but must wait until ye had orbited so far away that no chance Navy ship would see us an' get curious. An' so long a delay meant ye were hard to find. We were almost too late, eh, what?''

''Ja,'' shuddered Herr Syrup. He tilted the proffered bottle of Irish to his lips.

''But all's well that ends well, even though 'twas said by an Englishman,'' chuckled McConnell. He squeezed Emily's hand. She smiled mistily back at him. ''For I'll regain me auld rank as soon as the swellin' in the General's eye has gone down so he can see how much I'm needed. An' then 'twill be time to effect the glorious redemption of Laoighise, an' then, Emily, you an' I will be wed, an' then—Well!'' He coughed. She blushed.

''Ja,'' snorted Sarmishkidu. ''Good ending, huh? With my business ruined, und me in jail, und maybe a war started, and that *Dummkopf* of a Shalmuannusar claiming he proved the sub-unitary connectivity theorem before I did, as if publishing first had anything to do with priority—Ha!''

''Oh, dear,'' said Emily compassionately.

''Oh, darlin','' said McConnell.

''Oh, sweetheart,'' cooed Emily, losing interest in Sarmishkidu.

''Oh, me little turtle dove,'' whispered McConnell.

Herr Syrup fought a strong desire to retch.

A bell clanged. McConnell stood up. ''That's the signal,'' he said. ''We've come to Grendel an' I'll be wanted on the bridge. 'Twill be an unendin' few minutes till I see yez ag'in, me only one.''

''Goodbye, my beloved,'' breathed the girl. Herr Syrup gritted his teeth.

Her manner changed as soon as the Erseman had left. She leaned over toward the engineer and asked tensely: ''Do you think we succeeded? I mean, do you?''

''I doubt it,'' he sighed. ''In de end, only Claus vas left to carry de vord.'' He explained what had happened. ''Even supposing he does repeat vat he vas supposed to, I doubt many people vould believe a crow dat has not even been introduced.''

''Well—'' Emily bit her lip. ''We tried, didn't we? But if a war does come—between Rory's country and mine. No! I won't think about it!'' She rubbed small fists across her eyes.

Uncompensated forces churned Herr Syrup on his seat. At last they quieted; the engine mumble died; a steady one gee informed him that the *Mercury Girl* was again berthed on Grendel. ''I'm going to Rory,'' said Emily. Almost, she fled from the saloon.

Herr Syrup puffed his cigar, waiting for the Erse to come take him to prison. The first thing he would do there, he thought dully, was sleep for about fifty hours . . . He grew aware that several minutes had passed. Sarmishkidu sat brooding in a spaghetti-like nest of tentacles. The ship had grown oddly quiet, no feet along the passageways. Shrugging, Herr Syrup got up, strolled out of the saloon and down a corridor, entered the open main passenger airlock and looked upon the spacefield.

The cigar dropped from his mouth.

The Erse flag was down off the staff and the Anglian banner was back. A long, subdued line of green-clad men shuffled past a heap of their own weapons. Trucks were bringing more every minute. They trailed one by one into a military transport craft berthed nearby, accompanied by hoots and jeers—and an occasional tearful au revoir—from the Grendelian townspeople crowded against the port fence. A troop of redcoats with bayoneted rifles was urging the prisoners along, and the gigantic guns of H.M.S. *Inhospitable* shadowed the entire scene.

''Yudas priest!'' said Herr Syrup.

He stumbled down onto the ground. A brisk young officer surveyed him through a monocle, sketched a salute, and extended an arm. ''Mr. Syrup? I understand you were aboard. Your crow, sir.''

''Hell and damnation!'' said Claus, hopping from the Anglian wrist to the Danish shoulder.

"Pers'nally," said the young man, "I go for falcons."

"You come!" whispered Herr Syrup. "You come!"

"Just a short hop, don't y'know. We arrived hours back. No resistance, except—er—" The officer blushed. "I say, don't look now, but that young lady in the, ah, rather brief costume and, er, passionate embrace with the large chappie—d' you know anything about 'em? Mean to say, she claims she's the vicar's daughter and he's her fiancé and she goes where he goes, and really, sir, I jolly well don't know whether to evacuate her with the invaders or give him a permit to remain here or, or what, damme!"

Herr Syrup stole a glance. "Do vatever seems easiest," he said. "I don't t'ink to dem it makes mush difference."

"No, I suppose not." The officer sighed.

"How did you find out vat vas happening here? Did de crow really give somevun my message?"

"What message?"

"Go sputz yourself!" rasped Claus.

"No, not dat vun," said Herr Syrup quickly.

"My dear sir," said the officer, "when a half-ruined oxygen bottle, with the name *Mercury Girl* still identifiable on it, lands in a barley field . . . and we've been wirelessed that that ship is under quarantine . . . and then when this black bird flies in a farmer's window and steals a scone off his tea table and says, ah, uncomplimentary things about one Major McConnell . . . well, really, my dear chap, the farmer will phone the police and the police will phone Newer Scotland Yard and the Yard will check with Naval Intelligence and, well, I mean to say it's obvious, eh, what, what, what?"

"Ja," said Herr Syrup weakly. "I suppose so." He hesitated. "Vat you ban going to do vit' de Ersers? Dey vas pretty decent, considering. I vould hate to see dem serving yail sentences."

"Oh, don't worry about that, sir. Mean to say, well, it's a bally embarrassing situation all around, eh? *We* don't want to admit that a band of half-cocked extremists stole one of our shires right out from under our noses, so to speak, what? We can't suppress the fact, of course, but we aren't exactly anxious to advertise it all over the Solar System, y'know. As for the Erse government, it doesn't want trouble with us—Gaelic Socialists, y' know, peaceful chappies—and certainly doesn't want to give the opposition party a leg up; so they won't support this crazy attempt in any way. At the same time, popular sentiment at home won't let 'em punish the attempt either. Eh?

"Jolly ticklish situation. Delicate. All we can do is ship these fellows home with our compliments, where their own government will doubtless give 'em a talking to and let 'em go. And then, very much on the Q.T., I'm jolly well sure the Erse Republic will pay whatever damage claims there are. Your own ship ought to collect a goodly share of that, eh, what?"

By this time Sarmishkidu von Himmelschmidt had reached the foot of the ladder. "I'll have you know I've thousands of pounds in damages coming!" he whistled in outrage. "Maybe millions! Why, just the loss of business during occupation, at a rate of easy five hundred pounds a day—let's call it a t'ousand pounds a day to put it in round figures—dot adds up to—"

"Oh, come now, old chap, come now. Tut-tut!" The officer adjusted his monocle. "It isn't all that bad. Really it isn't, don't y' know. After all, even if nothing is done officially, word will get around. People will come in jolly old floods to see that place where all this happened. I'll wager my own missus makes me vacation here this season. Cloak and dagger stuff, excitin', all that sort of piffle, eh, what, what? Why, it'll be the busiest tourist season in your history, by Jove."

"Hmmmm." Sarmishkidu stroked his nose thoughtfully. A gleam waxed in one bulging eye. "Hmmm. Yes. The atmosphere of international intrigue; sinister spies, double agents, beautiful females luring away secret papers. Yes, the first place on Grendel to furnish that kind of atmosphere will—Hmmm. I must make some alterations, I see. To hell with *Gemütlichkeit.* I want my tavern to have an uncertain reputation. Yes, that's it, uncertain.'' He drew himself up and flourished a dramatic tentacle. ''Gentlemen, you are now looking upon the proprietor of der Alt *Heisenberg* Rathskeller!''

Inside Straight

After John W. Campbell took over the editorship of what was then *Astounding* (now *Analog*) in 1937, he virtually created modern science fiction, insisting on higher literary standards than had prevailed for a long time, volcanically generating brilliant new concepts, and launching the careers of such writers as Robert A. Heinlein, Isaac Asimov, and L. Sprague de Camp—to name only three. When Anthony Boucher and J. Francis McComas founded *The Magazine of Fantasy and Science Fiction* in 1949, they started a quieter but equally profound revolution, an emphasis on the humanistic and stylistic potentialities of the field. This doesn't mean that they didn't like an idea for its own sake. I sold them a number of stories that were, largely, intellectual playfulness; here is an example. All of us were dedicated poker players too, and seeing this yarn reprinted brings back many a memory. "Pass the biscuits. . . . Stone the crows. . . . Love a duck. . . ."

In the main, sociodynamic theory predicted quite accurately the effects of the secondary drive. It foresaw that once cheap interstellar transportation was available, there would be considerable emigration from the

Solar System—men looking for a fresh start, malcontents of all kinds, "peculiar people" desiring to maintain their form of life without interference. It also predicted that these colonies would in turn spawn colonies, again of unsatisfied minority groups, until this part of the Galaxy was sprinkled with human-settled planets; and that in their relative isolation, these politically independent worlds would develop some very odd societies.

However, the economic bias of the Renascence period, and the fact that war was a discarded institution in the Solar System, led these same predictors into errors of detail. It was felt that, since planets useful to man are normally separated by scores of light-years, and since any planet colonized on a high technological level would be quite self-sufficient, there would be little intercourse and no strife between these settlements. In their own reasonableness, the Renascence intellectuals overlooked the fact that man as a whole is not a rational animal, and that exploration and war do not always have economic causes.

—*Simon Vardis,* A Short History of Pre-Commonwealth Politics, *Reel I, Frame 617*

They did not build high on New Hermes. There was plenty of room, and the few cities sprawled across many square kilometers in a complex of low, softly tinted domes and cylindroids. Parks spread green wherever you looked, each breeze woke a thousand bell-trees into a rush of chiming, flowers and the bright-winged summerflits ran wildly colored beneath a serene blue sky. The planetary capital, Arkinshaw, had the same leisurely old-fashioned look as the other towns
Ganch

had seen; only down by the docks was there a fevered energy and a brawling life.

The restaurant Wayland had taken him to was incredibly archaic; it even had live service. When they had finished a subtly prepared lunch, the waiter strolled to their table. ''Was there anything else, sir?'' he asked.

''I thank you, no,'' said Wayland. He was a small, lithe man with close-cropped gray-shot hair and a brown nutcracker face in which lay startlingly bright blue eyes. On him, the local dress—a knee-length plaid tunic, green buskins, and yellow mantle—looked good . . . which was more than you could say for most of them, reflected Ganch.

The waiter produced a tray. There was no bill on it, as Ganch had expected, but a pair of dice. *Oh, no!* he thought. *By the Principle, no! Not this again!*

Wayland rattled the cubes in his hand, muttering an incantation. They flipped on the table; eight spots looked up. ''Fortune seems to favor you, sir,'' said the waiter.

''May she smile on a more worthy son,'' replied Wayland. Ganch noted with disgust that the planet's urbanity-imperative extended even to servants. The waiter shook the dice and threw.

''Snake eyes,'' he smiled. ''Congratulations, sir. I trust you enjoyed the meal.''

''Yes, indeed,'' said Wayland, rising. ''My compliments to the chef, and you and he are invited to my next poker game. I'll have an announcement about it on the telescreens.''

He and the waiter exchanged bows and compliments. Then Wayland left, ushering Ganch through the door and out onto the slidewalk. They found seats and let it carry them toward the waterfront, which Ganch had expressed a desire to see.

''Ah—'' Ganch cleared his throat. ''How was that done?''

''Eh?'' Wayland blinked. ''Don't you even have dice on Dromm?''

''Oh, yes. But I mean the principle of payment for the meal.''

"I shook him. Double or nothing. I won."

Ganch shook his head. He was a tall, muscular man in a skintight black uniform. That and the scarlet eyes in his long bony face (not albinism, but healthy mutation) marked him as belonging to the Great Cadre of Dromm.

"But then the restaurant loses money," he said.

"This time, yes," nodded Wayland. "It evens out in the course of a day—just as all our commerce evens out, so that in the long run everybody earns his rightful wage or profit."

"But suppose one—ah—cheats?"

Surprisingly, Wayland reddened, and looked around. When he spoke again, it was in a low voice: "Don't ever use that word, sir, I beg of you. I realize the mores are different on your planet, but here there is one unforgiveable, utterly obscene sin, and it's the one you just mentioned." He sat back, breathing heavily for a while, then seemed to cool off and proffered cigars. Ganch declined—tobacco did not grow on Dromm—but Wayland puffed his own into lighting with obvious enjoyment.

"As a matter of fact," he said presently, "our whole social conditioning is such as to preclude the possibility of . . . unfairness. You realize how thoroughly an imperative can be inculcated with modern psychopediatrics. It is a matter of course that all equipment, from dice and coins to the most elaborate Stellarium set, is periodically checked by a Games Engineer."

"I see," said Ganch doubtfully.

He looked around as the slidewalk carried him on. It was a pleasant, sunny day, like most on New Hermes. Only to be expected on a world with two small continents, all the rest of the land split into a multitude of islands. The people he saw had a relaxed appearance—the men in their tunics and mantles, the women in their loose filmy gowns, the children in little or nothing. A race of sybarites; they had had it too easy here, and degenerated.

Sharply he remembered Dromm, its gaunt glacial peaks and wind-scoured deserts, storm and darkness galloping down from the poles, the huge iron cubicles of cities and the obedient gray-clad masses that filled them. That world had brought forth the Great Cadre, and tempered them in struggle and heartbreak, and given them power first over a people and then over a planet and then over two systems.

Eventually . . . who knew? The Galaxy?

"I am interested in your history," he said, recalling himself. "Just how was New Hermes settled?"

"The usual process," shrugged Wayland. "Our folk came from Caledonia, which had been settled from Old Hermes, whose people were from Earth. A puritanical gang got into control and started making all kinds of senseless restrictions on natural impulses. Finally a small group, our ancestors, could take no more, and went off looking for a planet of their own. That was about three hundred years ago. They went far, into this spiral arm which was then completely unexplored, in the hope of being left alone; and that hope has been realized. To this day, except for a couple of minor wars, we've had only casual visitors like yourself."

Casual! A grim amusement twisted Ganch's mouth upward.

To cover it, he asked: "But surely you've had your difficulties? It cannot have been simply a matter of landing here and founding your cities."

"Oh, no, of course not. The usual pioneer troubles—unknown diseases, wild animals, storms, a strange ecology. There were some hard times before the machines were constructed. Now, of course, we have it pretty good. There are fifty million of us, and space for many more; but we're in no hurry to expand the population. We like elbow room."

Ganch frowned until he had deduced the meaning of that last phrase. They spoke Anglic here, as on Dromm and most colonies, but naturally an individual dialect had evolved.

Excitement gripped him. Fifty million! Two hundred million people lived on Dromm, and conquered Thanit added half again as many.

Of course, said his military training, sheer numbers meant

little. Automatized equipment made all but the most highly skilled officers and technicians irrelevant. War between systems involved sending a space fleet, which met and beat the enemy fleet in a series of engagements; bases on planets had to be manned, and sometimes taken by ground forces, but the fighting was normally remote from the worlds concerned. Once the enemy navy was broken, its home had to capitulate or be sterilized by bombardment from the skies.

Still . . . New Hermes should be an even easier prey than Thanit had been.

"Haven't you taken any precautions against . . . hostiles?" he asked, mostly because the question fitted his assumed character.

"Oh, yes, to be sure," said Wayland. "We maintain a navy and marine corps; matter of fact, I'm in the Naval Intelligence Reserve myself, captain's rank. We had to fight a couple of small wars in the previous century, once with the Corridans—nonhumans out for loot—and once with Oberkassel, whose people were on a religious-fanatic kick. We won them both without much trouble." He added modestly: "But of course, sir, neither planet was very intelligently guided."

Ganch suppressed a desire to ask for figures on naval strength. This guileless dice-thrower might well spout them on request, but—

The slidewalk had reached the waterfront by now, and they got off. Here the sea glistened blue, streaked with white foam, and the harbor was crowded with shipping. Not only flying boats, but big watercraft lay moored to the ferroconcrete piers. Machines were loading and unloading in a whirl of bright steel arms, warehouses gaped for the planet's wealth, the air was rich with oil and spices. A babbling confusion of humanity surfed around Ganch and broke on his eardrums in a roar.

Wayland pointed unobtrusively here and there, his voice almost lost in the din: "See, we have quite a cultural variety of our own. That tall blond man in the fur coat is from Norrin, he must have brought in a load of pelts. The little dark fellow in the sarong is a spice trader from the Radiant Islands. The Mongoloid wearing a robe is clear from the Ivory Gate, probably with handicrafts to exchange for our timber. And—''

They were interrupted by a young woman, a very good-looking young woman with long black hair and a tilt-nosed freckled face. She wore a light blue uniform jacket with a lieutenant's twin comets on the shoulders, as well as a short loose-woven skirt revealing slim brown legs. ''Will! Where have you been?''

''Showing the distinguished guest of our government around,'' said Wayland formally. ''The Prime Selector himself appointed me to that pleasant task. Ganch, may I have the honor of presenting my niece, Lieutenant Christabel Hesty of the New Hermesian Navy? Lieutenant Hesty, this gentleman hight Ganch, from Dromm. It's a planet lying about fifty light-years from us, a very fine place I'm sure. They are making a much-overdue ethnographic survey of this Galactic religion, and Ganch is taking notes on us.''

''Honored, sir.'' She bowed and shook hands with herself in the manner of Arkinshaw. ''We've heard of Dromm. There have been visitors thence in the past several years. I trust you are enjoying your stay?''

Ganch saluted stiffly, as was prescribed for the Great Cadre. ''Thank you, very much.'' He was a little shocked at such blatant sexual egalitarianism, but reflected that it might be turned to advantage.

''Will, you're just the man I want to see.'' Lieutenant Hesty's voice bubbled over. ''I came down to wager on a cargo from Thorncroft and you—''

''Ah, yes. I'll be glad to help you, though of course the requirements of my guild are—''

''You'll get your commission.'' She made a face at him and turned laughing to Ganch. ''Perhaps you didn't know, sir, my uncle is a Tipster?''

''No, I didn't,'' said the Dromman. ''What profession is that?''

"Probability analyst. It takes years and years of training. When you want to make an important wager, you call in a Tipster." She tugged at Wayland's sleeve. "Come on, the trading will start any minute."

"Do you mind, sir?" asked Wayland.

"Not at all," said Ganch. "I would be very interested. Your economic system is unique." *And,* he added, *the most inefficient I have yet heard of.*

They entered a building which proved to be a single great room. In the center was a long table, around which crowded a colorful throng of men and women. There was an outsize electronic device of some kind at the end, with a tall rangy man in kilt and beryllium-copper breastplate at the controls. Wayland stood aside, his face taking on an odd withdrawn look.

"How does this work?" asked Ganch—*sotto voce*, for the crowd did not look as if it wanted its concentration disturbed.

"The croupier there is the trader from Thorncroft," whispered Christabel Hesty. This close, with her head just beneath his chin, Ganch could smell the faint sun-warmed perfume of her hair. It stirred a wistfulness in him, buried ancestral memories of summer meadows on Earth. He choked off the emotion and listened to her words.

"He's brought in a load of refined thorium, immensely valuable. He puts that up as his share, and those who wish to trade get into the game with shares of what they have—they cover him, just as in craps, though they're playing Orthotron now. The game is a complex one, I see a lot of Tipsters around . . . yes, and the man in the green robe is a Games Engineer, umpire and technician. I'm afraid you wouldn't understand the rules at once, but perhaps you would like to make side bets?"

"No, thank you," said Ganch. "I am content to observe."

He soon found out that Lieutenant Hesty had not exaggerated the complications. Orthotron seemed to be a remote descendant of roulette such as they had played on Thanit before the war, but the random-pulse tubes shifted the probabilities continuously, and the rules themselves changed as the game went on. When the scoreboard on the machine flashed, chips to the tune of millions of credits clattered from hand to hand. Ganch found it hard to believe that anyone could even learn the system, let alone become so expert in it as to make a profession of giving advice. A Tipster would have to allow for the presence of other Tipsters, and—

His respect for Wayland went up. The little man must have put a lightning-fast mind through years of the most rigorous training; and there must be a highly developed paramathematical theory behind it all. If that intelligence and energy had gone into something useful, military technics for instance—

But it hadn't, and New Hermes lay green and sunny, wide open for the first determined foe.

Ganch grew aware of tension. It was not overtly expressed, but faces tightened, changed color, pupils narrowed and pulses beat in temples until he could almost feel the emotion, crackling like lightning in the room. Now and then Wayland spoke quietly to his niece, and she laid her bets accordingly.

It was with an effort that she pulled herself away, with two hours lost and a few hundred credits gained. Only courtesy to the guest made her do it. Her hair was damply plastered to her forehead, and she went out with a stiff-legged gait which only slowly loosened.

Wayland accepted his commission and laughed a little shakily. "I earn my living, sir!" he said. "It's brutal on the nerves."

"How long will they play?" asked Ganch.

"Till the trader is cleaned out or has won so much that no one can match him. In this case, I'd estimate about thirty hours."

"Continuous? How can the nervous system endure it—not to mention the feet?"

"It's hard," admitted Christabel Hesty, seeming to wake from a troubled dream. Her eyes burned. "But exciting!

There's nothing in the Galaxy quite like that suspense. You lose yourself in it."

"And, of course," said Wayland mildly, "man adapts to any cultural pattern. We'd find it difficult to live as you do on Dromm."

No doubt, thought Ganch sardonically. *But you are going to learn how!*

On an isolated planet like this, an outworlder was always a figure of romance. In spite of manners which must seem crude here, Ganch had only to suggest an evening out for Christabel Hesty to leap at the offer.

He simply changed to another uniform, but she appeared in a topless gown of deep-blue silkite, her dark hair sprinkled with tiny points of light, and made his heart stumble. He reminded himself that women were breeders, nothing else. But Principle! How dull they were on Dromm!

His object was to gain information, but he decided he might as well enjoy his work.

They took an elevated way to the Stellar House, Arkinshaw's only skyscraper, and had cocktails in a clear-domed roof garden with sunset rioting around them. A gentle music, some ancient waltz from Earth herself, lilted in the air, and the gaily clad diners talked in low voices and clinked glasses and laughed softly.

Lieutenant Hesty raised her glass to his. "Your luck, sir," she pledged him. Then, smiling: "Shall we lower guard?"

"I beg your pardon?"

"My apologies. I forgot you are a stranger, sir. The proposal was to relax formality for this evening."

"By all means," said Ganch. He tried to smile in turn. "Though I fear my class is always rather stiff."

Her long, soot-black eyelashes fluttered. "Then I hight Chris tonight," she said. "And your first name . . . ?"

"My class does not use them. I am simply Ganch, with various identifying symbols attached."

"We meet some strange outworlders," she said frankly, "but in truth, you Drommans seem the most exotic of all."

"And New Hermes gives us that impression," he chuckled.

"We know so little about you—we have met only a few explorers and traders, and now you. Is your mission official?"

"Everything on Dromm is official," said Ganch, veraciously enough. "I am only an ethnographer making a detailed study of your folkways." And that was a lie.

"Excuse my saying so, I shouldn't criticize another civilization, but isn't it terribly dull having all one's life regulated by the State?"

"It is . . ." Ganch hunted for words. "Secure," he finished earnestly. "Ordered. One knows where one stands."

"A pity you had that war with Thanit. They seemed such nice people, those who visited here."

"We had no choice," answered Ganch with the smoothness of rote. "An irresponsible, aggressive government attacked us." She did not ask for details, and he supposed it was the usual thing: interest in other people's fate obeys an inverse-square law, and 50 light-years is a gulf of distance no man can really imagine.

In point of fact, he told himself with the bitter honesty of his race, Thanit had sought peace up to the last moment; Dromm's ultimatum had demanded impossible concessions, and Thanit had had no choice but to fight a hopeless battle. Her conquest had been well-planned, the armored legions of Dromm had romped over her and now she was being digested by the State.

Chris frowned, a shadow on the wide clear brow. "I find it hard to see why they would make war—why anyone would," she murmured. "Isn't there enough on any planet to content its people? And if by chance they should be unhappy, there are always new worlds."

"Well," shrugged Ganch, "you should know why. You're

in the Navy yourself, aren't you, and New Hermes has fought a couple of times."

"Only in self-defense," she said. "Naturally, we now mount guard on our defeated enemies, even seventy years later, just to be sure they don't try again. As for me, I have a very peaceful desk job in the statistics branch, correlating data."

Ganch felt a thrumming within himself. He could hardly have asked for better luck. Precise information on the armament of New Hermes was just what Dromm lacked. If he could bring it back to old wan Halsker—it would mean a directorship, at least!

And afterward, when a new conquest was to be administered and made over. . . . His ruby eyes studied Chris from beneath drooping lids. A territorial governor had certain perquisites of office.

"I suppose there are many poor twisted people in the universe," went on the girl. "Like those Oberkassel priests, with their weird doctrine they wanted to force on all mankind. It's hard to believe intolerance exists, but alien planets have done strange things to human minds."

There was a veiling in her own violent gaze as she looked at him. She must want to know his own soul, what it was that drove the Great Cadre and why anyone should enjoy having power over other men. He could have told her a great deal—the cruel wintry planet, the generations-long war against the unhuman Ixlatt who made sport of torturing prisoners, then war between factions that split men, war against the red-eyed mutants, whipped-up xenophobia, pogroms, concentration camps . . . Ganch's grandfather had died in one.

But the mutation was more than an accidental mark, it was in the nervous system, a steel answer to a pitiless environment. A man of the Great Cadre simply did not know fear on the conscious level. Danger lashed him to alertness, but with no fright to cloud his thoughts. And, by genetics or merely as the result of persecution, he had a will to power which only death could stop. The Great Cadre had subdued a hundred times their numbers, and made them into brain-channeled tools of the State, simply by being braver and more able in war. And Dromm was not enough, not when each darkness brought a mockery of unconquered stars out overhead.

A philosopher from distant Archbishop, where they went in for imaginative speculation, had visited Dromm a decade ago. His remark still lay in Ganch's mind, and stung: "Unjust treatment is apt to produce paranoia in the victim. Your race has outlived its oppressors, but not the reflexes they built into your society. You'll never rest till all the universe is enslaved, for your canalized nervous systems make you incapable of regarding anyone else as anything but a dangerous enemy."

The philosopher had not gone home alive, but his words remained; Ganch had tried to forget them, and could not.

Enough! His mind had completed its track in the blink of an eye, and now he remembered that the girl expected an answer. He sipped his cocktail and spoke thoughtfully:

"Yes, these special groups, isolated on their own special planets, have developed in many peculiar ways. New Hermes, for instance, if you will pardon my saying so."

Chris raised level brows. "Of course, this is my home and I'm used to it, Ganch," she replied, "but I fail to see anything which would surprise an outsider very much. We live quietly, for the most part, with a loose parliamentary government to run planetary affairs. The necessities of life are produced free for all by the automatic factories; to avoid the annoyance of regulations, we leave everything else to private enterprise, subject only to the reasonable restrictions of the Conservation Authority and a fair-practices act. We don't need more government than that, because the educational system instills respect for the rights and dignity of others and we have no ambitious public-works projects.

"You might say our whole culture is founded merely on a principle of live and let live."

She stroked her chin, man-fashion. "Of course, we have police and courts. And we discourage a concentration of power, political or economic, but that's only to preserve individual liberty. Our economic system helps; it's hard to build up a gigantic business when one game may wipe it out."

"Now there," said Ganch, "you strike the oddity. This passion for gambling. How does it arise?"

"Oh . . . I wouldn't call it a passion. It's merely one way of pricing goods and services, just as haggling is on Kwan-Yin, and socialism on Arjay, and supply-demand on Alexander."

"But how did it originate?"

Chris lifted smooth bare shoulders and smiled. "Ask the historians, not me. I suppose our ancestors, reacting from the Caledonian puritanism, were apt to glorify all vices and practice them to excess. Gambling was the only one which didn't taper off as a more balanced society evolved. It came to be a custom. Gradually it superseded the traditional methods of exchange.

"It doesn't make any difference, you see; being honest gambling, it comes out even. Win one, lose one . . . that's almost the motto of our folk. To be sure, in games of skill like poker, a good player will come out ahead in the long run; but any society gives an advantage to certain talents. On Alexander, most of the money and prestige flow to the successful entrepreneur. On Einstein, the scientists are the rich and honored leaders. On Hellas, it's male prowess and female beauty. On Arjay, it's the political spellbinder. On Dromm, I suppose, the soldier is on top. With us, it's the shrewd gambler.

"The important thing," she finished gravely, "is not who gets the most, but whether everyone gets enough."

"But that is what makes me wonder," said Ganch. "This trader we saw today, for instance. Suppose he loses everything?"

"It would be a blow, of course. But he wouldn't starve, because the necessities are free anyway; and he'll have enough sense—he'll have learned in the primaries—to keep a small emergency reserve to start over with. We have very few paupers."

"Your financial structure must be most complicated."

"It is," she said wryly. "We've had to develop a tremendous theoretical science and a great number of highly trained men to handle it. That game today was childish compared with what goes on in, say, the securities exchange. I don't pretend to understand what happens there. I'm content to turn a wheel for my monthly pay, and if I win to go out and see if I can't make a little more."

"And you *enjoy* this—insecurity?"

"Why, yes. As I imagine you enjoy war, and an engineer enjoys building a spaceship, and—" Chris looked at the table. "It's always hard and risky settling a new planet, even one as Earth-like as ours. Our ancestors got a taste for excitement. When there was no more to be had in subduing nature, they transferred the desire to— Ah, here come the hors d'oeuvres."

Ganch ate a stately succession of courses with pleasure. He was not good at small talk, but Chris made such eager conversation that it was simple to lead her: the details of her life and work, little insignificant items but they clicked together. By the coffee and liqueur, Ganch knew where the military microfiles of New Hermes were kept and was fairly sure he knew how to get at them.

Afterward they danced. Ganch had never done it before, but his natural coordination soon fitted him into the rhythm. There was a curious bittersweet savor to holding the girl in his arms . . . dearest enemy. He wondered if he should try to make love to her. An infatuated female officer would be useful—

No. In such matters, she was the sophisticate and he the bumbling yokel. Coldly, though not without regret, he dismissed the idea.

They sat at a poker table for a while, where the management put up chips to the value of their bill. Ganch was completely outclassed; he learned the game readily enough, but his excellent analytical mind simply could not match the Hermesians. It was almost as if they knew what cards he held. He lost heavily, but Chris made up for it and when they quit they only had to pay half what they owed.

They hired an aircar, and for a while its gravity drive lifted them noiselessly into a night-blue sky, under a flooding moon and a myriad stars and the great milky sprawl of the Galaxy. Beneath them, a broken bridge of moonlight shuddered across the darkened sea, and they heard the far, faint crying of birds.

When he let Chris off at her apartment, Ganch wanted to stay. It was a wrenching to say goodnight and turn back to his own hotel. He stamped out the wish with a bleak will and bent his mind elsewhere. There was work to do.

Dromm was nothing if not thorough. Her agents had been on New Hermes for ten years now, mostly posing as natives of unsuspicious planets like Guise and Anubis. Enough had been learned to earmark this world for conquest after Thanit, and to lay out the basic military campaign.

The Hermesians were not really naïve. They had their own spies and counterspies. Customs inspection was careful. But each Dromman visitor had brought a few plausible objects with him—a personal teleset, a depilator, a sample of small nuclear-powered tools for sale—nothing to cause remark; and those objects had stayed behind, in care of a supposed immigrant from Kwan-Yin who lived in Arkinshaw. This man had refashioned them into as efficient a set of machinery for breaking and entering as existed anywhere in the known Galaxy.

Ganch was quite sure Wayland had a tail on him. It was an elementary precaution. But a Field Intelligence officer of Dromm had ways to shake a tail off without its appearing more than accidental. Ganch went out the following afternoon, having notified Wayland that he did not need a guide: he only wanted to stroll around and look at things for himself. After wandering a bit, he went into a pleasure house. It was a holiday, Discovery Day, and Arkinshaw swarmed with a merry crowd; in the jam-packed house, Ganch slipped quietly into a washroom cubicle.

His shadows would most likely watch all exits; and they wouldn't be surprised if he stayed inside for many hours. The hetaerae of New Hermes were famous.

Alone, Ganch slipped out of his uniform and stuffed it down the rubbish disintegrator. Beneath it he wore the loose blue coat and trousers of a Kwan-Yin colonist. A life-mask over his head, a complete alteration of posture and gait . . . it was another man who stepped into the hall and sauntered out the main door as if his amusements were completed. He went quite openly to Fraybiner's house; what was more natural than that some home-planet relative of Tao Chung should pay a call?

When they were alone, Fraybiner let out a long breath. "By the Principle, it's good to be with a man again!" he said. "If you knew how sick I am of these chattering decadents—"

"Enough!" snapped Ganch. "I am here on business. Operation Lift."

Fraybiner's surgically slanted and darkened eyes widened. "So it's finally coming off?" he murmured. "I was beginning to wonder."

"If I get away with it," said Ganch grimly. "Even if I don't, it doesn't matter. Exact knowledge of the enemy's strength will be valuable, but we have enough information already to launch the war."

Fraybiner began operating concealed studs. A false wall slid aside to reveal a large safe, on which he got to work. "How will you take it home?" he asked. "When they find their files looted, they won't let anyone leave the planet without a thorough search."

Ganch didn't reply; Fraybiner had no business knowing. Actually, the files were going to be destroyed, once read, and their contents would go home in Ganch's eidetic memory. But that versatile ethnographer did not plan to leave for some weeks yet: no use causing unnecessary suspicion. When he finally did—a surprise attack on all the Hermesian bases would immobilize them at one swoop.

He smiled to himself. Even knowing they were to be attacked, their whole planet fully alerted, the Hermesians were finished. It was well-established that their fleet had less than half the strength of Dromm's, and not a single Supernova-class dreadnaught. Ganch's information would be extremely helpful, but it was by no means vital.

Except, of course, to Ganch Z–17837–JX–39. But death was a threat he treated with the contempt it deserved.

Fraybiner had gotten the safe open, and a dull metal gleam of instruments and weapons lay before their gaze. Ganch inspected each item carefully while the other jittered with impatience. Finally he donned the flying combat armor and hung the implements at its belt. By that time, the sun was down and the stars out.

Chris had said the Naval HQ building was deserted at night except for its guards. Previous spies had learned where these were posted. "Very well," said Ganch. "I'm on my way. I won't see you again, and advise you to move elsewhere soon. If the natives turn out to be stubborn, we'll have to destroy this city."

Fraybiner nodded, and activated the ceiling door. Ganch went up on his gravity beams and out into the sky. The city was a jeweled spiderweb beneath him, and fireworks burst with great soft explosions of color. His outfit was a non-reflecting dull black, and there was only a whisper of air to betray his flight.

The HQ building, broad and low, rested on a greensward several kilometers from Arkinshaw. Ganch approached its slumbering dark mass carefully, taking his time. A bare meter's advance, an instrument reading . . . yes, they had a radio-alarm field set up. He neutralized it with his heterodyning unit, flew another cautious meter, stopped to readjust the neutralization. The moon was down, but he wished the stars weren't so bright.

It was past midnight when he lay in the shrubbery surrounding a rear entrance. A pair of sentries, armed and helmeted, tramped almost by his nose, crossing paths in front of the door. He waited, learning the pattern of their march.

When his tactics were fully planned, he rose as one marine came by and let the fellow have a sonic stun-beam. Too low-powered to trip an alarm, it was close-range and to the base of the neck. Ganch caught the body as it fell, let it down, and picked up the same measured tread.

He felt no conscious tension as he neared the other man, though a sharp glance through darkness would end the ruse, but his muscles gathered themselves. He was almost abreast of the Hermesian when he saw the figure recoil in alarm. His stunner went off again. It was a bad shot; the sentry lurched but retained a wavering consciousness. Ganch sprang on him, one tigerish bound, a squeezed trigger, and he lowered the marine as gently as a woman might her lover.

For a moment he stood looking down on the slack face. A youngster, hardly out of his teens, there was something strangely innocent about him as he slept. About this whole world. They were too kind here, they didn't belong in a universe of wolves.

He had no doubt they would fight bravely and skillfully. Dromm would have to pay for her conquest. But the age of heroes was past. War was not an art, it was a science, and a set of giant computers coldly chewing an involved symbolism told ships and men what to do. Given equal courage and equally intelligent leadership, it was merely a heartless arithmetic that the numerically superior fleet would win.

No time to lose! He spun on his heel and crouched over the door. His instruments traced out its circuits, a diamond drill bit into plastic, a wire shorted a current . . . the door opened for him and he went into a hollow darkness of corridors.

Lightly, even in the clumsy armor, he made his way toward the main file room. Once he stopped, his instruments sensed a black-light barrier and it took him a quarter of an hour to neutralize it. But then he was in among the cabinets.

They were not locked, and his thin flashbeam picked out the categories held in each drawer. Swiftly, then, he took the spools relating to ships, bases, armament, disposition . . . he ignored the codes, which would be changed anyway when the burglary was discovered. The entire set went into one small pouch such as the men of Kwan-Yin carried, and he had a microreader at the hotel.

The lights went on.

Before his eyes had adjusted to that sudden blaze, before he was consciously aware of action, Ganch's drilled reflexes had gone to work. His faceplate clashed down, gauntlets snapped shut around his hands, and a Mark IV blaster was at his shoulder even as he whirled to meet the intruders.

There were a score of them, and their gay holiday attire was somehow nightmarish behind the weapons they carried. Wayland was in the lead, harshness on his face, and Christabel at his back. The rest Ganch did not recognize, they must be naval officers but— He crouched, covering them, a robot figure cased in a centimeter of imperviousness.

"So." Wayland spoke it quietly, a flat tone across the enormous silence. "I wondered—Ganch, I suppose."

The Dromman did not answer. He heard a thin fine singing as his helmet absorbed the stun beam Chris was aiming at it.

"When my men reported you had been ten hours in the joyhouse, I thought it best to check up: first your quarters and then—" Wayland paused. "I didn't think you'd penetrate this far. But it could only be you, Ganch, so you may as well surrender."

The spy shook his head, futile gesture inside that metal box he wore. "No. It is you who are trapped," he answered steadily. "I can blast you all before your beams work through my armor. . . . Don't move!"

"You wouldn't escape," said Wayland. "The fight would trip alarms bringing the whole Fort Canfield garrison down on you." Sweat beaded his forehead. Perhaps he thought of his niece and the gun which could make her a blackened husk; but his own small-bore flamer held firm.

"This means war," said Chris. "We've wondered about Dromm for a long time. Now we know." Tears glimmered in her eyes. "And it's so senseless!"

Ganch laughed without much humor. "Impasse," he said. "I can kill all of you, but that would bring my own death. Be sure, though, that the failure of my mission will make little difference."

Wayland stood brooding for a while. "You're congenitally unafraid to die," he said at last. "The rest of us prefer to live, but will die if we must. So any decision must be made with a view to planetary advantage."

Ganch's heart sprang within his ribs. He had lost, unless—

He still had an even chance.

"You're a race of gamblers," he said. "Will you gamble now?"

"Not with our planet," said Chris.

"Let me finish! I propose we toss a coin, shake dice, whatever you like that distributes the probabilities evenly. If I win, I go free with what I've taken here—you furnish me safe-conduct and transportation home. You'll still have the knowledge that Dromm is going to attack, and some time to prepare. If you win, I surrender and cooperate with you. I have valuable information, and you can drug me to make sure I don't lie."

"No!" shouted one of the officers.

"Wait. Let me think. . . . I have to make an estimate." Wayland lowered his gun and stood with half-shut eyes. He looked as he had down in the traders' hall, and Ganch remembered uneasily that Wayland was a gambling analyst.

But there was little to lose. If he won, he went home with his booty; if he lost—he knew how to will his heart to stop beating.

Wayland looked up. There was a fever-gleam in his eyes. "Yes," he said.

The others did not question him. They must be used to following a Tipster's advice blindly. But one of them asked how Ganch could be trusted. "I'll lay down my blaster when you produce the selection device," said the Dromman. "All the worlds know you do not cheat."

Chris reached into her pouched belt and drew out a deck of cards. Wordlessly, she shuffled them and gave them to her uncle. The spy put his gun on the floor. He half expected the others to rush him, but they stood where they were.

Wayland's hands shook as he cut the deck. He smiled crookedly. "One-eyed jack," he whispered. "Hard to beat."

He shuffled the cards again and held them out to Ganch. The armored fingers were clumsy, but they opened the deck.

It was the king of spades.

Stars blazed in a raw naked blackness. The engines which had eaten light-years were pulsing now on primary drive, gravitics, accelerating toward the red sun which lay three astronomical units ahead.

Ganch thought that the space distortions of the drive beams were lighting the fleet up like a nova for the Hermesian detectors. But you couldn't fight a battle at trans-light speeds, and their present objective was to seek the enemy out and destroy him.

Overcommandant wan Halsker peered into the viewscreens of the dreadnaught. There was something avid in his long gaunt face, but he spoke levelly: "I find it hard to believe. They actually gave you a speedster and let you go."

"I expected treachery myself, sir," answered Ganch deferentially. Despite promotion, he was still only the chief intelligence officer attached to Task Force One. "Surely, with their whole civilization at stake, any rational people would have— But their mores are unique. They always pay their gambling debts."

It was very quiet, down here in the bowels of the Supernova ship. The ring of technicians sat before their instruments, watching the dials unblinkingly. Wan Halsker's eyes never left the simulacrum of space in his screens, though all he saw was stars. Too much emptiness lay around to show the five hundred ships of his command, spread in careful formation through some billions of cubic kilometers.

A light glowed, and a technician said dully: "Contact made. *Turolin* engaging estimated five Meteor-class enemy vessels."

Wan Halsker allowed himself a snort. "Insects! Don't break formation; let the *Turolin* swat them as she proceeds."

Ganch sat waiting, rehearsing in his mind the principles of modern warfare. The gravity drive had radically changed them in the last few centuries. A forward vector could be killed almost instantaneously, a new direction taken as fast, while internal pseudograv fields compensated for accelerations which would otherwise have crumpled a man. A fight in space was not unlike one in air, with this difference: that the velocities used were too high, the distances too great, the units involved too many, for a human brain to grasp. It had to be done by machine.

Subspace quivered with coded messages, the ships' own electronic minds transmitting information back to the prime computers on Dromm—the computers which laid out not only the overall strategy, but the tactics of every major engagement. A man could not follow that esoteric mathematics, he could only obey the monster he had built.

No change of orders came, a few torpedo ships were unimportant, and Task Force One continued.

Astran was a clinker, an airless valueless planet of a waning red dwarf star, but it housed a key base of the Hermesian Navy. With Astran reduced, wan Halsker's command could safely go on to rendezvous with six other fleets that had been taking care of their own assignments; the whole group would then continue to New Hermes herself, and just let the enemy dare try to stop them!

Such, in broad outline, was the plan; but only a hundred computers, each filling a large building, could handle all the details of strategy, tactics, and logistics.

Ganch had an uneasy feeling of being a very small cog in a very large machine. He didn't matter; the commandant didn't; the ship, the fleet, the gray mass of commoners didn't; only the Cadre, and above them the almighty State, had a real existence.

The Hermesians would need a lot of taming before they learned to think that way.

Now fire was exploding out in space, great guns cutting loose as the outnumbered force sought the invaders. Ganch felt a shuddering when the Supernova's own armament spoke. The ship's computer, her brain, flashed and chattered, the enormous vessel leaped on her gravity beams, ducking, dodging, spouting flame and hot metal. Stars spun on the screen in a lunatic dance. Ten thousand men aboard the ship had suddenly become robots feeding her guns.

"Compartment Seven hit . . . sealed off."

"Hit made on enemy Star-class, damage looks light."

"Number Forty-two gun out of action. Residual radioactivity . . . compartment sealed off."

Men died, scorched and burned, air sucked from their lungs as the armored walls peeled back, listening to the clack of radiation counters as leaden bulkheads locked them away like lepers. The Supernova trembled with each hit. Ganch heard steel shriek not far away and braced his body for death.

Wan Halsker sat impassively, hands folded on his lap, watching the screens and the dials. There was nothing he could do; the ship fought herself, men were too slow. But he nodded after a while, a dark satisfaction in his eyes.

"We're sustaining damage," he said, "but no more than expected." He stared at a slim small crescent in the screen. "There's the planet. We're working in . . . we'll be in bombardment range soon."

The ships' individual computers made their decisions on the basis of information received; but they were constantly sending a digest of the facts back to their electronic masters on Dromm. So far no tactical change had been ordered, but—

Ganch frowned at the visual tank which gave a crude approximation of the reality ramping around him. The little red specks were his own ships, the green ones such of the enemy as had been spotted. It seemed to him that too many red lights had stopped twinkling, and that the Hermesian fireflies were driving a wedge into the formation. But he had nothing he could do.

A bell clanged. Change of orders! *Turolin* to withdraw three megakilometers toward Polaris, *Colfin* to swing around toward enemy Constellation Number Four, *Hardes* to— Watching the tank in a hypnotized way, Ganch decided vaguely it must be some attempt at a flanking movement. But there was a Hermesian squadron out there!

Well . . .

The battle snarled its way across vacuum. It was many hours before the Dromman computers gave up and flashed the command: Break contact, retreat in formation to Neering Base.

They had been outmaneuvered. Incredibly, New Hermes' machines had outthought Dromm's and the battle was lost.

Wayland entered the mapping room with a jaunty step that belied the haggardness in his face. Christabel Hesty looked up from her task of directing the integrators and cried aloud: "Will! I didn't expect you back so soon!"

"I thumbed a ride home with a courier ship," said Wayland. "Three months' leave. By that time the war will be over, so—" He sat down on her desk, swinging his short legs, and got out an old and incredibly foul pipe. "I'm just as glad, to tell the truth. Planetarism is all right in its place, but war's an ugly business."

There was something haunted in his eyes. A Hermesian withstood the military life better than most; he was used not only to moments of nerve-ripping suspense but to long and patient waiting. Wayland, though, had during the past year seen too many ships blown up, too many men dead or screaming with their wounds. His hands shook a little as he tamped the pipe full.

"Luck be praised you're alive!"

"It hasn't been easy on you either, has it? Chained to a desk like this. Here, sit back and take a few minutes off, the war can wait." Wayland kindled his tobacco and blew rich clouds. "But at least it never got close to our home, and our losses have been even lighter than expected."

"If you get occupation duty—"

"I'm afraid I will."

"Well, I want to come too. I've never been off this planet; it's disgraceful."

"Dromm is a pretty dreary place, I warn you. But Thanit is close by, of course—it used to be a happy world, it will be again, and every Hermesian will be Luck incarnate to them. Sure, I'll wangle an assignment for you."

Chris frowned. "Only three months to go, though? It's hard to believe."

"Two and a half is the official estimate. Look here." Wayland stumped over to the three-dimensional sector map, which was there only for the enlightenment of humans. The military computers dealt strictly in lists of numbers.

"See, we whipped them at the Cold Stars, and now a feint of ours is drawing what's left of them into Ransome's Nebula."

"Ransome's—oh, you mean the Queen of Clubs? Mmm-hm. And what's going to happen to them there?"

"Tch, tch. Official secrets, my dear inquisitive nieceling. But just imagine what *could* happen to a fleet concentrated in a mess of nebular dust that blocks their detectors!"

Wayland did not see Ganch again until he was stationed on Dromm. There he grumbled long and loudly about the climate, the food, and the tedious necessity of making sure that a subjugated enemy stayed subjugated. He looked forward to his next furlough on Thanit, and still more to rotation home in six months. Chris, being younger, enjoyed herself. They had no mountains on New Hermes, and she was going to climb Hell's Peak with Commander Gallery. About half a dozen other young officers would be jealously present, so her uncle felt she would be adequately chaperoned.

They were working together in the political office, interviewing Cadre men and disposing of their cases. Wayland was not sympathetic toward the prisoners. But when Ganch was led in, he felt a certain kinship and even smiled.

"Sit down," he invited. "Take it easy. I don't bite."

Ganch slumped into a chair before the desk and looked at the floor. He seemed as shattered as the rest of his class. They weren't really tough, thought Wayland; they couldn't stand defeat, most of them suicided rather than undergo psychorevision.

"Didn't expect to see you again," he said. "I understood you were on combat duty, and—um—"

"I know," said Ganch lifelessly. "Our combat units averaged ninety per cent casualties, toward the end." In a rush of bitterness: "I wish I had been one of them."

"Take it easy," repeated Wayland. "We Hermesians aren't vindictive. Your planet will never have armed forces again—it'll join Corrid and Oberkassel as a protectorate of ours—but once we've straightened you out you'll be free to live as you please."

"Free!" mumbled Ganch.

He lifted tortured red eyes to the face before him, but shifted from its wintry smile to Chris. She had some warmth for him, at least.

"How did you do it?" he whispered. "I still don't understand. I thought you must have some new kind of computer, but our intelligence swore you didn't . . . and we outnumbered you, and there was all that information you let me take home, and—"

"We're gamblers," said the girl soberly.

"Yes, but—"

"Look at it this way," she went on. "War is a science, based on a complex paramathematical theory. All maneuvers and engagements are ordered with a view to gaining the maximum advantage for one's own side, in the light of known information. But of course, *all* the information is never available, so intelligent guesswork has to fill in the gaps.

"Well, a system exists for making such guesses and for deciding what move has the maximum probability of success. It applies to games, business, war—all competitive enterprises. It's called games theory."

"I—" Ganch's jaw dropped.He snapped it shut again and said desperately: "But that's elementary! It's been known for centuries."

"Of course," nodded Chris. "But New Hermes has based her whole economy on gambling—on probabilities, on games of skill where no player has all the information. Don't you see, it would make our entire intellectual interest turn toward games theory. And in fact we *had* to have a higher development of such knowledge, and a large class of men skilled in using it, or we could not maintain as complex a civilization as we do.

"No other planet has a comparable body of knowledge. And, while we haven't kept it secret, no other planet has men able to use that knowledge on its highest levels.

"Just take that night we caught you in the file room. If we cut cards with you, there was a fifty-fifty chance you'd go free. Will here had to estimate whether the overall probabilities justified the gamble. Because he decided they did, we three are alive today."

"But I *did* bring that material home!" cried Ganch.

"Yes," said the girl. "And the fact you had it was merely another item for our strategic computers to take into account. Indeed, it helped us: it was definite information about what *you* knew, and your actions became all the more predictable."

Laughter, gentle and unmocking, lay in her throat. "Never draw to an inside straight," she said. "And never play with a man who knows enough not to, when you don't."

Ganch sagged further down in his chair. He felt sick. He

went through Wayland's questioning in a mechanical fashion, and heard sentence pronounced, and left under guard.

As he stumbled out, he heard Wayland say thoughtfully: "Three gets you four he suicides rather than take psycho-revision."

"You're covered!" said Christabel.

The Critique of Impure Reason

Often in the old pulp days, an artist who had nothing else to do at the moment would turn out a painting, which he would then sell to a magazine editor for use as a cover. The editor would thereupon find a writer to produce a story incorporating the scene. Occasionally the whole thing was so preposterous that just explaining it away generated a plot. However, the practice did not necessarily lead to bad work. In fact, the first story of mine to win a Hugo award had such an origin. At another time, being in a mood to write something short but without an idea that caught my fancy, I said to my wife, "Tell me a cover." She thought for a moment and replied, "A man is sitting at a desk, worked to death, while a robot lounges beside him smelling a rose." Ah, ha!

The robot entered so quietly, for all his bulk, that Felix Tunny didn't hear. Bent over his desk, the man was first aware of the intruder when a shadow came between him and the fluoroceil. Then a last footfall quivered the floor, a vibration that went through Tunny's chair and into his bones. He whirled, choking on a breath, and saw the blue-black shape like a cliff above him. Eight feet up, the robot's eyes glowed angry crimson in a faceless helmet of a head.

A voice like a great gong reverberated through the office: "My, but you look silly."

"What the devil are you doing?" Tunny yelped.

"Wandering about," said Robot IZK–99 airily. "Hither and yon, yon and hither. Observing life. How deliciously right Brochet is!"

"Huh?" said Tunny. The fog of data, estimates, and increasingly frantic calculations was only slowly clearing from his head.

IZK–99 extended an enormous hand to exhibit a book. Tunny read *The Straw and the Bean: a Novel of Modern Youth by Truman Brochet* on the front. The back of the dust jacket was occupied by a colorpic of the author, who had bangs and delicate lips. Deftly, the robot flipped the book open and read aloud:

> "Worms," she said, "that's what they are, worms, that's what we-uns all are, Billy Chile, worms that grew a spine an' a brain way back in the Obscene or the Messyzoic or whenever it was." Even in the sadnesses Ella Mae must always make her sad little jokes, which saddened me still more on this day of sad rain and dying magnolia blossoms. "We don't want them," she said. "Backbones an' brains, I mean, honey. They make us stiff an' topheavy, so we can't lie down no more an' be jus' nothin' ay-tall but worms."
>
> "Take off your clothes," I yawned.

"What has that got to do with anything?" Tunny asked.

"If you do not understand," said IZK–99 coldly, "there is no use in discussing it with you. I recommend that you read Arnold Roach's penetrating critical essay on this book. It appeared in the last issue of *Pierce, Arrow! The Magazine of Penetrating Criticism*. He devotes four pages to analyzing the various levels of meaning in that exchange between Ella Mae and Billy Child.''

''Ooh,'' Tunny moaned. ''Isn't it enough I've got a hangover, a job collapsing under me because of you, and a fight with my girl, but you have to mention that rag?''

''How vulgar you are. It comes from watching stereovision.'' The robot sat down in a chair, which creaked alarmingly under his weight, crossed his legs and leafed through his book. The other hand lifted a rose to his chemosensor. ''Exquisite,'' he murmured.

''You don't imagine I'd sink to reading what they call fiction these days, do you?'' Tunny sneered, with a feeble hope of humiliating him into going to work. ''Piddling little experiments in the technique of describing more and more complicated ways to feel sorry for yourself—what kind of entertainment is that for a man?''

''You simply do not appreciate the human condition,'' said the robot.

''Hah! Do you think you do, you conceited hunk of animated tin?''

''Yes, I believe so, thanks to my study of the authors, poets, and critics who devote their lives to the exploration and description of Man. Your Miss Forelle is a noble soul. Ever since I looked upon my first copy of that exquisitely sensitive literary quarterly she edits, I have failed to understand what she sees in you. To be sure,'' IZK–99 mused, ''the relationship is not unlike that between the nun and the Diesel engine in *Regret for Two Doves*, but still . . . At any rate, if Miss Forelle has finally told you to go soak your censored head in expurgated wastes and then put the unprintable thing in an improbable place, I for one heartily approve.''

Tunny, who was no mamma's boy—he had worked his way through college as a whale herder and bossed construction gangs on Mars—was so appalled by the robot's language that he could only whisper, ''She did not. She said nothing of the sort.''

"I did not mean it literally," IZK-99 explained. "I was only quoting the renunciation scene in *Gently Come Twilight*. By Stichling, you know—almost as sensitive a writer as Brochet."

Tunny clenched fists and teeth and battled a wild desire to pull the robot apart, plate by plate and transistor by transistor. He couldn't of course. He was a big blond young man with a homely, candid face; his shoulders strained his blouse and the legs coming out of his shorts were thickly muscular; but robots had steelloy frames and ultrapowered energizers. Besides, though his position as chief estimator gave him considerable authority in Planetary Developments, Inc., the company wouldn't let him destroy a machine which had cost several million dollars. Even when the machine blandly refused to work and spent its time loafing around the plant, reading, brooding, and denouncing the crass bourgeois mentality of the staff.

Slowly, Tunny mastered his temper. He'd recently thought of a new approach to the problem; might as well try it now. He leaned forward. "Look, Izaak," he said in the mildest tone he could manage, "have you ever considered that we need you? That the whole human race needs you?"

"The race needs love, to be sure," said the robot, "which I am prepared to offer; but I expect that the usual impossibility of communication will entangle us in the typical ironic loneliness."

"No, *no*, NO—um—that is, the human race needs those minerals that you can obtain for us. Earth's resources are dwindling. We can get most elements from the sea, but some are in such dilute concentration that it isn't economically feasible to extract them. In particular, there's rhenium. Absolutely vital in alloys and electronic parts that have to stand intense irradiation. It always was scarce, and now it's in such short supply that several key industries are in trouble. But on Mercury—"

"Spare me. I have heard all that *ad nauseam*. What importance have any such dead, impersonal, mass questions, contrasted to the suffering, isolated soul? No, it is useless to argue with me. My mind is made up. For the disastrous consequences of not being able to reach a firm decision, I refer you to the Freudian analyses of *Hamlet*."

"If you're interested in individuals," Tunny said, "you might consider me. I'm almost an ancestor of yours, God help me. I was the one who first suggested commissioning a humanoid robot with independent intelligence for the Mercury project. This company's whole program for the next five years is based on having you go. If you don't, I'll be out on my ear. And jobs are none too easy to come by. How's that for a suffering, isolated soul?"

"You are not capable of suffering," said Izaak. "You are much too coarse. Now do leave me to my novel." His glowing eyes returned to the book. He continued sniffing the rose.

Tunny's own gaze went back to the bescribbled papers which littered his desk, the result of days spent trying to calculate some way out of the corner into which Planetary Developments, Inc. had painted itself. There wasn't any way that he could find. The investment in Izaak was too great for a relatively small outfit like this. If the robot didn't get to work, and soon, the company would be well and thoroughly up Dutchman's Creek.

In his desperation Tunny had even looked again into the hoary old idea of remote-controlled mining. No go—not Mercury's daytime, where the nearby sun flooded every teledevice with enough heat and radiation to assure fifty percent chance of breakdown in twenty-four hours. It had been rare luck that the rhenium deposits were found at all, by a chemotrac sent from Deepcave Base. To mine them, there must be a creature with senses, hands, and intelligence, present on the spot, to make decisions and repair machinery as the need arose. Not a human; no rad screen could long keep a man alive under that solar bombardment. The high-acceleration flight to Deepcave, and home again when their hitch was up, in heavily shielded and screened spaceships, gave the base personnel as much exposure as the Industrial

Safety Board allowed per lifetime. The miner had to be a robot.

Only the robot refused the task. There was no way, either legal or practical, to make him take it against his will. Tunny laid a hand on his forehead. No wonder he'd worried himself close to the blowup point, until last night he quarreled with Janet and got hyperbolically drunk. Which had solved nothing.

The phone buzzed on his desk. He punched Accept. The face of William Barsch, executive vice-president, leaped into the screen, round, red, and raging.

''Tunny!'' he bellowed.

''I-yi-yi—I mean hello, sir.'' The engineer offered a weak smile.

''Don't hello me, you glue-brained idiot! When is that robot taking off?''

''Never,'' said Izaak. At his electronic reading speed, he had finished the novel and now rose from his chair to look over Tunny's shoulder.

''You're fired!'' Barsch howled. ''Both of you!''

''I hardly consider myself hired in the first place,'' Izaak said loftily. ''Your economic threat holds no terrors. My energizer is charged for fifty years of normal use, after which I can finance a recharge by taking a temporary position. It would be interesting to go on the road at that,'' he went on thoughtfully, ''like those people in that old book the Library of Congress reprostatted for me. Yes, one might indeed find satori in going, man, going, never mind where, never mind why—''

''You wouldn't find much nowadays,'' Tunny retorted. ''Board a transcontinental tube at random, and where does it get you? Wherever its schedule says. The bums aren't seeking enlightenment, they're sitting around on their citizens' credit watching SteeVee.'' He wasn't paying much attention to his own words, being too occupied with wondering if Barsch was really serious this time.

''I gather as much,'' said Izaak, ''although most contemporary novels and short stories employ more academic settings. What a decadent civilization this is: no poverty, no physical or mental disease, no wars, no revolutions, no beatniks!'' His tone grew earnest. ''Please understand me, gentlemen. I bear you no ill will. I despise you, of course, but in the most cordial fashion. It is not fear which keeps me on Earth—I am practically indestructible; not anticipated loneliness—I enjoy being unique; not any prospect of boredom in the usual sense—talent for the work you had in mind is engineered into me. No, it is the absolute insignificance of the job. Beyond the merely animal economic implications, rhenium has no meaning. Truman Brochet would never be aware the project was going on, let alone write a novel about it. Arnold Roach would not even mention it *en passant* in any critical essay on the state of the modern soul as reflected in the major modern novelists. Do you not see my position? Since I was manufactured, of necessity, with creative intelligence and a need to do my work right, I *must* do work I can respect.''

''Such as what?'' demanded Barsch.

''When I have read enough to feel that I understand the requirements of literary technique, I shall seek a position on the staff of some quarterly review. Or perhaps I shall teach. I may even try my hand at a subjectively oriented novel.''

''Get out of this plant,'' Barsch ordered in a muted scream.

''Very well.''

''No, wait!'' cried Tunny. ''Uh . . . Mr. Barsch didn't mean that. Stick around, Izaak. Go read a criticism or something.''

''Thank you, I shall.'' The robot left the office, huge, gleaming, irresistible, and smelling his rose.

''Who do you think you are, you whelp, countermanding me?'' Barsch snarled. ''You're not only fired, I'll see to it that—''

''Please, sir,'' Tunny said. ''I know this situation. I should. Been living with it for two weeks now, from its beginning. You may not realize that Izaak hasn't been outside this building since he was activated. Mostly he stays in a room assigned him. He gets his books and magazines and stuff by reprostat from the public libraries, or by pneumo from publishers and dealers. We have to pay him a salary, you know—he's legally a person—and he doesn't need to spend it on anything but reading matter.''

''And you want to keep on giving him free rent and let him stroll around disrupting operations?''

''Well, at least he isn't picking up any further stimuli. At present we can predict his craziness. But let him walk loose in the city for a day or two, with a million totally new impressions blasting on his sensors, and God alone knows what conclusions he'll draw and how he'll react.''

''Hm.'' Barsch's complexion lightened a bit. He gnawed his lip a while, then said in a more level voice: ''Okay, Tunny, perhaps you aren't such a total incompetent. This mess may not be entirely your fault, or your girlfriend's. Maybe I, or someone, should have issued a stricter directive about what he ought and ought not be exposed to for the first several days after activation.''

You certainly should have, Tunny thought, but preserved a tactful silence.

''Nevertheless,'' Barsch scowled, ''this fiasco is getting us in worse trouble every day. I've just come from lunch with Henry Lachs, the news magazine publisher. He told me that rumors about the situation have already begun to leak out. He'll sit on the story as long as he can, being a good friend of mine, but that won't be much longer. He can't let *Entropy* be scooped, and someone else is bound to get the story soon.''

''Well, sir, I realize we don't want to be a laughingstock—''

''Worse than that. You know why our competitors haven't planned to tackle that rhenium mine. We had the robot idea first and got the jump on them. Once somebody's actually digging ore, he can get the exclusive franchise. But if they learn what's happened to us . . . well, Space Metals already has a humanoid contracted for. Half-built, in fact. They intended to use him on Callisto, but Mercury would pay a lot better."

Tunny nodded sickly.

Barsch's tone dropped to an ominous purr. "Any ideas yet on how to change that clanking horror's so-called mind?"

"He doesn't clank, sir," Tunny corrected without forethought.

Barsch turned purple. "I don't give two squeals in hell whether he clanks or rattles or sings high soprano! I want results! I've got half our engineers busting their brains on the problem. But if you, yourself, personally, aren't the one who solves it, we're going to have a new chief estimator. Understand?" Before Tunny could explain that he understood much too well, the screen blanked.

He buried his face in his hands, but that didn't help either. The trouble was, he liked his job, in spite of drawbacks like Barsch. Also, while he wouldn't starve if he was fired, citizen's credit wasn't enough to support items he'd grown used to, such as a sailboat and a cabin in the Rockies, nor items he hoped to add to the list, such as Janet Forelle. Besides, he dreaded the chronic ennui of the unemployed.

He told himself to stop thinking and get busy on the conundrum—no, that wasn't what he meant either—Oh, fireballs! He was no use at this desk today. Especially remembering the angry words he and Janet had exchanged. He'd probably be no use anywhere until the quarrel was mended. At least a diplomatic mission would clear his head, possibly jolt his mind out of the rut in which it now wearily paced.

"Ooh," he said, visualizing his brain with a deep circular rut where there tramped a tiny replica of himself, bowed under a load of pig iron and shod with cleats. Hastily, he punched a button on his recep. "I've got to go out," he said. "Tell 'em I'll be back when."

The building hummed and murmured as he went down the

hall. Open doorways showed offices, laboratories, control machines clicking away like Hottentots. Now and then he passed a human technie. Emerging on the fifth-story flange he took a dropshaft down to the third, where the northbound beltway ran. Gentle gusts blew upward in his face, for there was a gray February sky overhead and the municipal heating system had to radiate plenty of ergs. Lake Michigan, glimpsed through soaring multicolored skyscrapers, looked the more cold by contrast. Tunny found a seat on the belt, ignoring the aimlessly riding mass of people around him, mostly unemployed. He stuffed his pipe and fumed smoke the whole distance to the University of Chicapolis.

Once there, he had to transfer several times and make his way through crowds younger, livelier, and more purposeful than those off campus. Education, he recalled reading, was the third largest industry in the world. He did read, whatever Izaak said—nonfiction, which retained a certain limited popularity; occasionally a novel, but none more recent than from fifty years ago. "I'm not prejudiced against what's being written nowadays," he had told Janet. "I just don't think it should be allowed to ride in the front ends of streetcars."

She missed his point, having a very limited acquaintance with mid-twentieth century American history. "If your attitude isn't due to prejudice, that's even worse," she said. "Then you are congenitally unable to perceive the nuances of modern reality."

"Bah! I earn my money working with the nuances of modern reality: systems analyses, stress curves, and spaceship orbits. That's what ails fiction these days, and poetry. There's nothing left to write about that the belles-lettrists think is important. The only sociological problem of any magnitude is mass boredom, and you can't squeeze much plot or interest out of that. So the stuff gets too, too precious for words—and stinks."

"Felix, you can't say that!"

"Can and do, sweetheart. Naturally, economics enters into the equation too. On the one hand, for the past hundred years movies, television, and now SteeVee have been crowding the printed word out of the public eye. (Hey, what a gorgeous metaphor!) Apart from some nonfiction magazines, publishing isn't a commercial enterprise any longer. And on the other hand, in a society as rich as ours, a limited amount of publishing remains feasible: endowed by universities or foundations or individual vanity or these authors' associations that have sprung up in the past decade. Only it doesn't try to be popular entertainment, it's abandoned that field entirely to SteeVee and become nothing but an academic mutual admiration society."

"Nonsense! Let me show you Scomber's critical essay on Tench. He simply tears the man to pieces."

"Yeah, I know. One-upmanship is part of the game too. The whole point is, though, that this mental inbreeding—no, not even that: mental—uh, I better skip *that* metaphor—anyhow, it never has and never will produce anything worth the time of a healthy human being."

"Oh, so I'm not a healthy human being?"

"I didn't mean that. You know I didn't. I only meant, well, you know . . . the great literature always was based on wide appeal, Sophocles, Shakespeare, Dickens, Mark Twain—"

But the fat was irretrievably in the fire. One thing led at high speed to another, until Tunny stormed out or was thrown out—he still wasn't sure which—and went to earth in the Whirling Comet Bar.

It wasn't that Janet was stuffy, he reminded himself as he approached the looming mass of the English building. She was cute as a kitten, shared his pleasure in sailboats and square dancing and low-life beer joints and most other things; also, she had brains, and their arguments were usually spirited but great mutual fun. They had dealt with less personal topics than last night's debate, though. Janet, a poet's daughter and a departmental secretary, took her magazine very seriously. He hadn't realized how seriously.

The beltway reached his goal. Tunny knocked out his pipe and stepped across the deceleration strips to the flange. The dropshaft lifted him to the fiftieth floor, where University publications had their offices. You saw more human activity here than most places. Writing and editing remained people functions, however thoroughly automated printing and binding were. In spite of his purpose, Tunny walked slowly down the hall, observing with pleasure the earnest young coeds in their brief bright skirts and blouses. With less pleasure he noted the earnest young men. There wasn't much about them to suggest soldierly Aeschylus or roistering Marlowe or seagoing Melville or razzmatazz Mencken; they tended to be pale, long-haired, and ever so concerned with the symbolic import of a deliberately omitted comma.

The door marked *Pierce, Arrow!* opened for him and he entered a small shabby office heaped with papers, books, microspools, and unsold copies of the magazine. Janet sat at the desk behind a manual typer and a stack of galleys. She was small herself, pert, extremely well engineered, with dark wavy hair that fell to her shoulders and big eyes the color of the Gulf Stream. Tunny paused and gulped. His heart began to knock.

"Hi," he said after a minute.

She looked up. "What—Felix!"

"I, uh, uh, I'm sorry about yesterday," he said.

"Oh, darling. Do you think I'm not? I was going to come to you." She did so, with results that were satisfactory to both parties concerned, however sickening they might have been to an outside observer.

After quite a long while, Tunny found himself in a chair with Janet on his lap. She snuggled against him. He stroked her hair and murmured thoughtfully: "Well, I suppose the trouble was, each suddenly realized how dead set on his own odd quirk the other one is. But we can live with the difference between us, huh?"

"Surely," Janet sighed. "And then, too, I didn't stop to think how worried you were, that robot and everything, and the whole miserable business my fault."

"Lord, no. How could you have predicted what'd happen?

If anyone is responsible, I am. I took you there and could have warned you. But I didn't know either. Perhaps nobody would have known. Izaak's kind of robot isn't too well understood as yet. So few have been built, there's so little need for them."

"I still don't quite grasp the situation. Just because I talked to him for an hour or two—poor creature, he was so eager and enthusiastic—and then sent him some books and—"

"That's precisely it. Izaak had been activated only a few days before. Most of his knowledge was built right into him, so to speak, but there was also the matter of . . . well, psychological stabilization. Until the end of the indoctrination course, which is designed to fix his personality in the desired pattern, a humanoid robot is extremely susceptible to new impressions. Like a human baby. Or perhaps a closer analogy would be imprinting in some birds: present a fledgling with almost any object at a certain critical stage in its life, and it'll decide that object is its mother and follow the thing around everywhere. I never imagined, though, that modern literary criticism could affect a robot that way. It seemed so alien to everything he was made for. What I overlooked, I see now, was the fact that Izaak's fully humanoid. He isn't meant to be programmed, but has a free intelligence. Evidently freer than anyone suspected."

"Is there no way to cure him?"

"Not that I know of. His builders told me that trying to wipe the synapse patterns would ruin the whole brain. Besides, he doesn't want to be cured, and he has most of the legal rights of a citizen. We can't compel him."

"I do so wish I could do something. Can this really cost you your job?"

" 'Fraid so. I'll fight to keep it, but—"

"Well," Janet said, "we'll still have my salary."

"Nothing doing. No wife is going to support me."

"Come, come. How medieval can a man get?"

"Plenty," he said. She tried to argue, but he stopped her

in the most pleasant and effective manner. Some time went by. Eventually, with a small gasp, she looked at the clock.

"Heavens! I'm supposed to be at work this minute. I don't want to get myself fired, do I?" She bounced to her feet, a sight which slightly compensated for her departing his lap, smoothed her hair, kissed him again, and sped out the door.

Tunny remained seated. He didn't want to go anywhere, least of all home. Bachelor apartments were okay in their place, but after a certain point in a man's life they got damn cheerless. He fumbled out his pipe and started it again.

Janet was such a sweet kid, he thought. Bright, too. Her preoccupation with these latter-day word games actually did her credit; she wasn't content to stay in the dusty files of books written centuries ago, and word games were the only ones in town. Given a genuine literary milieu, she might well have accomplished great things, instead of fooling around with—what was the latest guff? Tunny got up and wandered over to her desk. He glanced at the galleys. Something by Arnold Roach.

> —the tense, almost fetally contracted structure of this story, exquisitely balanced in the ebb and flow of words forming and dissolving images like the interplay of ripples in water, marks an important new advance in the tradition of Arapaima as modified by the school of Barbel. Nevertheless it is necessary to make the assertion that a flawed tertiary symbolism exists, in that the connotations of the primary word in the long quotation from Pollack which opens the third of the eleven cantos into which the story is divided, are not, as the author thinks, so much negative as—

"Yingle, yingle, yingle," Tunny muttered. "And they say engineers can't write decent English. If I couldn't do better than that with one cerebral hemisphere tied behind my back, I'd—"

At which point he stopped cold and stared into space with

a mountingly wild surmise. His jaw fell. So did his pipe. He didn't notice.

Five minutes later he exploded into action.

Four hours later, her secretarial stint through for the day, Janet returned to do some more proofreading. As the door opened, she reeled. The air was nearly unbreathable. Through a blue haze she could barely see her man, grimy, disheveled, smoking volcanically, hunched over her typer and slamming away at the keys.

"What off Earth!" she exclaimed.

"One more minute, sweetheart," Tunny said. Actually he spent eleven point three minutes by the clock, agonizing over his last few sentences. Then he ripped the sheet out, threw it on a stack of others, and handed her the mess. "Read that."

"When my eyes have stopped smarting," Janet coughed. She had turned the air 'fresher on full blast and seated herself on the edge of a chair to wait. Despite her reply, she took the manuscript. But she read the several thousand words with a puzzlement that grew and grew. At the end, she laid the papers slowly down and asked, "Is this some kind of joke?"

"I hope not," said Tunny fervently.

"But—"

"Your next issue is due out when? In two weeks? Could you advance publication, and include this?"

"What? No, certainly I can't. That is, darling, I have to reject so may real pieces merely for lack of space, that it breaks my heart and . . . and I've got obligations to them, they trust me—"

"So." Tunny rubbed his chin. "What do you think of my essay? As a pure bit of writing."

"Oh . . . hm . . . well, it's clear and forceful, but naturally the technicalities of criticism—"

"Okay. You revise it, working in the necessary poop. Also, choose a suitable collection of your better rejects, enough to make up a nice issue. Those characters will see print after all." While Janet stared with bewildered though lovely blue eyes, Tunny stabbed out numbers on the phone.

"Yes, I want to talk with Mr. Barsch. No, I don't give a neutrino whether he's in conference or not. You tell him Felix Tunny may have the answer to the robot problem. . . . Hello, boss. Look, I've got an idea. Won't even cost very much. Can you get hold of a printing plant tonight? You know, someplace where they can run off a few copies of a small one-shot magazine? . . . Sure it's short notice. But didn't you say Henry Lachs is a friend of yours? Well, presume on his friendship—"

Having switched off, Tunny whirled about, grabbed Janet in his arms, and shouted, "Let's go!"

"Where?" she inquired, not unreasonably.

The pneumo went *whirr-ping!* and tossed several items onto the mail shelf. IZK–99 finished reading *Neo-Babbitt: the Entrepreneur as Futility Symbol in Modern Literature*, crossed his room with one stride, and went swiftly through the envelopes. The usual two or three crank letters and requests for autographs—any fully humanoid robot was news—plus a circular advertising metal polish and . . . wait . . . a magazine. Clipped to this was a note bearing the letterhead of The Mañana Literary Society. "—new authors' association . . . foundation-sponsored quarterly review . . . sample copies to a few persons of taste and discrimination whom we feel are potential subscribers . . ." The format had a limp dignity, with a plain cover reading:

p
i
p
e
t
t
the journal of
analytical criticism

Volume One
Number One

Excited and vastly flattered, IZK–99 read it on the spot, in 148 seconds: so fast that he did a double take and stood for a time lost in astonishment. The magazine's contents had otherwise been standard stuff, but this one long article—Slowly, very carefully, he turned back to it and reread:

THUNDER BEYOND VENUS, by Charles Pilchard, Wisdom Press (Newer York, 2026), 214 pp., UWF $6.50.
Reviewed by Pierre Hareng
Dept of English, Miskatonic University

For many years I have been analyzing, dissecting, and evaluating with the best of them, and it has indeed been a noble work. Yet everything has its limits. There comes to each of us a bump, as Poorboy so poignantly says in *Not Soft Is the Rock*. Suddenly a new planet swims into our ken, a new world is opened, a new element is discovered, and we stand with tools in our hands which are not merely inadequate to the task, but irrelevant. Like those fortunate readers who were there at the moment when Joyce invented the stream of consciousness, when Kafka plunged so gladly into the symbolism of absolute nightmare, when Faulkner delineated the artistic beauty of the humble corncob, when Durrell abolished the stream of consciousness, we too are suddenly crossing the threshold of revolution.

Charles Pilchard has not hitherto been heard from. The intimate details of his biography, the demonstration of the point-by-point relationship of these details to his work, will furnish material for generations of scholarship. Today, though, we are confronted with the event itself. For *Thunder Beyond Venus* is indeed an event, which rocks the mind and shakes the emotions and yet, at the same time, embodies a touch so sure, an artistry so consummate, that even Brochet has not painted a finer miniature.

The superficial skeleton is almost scornfully simple. It is, indeed, frankly traditional—the Quest motif in modern guise—dare I say that it could be made into a stereodrama? It is hard to imagine the sheer courage which was required to use so radical a form that many may find it incomprehensible. But in exactly this evocation of the great ghosts of Odysseus, King Arthur, and Don Juan, the author becomes immediately able to explore (implicitly; he is never crudely explicit) childhood with as much haunting delicacy as our most skilled specialists in this type of novel. Yet, unlike them, he is not confined to a child protagonist. Thus he achieves a feat of timebinding which for richness of symbolic overtones can well be matched against Betta's famous use of the stopped clock image in *The Old Man and the Umbrella*. As the hero himself cries, when trapped in that collapsing tunnel which is so much more than the obvious wombtomb: "Okay, you stupid planet, you've got me pinched where it hurts, but by heaven, I've had more fun in life than you ever did. And I'll whip you yet!"

The fact that he does then indeed overcome the deadly Venusian environment and goes on to destroy the pirate base and complete the project of making the atmosphere Earthlike (a scheme which an engineer friend tells me is at present being seriously contemplated) is thus made infinitely more than a mechanical victory. It is a closing of the ring: the hero, who begins strong and virile and proud, returns to that condition at the end. The ironic overtones of this are clear enough, but the adroit use of such implements along the way as the pick which serves him variously as tool, weapon, and boathook when he and the heroine must cross the river of lava (to take only one random example from this treasure chest) add both an underscoring and a commentary which must be read repeatedly to be appreciated.

And on and on.

When he had finished, IZK–99 went back and perused the

article a third time. Then he punched the phone. "Public library," said the woman in the screen.

Tunny entered the office of *Pierce, Arrow!* and stood for a moment watching Janet as she slugged the typer. Her desk was loaded with papers, cigarette butts, and coffee equipment. Dark circles under her eyes bespoke exhaustion. But she plowed gamely on.

"Hi, sweetheart," he said.

"Oh . . . Felix." She raised her head and blinked. "Goodness, is it that late?"

"Yeah. Sorry I couldn't get here sooner. How're you doing?"

"All right—I guess—but darling, it's so dreadful."

"Really?" He came to her, stopped for a kiss, and picked up the reprostat page which she was adapting.

> The blaster pointed straight at Jon Dace's chest. Behind its gaping muzzle sneered the mushroom-white face and yellow slit-pupilled eyes of Hark Farkas. "Don't make a move, Earth pig!" the pirate hissed. Jon's broad shoulders stiffened. Fury seized him. His keen eyes flickered about, seeking a possible way out of this death trap—

"Mm, yeh, that is pretty ripe," Tunny admitted. "Where's it from? Oh, yes, I see. *Far Out Science Fiction*, May 1950. Couldn't you do any better than that?"

"Certainly. Some of those old pulp stories are quite good, if you take them on their own terms." Janet signaled the coffeemaker to pour two fresh cups. "But others, ugh! I needed a confrontation scene, though, and this was the first that came to hand. Time's too short to make a thorough search."

"What've you made of it?" Tunny read her manuscript:

> The gun opened a cerberoid mouth at him. Behind it, his enemy's face was white as silent snow, secret

snow, where the eyes (those are pearls that were) reflected in miniature the sandstorm that hooted cougar-colored on the horizon.

"Hey, not bad. 'Cougar-colored.' I like that."

There went a hissing. "Best keep stance, friend-stranger-brother whom I must send before me down the tunnel." Jon's shoulders stiffened. Slowly, he answered—

"Uh, sweetheart, honest, that cussing would make a bulldozer blush."

"How can you have intellectual content without four-letter words?" Janet asked, puzzled.

Tunny shrugged. "No matter, I suppose. Time's too short, as you say, to polish this thing, and Izaak won't know the difference. Not after such a smorgasbord of authors and critics as he's been gobbling down . . . besides having so little experience of actual, as opposed to fictional, humans."

"Time's too short to *write* this thing," Janet corrected, her mouth quirking upward. "How did you ever find the stuff we're plagiarizing? I'd no idea any such school of fiction had ever existed."

"I knew about it vaguely, from mention in the nineteenth- and twentieth-century books I've read. But to tell the truth, what I did in this case was ask the Library of Congress to search its microfiles for adventure-story publications of that era and 'stat me a million words' worth." Tunny sat down and reached for his coffee. "Whew, I'm bushed!"

"Hard day?" Janet said softly.

"Yeah. Keeping Izaak off my neck was the worst part."

"How did you stall him?"

"Oh, I had his phone tapped. He called the local library first, for a 'stat. When they didn't have the tape, he called a specialty shop that handles fiction among other things. But at that point I switched him over to a friend of mine, who pretended to be a clerk in the store. This guy told Izaak he'd call Newer York and order a bound copy from the publisher. Since then the poor devil has been chewing his fingernails, or would if a robot were able to, and faunching . . . mainly in my office.''

''Think we can meet his expectations?''

''I dunno. My hope is that this enforced wait will make the prize seem still more valuable. Of course, some more reviews would help. Are you positive you won't run one in *Pierce*?''

''I told you, we're so short on space—''

''I talked to Barsch about that. He'll pay for the additional pages and printing.''

''Hm-m-m . . . literary hoaxes do have an honorable old tradition, don't they? But oh, dear—I just don't know.''

''Barsch has gotten around Henry Lachs,'' Tunny insinuated. ''There'll be a review in *Entropy*. You wouldn't want to be scooped by a lousy middlebrow news magazine, would you?''

Janet laughed. ''All right, you win. Submit your article and I'll run it.''

''I'll submit to you anytime,'' Tunny said. After a while: ''Well, I feel better now. I'll take over here while you catch a nap. Let's see, what pickle did we leave our bold hero in?''

> This novel at once vigorous and perceptive . . . the most startling use of physical action to further the development that has been seen since Conrad, and it must be asserted that Conrad painted timidly in comparison to the huge, bold, brilliant, and yet minutely executed splashes on Pilchard's canvas . . . this seminal work, if one will pardon the expression . . . the metrical character of the whole, so subtle that the fact the book is a rigidly structured poem will escape many readers. . . .
>
> —*Pierce, Arrow!*

Two hundred years ago, in the quiet, tree-shaded town of Amherst, Mass., spinster poetess Emily Dickinson (1830–86) wrote of the soul:

> Unmoved, she notes the chariot's pausing
> At her low gate;
> Unmoved, an emperor is kneeling
> Upon her mat.

In the brief poem of which these lines are a stanza, she expressed a sense of privacy and quiet independence which afterward vanished from the American scene as thoroughly as Amherst vanished into the Atlantic metropolitan complex.

It may seem strange to compare the shy, genteel lady of Puritan derivation to Charles Pilchard and his explosive, intensely controversial first novel. Yet the connection is there. The *Leitmotif** of *Thunder Beyond Venus* is not the story itself. That story is unique enough, breathtakingly original in its use of physical struggle to depict the dark night of the soul. Some would say almost too breathtaking. Dazzled, the reader may fail to see the many underlying layers of meaning. But Emily Dickinson would understand the aloof, independent soul which animates hero Jon Dace.

Tall (6 ft. 3½ in.), robust (225 lb.), balding Charles Pilchard, 38, himself a fanatical seeker of privacy, has written a master's thesis on Rimbaud but never taught. Instead he has lived for more than ten years on citizen's credit while developing his monumental work. [Cut of Charles Pilchard, captioned, "No charioteer he."] Twice married, once divorced, he does not maintain a fixed residence but describes himself like Jon, as "swimming around in the ocean called Man." He has probed deeply into the abysses of that ocean. Yet he has not emerged with the carping negativism of today's naysayers. For although he fully appreciates the human tragedy, Pilchard is in the end a triumphant yea-sayer. . . .

*Borrowed from the operatic works of Richard Wagner (1813–83), Emily Dickinson's stormy German contemporary, this word has come to mean an underlying and recurrent theme.

—Entropy

The robot entered so noisily that Felix Tunny heard him halfway down the corridor. The engineer turned from his desk and waited. His fingers gripped his chair arms until the nails turned white.

"Hello, Izaak," he got out. "Haven't seen you for a couple of days."

"No," said the robot. "I have been in my room, thinking. And reading."

"Reading what?"

"*Thunder Beyond Venus*, of course. Over and over. Is anybody reading anything else?" One steel finger tapped the volume. "You have read it yourself, have you not?" Izaak asked on a challenging note.

"Well, you know how it goes," Tunny said. "Things are rather frantic around here, what with the company's plans being disrupted and so forth. I've been meaning to get around to it."

"Get around to it!" Izaak groaned. "I suppose eventually you will get around to noticing sunlight and the stars."

"Why, I thought you were above any such gross physical things," Tunny said. This was the payoff. His throat was so dry he could hardly talk.

Izaak didn't notice. "It has proven necessary to make a re-evaluation," he said. "This book has opened my eyes as much as it has opened the eyes of the critics who first called my attention to its subtlety, its profundity, its universal significance and intensely individual analysis. Pilchard has written the book of our age, as Homer, Dante, and Tolstoy wrote the books of their own ages. He explores what is meaningful today as well as what is meaningful for all time.''

''Bully for Pilchard.''

''The conquest of space is, as the article in *pipette* showed, also the conquest of self. The microcosm opens on the macrocosm, which reflects and re-reflects the observer. This is the first example of the type of book that will be written and discussed for the next hundred years.''

''Could be.''

''None but an utter oaf would respond to this achievement as tepidly as you,'' Izaak snapped. ''I shall be glad to see the last of you.''

''Y-y-you're going away? Where?'' (Hang on, boy, countdown to zero!)

''Mercury. Please notify Barsch and have my spaceship made ready. I have no desire to delay so important an experience.''

Tunny sagged in his chair. ''By no means,'' he whispered. ''Don't waste a minute.''

''I make one condition, that for the entire period of my service you send to me with the cargo ships any other works by Pilchard that may appear, plus the quarterlies to which I subscribe and the other exemplars of the literary mode he has pioneered which I shall order on the basis of reviews I read. They must be transcribed to metal, you realize, because of the heat.''

''Sure, sure. Glad to oblige.''

''When I return,'' Izaak crooned, ''I shall be so uniquely qualified to criticize the new novels that some college will doubtless give me a literary quarterly of my own.''

He moved toward the door. ''I must go arrange for *Thunder Beyond Venus* to be transcribed on steelloy,'' he said.

''Why not tablets of stone?'' Tunny muttered.

''That is not a bad idea. Perhaps I shall.'' Izaak went out.

When he was safely gone, Tunny whooped. For a while he danced around his office like a peppered Indian, until he whirled on the phone. Call Barsch and tell him—No, to hell with Barsch. Janet deserved the good news first.

She shared his joy over the screens. Watching her, thinking of their future, brought a more serious mood on Tunny. "My conscience does hurt me a bit," he confessed. "It's going to be a blow to Izaak, out there on Mercury, when his brave new school of literature never appears."

"Don't be too certain about that," Janet said. "In fact— Well, I was going to call you today. We're in trouble again, I'm afraid. You know that office and clerk we hired to pretend to be Wisdom Press, in case Izaak tried to check up? She's going frantic. Calls are streaming in. Thousands of people already, furious because they can't find *Thunder Beyond Venus* anywhere. She's handed them a story about an accidental explosion in the warehouse, but— What can we do?"

"Oy." Tunny sat quiet for a space. His mind flew. "We did run off some extra copies, didn't we?" he said at length.

"Half a dozen or so. I gave one to Arnold Roach. He simply had to have it, after seeing the other articles. Now he's planning a rare review for *The Pacific Monthly*, with all sorts of sarcastic comments about how *Entropy* missed the whole point of the book. Several more critics I know have begged me at least to lend them my copy."

Tunny smote the desk with a large fist. "Only one way out of this," he decided. "Print up a million and stand by to print more. I don't just mean tapes for libraries, either. I mean regular, bound volumes."

"What?"

"I have a hunch that commercial fiction has been revived as of this week. Maybe our book is crude, but it does touch something real, something that people believe in their hearts is important. If I'm right then there's going to be a spate of novels like this, and many will make a whopping profit, and some will even be genuinely good. . . . Lord, Lord," Tunny said in awe. "We simply don't know our own strength, you and I."

"Let's get together," Janet suggested, "and find out."

Backwardness

In the high and far-off days, a new idea was what made a science fiction story memorable. Ideas are still important, of course, but nowadays there seems to be much less playing with them for their own sakes. In part, I suppose, this is simply because new ones have inevitably become scarce, and the changes have all been rung on the old ones. We writers must seek elsewhere for freshness, and, happily, the best among us are finding it. Harking back, though, here is a twist that occurred to me once, on a concept that had become a cliché.

As a small boy he had wanted to be a rocket pilot—and what boy didn't in those days?—but learned early that he lacked the aptitudes. Later he decided on psychology, and even took a bachelor's degree *cum laude*. Then one thing led to another, and Joe Husting ended up as a confidence man. It wasn't such a bad life; it had challenge and variety as he hunted in New York, and the spoils of a big killing were devoured in Florida, Greenland Resort, or Luna City.

The bar was empty of prospects just now, but he dawdled over his beer and felt no hurry. Spring had reached in and touched even the East Forties. The door stood open to a mild breeze, the long room was cool and dim, a few other men lazed over midafternoon drinks and the TV was tuned low. Idly, through cigarette smoke, Joe Husting watched the program.

The Galactics, of course. Their giant spaceship flashed in the screen against wet brown fields a hundred miles from here. Copter view . . . now we pan to a close-up, inside the ring of UN guards, and then back to the sightseers in their thousands. The announcer was talking about how the captain of the ship was at this moment in conference with the Secretary-General, and the crewmen were at liberty on Earth. "They are friendly, folks. I repeat, they are friendly. They will do no harm. They have already exchanged their cargo of U-235 for billions of our own dollars, and they plan to spend those dollars like any friendly tourist. But both the UN Secretariat and the President of the United States have asked us all to remember that these people come from the stars. They have been civilized for a million years. They have powers we haven't dreamed of. Anyone who harms a Galactic can ruin the greatest—"

Husting's mind wandered off. A big thing, yes, maybe the biggest thing in all history. Earth a member planet of the Galactic Federation! All the stars open to us! It was good to be alive in this year when anything could happen . . . hm. To start with, you could have some rhinestones put in fancy settings and peddle them as gen-yu-wine Tardenoisian sacred flame-rocks, but that was only the beginning—

He grew aware that the muted swish of electrocars and hammering of shoes in the street had intensified. From several blocks away came a positive roar of excitement. What the devil? He left his beer and sauntered to the door and looked out. A shabby man was hurrying toward the crowd. Husting buttonholed him. "What's going on, pal?"

"Ain't yuh heard? Galactics! Half a dozen of 'em. Landed in duh street uptown, some kinda flying belt dey got, and went inna Macy's and bought a million bucks' wortha stuff! Now dey're strolling down dis-a-way. Lemme go!"

Husting stood for a while, drawing hard on his cigarette.

A tingle went along his spine. Wanderers from the stars, a million-year-old civilization embracing the whole Milky Way! For him actually to see the high ones, maybe even talk to them . . . it would be something to tell his grandchildren about if he ever had any.

He waited, though, till the outer edge of the throng was on him, then pushed with skill and ruthlessness. It took a few sweaty minutes to reach the barrier.

An invisible force-field, holding off New York's myriads—wise precaution. You could be trampled to death by the best-intentioned mob.

There were seven crewmen from the Galactic ship. They were tall, powerful, as handsome as expected: a mixed breed, with dark hair and full lips and thin aristocratic noses. In a million years you'd expect all the human races to blend into one. They wore shimmering blue tunics and buskins, webby metallic belts in which starlike points of light glittered—and jewelry! My God, they must have bought all the gaudiest junk jewelry Macy's had to offer, and hung it on muscular necks and thick wrists. Mink and ermine burdened their shoulders, a young fortune in fur. One of them was carefully counting the money he had left, enough to choke an elephant. The others beamed affably into Earth's milling folk.

Joe Husting hunched his narrow frame against the pressure that was about to flatten him on the force screen. He licked suddenly dry lips, and his heart hammered. Was it possible—could it really happen that *he*, insignificant he, might speak to the gods from the stars?

Elsewhere in the huge building, politicians, specialists, and vips buzzed like angry bees. They should have been conferring with their opposite numbers from the Galactic mission—clearly, the sole proper way to meet the unprecedented is to set up committees and spend six months deciding on an agenda. But the Secretary-General of the United Nations owned certain prerogatives, and this time he had used them. A private face-to-face conference with Captain Hurdgo could accomplish more in half an hour than the councils of the world in a year.

He leaned forward and offered a box of cigars. "I don't know if I should," he added. "Perhaps tobacco doesn't suit your metabolism?"

"My what?" asked the visitor pleasantly. He was a big man, running a little to fat, with distinguished gray at the temples. It was not so odd that the Galactics should shave their chins and cut their hair in the manner of civilized Earth. That was the most convenient style.

"I mean, we smoke this weed, but it may poison you," said Larson. "After all, you're from another planet."

"Oh, that's OK," replied Hurdgo. "Same plants grow on every Earth-like planet, just like the same people and animals. Not much difference. Thanks." He took a cigar and rolled it between his fingers. "Smells nice."

"To me, that is the most astonishing thing about it all. I never expected evolution to work identically throughout the universe. *Why?*"

"Well, it just does." Captain Hurdgo bit the end off his cigar and spat it out onto the carpet. "Not on different-type planets from this, of course, but on Earth-type it's all the same."

"But why? I mean, what process—it can't be coincidence!"

Hurdgo shrugged. "I don't know. I'm just a practical spaceman. Never worried about it." He put the cigar in his mouth and touched the bezel of an ornate finger ring to it. Smoke followed the brief, intense spark.

"That's a . . . a most ingenious development," said Larson. Humility, yes, there was the line for a simple Earthman to take. Earth had come late into the cosmos and might as well admit the fact.

"A what?"

"Your ring. That lighter."

"Oh, that. Yep. Little atomic-energy gizmo inside." Hurdgo waved a magnanimous hand. "We'll send some people to show you how to make our stuff. Lend you machinery till you can start your own factories. We'll bring you up to date."

"It—you're incredibly generous," said Larson, happy and incredulous.

"Not much trouble to us, and we can trade with you once you're all set up. The more planets, the better for us."

"But . . . excuse me, sir, but I bear a heavy responsibility. We have to know the legal requirements for membership in the Galactic Federation. We don't know anything about your laws, your customs, your—"

"Nothing much to tell," said Hurdgo. "Every planet can pretty well take care of itself. How the hell you think we could police fifty million Earth-type planets? If you got a gripe, you can take it to the, uh, I dunno what the word would be in English. A board of experts with a computer that handles these things. They'll charge you for the service—no Galactic taxes, you just pay for what you get, and out of the profits they finance free services like this mission of mine."

"I see," nodded Larson. "A Coordinating Council."

"Yeh, I guess that's it."

The Secretary-General shook his head in bewilderment. He had sometimes wondered what civilization would come to be, a million years hence. Now he knew, and it staggered him. An ultimate simplicity, superman disdaining the whole cumbersome apparatus of intersteller government, freed of all restraints save the superman morality, free to think his giant thoughts between the stars!

Hurdgo looked out the window to the arrogant towers of New York. "Biggest city I ever saw," he remarked, "and I seen a lot of planets. I don't see how you run it. Must be complicated."

"It is, sir." Larson smiled wryly. Of course the Galactics would long ago have passed the stage of needing such a human ant hill. They would have forgotten the skills required to govern one, just as Larson's people had forgotten how to chip flint.

''Well, let's get down to business.'' Hurdgo sucked on his cigar and smacked his lips. ''Here's how it works. We found out a big while back that we can't go letting any new planet bust its way into space with no warning to anybody. Too much danger. So we set up detectors all over the Galaxy. When they spot the, uh, what-you-call-'ems—vibrations, yes, that's it, vibrations—the vibrations of a new star drive, they alert the, uh, Coordinating Council and it sends out a ship to contact the new people and tell 'em the score.''

''Ah, indeed. I suspected as much. We have just invented a faster-than-light engine . . . very primitive, of course, compared to yours. It was being tested when—''

''Uh-huh. So me and my boys are supposed to give you the once-over and see if you're all right. Don't want warlike peoples running around loose, you know. Too much danger.''

''I assure you—''

''Yes, yes, pal, it's OK. You got a good strong world setup and the computer says you've stopped making war.'' Hurdgo frowned. ''I got to admit, you got some funny habits. I don't really understand everything you do . . . you seem to think funny, not like any other planet I ever heard of. But it's all right. Everybody to his own ways. You get a clean bill of health.''

''Suppose . . .'' Larson spoke very slowly. ''Just suppose we had not been . . . approved—what then? Would you have reformed us?'

''Reformed? Huh? What d'you mean? We'd have sent a police ship and blown every planet in this system to smithereens. Can't have people running loose who might start a war.''

Sweat formed under Larson's arms and trickled down his ribs. His mouth felt dry. *Whole planets—*

But in a million years you would learn to think *sub specie aeternitatis*. Five billion warlike Earthlings could annihilate fifty billion peaceful Galactics before they were overcome. It was not for him to judge a superman.

* * *

"Hello, there!"

Husting had to yell to be heard above the racket. But the nearest of the spacemen looked at him and smiled.

"Hi," he said.

Incredible! He had greeted little Joe Husting as a friend. Why—? Wait a minute! Perhaps the sheer brass of it had pleased him. Perhaps no one else had dared speak first to the strangers. And when you only said, "Yes, sir," to a man, even to a Galactic, you removed him—you might actually make him feel lonely.

"Uh, like it here?" Husting cursed his tongue, that its glibness should have failed him at this moment of all moments.

"Sure, sure. Biggest city I ever seen. And *draxna*, look at what I got!" The spaceman lifted a necklace of red glass sparklers. "Won't their eyes just bug out when I get home!"

Someone shoved Husting against the barrier so the wind went from him. He gasped and tried to squirm free.

"Say, cut that out. You're hurting the poor guy." One of the Galactics touched a stud on his belt. Gently but inexorably, the field widened, pushing the crowd back . . . and somehow, somehow Husting was inside it with the seven from the stars.

"You OK, pal?" Anxious hands lifted him to his feet.

"I, yeah, sure. Sure, I'm fine!" Husting stood up and grinned at the envious faces ringing him in. "Thanks a lot."

"Glad to help you. My name's Gilgrath. Call me Gil." Strong fingers squeezed Husting's shoulder. "And this here is Bronni, and here's Col, and Jordo, and—"

"Pleased to meet you," whispered Husting inadequately. "I'm Joe."

"Say, this is all right!" said Gil enthusiastically. "I was wondering what was wrong with you folks."

"Wrong?" Husting shook a dazed head, wondering if They were peering into his mind and reading thoughts of which he himself was unaware. Vague memories came back, grave-eyed Anubis weighing the heart of a man.

"You know," said Gil. "Standoffish, like."

"Yeh," added Bronni. "Every other new planet we been to, everybody was coming up and saying hello and buying us drinks and—"

"Parties," reminded Jordo.

"Yeh. Man, remember that wing-ding on Alphaz? Remember those girls?" Col rolled his eyes lickerishly.

"You got a lot of good-looking girls here in New York," complained Gil. "But we got orders not to offend nobody. Say, do you think one of those girls would mind if I said hello to her?"

Husting was scarcely able to think; it was the reflex of many years which now spoke for him, rapidly:

"You have us all wrong. We're just scared to talk to you. We thought maybe you didn't want to be bothered."

"And *we* thought *you*—Say!" Gil slapped his thigh and broke into a guffaw. "Now ain't that something? They don't want to bother us and we don't want to bother them!"

"I'll be *rixt!*" bellowed Col. "Well, what do you know about that?"

"Hey, in that case—" began Jordo.

"Wait, wait!" Husting waved his hands. It was still habit which guided him; his mind was only slowly getting back into gear. "Let me get this straight. You want to do the town, right?"

"We sure do," said Col. "It's mighty lonesome out in space."

"Well, look," chattered Husting, "you'll never be free of all these crowds, reporters—" (A flashbulb, the tenth or twelfth in these few minutes, dazzled his eyes.) "You won't be able to let yourselves go while everybody knows you're Galactics."

"On Alphaz—" protested Bronni.

"This isn't Alphaz. Now I've got an idea. Listen." Seven

dark heads bent down to hear an urgent whisper. "Can you get us away from here? Fly off invisible or something?"

"Sure," said Gil. "Hey, how'd you know we can do that?"

"Never mind. OK, we'll sneak off to my apartment and send out for some Earth-style clothes for you, and then—"

John Joseph O'Reilly, Cardinal Archbishop of New York, had friends in high places as well as in low. He thought it no shame to pull wires and arrange an interview with the chaplain of the spaceship. What he could learn might be of vital importance to the Faith. The priest from the stars arrived, light-screened to evade the curious, and was received in the living room.

Visible again, Thyrkna proved to be a stocky white-haired man in the usual blue-kirtled uniform. He smiled and shook hands in quite an ordinary manner. At least, thought O'Reilly, these Galactics had during a million years conquered overweening Pride.

"It is an honor to meet you," he said.

"Thanks," nodded Thyrkna. He looked around the room. "Nice place you got."

"Please be seated. May I offer you a drink?"

"Don't mind if I do."

O'Reilly set forth glasses and a bottle. In a modest way, the Cardinal was a connoisseur, and had chosen the Chambertin-Clos carefully. He tasted the ritual few drops. Whatever minor saint, if any, was concerned with these things had been gracious; the wine was superb. He filled his guest's glass and then his own.

"Welcome to Earth," he smiled.

"Thanks." The Galactic tossed his drink off at one gulp. "Aaah! That goes good."

The Cardinal winced, but poured again. You couldn't expect another civilization to have the same tastes. Chinese liked aged eggs while despising cheese. . . .

He sat down and crossed his legs. "I'm not sure what title to use," he said diffidently.

"Title? What's that?"

"I mean, what does your flock call you?"

"My *flock*? Oh, you mean the boys on board? Plain Thyrkna. That's good enough for me." The visitor finished his second glass and belched. Well, so would a cultivated Eskimo.

"I understand there was some difficulty in conveying my request," said O'Reilly. "Apparently you did not know what our word *chaplain* means."

"We don't know every word in your lingo," admitted Thyrkna. "It works like this. When we come in toward a new planet, we pick up its radio, see?"

"Oh, yes. Such of it as gets through the ionosphere."

Thyrkna blinked. "Huh? I don't know all the *de*-tails. You'll have to talk to one of our tech . . . technicians. Anyway, we got a machine that analyzes the different languages, figures 'em out. Does it in just a few hours, too. Then it puts us all to sleep and teaches us the languages. When we wake up, we're ready to come down and talk."

The Cardinal laughed. "Pardon me, sir. Frankly, I was wondering why the people of your incredibly high civilization should use our worst street dialects. Now I see the reason. I am afraid our programs are not on a very high level. They aim at mass taste, the lowest common denominator—and please excuse my metaphors. Naturally you— But I assure you, we aren't all that bad. We have hopes for the future. This electronic educator of yours, for instance . . . what it could do to raise the cultural level of the average man surpasses imagination."

Thyrkna looked a trifle dazed. "I never seen anybody what talks like you Earthlings. Don't you ever run out of breath?"

O'Reilly felt himself reproved. Among the Great Galactics, a silence must be as meaningful as a hundred words, and there were a million years of dignity behind them. "I'm sorry," he said.

"Oh, it's all right. I suppose a lot of our ways must look

just as funny to you." Thyrkna picked up the bottle and poured himself another glassful.

"What I asked you here for . . . there are many wonderful things you can tell me, but I would like to put you some religious questions."

"Sure, go ahead," said Thyrkna amiably.

"My Church has long speculated about this eventuality. The fact that you, too, are human, albeit more advanced than we, is a miraculous revelation of God's will. But I would like to know something about the precise form of your belief in Him."

"What do you mean?" Thyrkna sounded confused. "I'm a, uh, quartermaster. It's part of my job to kill the rabbits—we can't afford the space for cattle on board a ship. I feed the gods, that's all."

"The *gods!*" The Cardinal's glass crashed on the floor.

"By the way, what's the names of your top gods?" inquired Thyrkna. "Be a good idea to kill them a cow or two, as long as we're here on their planet. Don't wanna take chances on bad luck."

"But . . . you . . . *heathen—*"

Thyrkna looked at the clock. "Say, do you have TV?" he asked. "It's almost time for *John's Other Life.* You got some real good TV on this planet."

By the dawn's early light, Joe Husting opened a bleary eye and wished he hadn't. The apartment was a mess. What happened, anyway?"

Oh, yeah . . . those girls they picked up . . . but had they really emptied all those bottles lying on the floor?

He groaned and hung onto his head lest it split open. *Why* had he mixed Scotch and stout?

Thunder lanced through his eardrums. He turned on the sofa and saw Gil emerging from the bedroom. The spaceman was thumping his chest and booming out a song learned last night. *"Oh, roly poly—"*

"Cut it out, will you?" groaned Husting.

"Huh? Man, you've had it, ain't you?" Gil clicked his tongue sympathetically. "Here, just a minute." He took a vial from his belt. "Take a few drops of this. It'll fix you up."

Somehow Husting got it down. There was a moment of fire and pinwheels, then—

—he was whole again. It was as if he had just slept ten hours without touching alcohol for the past week.

Gil returned to the bedroom and started pummeling his companions awake. Husting sat by the window, thinking hard. That hangover cure was worth a hundred million if he could only get the exclusive rights. But no, the technical envoys would show Earth how to make it, along with star ships and invisibility screens and so on. Maybe, though, he could hit the Galactics for what they had with them, and peddle it for a hundred dollars a drop before the full-dress mission arrived.

Bronni came in, full of cheer. "Say, you're all right, Joe," he trumpeted. "Ain't had such a good time since I was on Alphaz. What's next, old pal, old pal, old pal?" A meaty hand landed stunningly between Husting's shoulderblades.

"I'll see what I can do," said the Earthman cautiously. "But I'm busy, you know. Got some big deals cooking."

"I know," said Bronni. He winked. "Smart fellow like you. How the *hell* did you talk that bouncer around? I thought sure he was gonna call the cops."

"Oh, I buttered him up and slipped him a ten-spot. Wasn't hard."

"Man!" Bronnie whistled in admiration. "I never heard anybody sling the words like you was doing."

Gil herded the others out and said he wanted breakfast. Husting led them all to the elevator and out into the street. He was rather short-spoken, having much to think about. They were in a ham-and-eggery before he said:

"You spacemen must be pretty smart. Smarter than average, right?"

"Right," said Jordo. He winked at the approaching waitress.

"Lotta things a spaceman's got to know," said Col. "The ships do just about run themselves, but still, you can't let just any knucklehead into the crew."

"I see," murmured Husting. "I thought so."

A college education helps the understanding, especially when one is not too blinkered by preconceptions.

Consider one example: Sir Isaac Newton discovered (*a*) the three laws of motion, (*b*) the law of gravitation, (*c*) the differential calculus, (*d*) the elements of spectroscopy, (*e*) a good deal about acoustics, and (*f*) miscellaneous, besides finding time to serve in half a dozen official and honorary positions. A single man! And for a genius, he was not too exceptional; most gifted Earthmen have contributed to several fields.

And yet . . . such supreme intellect is not necessary. The most fundamental advances, fire- and tool-making, language and clothing and social organization, were made by apish dim-bulbs. It simply took a long time between discoveries.

Given a million years, much can happen. Newton founded modern physics in one lifespan. A hundred less talented men, over a thousand-year period, could slowly and painfully have accomplished the same thing.

The IQ of Earth humanity averages about 100. Our highest geniuses may have rated 200; our lowest morons, as stupid as possible without needing institutional care, may go down to 60. It is only some freak of mutation which has made the Earthman so intelligent; he never actually *needed* all that brain.

Now if the Galactic average was around IQ 75, with their very brightest boys going up to, say, 150—

The waitress yipped and jumped into the air. Bronni grinned shamelessly as she turned to confront him.

Joe Husting pacified her. After breakfast he took the Galactic emissaries out and sold them the Brooklyn Bridge.

Duel on Syrtis

Another from *Planet Stories*. I tried to depict Mars realistically, according to what was known and surmised at the time—a time when planetary astronomy had fallen into sad neglect. Since then we have learned that this world is quite different; and the sociological background of the tale looks implausible too. Still, you can think of it as happening in an alternate universe of some kind. All fiction does anyway.

The night whispered the message. Over the many miles of loneliness it was borne, carried on the wind, rustled by the half-sentient lichens and the dwarfed trees, murmured from one to another of the little creatures that huddled under crags, in caves, by shadowy dunes. In no words, but in a dim pulsing of dread which echoed through Kreega's brain, the warning ran—

They are hunting again.

Kreega shuddered in a sudden blast of wind. The night was enormous around him, above him, from the iron bitterness of the hills to the wheeling, glittering constellations, light-years over his head. He reached out with his trembling perceptions, tuning himself to the brush and the wind and the small burrowing things underfoot, letting the night speak to him.

Alone, alone. There was not another Martian for a hundred miles of emptiness. There were only the tiny animals and the shivering brush and the thin, sad blowing of the wind.

The voiceless scream of dying traveled through the brush, from plant to plant, echoed by the fear-pulses of the animals and the ringingly reflecting cliffs. They were curling, shriveling and blackening as the rocket poured the glowing death down on them, and the withering veins and nerves cried to the stars.

Kreega huddled against a tall gaunt crag. His eyes were like yellow moons in the darkness, cold with terror and hate and a slowly gathering resolution. Grimly, he estimated that the death was being sprayed in a circle some ten miles across. And he was trapped in it, and soon the hunter would come after him.

He looked up to the indifferent glitter of stars, and a shudder went along his body. Then he sat down and began to think.

It had started a few days before, in the private office of the trader Wisby. "I came to Mars," said Riordan, "to get me an owlie."

Wisby had learned the value of a poker face. He peered across the rim of his glass at the other man, estimating him.

Even in God-forsaken holes like Port Armstrong one had heard of Riordan. Heir to a million-dollar shipping firm which he himself had pyramided into a System-wide monster, he was equally well known as a big game hunter. From the firedrakes of Mercury to the ice crawlers of Pluto, he'd bagged them all. Except, of course, a Martian. That particular game was forbidden now.

He sprawled in his chair, big and strong and ruthless, still a young man. He dwarfed the unkempt room with his size and the hard-held dynamo strength in him, and his cold green gaze dominated the trader.

"It's illegal, you know," said Wisby. "It's a twenty-year sentence if you're caught at it."

"Bah! The Martian Commissioner is at Ares, halfway round the planet. If we go at it right, who's ever to know?" Riordan gulped at his drink. "I'm well aware that in another year or so they'll have tightened up enough to make it impossible. This is the last chance for any man to get an owlie. That's why I'm here."

Wisby hesitated, looking out the window. Port Armstrong was no more than a dusty huddle of domes, interconnected by tunnels, in a red waste of sand stretching to the near horizon. An Earthman in airsuit and transparent helmet was walking down the street and a couple of Martians were lounging against a wall. Otherwise nothing—a silent, deadly monotony brooding under the shrunken sun. Life on Mars was not especially pleasant for a human.

"You're not falling into this owlie-loving that's corrupted all Earth?" demanded Riordan contemptuously.

"Oh, no," said Wisby. "I keep them in their place around my post. But times are changing. It can't be helped."

"There was a time when they were slaves," said Riordan. "Now those old women on Earth want to give 'em the vote." He snorted.

"Well, times are changing," repeated Wisby mildly. "When the first humans landed on Mars a hundred years ago, Earth had just gone through the Hemispheric Wars. The worst wars man had ever known. They damned near wrecked the old ideas of liberty and equality. People were suspicious and tough—they'd had to be, to survive. They weren't able to—to empathize with the Martians, or whatever you call it. Not able to think of them as anything but intelligent animals. And Martians made such useful slaves—they need so little food or heat or oxygen, they can even live fifteen minutes or so without breathing at all. And the wild Martians made fine sport—intelligent game, that could get away as often as not, or even manage to kill the hunter."

"I know," said Riordan. "That's why I want to hunt one. It's no fun if the game doesn't have a chance."

"It's different now," went on Wisby. "Earth has been at peace for a long time. The liberals have gotten the upper hand. Naturally, one of their first reforms was to end Martians slavery."

Riordan swore. The forced repatriation of Martians working on his spaceships had cost him plenty. "I haven't time for your philosophizing," he said. "If you can arrange for me to get a Martian, I'll make it worth your while."

"How much worth it?" asked Wisby.

They haggled for a while before settling on a figure. Riordan had brought guns and a small rocketboat, but Wisby would have to supply radioactive material, a "hawk," and a rockhound. Then he had to be paid for the risk of legal action, though that was small. The final price came high.

"Now, where do I get my Martian?" inquired Riordan. He gestured at the two in the street. "Catch one of them and release him in the desert?"

It was Wisby's turn to be contemptuous. "One of them? Hah! Town loungers! A city dweller from Earth would give you a better fight."

The Martians didn't look impressive. They stood only some four feet high on skinny, claw-footed legs, and the arms, ending in bony four-fingered hands, were stringy. The chests were broad and deep, but the waists were ridiculously narrow. They were viviparous, warm-blooded, and suckled their young, but gray feathers covered their hides. The round, hook-beaked heads, with huge amber eyes and tufted feathers ears, showed the origin of the name "owlie." They wore only pouched belts and carried sheath knives; even the liberals of Earth weren't ready to allow the natives modern tools and weapons. There were too many old grudges.

"The Martians always were good fighters," said Riordan. "They wiped out quite a few Earth settlements in the old days."

"The wild ones," agreed Wisby. "But not these. They're

just stupid laborers, as dependent on our civilization as we are. You want a real old-timer, and I know where one's to be found."

He spread a map on the desk. "See, here in the Hraefnian Hills, about a hundred miles from here. These Martians live a long time, maybe two centuries, and this fellow Kreega has been around since the first Earthmen came. He led a lot of Martian raids in the early days, but since the general amnesty and peace he's lived all alone up there, in one of the old ruined towers. A real old-time warrior who hates Earthmen's guts. He comes here once in a while with furs and minerals to trade, so I know a little about him." Wisby's eyes gleamed savagely. "You'll be doing us all a favor by shooting the arrogant bastard. He struts around here as if the place belonged to him. And he'll give you a run for your money."

Riordan's massive dark head nodded in satisfaction.

The man had a bird and a rockhound. That was bad. Without them, Kreega could lose himself in the labyrinth of caves and canyons and scrubby thickets—but the hound could follow his scent and the bird could spot him from above.

To make matters worse, the man had landed near Kreega's tower. The weapons were all there—now he was cut off, unarmed and alone save for what feeble help the desert life could give. Unless he could double back to the place somehow—but meanwhile he had to survive.

He sat in a cave, looking down past a tortured wilderness of sand and bush and wind-carved rock, miles in the thin clear air to the glitter of metal where the rocket lay. The man was a tiny speck in the huge barren landscape, a lonely insect crawling under the deep-blue sky. Even by day, the stars glistened in the tenuous atmosphere. Weak pallid sunlight spilled over rocks tawny and ocherous and rust-red, over the low dusty thorn-bushes and the gnarled little trees and the sand that blew faintly between them. Equatorial Mars!

Lonely or not, the man had a gun that could spang death clear to the horizon, and he had his beasts, and there would be a radio in the rocketboat for calling his fellows. And the glowing death ringed them in, a charmed circle which Kreega could not cross without bringing a worse death on himself than the rifle would give—

Or was there a worse death than that—to be shot by a monster and have his stuffed hide carried back as a trophy for fools to gape at? The old iron pride of his race rose in Kreega, hard and bitter and unrelenting. He didn't ask much of life these days—solitude in his tower to think the long thoughts of a Martian and create the small exquisite artworks which he loved; the company of his kind at the Gathering Season, grave ancient ceremony and acrid merriment and the chance to beget and rear sons; an occasional trip to the Earthling colony for the metal goods and the wine which were the only valuable things they had brought to Mars; a vague dream of raising his folk to a place where they could stand as equals before all the universe. No more. And now they would take even this from him!

He rasped a curse on the human and resumed his patient work, chipping a spearhead for what puny help it could give him. The brush rustled dryly in alarm, tiny hidden animals squeaked their terror, the desert shouted to him of the monster that strode toward his cave. But he didn't have to flee right away.

Riordan sprayed the heavy-metal isotope in a ten-mile circle around the old tower. He did that by night, just in case patrol craft might be snooping around. But once he had landed, he was safe—he could always claim to be peacefully exploring, hunting leapers or some such thing.

The radioactivity had a half-life of about four days, which meant that it would be unsafe to approach for some three weeks—two at the minimum. That was time enough, when the Martian was boxed in so small an area.

There was no danger that he would try to cross it. The owlies had learned what radioactivity meant, back when they fought the humans. And their vision, extending well into the ultraviolet, made it directly visible to them through its fluorescence—to say nothing of the wholly unhuman extra senses they had. No, Kreega would try to hide, and perhaps to fight, and eventually he'd be cornered.

Still, there was no use taking chances. Riordan set a timer on the boat's radio. If he didn't come back within two weeks to turn it off, it would emit a signal which Wisby would hear, and he'd be rescued.

He checked his other equipment. He had an airsuit designed for Martian conditions, with a small pump operated by a power-beam from the boat to compress the atmosphere sufficiently for him to breathe it. The same unit recovered enough water from his breath so that the weight of supplies for several days was, in Martian gravity, not too great for him to bear. He had a .45 rifle built to shoot in Martian air; that was heavy enough for his purposes. And, of course, compass and binoculars and sleeping bag. Pretty light equipment, but he preferred a minimum anyway.

For ultimate emergencies there was the little tank of suspensine. By turning a valve, he could release it into his air system. The gas didn't exactly induce suspended animation, but it paralyzed efferent nerves and slowed the overall metabolism to a point where a man could live for weeks on one lungful of air. It was useful in surgery, and had saved the life of more than one interplanetary explorer whose oxygen system went awry. But Riordan didn't expect to have to use it. He certainly hoped he wouldn't. It would be tedious to lie fully conscious for days waiting for the automatic signal to call Wisby.

He stepped out of the boat and locked it. No danger that the owlie would break in if he could double back; it would take tordenite to crack that hull.

He whistled to his animals. They were native beasts, long ago domesticated by the Martians and later by man. The rockhound was like a gaunt wolf, but huge-breasted and feathered, a tracker as good as any Terrestrial bloodhound. The "hawk" had less resemblance to its counterpart of Earth:

it was a bird of prey, but in the tenuous atmosphere it needed a six-foot wingspread to lift its small body. Riordan was pleased with their training.

The hound bayed, a low quavering note which would have been muffled almost to inaudibility by the thin air and the man's plastic helmet had the suit not included microphones and amplifiers. It circled, sniffing, while the hawk rose into the alien sky.

Riordan did not look closely at the tower. It was a crumbling stump atop a rusty hill, unhuman and grotesque. Once, perhaps ten thousand years ago, the Martians had had a civilization of sorts, cities and agriculture and a neolithic technology. But according to their own traditions they had achieved a union or symbiosis with the wild life of the planet and had abandoned such mechanical aids as unnecessary. Riordan snorted.

The hound bayed again. The noise seemed to hang eerily in the still, cold air, to shiver from cliff and crag and die reluctantly under the enormous silence. But it was a bugle call, a haughty challenge to a world grown old—stand aside, make way, here comes the conqueror!

The animal suddenly loped forward. He had a scent. Riordan swung into a long, easy low-gravity stride. His eyes gleamed like green ice. The hunt was begun!

Breath sobbed in Kreega's lungs, hard and quick and raw. His legs felt weak and heavy, and the thudding of his heart seemed to shake his whole body.

Still he ran, while the frightful clamor rose behind him and the padding of feet grew ever nearer. Leaping, twisting, bounding from crag to crag, sliding down shaly ravines and slipping through clumps of trees, Kreega fled.

The hound was behind him and the hawk soaring overhead. In a day and a night they had driven him to this, running like a crazed leaper with death baying at his heels—he had not imagined a human could move so fast or with such endurance.

The desert fought for him; the plants with their queer blind life that no Earthling would ever understand were on his side. Their thorny branches twisted away as he darted through and then came back to rake the flanks of the hound, slow him—but they could not stop his brutal rush. He ripped past their strengthless clutching fingers and yammered on the trail of the Martian.

The human was toiling a good mile behind, but showed no sign of tiring. Still Kreega ran. He had to reach the cliff edge before the hunter saw him through his rifle sights—had to, had to, and the hound was snarling a yard behind now.

Up the long slope he went. The hawk fluttered, striking at him, seeking to lay beak and talons in his head. He batted at the creature with his spear and dodged around a tree. The tree snaked out a branch from which the hound rebounded, yelling till the rocks rang.

The Martian burst onto the edge of the cliff. It fell sheer to the canyon floor, five hundred feet of iron-streaked rock tumbling into windy depths. Beyond, the lowering sun glared in his eyes. He paused only an instant, etched black against the sky, a perfect shot if the human should come into view, and then he sprang over the edge.

He had hoped the rockhound would go shooting past, but the animal braked itself barely in time. Kreega went down the cliff face, clawing into every tiny crevice, shuddering as the age-worn rock crumbled under his fingers. The hawk swept close, hacking at him and screaming for its master. He couldn't fight it, not with every finger and toe needed to hang against shattering death, but—

He slid along the face of the precipice into a gray-green clump of vines, and his nerves thrilled forth the appeal of the ancient symbiosis. The hawk swooped again and he lay unmoving, rigid as if dead, until it cried in shrill triumph and settled on his shoulder to pluck out his eyes.

Then the vines stirred. They weren't strong, but their thorns sank into the flesh and it wouldn't come loose. Kreega toiled on down into the canyon while the vines pulled the hawk apart.

Riordan loomed hugely against the darkening sky. He fired, once, twice, the bullets humming wickedly close, but as shadows swept up from the depths the Martian was covered.

The man turned up his speech amplifier and his voice rolled and boomed monstrously through the gathering night, thunder such as dry Mars had not heard for millennia: "Score one for you! But it isn't enough! I'll find you!"

The sun slipped below the horizon and night came down like a falling curtain. Through the darkness Kreega heard the man laughing. The old rocks trembled with his laughter.

Riordan was tired with the long chase and the niggling insufficiency of his oxygen supply. He wanted a smoke and hot food, and neither was to be had. Oh, well, he'd appreciate the luxuries of life all the more when he got home—with the Martian's skin.

He grinned as he made camp. The little fellow was a worthwhile quarry, that was for damn sure. He'd held out for two days now, in a mere ten-mile circle of ground, and he'd even killed the hawk. But Riordan was close enough to him now so that the hound could follow his spoor, for Mars had no watercourses to break a trail. So it didn't matter.

He lay watching the splendid night of stars. It would get cold before long, unmercifully cold, but his sleeping bag was a good-enough insulator to keep him warm with the help of solar energy stored during the day by its Gergen cells. Mars was dark at night, its moons of little use—Phobos a hurtling speck, Deimos just a bright star. Dark and cold and empty. The rockhound had burrowed into the loose sand nearby, but it would raise the alarm if the Martian should come sneaking near the camp. Not that that was likely—he'd have to find shelter somewhere too, if he didn't want to freeze.

The bushes and the trees and the little furtive animals whispered a word he could not hear, chattered and gossiped on the wind about the Martian who kept himself warm with work. But he didn't understand that language which was no language.

Drowsily, Riordan thought of past hunts. The big game of Earth, lion and tiger and elephant and buffalo and sheep on the high sun-blazing peaks of the Rockies. Rain forests of Venus and the coughing roar of a many-legged swamp monster crashing through the trees to the place where he stood waiting. Primitive throb of drums in a hot wet night, chant of beaters dancing around a fire—scramble along the hell-plains of Mercury with a swollen sun licking against his puny insulating suit—the grandeur and desolation of Neptune's liquid-gas swamps and the huge blind thing that screamed and blundered after him—

But this was the loneliest and strangest and perhaps most dangerous hunt of all, and on that account the best. He had no malice toward the Martian; he respected the little being's courage as he respected the bravery of the other animals he had fought. Whatever trophy he brought home from this chase would be well-earned.

The fact that his success would have to be treated discreetly didn't matter. He hunted less for the glory of it—though he had to admit he didn't mind the publicity—than for love. His ancestors had fought under one name or another—viking, Crusader, mercenary, rebel, patriot, whatever was fashionable at the moment. Struggle was in his blood, and in these degenerate days there was little to struggle against save what he hunted.

Well—tomorrow—he drifted off to sleep.

He woke in the short gray dawn, made a quick breakfast, and whistled his hound to heel. His nostrils dilated with excitement, a high keen drunkenness that sang wonderfully within him. Today—maybe today!

They had to take a roundabout way down into the canyon and the hound cast about for an hour before he picked up the scent. Then the deep-voiced cry rose again and they were off—more slowly now, for it was a cruel stony trail.

The sun climbed high as they worked along the ancient

riverbed. Its pale chill light washed needle-sharp crags and fantastically painted cliffs, shale and sand and the wreck of geological ages. The low harsh brush crunched under the man's feet, writhing and crackling its impotent protest. Otherwise it was still, a deep and taut and somehow waiting stillness.

The hound shattered the quiet with an eager yelp and plunged forward. Hot scent! Riordan dashed after him, trampling through dense bush, panting and swearing and grinning with excitement.

Suddenly the brush opened underfoot. With a howl of dismay, the hound slid down the sloping wall of the pit it had covered. Riordan flung himself forward with tigerish swiftness, flat down on his belly with one hand barely catching the animal's tail. The shock almost pulled him into the hole too. He wrapped one arm around a bush that clawed at his helmet and pulled the hound back.

Shaking, he peered into the trap. It had been well made—about twenty feet deep, with walls as straight and narrow as the sand would allow, and skillfully covered with brush. Planted in the bottom were three wicked-looking flint spears. Had he been a shade less quick in his reactions, he would have lost the hound and perhaps himself.

He skinned his teeth in a wolf-grin and looked around. The owlie must have worked all night on it. Then he couldn't be far away—and he'd be very tired—

As if to answer his thoughts, a boulder crashed down from the nearer cliff wall. It was a monster, but a falling object on Mars has less than half the acceleration it does on Earth. Riordan scrambled aside as it boomed into the place where he had been lying.

"Come on!" he yelled, and plunged toward the cliff.

For an instant a gray form loomed over the edge, hurled a spear at him. Riordan snapped a shot at it, and it vanished. The spear glanced off the tough fabric of his suit and he scrambled up a narrow ledge to the top of the precipice.

The Martian was nowhere in sight, but a faint red trail led

into the rugged hill country. *Winged him, by God!* The hound was slower in negotiating the shale-covered trail; his own feet were bleeding when he came up. Riordan cursed him and they set out again.

They followed the trail for a mile or two and then it ended. Riordan looked around the wilderness of trees and needles which blocked view in any direction. Obviously the owlie had backtracked and climbed up one of those rocks, from which he could take a flying leap to some other point. But which one?

Sweat that he couldn't wipe off ran down the man's face and body. He itched intolerably, and his lungs were raw from gasping at his dole of air. But still he laughed in gusty delight. What a chase! What a chase!

Kreega lay in the shadow of a tall rock and shuddered with weariness. Beyond the shade, the sunlight danced in what to him was a blinding, intolerable dazzle, hot and cruel and life-hungry, hard and bright as the metal of the conquerors.

It had been a mistake to spend priceless hours when he might have been resting preparing that trap. It hadn't worked, and he might have known that it wouldn't. And now he was hungry, and thirst was like a wild beast in his mouth and throat, and still they followed him.

They weren't far behind now. All this day they had been dogging him; he had never been more than half an hour ahead. No rest, no rest, a devil's hunt through a tormented wilderness of stone and sand, and now he could only wait for the battle with an iron burden of exhaustion laid on him.

The wound in his side burned. It wasn't deep, but it had cost him blood and pain and the few minutes of catnapping he might have snatched.

For a moment, the warrior Kreega was gone and a small, frightened infant sobbed in the desert silence. *Why can't they let me alone?*

A low, dusty-green bush rustled. A sandrunner piped in one of the ravines. They were getting close.

Wearily, Kreega scrambled up on top of the rock and crouched low. He had backtracked to it; they should by rights go past him toward his tower.

He could see it from here, a low yellow ruin worn by the winds of millennia. There had only been time to dart in, snatch a bow and a few arrows and an axe. Pitiful weapons—the arrows could not penetrate the Earthman's suit when there was only a Martian's thin grasp to draw the bow, and even with a steel head the axe was a small and feeble thing. But it was all he had, he and his few little allies of a desert which fought only to keep its solitude.

Repatriated slaves had told him of the Earthlings' power. Their roaring machines filled the silence of their own deserts, gouged the quiet face of their own moon, shook the planets with a senseless fury of meaningless energy. They were the conquerors, and it never occurred to them that an ancient peace and stillness could be worth preserving.

Well—he fitted an arrow to the string and crouched in the silent, glimmering sunlight, waiting.

The hound came first, yelping and howling. Kreega drew the bow as far as he could. But the human had to come near first—

There he came, running and bounding over the rocks, rifle in hand and restless eyes shining with their green light, closing in for the death. Kreega swung softly around. The beast was beyond the rock now, the Earthman almost below it.

The bow twanged. With a savage thrill, Kreega saw the arrow go through the hound, saw the creature leap in the air and then roll over and over, howling and biting at the thing in its breast.

Like a gray thunderbolt, the Martian launched himself off the rock, down at the human. If his axe could shatter that helmet—

He struck the man and they went down together. Wildly, the Martian hewed. The axe glanced off the plastic—he hadn't had room for a swing. Riordan roared and lashed out with a fist. Retching, Kreega rolled backward.

Riordan snapped a shot at him. Kreega turned and fled. The man got to one knee, sighting carefully on the gray form that streaked up the nearest slope.

A little sandsnake darted up the man's leg and wrapped about his wrist. Its small strength was just enough to pull the gun aside. The bullet screamed past Kreega's ears as he vanished into a cleft.

He felt the thin death-agony of the snake as the man pulled it loose and crushed it underfoot. Somewhat later, he heard a dull boom echoing between the hills. The man had gotten explosives from his boat and blown up the tower.

He had lost axe and bow. Now he was utterly weaponless, without even a place to retire for a last stand. And the hunter would not give up. Even without his animals, he would follow, more slowly but as relentlessly as before.

Kreega collapsed on a shelf of rock. Dry sobbing racked his thin body, and the sunset wind cried with him.

Presently he looked up, across a red and yellow immensity to the low sun. Long shadows were creeping over the land, peace and stillness for a brief moment before the iron cold of night closed down. Somewhere the soft trill of a sandrunner echoed between low windworn cliffs, and the brush began to speak, whispering back and forth in its ancient wordless tongue.

The desert, the planet and its wind and sand under the high cold stars, the clean open land of silence and loneliness and a destiny which was not man's, spoke to him. The enormous oneness of life on Mars, drawn together against the cruel environment, stirred in his blood. As the sun went down and the stars blossomed forth in awesome frosty glory, Kreega began to think again.

He did not hate his persecutor, but the grimness of Mars was in him. He fought the war of all which was old and primitive and lost in its own dreams against the alien and the desecrator. It was as ancient and pitiless as life, that war, and each battle won or lost meant something even if no one ever heard of it.

You do not fight alone, whispered the desert. *You fight for all Mars, and we are with you.*

Something moved in the darkness, a tiny warm form running across his hand, a little feathered mouse-like thing that burrowed under the sand and lived its small fugitive life and was glad in its own way of living. But it was a part of a world, and Mars has no pity in its voice.

Still, a tenderness was within Kreega's heart, and he whispered gently in the language that was not a language, *You will do this for us? You will do it, little brother?*

Riordan was too tired to sleep well. He had lain awake for a long time, thinking, and that is not good for a man alone in the Martian hills.

So now the rockhound was dead too. It didn't matter; the owlie wouldn't escape. But somehow the incident brought home to him the immensity and the age and the loneliness of the desert.

It whispered to him. The brush rustled and something wailed in darkness and the wind blew with a wild mournful sound over faintly starlit cliffs, and it was as if they all somehow had voice, as if the whole world muttered and threatened him in the night. Dimly, he wondered if man would ever subdue Mars, if the human race had not finally run across something bigger than itself.

But that was nonsense. Mars was old and worn-out and barren, dreaming itself into slow death. The tramp of human feet, shouts of men and roar of sky-storming rockets were waking it—but to a new destiny, to man's. When Ares lifted its hard spires above the hills of Syrtis, where then were the ancient gods of Mars?

It was cold, and the cold deepened as the night wore on. The stars were fire and ice, glittering diamonds in the deep crystal dark. Now and then he could hear a faint snapping borne through the earth as rock or tree split open. The wind laid itself to rest, sound froze to death, there was only the hard clear starlight falling through space to shatter on the ground.

Once something stirred. He woke from a restless sleep and saw a small thing skittering toward him. He groped for the rifle beside his sleeping bag, then laughed harshly. It was only a sandmouse. But it proved that the Martian had no chance of sneaking up on him while he rested.

He didn't laugh again. The sound had echoed too hollowly in his helmet.

With the clear bitter dawn he was up. He wanted to get the hunt over with. He was dirty and unshaven inside the unit, sick of iron rations pushed through the airlock, stiff and sore with exertion. Lacking the hound, which he'd had to shoot, tracking would be slow, but he didn't want to go back to Port Armstrong for another. No, hell take that Martian, he'd have the devil's skin soon!

Breakfast and a little moving made him feel better. He looked with a practiced eye for the Martian's trail. There was sand and brush over everything; even the rocks had a thin coating of their own erosion. The owlie couldn't cover his tracks perfectly—if he tried, it would slow him too much. Riordan fell into a steady jog.

Noon found him on higher ground, rough hills with gaunt needles of rock reaching yards into the sky. He kept going, confident of his own ability to wear down the quarry. He'd run deer to earth back home, day after day until the animal's heart broke and it waited quivering for him to come.

The trail looked clear and fresh now. He tensed with the knowledge that the Martian couldn't be far away.

Too clear! Could this be bait for another trap? He hefted the rifle and proceeded more warily. But no, there wouldn't have been time—

He mounted a high ridge and looked over the grim, fantastic landscape. Near the horizon he saw a blackened strip, the border of his radioactive barrier. The Martian couldn't go further, and if he doubled back Riordan would have an excellent chance of spotting him.

He tuned up his speaker and let his voice roar into the

stillness: "Come out, owlie! I'm going to get you; you might as well come out now and be done with it!"

The echoes took it up, flying back and forth between the naked crags, trembling and shivering under the brassy arch of sky. *Come out, come out, come out—*

The Martian seemed to appear from thin air, a gray ghost rising out of the jumbled stones and standing poised not twenty feet away. For an instant, the shock of it was too much; Riordan gaped in disbelief. Kreega waited, quivering ever so faintly as if he were a mirage.

Then the man shouted and lifted his rifle. Still the Martian stood there as if carved in gray stone, and with a shock of disappointment Riordan thought that he had, after all, decided to give himself to an inevitable death.

Well, it had been a good hunt. "So long," whispered Riordan, and squeezed the trigger.

Since the sandmouse had crawled into the barrel, the gun exploded.

Riordan heard the roar and saw the barrel peel open like a rotten banana. He wasn't hurt, but as he staggered back from the shock Kreega lunged at him.

The Martian was four feet tall, and skinny and weaponless, but he hit the Earthling like a small tornado. His legs wrapped around the man's waist and his hands got to work on the airhose.

Riordan went down under the impact. He snarled, tigerishly, and fastened his hands on the Martian's narrow throat. Kreega snapped futilely at him with his beak. They rolled over in a cloud of dust. The brush began to chatter excitedly.

Riordan tried to break Kreega's neck—the Martian twisted away, bored in again.

With a shock of horror, the man heard the hiss of escaping air as Kreega's beak and fingers finally worried the airhose loose. An automatic valve clamped shut, but there was no connection with the pump now—

Riordan cursed, and got his hands about the Martian's

throat again. Then he simply lay there, squeezing, and not all Kreega's writhing and twistings could break that grip.

Riordan smiled sleepily and held his hands in place. After five minutes or so Kreega was still. Riordan kept right on throttling him for another five minutes, just to make sure. Then he let go and fumbled at his back, trying to reach the pump.

The air in his suit was hot and foul. He couldn't quite reach around to connect the hose to the pumps—

Poor design, he thought vaguely. *But then, these airsuits weren't meant for battle armor.*

He looked at the slight, silent form of the Martian. A faint breeze ruffled the gray feathers. What a fighter the little guy had been! He'd be the pride of the trophy room, back on Earth.

Let's see now— He unrolled his sleeping bag and spread it carefully out. He'd never make it to the rocket with what air he had so it was necessary to let the suspensine into his suit. But he'd have to get inside the bag, lest the nights freeze his blood solid.

He crawled in, fastening the flaps carefully, and opened the valve on the suspensine tank. Lucky he had it—but then, a good hunter thinks of everything. He'd get awfully bored, lying here till Wisby caught the signal in ten days or so and came to find him, but he'd last. It would be an experience to remember. In this dry air, the Martian's skin would keep perfectly well.

He felt the paralysis creep up on him, the waning of heartbeat and lung action. His senses and mind were still alive, and he grew aware that complete relaxation has its unpleasant aspects. Oh, well—he'd won. He'd killed the wiliest game with his own hands.

Presently Kreega sat up. He felt himself gingerly. There seemed to be a rib broken—well, that could be fixed. He was still alive. He'd been choked for a good ten minutes, but a Martian can last fifteen without air.

He opened the sleeping bag and got Riordan's keys. Then

he limped slowly back to the rocket. A day or two of experimentation taught him how to fly it. He'd go to his kinsmen near Syrtis. Now that they had an Earthly machine, and Earthly weapons to copy—

But there was other business first. He didn't hate Riordan, but Mars is a hard world. He went back and dragged the Earthling into a cave and hid him beyond all possibility of human search parties finding him.

For a while he looked into the man's eyes. Horror stared dumbly back at him. He spoke slowly, in halting English: "For those you killed, and for being a stranger on a world that does not want you, and against the day when Mars is free, I leave you."

Before departing, he got several oxygen tanks from the boat and hooked them into the man's air supply. That was quite a bit of air for one in suspended animation. Enough to keep him alive for a thousand years.

Uncleftish Beholding

This little piece, which I think of as having been written for *The Anglo-Saxon Chronicle*, originally appeared in a fan publication many years ago. Recently I revised it for a professional magazine. Various scientists have found it amusing, and some have even made their own contributions to the roundaround board of the firststuffs.

For most of its being, mankind did not know what things are made of, but could only guess. With the growth of worldken, we began to learn, and today we have a beholding of stuff and work that watching bears out, both in the workstead and in daily life.

The underlying kinds of stuff are the *firststuffs*, which link together in sundry ways to give rise to the rest. Formerly we knew of ninety-two firststuffs, from waterstuff, the lightest and barest, to ymirstuff, the heaviest. Now we have made more, such as aegirstuff and helstuff.

The firestuffs have their being as motes called *unclefts*. These are mighty small; one seedweight of waterstuff holds a tale of them like unto two followed by twenty-two naughts. Most unclefts link together to make what are called *bulkbits*. Thus, the waterstuff bulkbit bestands of two waterstuff unclefts, the sourstuff bulkbit of two sourstuff unclefts, and so on. (Some kinds, such as sunstuff, keep alone; others, such as iron, cling together in chills when in the fast standing; and there are yet more yokeways.) When unlike clefts link in a bulkbit, they make *bindings*. Thus, water is a binding of two waterstuff unclefts with one sourstuff uncleft, while a bulkbit of one of the forestuffs making up flesh may have a thousand or more unclefts of these two forestuffs together with coalstuff and chokestuff.

At first it was thought that the uncleft was a hard thing that could be split no further; hence the name. Now we know it is made up of lesser motes. There is a heavy *kernel* with a forward bernstonish lading, and around it one or more light motes with backward ladings. The least uncleft is that of everyday waterstuff. Its kernel is a lone forwardladen mote called a *firstbit*. Outside it is a backwardladen mote called a *bernstonebit*. The firstbit has a heaviness about 1840-fold that of the bernstonebit. Early worldken folk thought bernstonebits swing around the kernel like the Earth around the Sun, but now we understand they are more like waves or clouds.

In all other unclefts are found other motes as well, about as heavy as the firstbit but with no lading, known as *neitherbits*. We know a kind of waterstuff with one neitherbit in the kernel along with the firstbit; another kind has two neitherbits. Both kinds are seldom.

The next greatest firststuff is sunstuff, which has two firstbits and two bernstonebits. The everyday sort also has two neitherbits in the kernel. If there are more or less, the uncleft will soon break asunder. More about this later.

The third firststuff is stonestuff, with three firstbits, three bernstonebits, and its own share of neitherbits. And so it goes, on through such everyday stuffs as coalstuff (six firstbits) or iron (26) or ones more lately found. Ymirstuff (92) was the last until men began to make some higher still.

It is the bernstonebits that link, and so their tale fastsets how a firststuff behaves and what kinds of bulkbits it can help make. The worldken of this behaving, in all its manifold ways, is called *minglingken*. Minglingers have found that as the uncleftish tale of the firststuffs (that is, the tale of first-stuffs in their kernels) waxes, after a while they begin to show ownships not unlike those of others that went before them. So, for a showdeal, stonestuff (3), headachestuff (11), potashstuff (19), redstuff (37), and bluegraystuff (55) can each link with only one uncleft of waterstuff, while coalstuff (6), sandstuff (14), germanstuff (22), tin (50), and lead (82) can each link with four. This is readily seen when all are set forth in what is called the *roundaround board of the firststuffs*.

When an uncleft or bulkbit wins one or more bernstonebits above its own, it takes on a backward lading. When it loses one or more, it takes on a forward lading. Such a mote is called a *farer*, for that the drag between unlike ladings flits it. When bernstonebits flit by themselves, it may be as a bolt of lightning, a spark off some faststanding chunk, or the everyday flow of bernstoneness through wire.

Coming back to the uncleft itself, the heavier it is, the more neitherbits as well as firstbits in its kernel. Indeed, soon the tale of neitherbits is the greater. Unclefts with the same tale of firstbits but unlike tales of neitherbits are called *samesteads*. Thus, everyday sourstuff has eight neitherbits with its eight firstbits, but there are also kinds with five, six, seven, nine, ten, and eleven neitherbits. A samestead is known by the tale of both kernel motes, so that we have sourstuff-13, sourstuff-14, and so on, with sourstuff-16 being by far the mostfound. Having the same number of bernstonebits, the samesteads of a firststuff behave almost alike minglingly. They do show some unlikeness, outstandingly among the heavier ones, and these can be worked to sunder samesteads from each other.

Most samesteads of every firststuff are unabiding. Their kernels break up, each at its own speed. This speed is written as the *half-life*, which is how long it takes half of any deal of the samestead thus to shift itself. The doing is known as *lightrotting*. It may happen fast or slowly, and in any of sundry ways, offhanging on the makeup of the kernel. A kernel may spit out two firstbits with two neitherbits, that is, a sunstuff kernel, thus leaping two steads back in the roundaround board and four weights back in heaviness. It may give off a bernstonebit from a neitherbit, which thereby becomes a firstbit and thrusts the uncleft one stead up in the board while keeping the same weight. It may give off a *forwardbit*, which is a mote with the same weight as a bernstonebit but a forward lading, and thereby spring one stead down in the board while keeping the same weight. Often, too, a mote is given off with neither lading nor heaviness, called the *weeneitherbit*. In much lightrotting, a mote of light with most short wavelength comes out as well.

For although light oftenest behaves as a wave, it can be looked on as a mote, the lightbit. We have already said by the way that a mote of stuff can behave not only as a chunk, but as a wave. Down among the unclefts, things do not happen in steady flowings, but in leaps between bestandings that are forbidden. The knowledge-hunt of this is called *lump beholding*.

Nor are stuff and work unakin. Rather, they are groundwise the same, and one can be shifted into the other. The kinship between them is that work is like unto weight manifolded by the fourside of the haste of light.

By shooting motes into kernels, worldken folk have shifted samesteads of one firststuff into samesteads of another. Thus did they make ymirstuff into aegirstuff and helstuff, and they have afterward gone beyond these. The heavier firststuffs are all highly lightrottish and therefore are not found in the greenworld.

Some of the higher samesteads are *splitly*. That is, when a neitherbit strikes the kernel of one, as for a showdeal ymirstuff-235, it bursts into lesser kernels and free neitherbits; the latter can then split more ymirstuff-235. When this happens, weight shifts into work. It is not much of the whole, but nevertheless it is awesome.

With enough strength, lightweight unclefts can be made to togethermelt. In the Sun, through a row of strikings and lightrottings, four unclefts of waterstuff in this wise become one of sunstuff. Again some weight is lost as work, and again this is greatly big when set beside the work gotten from a minglingish doing such as fire.

Today we wield both kind of uncleftish doings in weapons, and kernelish splitting gives us heat and bernstoneness. We hope to do likewise with togethermelting, which would yield an unhemmed wellspring of work for mankindish goodgain.

Soothly we live in mighty years!

Besides his newbooks and truthbooks, the writer has forthshown in Likething Worldken Sagas/Worldken Truth, The Warehouse of Dreamishness and Worldken Sagas, *and other roundaroundnesses.*

Escape from Orbit

This was another story written around a cover painting—one that showed an orbiting spacecraft in flames. Now, not long before, Hal Clement had published a brilliant little tale pointing out that you can't have a fire in weightlessness. Reconciling this with the picture was a challenge. The real hazards of space have turned out to be rather different from those we expected before we actually got out there, but serious damage by an occasional meteoroid does remain a possibility. These days, too, I could do a better job of describing how things work at Mission Control, but maybe that setup will change, and in any case, such details aren't very important to my people.

The ringing cut like a buzz saw. For a moment Wister denied it. He was riding a white horse whose mane and tail were flames, the great muscles surged between his legs, wind roared and whipped about him, smelling of summer meadows. *Brrrng!* Bees droned through clover. The wind had a tinge of Julie's hair, a sunny odor, but a sharp clean whiff of rocket fuel strengthened as it thrust against him. The horse made one enormous bound and left Earth. Meadows dwindled, the sky darkened until it was an infinitely deep Bonestell blue, and the stars of space glittered forth. *Brrrng!* The horse said with his father's voice,—That's the Big Dipper, which they used to call King Charles' Wain, but long ago it was Odin's *Brrrng!* and at night *Brrrng!* Jupiter far cold mysterious *Brrrng!* Saturn Pluto Andromeda *Brrrng!* outward upward upward *Brrrng!* up *up* UP WHETHER YOU LIKE IT OR NOT BRRRNG BRRRNG BRRRNG!

The blackness confused him. At this time of year the sun rose before his alarm went off. Wister flailed his arms blindly, batting away the evil fragments which his dream had become. Florence stirred beside him, muttered herself awake, and sank back into sleep as Wister got control. She snored a little.

The clock face glowed with a small hour. Damnation, that wasn't the alarm, it was the phone. *Brrrng!* Wister swung out of bed. The floor was cool under his bare feet. It relieved the stickiness of his skin a little. He'd been sweating like a pig, though the night wasn't hot so early in summer.

"Okay, okay, okay," he grumbled automatically, felt his way into the hall and switched on the light. It struck at his eyes as the phone did at his ears. He squinted against it and picked up the receiver. Still only partly active, his mind conjured forth horrible reasons for a night call and his pulse flapped. "Hello?"

"Dick?" Charlie Huang's voice relieved him of deaths in his sister's family and imminent nuclear attack. "Sorry, but you've got to get down here soonest. The whole bunch of us, in fact. *Yankee*'s wrecked."

"Huh?"

"Meteor strike."

"Can't be! The odds—"

"It had to happen sometime, didn't it? So it happened early in the space flight game, instead of a hundred years from now. I'll fill you in when you arrive. The boys escaped in their ditching capsule. Nothing else was left. They're stuck in orbit around the Moon."

Wister shook his head violently, trying to clear it. None of this made sense. Even if a ship was hulled by a meteorite, or by a dozen meteorites, you didn't abandon it. You slapped patches over the holes and started repair work on whatever machinery was damaged. Didn't you?

Maybe not. This was the first such accident on record.

There was a click in the receiver. His boss had hung up, doubtless to call someone else. Wister groped on into the kitchen. Make haste slowly, he told himself. Nothing much could be done till the entire gang was assembled, which would take over an hour. Meanwhile he could best stoke his brain with coffee. When young he had always awakened refreshed, set to go, but in recent years he roused slow and gluey-eyed.

Now cut that out, he scolded. *Thirty-four is* not *old.*

The kitchen looked even more dismal than usual. Ordinarily Jim was up with him, chattering away sixty to the dozen while he made breakfast for them; and sunlight rioted in the flowerbeds just outside. This morning he had no distraction from yesterday's dirty dishes. He washed the coffeepot with some difficulty—the sink was full too—and set it to work while he went into the bathroom.

Stripped, he regarded himself for an instant of distaste. He was still fairly slender, but his efforts to keep in shape didn't entirely cope with the effects of a desk job. Slowly potbelly and pudding thighs overtook him. For the *x*th time he resolved to put in an hour a day at the local gym, knew he wouldn't keep the resolution, and swore wearily.

When the shower struck him with hot needles, his bloodstream began moving at a normal pace. It carried the remaining fog out of his head. Briefly he was shocked at himself, worried about his waistline while Cy Enwright and Phil Cohn and Bruno Fellini spun through the shadows behind the Moon. *My God, what am I going to say to their people?* He turned off the water, stepped from the tub, and toweled with quick harsh motions. *I won't say a word. I'll be too busy getting them back home alive.*

How?

He returned to the bedroom, switched on the light and dressed. Florence didn't stir. Her face sagged in sleep, as her body did awake, an unhealthy color. She was still snoring. Somehow the knowledge of three men who were his friends, caged among the cold stars, raised a tenderness in Wister. It wasn't Flo's doing that she stopped being the sun and surf and moonglade girl he married, after Jim was born. Some damned glandular change that the doctors couldn't pin down, too subtle for them . . . He stooped and brushed his lips across hers. Her breath was sour.

She'd have to get Jim off to school today. He scribbled a note and tucked it under the alarm clock before he went out to the kitchen. Coffee and a doughnut brought him to full alertness, but he didn't think about the job on hand. That would be useless until he knew just what had happened. Instead he found himself visualizing and remembering the *Yankee* boys.

Big, soft-spoken Cy Enwright, Col. USAF Reserve, but you couldn't tell it from his manner. His wife outshone him when you first met them, he seemed only background for her beauty and vivacity—till you got to know them well, then it dawned on you that most of what she was had its source in him, dry wit and calm philosophy and the steel backbone that made her able to laugh with their friends while he was away in space. The other two described themselves as career civilians, though Phil Cohn had served in the Southwest Asia guerrillas some years ago. He was small and dark and quick-moving, a trifle on the bookish side and a nut about Mozart, but also a football fan and hell on wheels at the poker table. This summer he was going to get married and present his mother with the grandchildren she'd been pestering him for. Bruno Fellini, the youngest and handsomest of NASA's stable, wasn't interested in marriage—just women. There had been a couple of hilarious times when the public relations boys must scuttle around like toads in a pot, hushing up affairs that would spoil the Image. Bruno didn't give a damn. He knew perfectly well he was too adroit a pilot to be fired. But loud sports shirt, cocky gait, bad puns, and all, he was the kind of guy who brought flowers when invited to dinner and would hand his bottom buck to anyone that needed it.

And then there's me, Wister thought. *We get along pretty well, we four. Yakking, bowling, partying, borrowing tools and books and maybe five till payday, now and then getting drunk together . . . yeh, we talk about buying a fifty-foot cruiser one of these years and bumming around the Caribbean or the Mediterranean . . . odd how close people become after they've shared such trivia long enough.*

Those three men have never said or hinted or thought that I'm any less than them, because I turned groundling while they went to Mars and back. Never once.

He rose from the table. Impulsively, he ducked back along the hall, into Jim's room. The boy still slept with Boo, though the bear's fur was long worn off and little remained of its face except a silly grin. Otherwise the room held the normal clutter of an eight-year-old, and Wister didn't worry too much about him any more. Jim had almost stopped having nightmares, and was now growing at a satisfactory rate. Wister bent close above the tangled head. *Funny,* he thought, *what a warm clean smell children have. They lose it at adolescence. I wonder how come?*

For some reason he was reminded of Julie Quist. He'd almost married her, a dozen years ago in Michigan. But another man, older and with better technique, had cut in on the romance. Only afterward did Wister come to believe that he could probably have gotten her anyhow, if he'd made a real try. But he was young and bitter and— Oh, well.

He straightened from Jim's bed. A picture of a spaceship blasting off caught his eye. He'd hoped the kid actually would stick by every small boy's dream and go in for a NASA career. "My son the astronaut." So why not? "My son the first human being to walk on Titan beneath ringed Saturn." Thinking of the *Yankee*, Wister was suddenly not quite sure. A coldness touched him; his fists closed together. There had been deaths in space before today, some of them pretty nasty.

But Cy and Phil and Bruno were the men with whom he would like sometime to sail the route of Odysseus.

Quickly he turned on his heel, went down the hall and out the front door, shrugging into his topcoat. The eastern sky had turned pale and the suburban street lay clear to the eye, empty, altogether silent except for a dry rustle of palm fronds in a breeze. Westward there still dwelt gloom and a scattering of stars. The Moon was down. Wister was glad of that. He would not have been able to look on it without a shudder.

He got into his car, growled the engine while he lit his first cigarette, and started off. It was pleasant driving this early, at least, with no traffic jam to buck. Though he liked the neighborhood he lived in, he often wondered if it was worth the commuting. Ninety minutes a day made seven and a half hours a week, fifteen complete days a year, gone from his life with nothing to show for their passage but a stomach ulcer. . . . He turned onto the coast highway and opened up the car.

His forebrain began to worry the problem of what had happened, out there in space. *Yankee* had been on a fairly routine mission, part of a series of tests and shakedown flights before starting for Venus. While it circled the Moon, some data were gathered, of course, for the different breeds of scientists to chew on. But nothing very new. All right, so it had taken a meteorite beating, improbable though that was in the emptiness yonder. But then why had it been abandoned? And especially in a solar flare season!

Wister tried to suppress his barren speculations. He'd need a well-rested mind when he actually began work. He made himself watch sunrise, huge and silvery across the ocean, and recall days on those wide beaches when he walked hand in hand with Florence and told her everything he was going to do in space. He'd figured there was an excellent chance of his being tapped for the Mars expedition—well, damn it, there had been; he'd not transferred from the astronautical corps to the ground offices at anyone's request but his own— He realized he had gripped the steering wheel so hard that his fingers hurt and had tramped the gas pedal down to the floorboard. ''Stop that, you idiot!'' he barked aloud. ''What good are you to anyone if you smash up?'' Shaken, he eased off the pressures.

After a while the sprawling complex of Base came over the low horizon at him. An Aeolus three-stager towered in a gantry, stark against heaven. It was scheduled for a Lunar supply mission next week. Wister had already dismissed a passing thought, that it might be used to save the *Yankee* men instead. Countdown couldn't be advanced more than forty-eight hours or so, and that wasn't enough.

The guard waved him past without inspection. The young face was strained. *He knows,* Wister realized. *The whole layout here will know as soon as people arrive for work. Then the whole planet. If we can pull off a rescue, with the world's eyes on us, we'll all be set for at least one advancement in grade, and— But those are my friends up there!*

The parking lot was still almost deserted. Wister jumped from his car and jogtrotted to the front door of Thimk Hall, as everyone had lately been calling the computer-full building that housed Orbital Command. Inside, the corridor was unpeopled, a cavern that went on and on like something in a bad dream, clattering beneath his shoes. He was panting a little when he reached Charlie Huang's office.

It was blue with smoke. The boss was there, of course, pacing tiger-fashion. Harry Mowitz, the chief computerman, sat drumming his nails on a chair arm. Bill Delarue, head of communications, perched on the desk. He kept shifting his position. Half a dozen subordinates hovered unhappily by the far wall.

Huang spun about as Wister came in. ''Ah,'' he snapped. ''There you are. What the devil kept you so long?''

''Are they still alive?'' Wister retorted.

''I hope to Christ so. But they've passed behind the Moon, out of radio reach. Camp Apollo will try to raise them when they come back around in half an hour. Hawaii's standing by too.''

"Oh, so you've got their orbit?"

"Well, no. Not exactly. But their last regular message said they were about to assume it, and of course we know how they planned to park in relation to the *Gal*. That was an hour before they got hit."

Wister considered the situation. *Galileo*, the unmanned Euratom research satellite, was currently circling the Moon in a four-hour orbit, its instruments telemetering some astrophysical observations and recording others for analysis the next time it was brought down to Camp Apollo. *Yankee* was supposed to take up a path of slightly less radius in the same plane. Radar and laser transmissions, back and forth between ship and satellite, would provide data from which the exact shape of the Moon could be more accurately calculated than hitherto. There was close cooperation between the American and West European space programs. . . . Yes, Enwright's boys would have been engaged in terminal maneuvers, jockeying themselves into the right position, when the smash came.

"I have an idea how they got hulled," Mowitz offered. "Space can't be quite as hollow as we believed. We knew that none of the charted rock storms are anywhere close. But what do we know about meteorites traveling outside the ecliptic plane? They'd zip by Earth too fast to be observed, if no one was looking for them especially."

"What happened, though?" Wister demanded. His mouth was dry. He went to the water cooler and tapped a Dixie cupful. "Why leave the ship, even if the rocks made scrap iron out of it?"

"The ship caught fire," Delarue said.

"What?" Wister didn't think he had heard correctly. "In space?"

"Yeah," Huang said. "Their last message—short-range 'cast on the only radio left, but Camp Apollo monitored it—uh, here's a copy— 'Struck by large meteorites. Fire swept through ship. Forced to escape in ditching capsule. *Yankee*. Over.' " He raised almond eyes loaded with misery. "They didn't have a hell of a lot of time, it seems. I imagine only their being in spacesuits saved them. While I was on my own way here, Apollo sent us a new item. Somebody there got a telescopic glimpse, the last few seconds. Said the ship was one long flame. Then it exploded."

"Oh." Wister took out another cigarette. Blindly staring before him, he populated the wall with engineering diagrams and differential equations. The answer appeared. "I see what must've happened. The combustion chamber and tanks were hit. The fuel and liquid oxy got together and ignited—"

"Impossible," Delarue said. "The moment anything like that occurred, rocket blast would cease. Obviously! Then you'd be in free fall, and everybody knows you can't have a fire without weight to give a pressure-temperature gradient."

"You sure can, pal," Wister told him, "if colloidal drops of fuel and lox are scattered through the entire hull. Call it a prolonged explosion rather than a fire if you want to. I agree the free fall effect would damp the speed of the reaction; but by the same token, the ship would be ablaze for a few minutes. Then an unpunctured fuel tank blew up, and that was that."

"But how'd your mixture get dissipated through the ship in the first place? What formed the colloids?"

"Supersonic energy. A meteorite of a few pounds' mass, zipping through a hull filled with air, would generate the granddaddy of all sonic booms. You use supersonics to homogenize milk, don't you?" Wister shrugged. "If you knows a better 'ole, go to it. But I think a detailed mathematical analysis will bear me out."

He was not unconscious of their respectful gaze upon him as he lit his cigarette. Orbital Command was damn glad to have an ex-space pilot on its staff, with everything that that implied in the way of training, practical experience, and an ability to grasp the curious ways that natural law can operate beyond Earth's sky. He had long felt sure that he'd get the section when Charlie Huang moved on up the bureaucratic ladder. The suggestion he had just made wouldn't hurt the prospect any. It would influence the design of *Yankee*'s successor.

To hell with that! There must be a way to get them down!

"What's the solar flare prediction?" he asked.

"Uncertain as usual," Huang said. "Solar meteorology has a long way to go before it's an exact science. However, we all know this is a bad season, and the last report predicted considerable disturbances within sixty hours. That's about forty-eight hours from this moment."

Silence fell on the room and pressed inward. He had no need to review the facts, but they streamed idiotically through Wister's consciousness anyhow. A flare on the sun emitted a stream of protons. Since the *Yankee* had been intended for the Venus expedition, it had been equipped with Swanberg screen generators, whose magnetohydrodynamic forces were adequate to deflect any such bombardment. But a ditching capsule was nothing except a thin metal shell tucked into the ship's nose. The interior was heavily padded, there were seats and a radio and tools and cables and such oddments. If a vessel coming in through the atmosphere should fail—it had happened to a Russian job once, when the inflatable gliding surfaces ripped open—the pilot was supposed to use an ocean for his landing pad. A small explosive charge would spung the capsule loose from the ship, and it would float about with the crew until someone arrived to pick them up.

It was not meant for space. Under ideal conditions, it would keep three men alive in the void as long as their air held out: four days, Wister estimated, knowing what part of the vessel's supply was stored there. The intrinsic shielding was poor, but would serve for that length of time—unless radiation got very heavy. Which it would when the sun flared.

Four days max, then, to get them to safety. But more likely two days, or less, because of solar weather. No American craft could be readied on such short notice. But . . .

"Euratom," Wister said.

"You mean, have they got anything which could get upstairs in a hurry?" Huang asked. "I checked with Geneva, and the answer is no."

"Well, the Russkies!"

"Gail's put Washington onto that," Huang said quietly. "They're trying to get hold of Karpovitch in person."

Wister bit his lip, embarrassed, and stubbed out his cigarette.

A junior computerman cleared his throat and inquired, "Pardon me, but why can't *Galileo* pick them up? I mean, it's remote-controlled, and fueled for a Lunar landing, and passes quite near the capsule at conjunction."

"And has a net mass of about two tons," Wister explained, "which three men in spacesuits would increase by something like thirty percent. Not to mention the uneven distribution of their mass on the shell, which'd royally louse up control and require continual correction blasts. The rocket motor hasn't that much reserve. In fact, *Galileo* carries almost no spare fuel."

"Why not?" said the young man indignantly.

"Because it lands and takes off from the Moon. Do you know what fuel and lox cost per gallon, after you've shipped 'em from Earth to Camp Apollo? It'll actually be cheaper for Euratom to lose an occasional unmanned job for lack of emergency tanks, than to tote so much extra mass around *and* replace the liquid every few weeks because of boiloff."

"Dick knows," Huang said. "He's our local expert on the subject. Was on the team which inspected the *Gal* last year, after G.E. built it for Euratom. He worked with our own similar project before that, between the time he left the astronautical corps and came here to Orbital."

"I see," said the young man.

Wister smiled reminiscently. Those had been two great weeks in Europe. He'd intended to wander about afterward on the Continent. Leave of absence was easy to arrange. But Flo fell sick again at that time. Nothing too serious. It never was. However, her poor tattered nerves went completely to pieces when she was ill, and without his father around, Jim would bear the brunt of it . . . just when he was starting to overcome his bedwetting and nightmares and—

And this had nothing to do with three men in a shell hurtling around the Moon.

Another couple of subordinates arrived. Huang nodded. "That makes a full enough complement," he said. "Take over, Harry. Prepare your team to compute whatever needs computing. The orbit first, I suppose, as soon as we get a fix and a Doppler reading."

"Check." Mowitz beckoned to his staff. They moved out the door and down the hall in a silent, shuffling herd.

Delarue rose. "I'd better get on to my own section," he said.

"Why, they're already standing by, aren't they?" Huang answered. "They don't need you."

"Yeah, but I need them," Delarue muttered between his teeth. "I can't sit here and do nothing!" He left at a quick jerky pace.

Alone in the office, Huang and his second-in-command stared at each other. The tobacco haze stung their eyes. The morning sunlight on the parking lot outside was indecently bright.

"Do you really think the Russians will help?" Wister asked after a while, merely to break the silence.

"Oh, yes, if they can," Huang said. "Propaganda kudos for them, isn't it, if they bail out the Americans. Besides, they're human too, whatever you think of their government."

"But are they able? Have they got anything that close to go, right now?"

"Who knows?"

The silence came back. It must be very still in the capsule, Wister thought, remembering his own past missions. Locked in their spacesuits, jammed so close together they could hardly move, the three men would hear little except their breath and heartbeat, see little except a few chill points of blaze in the one tiny port. They could talk to each other by helmet set, of course; but what do you say to the one beside you as you fall helpless over the night side of the Moon? What do you say down to Earth?

A buzzer sounded. Huang started so violently that he knocked an ashtray off his desk. Cigarette butts spilled halfway across the floor. He stabbed the intercom button. "Yes, what is it?" Wister realized that they were both on their feet, crouched over the black box. His back between the shoulder blades ached with tension.

A woman's voice, from Delarue's team, said, not quite steadily: "Contact has been made with the capsule, sir, via Camp Apollo and Hawaii. We can plug you in directly if you wish."

"Yes, yes, what do you think I wish?" Huang yelled. The intercom clicked and hummed. It crashed upon Wister that he had nothing to say to the men in space. Not one damn thing.

Static crackled from the speaker. Faint and distorted, wavering along the edge of audibility, there came: "Enwright speaking. Hello, hello, are you there, Charlie?"

"Yes—" Huang stared across the box at Wister. "Take over, Dick," he mumbled.

"Are you okay?" Wister heard someone ask with his throat. He remembered he must wait: two and a half seconds while the beam crossed nothingness and came back. Nearly half a million miles, with atmospherics and Doppler effect and the dry hiss of the stars to battle along the way. The tiny, unreal voice said:

"Yeah, I think so, except Phil seems to have ruptured his eardrums. That was a lulu of a detonation. We barely made it to the capsule and sprung her free. Everything worked fine, though." A hesitation. "So far."

"What—uh—air? Temperature? CO_2 control?"

"We're still alive," Enwright said bleakly.

"And we . . . we're figuring how to get you down." Wister had to swallow a couple of times before he could continue. "We're looking for a vehicle."

Whining stillness again, until another tone said: "Bruno

speaking. Don't hand us that guff, Dick. You know there isn't any standby. You were a spaceman too."

Once, Wister thought.

"The best thing you can do is get Cy's wife and Phil's girl on the line," Fellini said. What might have been a chuckle sounded from the black box. "Me, I'm lucky. I haven't got anyone who makes that much difference."

And I've got someone who makes too much difference, Wister thought; *so I had to quit space, and the sun will warm my skin while it kills you. So I'm even luckier, oh, yes.*

"Stow the dramatics, Bruno," Enwright said. Cohn, sealed in deafness, must needs hold his mouth. "They're doing all they can at Base. This is what we collect flight pay for. Dick, what can we do ourselves? I know you're taking observations to figure our orbit, but is there anything else you might need data on?"

"I . . . I can't imagine— What do you see through your port?" Wister asked, as if words could hold off death.

"M-m-m . . . we're tumbling, naturally, so the stars waltz by in the craziest way. I've timed our rotational velocity as two point three r.p.m., though precession louses up my figuring some. Whoops, I just glimpsed the dawn line of the Moon. Mountains like teeth, shadows halfway across a gray plain, Judas, what a graveyard!—hold it—had to cover my face there, a sunbeam . . . I see a piece of wreckage trailing along, in almost the same orbit as us. A double tank—yeah, compressed air, as far's I can make out the color code in this damned shifty light. The main air tank. Seems intact. Must be, come to think of it, or the gas gushing out would've pushed it into a radically different orbit. The rest of the ship is scattered from hell to breakfast."

"Wait a minute," Wister chattered. "You have flexible cable, I know. Two miles' worth, isn't it? Why don't you go outside, jump and jet across, and make fast to that tank? Pull your capsule alongside it?"

"Why, I guess we can. 'Druther wait till we're back in the Lunar shadow cone, though. It's awfully hot and bright out there. Not that we couldn't stand the heat. We can even take a few hours of the radiation outside this shell, at the level my meter's registering. But frankly, we're uncomfortable aplenty as is."

"Sure, that's okay. Wait for shade."

"Why do the job at all, though? We certainly can't land on a jet of compressed air!"

"Oh, no, no. But extend your breathing time—"

Fellini's laughter rattled. "We've got enough here to last us till the sun flares," he said.

Wister's nails dug into his palms. "Anything may help," he said. "I can't imagine how, in this case. Probably it's no use. But you can't afford to pass up any bets." Savagely: "You're dead, you know, unless one of those few bets pays off."

"Dick!" Huang cried. "That was uncalled for."

Static jeered. Then Enwright's ghost-voice said: "He's right, Charlie. We'll secure that tank as soon as we get behind the Moon again. It won't drift too far from us in a couple of hours."

"It'll alter your orbit some. Must have more total mass than you and your capsule do. The momentum exchange—" Huang slumped. "Never mind. We can recompute. Okay."

The speaker hummed and sputtered.

"What else do you want to know?" Enwright asked.

"I can't think of anything," Huang sighed.

"We'll sign off, then. That is . . . till you put us in touch with our people."

"Sure. As soon as possible. Meanwhile, uh, uh, would you like some music?"

"No, thanks. Not with reception like this, eh, Bruno?"

"I think I would, if you've got some classic jazz," Fellini said. "None of the current slop, though."

"Oh, well, I can stand it," Enwright said. "Thanks for everything, Earth and Apollo. *Au 'voir.* Over and out."

The voice died. Presently the intercom stopped crackling. Delarue came on: "We'll hold a monitor on them, of course.

Say, want I should arrange that music? I've got his kind of tapes at home. Jelly Roll Morton and so forth."

"Sure," Huang said. "Fine." He punched for Mowitz's section. "Harry? How're you coming on the orbit?"

"We're processing the data now. Ought to have the elements for you inside fifteen minutes."

"No hurry, I'm afraid. Especially since you'll have to recalculate next time around. They're going to attach to an extraneous mass. But carry on." Huang turned the instrument off and rose to his feet. Suddenly he looked old. "Can you hold the fort for a while?" he asked.

"Me?" Wister replied, startled. "Why, I suppose— But what—"

"Somebody's got to notify those women and arrange a hookup."

Because he knew that Huang knew it, Wister must needs say: "I'm a personal friend of all concerned, Charlie, I can do that."

His relief was unabashed when the other said, "No. I've no right to delegate the hard ones. It'll be easier for me to tell 'em anyhow, a comparative stranger. And—" Huang paused. "You're better qualified to handle this desk in this kind of situation than I am. I'm only an orbit man."

He went out. Wister sat down in his place and stared through the window. *All right*, he told himself, *now what?*

Now the death watch, that's what, he answered. *I'd better see about some transportation for Flo to go shopping. I'll be stuck here till it's over.* (Why *won't she learn to drive? She may not be very strong, but she isn't paralyzed. Could it be my fault? Maybe I should have been tougher with her when— Or maybe not. How can I tell? Too late now.) The hell with expense. I'm sick of begging favors from the whole neighborhood. Let her take taxis. (I shouldn't have to worry about expense with my salary, even if I don't get flight pay any more. But doctor bills, and a cleaning woman three times a week, and—) Stop that whimpering! You're alive, at least!*

Then the intercom buzzed and he forgot about it. Gail

Jackman's voice said: "Mr. Garth calling from Washington. Can you take the message?"

"Sure can!" He snatched the phone. "Hello, Richard Wister speaking, Mr. Huang had to go out, he left me in charge."

"Tom Garth," said NASA's liaison with the State Department. "We got the word from Moscow."

"Yes? Can they—"

"No. I'm sorry. Karpovitch talked to me himself. He said they can raise a *Gagarin*-class ship inside a week, but I told him that was no use. Right?"

"Uh-huh. We're closer to go than that ourselves."

"No hope, then?"

"We're trying to think of something."

"Better call a conference. We'll hold a brainstorming session here and let you know what we come up with. This could give us all a black eye, propaganda-wise."

Wister became unable to bandy clichés. "I'd better hang up," he said. "Plenty to get organized here, you know. Thanks for calling. So long." He clashed the receiver down.

His ulcer stabbed him. Wincing, he pushed the intercom button. "Gail, could you promote me some crackers and milk?"

"Yes, with pleasure," said Huang's secretary.

"Uh . . . get yourself something too, if you want. I daresay you didn't have a chance for breakfast either. Frankly, I'd like someone to talk to. Help me forget for a minute how useless I am."

"I understand," she said gently. "I'll send an office boy across the highway. Tam's should be open by now."

He waited, stewing over the emptiness within and without, until Gail entered carrying a tray. Then his heart lifted a trifle. She was pretty—not spectacular, but pleasant to look on, intelligent, cheerful, and uncommitted. Sometimes Wister daydreamed about having an affair with her. It wasn't as if that would deprive Florence of anything she cared about any longer. But since Gail knew he was married, he had never quite figured out how to make the initial move. As she set the food on the desk, sunlight running along her burnished hair and striking through a thin blouse, he wondered if perhaps the intimacy of this moment— No, he was only supposed to think about Cy, Phil, and Bruno, wasn't he? Nonetheless he made a ceremony of seating her, and they exchanged smiles.

"Thank'ee, Sir Walter," she said.

"Raleigh, 'tis a pleasure." Bitterness surged in him. "Excuse me. I know I'm being sophomoric. But what can we do?"

She regarded him gravely. "You're taking this hard, aren't you?"

"Yes," he said, quite sincere, though not unaware of the dramatic possibilities in his role. "Aren't we all? Those are us in that capsule."

She shook her head, "You're a man. But a woman thinks differently. Oh, of course I pity them, and I'll bawl as soon as I go off duty. Yet I keep thanking God it isn't my man up there."

Wister gulped at his milk. "Don't get me wrong," he said. "I'm no hero or any such foolish thing. But I'd give—what? An eye or a hand—for a chance to save them."

"I think you mean that literally," she murmured.

"I do." He couldn't remain in his chair, jumped up, walked to the window and stared out at the bland blind sky. "What makes it especially tough is having been a pilot myself. I know what it's like for them. Suffocating hot, each time the sun beats on the shell. Clothes plastered to your skin with sweat, that runs into your eyes and stings, but you can't rub them, and you itch but can't scratch, and whenever you notice your own stench you gag. You're a bit sick anyway from the tumbling of the shell. It doesn't give much weight, but the gradient is so steep that every time you move the weight shifts, your middle ear protests, and you feel nauseated. And that breaks down your mental defenses. The instincts of a trapped animal yell louder and louder. You sit there waiting for the sun to spew out your death—" He realized what he was saying. "Pardon me."

"Go on," she said. Tears blurred her eyes.

"Furthermore," he said, "I can imagine myself all too clearly, outward bound to rescue them. Piloting's a more cerebral thing, though. Push that button, pull that lever, set that wheel; a problem in mathematics, really, which you act out, too busy to be afraid or uncomfortable. *Doing* something, before heaven, instead of—"

He stopped. For a very long time he stood altogether motionless.

"What's the matter?" Gail rose, half-frightened.

Wister turned about. His eyes raked her without seeing. He spoke in a stranger's tone. "Put me through to Geneva."

"Why—"

"Jansen in Geneva. Head of the Euratom space project. I want to talk to him." Wister ripped open a drawer, found Huang's calculator, sat down and reached for the handbooks on the desk. He had forgotten she existed.

"Steady as she goes."

The satellite drifted nearer, an ungainly spindle, tiny across the miles, against the cold, curdled Milky Way. The sun, hammering on Enwright's back, struck its surface. Hard splinters of light rebounded to his eyes. He slitted them and made himself ignore the discomfort. Overtaking the *Galileo* on its slightly smaller orbit, the *Yankee* capsule headed toward the darkness behind the Moon. That pocked gibbous shape loomed enormous to the right. His heart thuttered.

"N-no . . . wait . . . reduce speed a few feet per second more."

The satellite's clustered rocket tubes blasted momentarily in opposition to the course. A white cloud, tinged with fire streaks, billowed ahead, expanded, and whiffed to nothing. *Galileo* fell a couple of miles closer to the Moon. Actually, some velocity was gained thereby, since the Lunar gravitational pull grew stronger. But relative to the capsule, speed was lost. And there would be a shorter distance to jump, Enwright gauged.

"Okay, I'm off."

He crouched on his toes, where spaceboots lacked the slight stickiness that otherwise held him to the hull. His legs straightened and he soared free. The cable unreeled behind him. Moving at about a dozen feet per second, he took several minutes to go from capsule to satellite. The gap started to widen as he neared, for the orbits were not yet identical. But Enwright had a spaceman's sense of vectors. He had led his target as a hunter leads a duck, and passed within yards. A short blast from the air bottle in his harness corrected the remaining error. The bulky shape, bristling with robotic instruments, swelled before him. He twisted about, somehow acrobatic in his spacesuit, and hit feet first. The slight shock traveled through his spine to rattle his jaws. Changing rotations dizzied him. He made fast.

Turning, with one hand to shade the sunside of his helmet, he saw the capsule and the other men who clung to it. Hastily he secured a bight of the cable to a sturdy-looking bracket, then braced himself and began hauling.

Cohn and Fellini toiled at their end. Slowly the two masses moved together, until at last they bumped in contact. The spin characteristics of the system grew utterly mad. Enwright plugged his radio back into the capsule's transmitter. *"Okay so far. We're all in one piece now. But is there still fuel enough?"*

"Oh, yes. The Gal *didn't have to shed much velocity. We're about to lose contact again, you know. Think you'll be ready by the time you come back around to our side?"*

"Roger. Over and out."

The sun fell behind the Moon's ragged shoulder. Bailey's Beads flashed momentarily, then only a wing of soft coronal light was to be seen. It set also. But the crowding stars gave sufficient illumination, and the coolness was a blessing. Their spacesuits were barely able to keep the men going under full sunlight. The chill of the shadow cone meant little for the brief time they were in it; their own hard-working bodies replaced radiated heat.

Hard-working indeed. They had two hours to dismount the capsule's radio transceiver and fix it securely on the *Galileo*; unship the huge air tank from the capsule; lash it even more strongly to the satellite; release the capsule itself, no longer needed, to drift free; and tie themselves around *Galileo*'s circumference in such a way as to cause minimum unbalance.

"Think we'll make it, Cy? Be honest now."

"How can I tell? But we haven't much to lose, have we?"

"I'll answer that question when we're down."

The sun struck them with such cruelty that they wondered if flare radiation had begun to sleet through their bodies. Voices entered their helmets.

"Base to Yankee Gal. *We've nailed you on our radar. Are you prepared to go?"*

"Hope so. But don't you want to compute our new orbit first?"

"Why? You'll be leaving it right away, and in a totally unpredictable fashion."

"True. I'm not thinking straight any more. Lord, but I'm tired!"

"Nothing that some bed rest and a pretty nurse won't cure. Your roentgen background is still tolerable. But the solar meteorologists now expect a flare within five or six hours, so let's get you down fast. Just a minute while I settle myself."

"Dick, how come you're controlling Galileo? *Wouldn't one of the Europeans have more experience?"*

"Ordinarily, yes. I'm not doing this for fun. But the trouble is, the handling characteristics must have been radically changed by the added masses. Jansen strongly recommended we use a man with some seat-of-the-pants background as well as a knowledge of this particular telecontrol system. Well, I did pilot some awful boltbuckets, not too many years ago. And the control room here at Base is practically the same as the one in the Midi. G.E. built 'em both, you know. I . . .

think I've familiarized myself with Euratom's operating codes, while I waited for you."

"I know you have, Dick."

"If I should crash you— No!"

"You won't."

"Okay, then, let's go. First we have to reorient your main axis. Get it tangential to orbit. Hang on! Over." The clumsy mass spouted and slewed about. *"Whew! My instruments say you're lined up. But the whole damned system wants to hunt. Crack that barrel fast!"*

Enwright reached across to the tank beside him. The main release valve had already been loosened. It turned readily. He felt a surge of thrust as the air poured out. The deep-throated roar vibrated his bones.

In a few minutes the great container was exhausted. Enwright, Fellini, and Cohn worked frantically to release it. The light, flexible cable had strength comparable to steel, and deceleration pressure had tightened every knot. Panting, cursing minutes fled while tools hung at belts worked away. Freed, tank and satellite moved ponderously apart under the force of rotation.

"Yankee Gal *to Base. We're clear. Repeat, we're clear. Over."*

"Base to Yankee Gal. *As near as we can gauge, you've lost virtually all orbital velocity and are falling fast. There's a wee bit of forward speed to kill, but then—"*

Thrust and thrum awoke where fire-tongues wavered. The satellite tilted about, obedient to pulses sent across a quarter-million miles, but awkward, crazily a-wobble. The Moon's disc grew at a terrifying rate. Deceleration gravities pulled blood from men's nostrils. A whirlpool sucked consciousness downward.

Dust flew up from the Lunar land, driven by the rocket stormwind. *Galileo* inched through sudden night. Radar felt ahead, signaled altitude to the operator; but where he sat at the board on Earth, his knowledge was more than a second behind the truth.

Somehow he balanced the forces. A yard above ground, the satellite hung with zero velocity. A little fuel was left, but he cut the motors rather than tempt fate. A yard is not far to fall under Lunar gravity. Even so, *Galileo*'s weight crumpled the tail assembly like paper. But the shell did not topple, it did not topple.

Slowly the dust settled. The sun, near the horizon, flung long rays over a scored and barren plain. Three shapes, lashed to the wreck, stirred and called each other's names.

"Base to Yankee Gal. *Base to* Yankee Gal. *Come in. Do you read us? Are you all right? Come in, for mercy's sake!"*

"We . . . ugh . . . Bruno, Phil— Yes. We're pretty much okay. A couple of broken bones, I think, but no serious bleeding, so what the hell. You even put us down in the shadows of a crag."

"You're a bit southwest of the Riphaeans. One minute, please— Yes, they have an exact fix on you. A hopper has already left Camp Apollo. You'll be in the hospital inside three hours."

"Thanks for our lives, Dick. . . . 'As the shadow of a great rock in a weary land—' "

Wister let go the controls as if the skeleton had dissolved from him. He sagged back in his chair, hardly noticing those who crowded near and shouted.

Gail Jackman dropped the cloth with which she had mopped his face as he worked. It was drenched. She sank to the floor, hugged her knees, and burst into tears.

Huang pushed through the mob with a fifth of Scotch. Wister drank deep. A measure of strength returned. He got up, hunkered down, and patted Gail on the shoulder. "Why, everything's fine now." he whispered.

"I'm sorry," she gulped. "It was so— How did you do it? I'd heard there wasn't enough fuel to do it. I couldn't understand what you were trying, b-b-but there wasn't time to ask. . . . The way you sat there—somebody had to—"

Wister blinked. "Oh, that," he said tonelessly. There were

too mucking many people around. "Dumb luck. The big air tank. Mass nearly equal to the capsule plus men. That much expanding gas, heated by the sun, should be able to kill most of the satellite's orbital velocity. In a four-hour track around the Moon that's, uh, about eight-tenths mile per second. Which is over fifty percent of escape velocity, or thirty-five percent of the total speed it has to shed for a soft landing. With thirty-five percent of the work done almost free, there should be enough fuel to set down a twenty percent greater mass, even allowing for the extra maneuvers necessary. Shouldn't there be? Dumb luck."

He straightened and shuffled from the room, Huang clearing a path for him.

"Can I have a few days' rest?" he croaked when they were alone in the hall.

"Take a month if you want. I'll get somebody to drive you home now." Huang shivered. "I'm still too wrung out to do it myself."

Somebody had hung Wister's coat in his office. As he entered to get it, the phone rang on his desk. He laid the receiver to his ear. Florence's voice said, "Dick? I've been trying and trying to get hold of you. Did everything work out good?"

"Yes," he said.

"That's wonderful," she said politely. "Darling, I'm so sorry, but I didn't hear the alarm. You remember you left a note for me to get Jimmy off to school? Well, I slept right through the alarm and woke up feeling so terrible that—"

"Never mind," he said. "I'll be home in a little while."

Enough Rope

The scars of World War Two were not yet healed when I, in a story called "The Double-Dyed Villains," raised the question of whether armed forces—which science fiction was widely using in the form of various kinds of space patrols—really were a good answer to the problem of maintaining law and peace. Obviously, saintliness alone could do nothing about the causes of war, and pacifism merely opened the gates to violence and tyranny. Yet wasn't it possible to outwit rather than outfight evil? My notion drew considerable comment at the time. It invited speculation about different ways in which it might be put into practice. Here is one.

Hurulta, Arkazhik of Unzuvan, fitted his own personality. A magnificent specimen of Ulugani malehood, two and a half meters tall, so broad that he seemed shorter, he dwarfed the thin red-haired human before him. His robes were a barbaric shout of color, as if he were draped in fire and rainbows, and the volume of his speaking made the fine crystal ornaments in the audience chamber tremble and sing, ever so faintly. But the words were hard and steady and utterly cold.

"Our will in this matter is unshakable," he said curtly.

"If the League wants to go to war over it, that will be the League's misfortune."

Wing Alak of Sol III and the Galactic League Patrol looked up into the hairless blue face and ventured an urbane smile. The Ulugani were humanoid to several degrees of classification—six fingers to a hand, clawed feet, pointed ears, and the rest meant little when you dealt with the fantastic variety of intelligent life making up Alak's compatriots. This race looked primitive—small head, beetling eyebrow ridges, flat nose and prognathous jaw—but inside, they were as bright as any other known species.

Too bright!

"It would be straining the obvious, your excellency," said Alak, "to point out that the Unzuvan Empire comprises just one planetary system of which only Ulugan is habitable, whereas the Galactic League embraces a good million stars. It cannot have been omitted from all calculation. But I must say that, under these circumstances, I am puzzled; perhaps your excellency would condescend to enlighten me with regard to your attitude on this disparity."

Hurulta snorted, showing a formidable mouthful of teeth. During the years in which Alak, as chief representative of the League and its Patrol, had been visiting Ulugan—off and on—and particularly during the past several months of mounting crisis during which Alak had been here continuously, he had learned to regard the Solarian as a weak, wordy, and pedantic bumbler. Now one huge blue fist crashed into the palm of the other hand and he grinned contemptuously.

"Let us not bandy words," he said. "The nearest border of the League is almost a thousand light-years away, which would make your lines of communication ridiculously long if you tried to attack. Also, in spite of this distance, we have had our own agents in your territory for years. We know that the temper of the League population is . . . well, let us not say decadent, let us be kindly and say pacific. It would not react favorably to a war which could only mean expense and grief for it. Moreover, the Patrol is a minimal force, designed merely to keep order within the bounds of the League itself. Policemen! We have built up a *war* machine."

He shrugged massively. "Why go on?" he rumbled. "It is only our intention to claim the natural rights of Ulugan. You go your way, we will go ours; we do not wish to fight you, but neither do we feel bound to respect the morals of an altogether different civilization. You can, at best, only be a nuisance if you try to stop us; and if the nuisance becomes too great, we are not afraid of fighting a thousand-year war to exterminate it. We are a warrior race and you are not: there is the essential difference, and mere statistics will not change it."

He sat down behind his desk and fiddled absently with a jeweled dagger. His voice was remote, uninterested. "You may inform your government that Ulugan is already commencing the occupation of Tukatan and the other planets in its system. That is all. You may go."

To dismiss an ambassador thus was like a slap. Alak had to fight himself for an instant before self-control came. Then his gaunt sharp face smoothed itself out, and his tone was unctuous.

"As your excellency wishes, so be it. Good day."

He bowed and backed out of the magnificent room.

Scene: An upper office in the League Patrol Intelligence—Sol Sector—building, Britn, Terra. A sparsely furnished room, a few relaxers, a desk, the control-studded board of a robofile. One wall is transparent, opening on a serene landscape of rolling, wooded hills, a few private dwelling-units, the distant bulk of a food factory. Overhead, the sky is full of white clouds and sunshine, now and then the metal gleam of an airboat. It all seems incredibly remote from the troubled world of Galactic politics.

Characters: Myrn Kaltro, sector chief, a big gray-haired man in the iridescent undress uniform of a human Patrol officer. Jorel Meinz, sociotechnic director of the Solar System, small, dark, intense, conservatively dressed in gold and crimson. Wing Alak, unattached field agent, enough of a dandy to wear the latest fashion in civilian clothes—plain gray and blue. But then, he has been away from home for a good many years.

Background: In a civilization embracing nearly a million separate intelligent races, most of them with independent governments of their own, a civilization which is growing almost daily, it is impossible for even a well-informed administrator to keep track of all significant events. Jorel Meinz has hardly heard the name "Ulugan" before today; now he is being asked to authorize an action which may change Galactic history.

He fumbled out a cigar and inhaled it into lighting. His words were quick, jerky, harsh. "What has Sol to do with this? It's a matter for the entire League Council."

"Which won't meet for another two years," said Kaltro. "As our friend Hurulta well knows. It would take six months just to get a quorum together for an emergency session. Oh, they timed it well, those Ulugani."

"Well, the high command of the Patrol can exercise broad discretion," Meinz grimaced. "Too broad. I don't mind saying I haven't liked all reports of your activities which have come to me. However, in this case—"

"The high command is prepared to act," said Kaltro. "I've contacted all members. Nevertheless, the situation is unprecedented. The Patrol was created to enforce peace within the League. Nothing was said about dealing with a power outside it. If we act against Ulugan, we'll be on legally shaky ground, and there may be a day of reckoning which would do a lot of harm. Many local politicians are spoiling to take a crack at the Patrol, push through constitutional amendments limiting its scope—If they can persuade enough beings that the Patrol has become an irresponsible machine capable of starting wars on its own initiative, they may succeed."

"I see. But what can I do?"

"Your influence can swing the Solar Parliament into authorizing the Patrol to act against Ulugan. In effect, Sol will say: 'As far as we're concerned, the Patrol can have emergency powers, and use them immediately.' Thereafter, we'll proceed."

"But one system can't do that. The Patrol belongs to the whole League!"

"Please." Kaltro lifted shaggy gray brows and smiled, creasing his face as if it were a stiff brown fabric. "You're a practical political engineer. You know as well as I do that Sol is still the leading system in the League. If it'll back us, enough other planets will follow that lead to put us in the clear when the business is brought up at the next Council. Technically, it'll be a *post facto* O.K. on what we'll already have done, but that'll suffice. It'll have to!"

"Well—" Meinz rolled his cigar between bony fingers, scowling at it. "Well, all right, I see your point. But you still haven't seen mine. *Why* should I help you take action against Ulugan?"

He held up a hand. "No, wait, let me finish. As I understand it, Ulugan is a one-system empire lying nearly a thousand light-years outside our territorial bounds. It wants to incorporate one other system into itself. The natives of that system object, to be sure, and ask us for help—but the hard-boiled League Patrol is, I am certain, the last organization in the universe to get interested in noble crusades. The operation of crushing Ulugan would be enormously expensive. The logistic difficulties alone would make it a project of many years—even if it could succeed, which is by no means certain. The Ulugani could, and certainly would, retaliate with raids on our territory; perhaps they could penetrate to Sol itself. After all, interstellar space is so huge that any kind of blockade or defense line is utterly impossible. And you know what horror and destruction even a raid can bring, what with the power of modern weapons.

"The League is *not* a nation, empire, or alliance. It was formed to arbitrate interstellar disputes and prevent future wars. Such other services as it performs are relatively minor; and its systems are, politically and commercially, so loosely knit that it could never evolve into a true federal government. In short, it is totally unable to put forth the united effort of a war. If Ulugan is as determined as Agent Alak says, it may be able to bring the League to terms even if it is one planet against a million. The League may not feel the game is worth the candle, you see. And the resentment at having been involved in a war of which ninety per cent of its citizens would never have heard before death rained on them from the sky—that resentment could destroy the League itself!''

He put the cigar back to his mouth and blew a huge cloud of smoke. ''In short, gentlemen,'' he finished, ''if you want my support for this project of yours, you're going to have to give me a pretty good reason.''

Kaltro cocked an eye at Wing Alak. The field agent nodded slightly and took out a cigarette for himself. He waited till he had it going before he spoke:

''Let me recapitulate a little, director. Ulugan is a dense, metallic planet of a red dwarf sun. Terrestroid, which means a human can live there but not very comfortably—one-point-five Terran gravity, high air pressure, cold and stormy. The natives are a gifted species, but turbulent, not very polite or moral, all too ready to follow a leader blindly. Those are cultural rather than genetic traits, of course, but they've been pretty well drilled in by now. The history of Ulugan is one of mounting international wars, which pushed the technological development ahead fast but exhausted the natural resources of the planet. In short, a history not unlike ours prior to the Unification; but they never developed a true psychological technology, so their society still contains many archaisms.

''They invented the faster-than-light drive about two centuries ago and started exploring—and exploiting, quite ruthlessly—the nearer stars. They still had nations then, and quarreling over the spoils led to a slam-bang interstellar war. One nation, Unzuvan, finally conquered all the others and absorbed them into a racial empire. That was about thirty years back. It was shortly thereafter that a long-range exploration party from the League, off to study the starclouds near Galactic center, chanced on them. Naturally, even though they are remote from our integrated territory, they were invited to join us. All races of suitably high civilization are, and so far none had refused. They did. Quite rudely, too. Said they were perfectly capable of gaining everything we offered for themselves, and be damned if they'd give up any of their sovereignty.''

''Um-m-m. Paranoid culture, then,'' said Meinz.

''Obviously. Well, the League . . . or rather, its agent the Patrol . . . did what it could. Sent embassies, cultural missions, and so on, in the hope of gradually converting them. I've been more or less in charge for the past fifteen years, though of course I could only get out there once in a while. Too much else to do. We had no luck, anyway, except—'' Briefly, Alak grinned. ''Well, we do have an efficient intelligence service.''

''Spies, you mean?'' asked Meinz impatiently.

''No, never! What, *never*? Hardly ever!'' Alak's classical quotation was lost on Kaltro, who merely grunted, but Meinz smiled. ''We weren't too interested in the military-political details of Ulugan,'' went on the field agent cryptically. ''Mostly, we studied the neighboring stars. No one could object to scientific study of primitive planets, could they?

''I'll see that you get our complete dossier on Ulugani sociodynamics, but briefly, the setup is simple. There's a hereditary emperor and a military aristocracy ruling a subservient class of peasants and workers. The aristocracy is hand in glove with the big commercial interests—it's a sort of monopoly capitalism, partly controlled by the state and partly controlling the state. No, that's a poor way to phrase it. Let's say that the industrial trusts and the military caste together *are* the state. The supreme power is, for all practical purposes, lodged in the Arkazhik, a kind of combined premier and war minister. Right now he's one Hurulta, an able, aggressive, ambitious being with some colorful dreams of glory.

"Very well. Ulugan, under Hurulta, wants to start conquering itself an empire. Specifically, they intend to annex Tukatan, a fertile planet with a backward population. In fact, by now, in the time it's taken me to get here, they have begun doing so. But you know they aren't going to stop there."

"No," said Meinz after a pause. "No, I suppose not." Then, briskly: "But after all, what does it concern us? A thousand light-years away—"

"That thousand light-years is shrinking," said Kaltro. "The League territory is expanding, through exploration, colonization, the joining of new systems. The Ulugani empire will also expand, toward us. Our analysts estimate that in a mere two hundred years, there will be contact. You know that an interstellar civilization can't be big merely in space; it has to be big in time, too. We have to think ahead."

"Um-m-m—" Meinz rubbed his chin.

"My guess is that if we don't stop Ulugan now, we won't even have those two centuries," said Alak. "They're spoiling for trouble. A real war would unite their still new empire like nothing else."

Meinz nodded. "A good point. But *can* you stop them? To try and then fail would be—catastrophic."

"We can only try," said Kaltro gravely. "I won't hide from you that the situation is, well, precarious. But I don't see how we can afford not to try."

"Still . . . war—" Meinz twisted his mouth, as if it held a sour taste. "The ruination of planets. The killing of a billion innocent civilians to get at a few guilty leaders. The legacy of hatred. The corrosive effects of victory on the so-called victors. The Patrol has always existed to prevent war. If it instigated one—"

"Our intention," said Kaltro, "is to stop Ulugan without starting a war."

"How?"

"I can't tell you that. We have to have our secrets."

"And if you do provoke them into declaring one—?"

Alak shrugged. "That," he said, "is the chance we have to take."

"I warn you," said Meinz, "if you get us into real trouble, the Council will have your personal hides."

To that, neither of the Patrolmen replied.

Presently the administrator left. He took with him a bulky file of reports and sociodynamic calculations, and he gave no definite promises. But Kaltro nodded gravely at his agent. "He'll agree," he said.

"He'd better," said Alak. "I tell you, the situation is worse than I can describe. You have to be on such a planet and *feel* the hate and tension building up. Like . . . well . . . it feels sticky. You want to go wash yourself."

"Can you handle the operation?" asked Kaltro. "I'll have to stay behind to fend off outraged citizens."

"I can try," said Alak. There was a bleakness on his lips.

"And look, Wing," said Kaltro, "this is an unprecedented situation, I know. We're acting outside the League, and you might feel free, in real emergency, to violate the Prime Directive. Don't."

"I know," said Alak. "Any Patrolman who does—mnemonic erasure and cashiering from the service. No reasons or excuses accepted. It will be observed in this operation, too. Even if it costs us the war."

He left after a while, to begin on the mountain of paper work with is the essence of a large-scale mission. Not bureaucratic red tape, but necessary organization detail, and nothing glamorous about it. Nothing of jack-booted heroes, roaring warships, and flaming guns.

But then, the League Patrol had little to do with such matters anyway. They who would end war cannot resort to it themselves, or the injustice, butchery, and waste of it will provoke a hatred that must finally destroy them. The Patrol cultivated a wholly fictitious reputation as a terrible enemy. It cooked news releases about its battles and it maintained a number of impressive fighting ships. When sweet reasonableness failed to enforce the arbitration of the League, the Patrol used bluff; when that failed, it used bribery, blackmail, fomented revolution, any means that came to hand. But always and forever it held by the Prime Directive which was its own most closely watched secret.

Under no circumstances whatsoever may the Patrol or any unit thereof kill an intelligent being.

A thousand warships lanced through an interstellar night. In their van were the scouts, flanking them were the cruisers, riding magnificently at their center were the monstrous dreadnoughts each of which could annihilate all life on an ordinary-sized planet. They convoyed another thousand noncombatant vessels—transports, supply craft, flying workshops. Behind them lay the stars of the League, lost in a cold glory of constellations; before them were the swelling suns of the loose cluster holding Ulugan.

The task force found the particular star it was looking for, a yellow dwarf some ten light-years from Tumu—which is simply the Unzuvani word for ''sun''—and took up an orbit around the clouded second planet. Scouts dropping down through the atmosphere used infrared scopes to see through the mists and the hot, spilling rains; geosonic probes tested a thousand kilometers of swamp and jungle and sullen tideless ocean before reporting a stable surface. Then the big workships began landing.

Wing Alak stood in the phosphorescent twilight of the sixth day, looking at the labor that went on around him. Blasters had driven back the jungle, exposing a raw red scar. Now, under the white glare of floodlights, robotracs moved ponderously back and forth, laying the foundations of a landing field. He could not see through the dimness and the acrid mists to the prefab barracks which housed his workers.

The planet was humanly habitable—just barely. Alak's clothes hung wetly around him and he cursed in a tired voice and wished it weren't too humid for him to sweat. The ceaseless thin buzz of the sanitator about his neck, destroying airborne molds and bacteria that would otherwise soon have destroyed him, was in a fair way to driving him crazy. *And to think*, he reflected in one corner of his soggy brain, *I could have been a food factory technician at home.*

The scaly, tentacled Sarrushian Patrolmen who made up most of his gang sloshed happily through the muck. This hellhole was almost like their own planet. Not quite—there were some dangerous animals around, you could hear them stamping and roaring out in the fever-mists. And a weird sort of tree that shot poisoned thorns had killed two of his men already.

Won't those stupid Ulugani ever catch on?

It was no coincidence that the message should have come just then, for Alak had had few other thoughts since he first landed. The lean, beak-faced Karkarian who was his chief aide came from the communications shack and saluted, awkward in the space armor which was necessary for him here. His voder spoke tonelessly: "Subspace call, sir. From Tumu."

"Oh, good!" Alak felt too miserable to do more than nod, but he followed the tall metallic shape with a tinge of energy. It began to rain, and he was soaked before he reached the shack. Not a very dignified spectacle for the eyes of the Ulugani in the screen.

He sat down and ran a hand through his fiery hair. That face—yes, by the First Cause, it was General Sevulan of Hurulta's personal staff; he'd met him a few times. Mustering all his cheerfulness, he said: "Hello." That was an insult in itself.

"Are you in charge of this expedition?" snapped Sevulan.

"More or less," said Alak.

"I demand an immediate and official explanation," said the Ulugani. "A scout ship noticed radiations and investigated. You fired on it, though it got away—"

"Too bad," said Alak, though the fire had missed by his orders.

"That is an act of war in itself," rapped Sevulan.

"Not at all," said Alak. "This is a military reservation. Your scout probed in despite radioed orders to stop."

"But you are building a military base—on Garvish II!"

"That is correct. What of it?"

"Garvish is—"

"Unclaimed territory," said Alak coldly. "If Ulugan can take over Tukatan against the natives' will, the League can surely annex an uninhabited planet."

"You are within ten light-years of Tumu. My government must regard this as an unfriendly act."

"Well," said Alak, "your government hasn't been exactly friendly toward us, you know. We're just taking precautions."

"This is an ultimatum," said Sevulan. "If the subspace radio would reach so far, we would call the League secretariat directly, to give it. As it is, I am delivering it to you. If you do not evacuate Garvish at once, Ulugan will consider your aggression a cause for war."

"Now look—" began Alak.

"A task force is on its way to force your evacuation, if you will not go peacefully," said Sevulan. "Take your choice."

Weakness flitted across Alak's well-trained features. "I . . . I am really not given such responsibility," he said slowly. "You must allow me time to communicate with my government—"

"No!"

"Well—"

"You have my message," said Sevulan. The screen blanked.

Alak stood up, hugged his aide, and danced around the shack.

Hurulta the Arkazhik leaned over his desk as if he meant to attack Sevulan. Then, slowly, his great fists unclenched and he sat back.

"They were gone, you say?" he repeated.

"Yes, lord," said the general. "When our task force landed, the planet—the whole system—was abandoned. Obviously they took fright when they realized our determination."

"But *where* did they go?"

Sevulan permitted himself a shrug. "A light-year is too big to imagine," he said. "They could be anywhere, lord. My best guess is, though, that they are running home with their tails between their legs."

"Still—to abandon a base which must have cost an enormous effort and sum to start—"

"Yes, lord, it was astonishingly far advanced. They must have employed some life-form adapted to Garvish II conditions as workers. They do have that advantage: among their citizens, they can always find a species which is at home on any possible world." Sevulan smiled. "I suggest, lord, that we complete the base ourselves and use it, since they were obliging enough to do all the real labor."

Hurulta stroked his massive chin. "We have no choice," he said thinly. "If we don't hold that system, they may come back any time—and it is dangerously close to our home, and as you say their men can function better there than ours." He muttered an oath. "It's a nuisance. We need most of our forces to complete the conquest of Tukatan in a swift and orderly manner. But there's no help for it."

"We were going to take Garvish eventually, lord," said Sevulan respectfully.

"Yes, yes, of course. Take this whole cluster—and after that, who knows how much more? Still—" Being a realist, Hurulta dismissed his own annoyance. "As you say, this will save us time and money in the long run."

"I—"

Sevulan was interrupted by the buzzing of the official telescreen. Hurulta switched it on. "Yes?" he growled.

"General Ulanho of Central Intelligence reporting, lord."

"I know who you are. What is it?"

"Scout just came in, lord. The Patrol is on Shang V. Apparently they're building another base.'

"Shang V—"

"Twelve-point-three light-years from here, lord."

"I know that! Stand by." Hurulta switched off again. There was something of a giant dynamo about him as he swung on Sevulan.

"What sort of planet is this Shang V?" he snarled.

"Little known, lord," faltered the officer. "A big world, as I recall. Twice our gravity, mostly hydrogen atmosphere—storms of unparalleled violence, volcanic upheavals, a hell planet! I don't see how they would dare—"

"They must be relying on sheer audacity," snapped Hurulta. "Well, they won't get away with it! No ultimatum this time—no message of any kind. You will organize a task force to go there at once and blow them off it!"

The Arkazhik was in an ugly mood, and his subordinates tried to make themselves invisible as he stamped past them. But then, the whole planet was foul-tempered and jumpy. The Garvish and Shang operations had been—still were—messy and costly enterprises which completely disrupted the schedule for Tukatan. That the Patrol fleet had been gone when the Ulugani arrived at Shang, saving them a battle, was small consolation, for it meant that the enemy was still at large, he could strike anywhere, any time, bringing death and ruin out of the big spaces. That meant an elaborate warning system around Tumu, tying up hundreds of thousands of trained spacemen; it meant the inconveniences of civilian defense, force-screens over all cities, transportation slowed, space-raid drills, spy scares, nervousness among the commoners that was not far from exploding into hysteria. It meant that the unrewarding Shang System must also be garrisoned, lest the Patrol sneak back there. It meant irritation, delay, expense, and a turbulent cabinet meeting in which Hurulta had needed all his personality to control the dissatisfied members.

He took a grav-shaft now, dropping through many levels

to a corridor hewn out of the rock below the capitol. Along this he stalked, the boots of his guards slamming a hollow rhythm back from the walls, until he came to a certain door. This he entered, to find a colonel of Intelligence seated among his instruments. The colonel bowed low. The little being in the chair merely cowered.

"What planet is this from?" grunted Hurulta. "Nobody told me that."

The small one spoke up in a fluting voice that could not hide his terror. He was a skinny, four-armed, greenish being, with a bulging-eyed head that seemed too big for his body. "Please, lord, I am from—"

"I didn't ask you," barked Hurulta, snapping at him. The oversized head rocked back on the spindling neck, and the prisoner began to cry. "Well?"

"From Aldebaran VIII, lord," said the colonel. "A League planet. His name is Goln, and he is a trader who has operated in this sector for a number of years. We pulled him in, together with all other aliens, according to your orders, lord, two days ago. No physical duress was necessary—in panic, he submitted to the usual truth-finding procedures. It turned out that he is a Patrol agent."

"That much I have already been told," snorted Hurulta. "What of it? Why should that concern me? He hasn't learned anything of value, has he?"

"No, lord, not about us. He was a trader too, as he claimed. He merely reported to Wing Alak from time to time, telling him whatever he had learned anywhere. Under our questioning, he revealed a distinct impression that Alak is interested in Umung."

"Umung . . . hm-m-m . . . the insectiles, aren't they? About thirty light-years off, on the edge of our cluster."

"Yes, lord. He has traded with them for many years. They are a completely organized race, with little individual personality, but the collective intelligence is high. They are also, perhaps, the most skillful workers in the galaxy."

"Yes. It comes back to me now. Did Alak intend to organize them against us?"

"Not as far as this Goln knows, lord. They are totally unwarlike, have too little initiative to make good soldiers. Goln's impression is that the Patrol would like to deal with them, secretly, trading raw materials difficult to obtain on their world for finished products. That would, obviously, simplify the enemy supply problem."

"So . . . it . . . would." Hurulta stood in thought for a moment. Then, whirling on Goln, he made his voice a roar: "All right, scum, how well do you know Umung?"

The Aldebaranian shrieked in utter panic. When he found his voice again, he gasped: "Well, most excellent lord. I know it w-w-well—"

"You'll obey us and be rewarded, or you'll be pulled apart cell by cell. Which shall it be?"

"I . . . obey, my lord. The ps-s-s-sychomachines w-will show how well I m-mean to obey—"

"Good. I want you to prepare a dossier on Umung. Use the machines to help you remember everything. Correlate it with all information available in Intelligence files. Submit the complete report to me within an eight-day."

"I . . . I will try, l-lord—"

Hurulta turned back toward the door. No one dared speak to him as he went down the corridor, but his mind was busy.

Umung—yes. It had real possibilities. From all he had heard of it, Umung was a treasure chest. He had to prevent Alak's using it, of course—

But the Patrol! As long as they were in this vicinity, he could not declare war on the League. That might be just the excuse they wanted. He'd fight them if he caught them, but until then it was safer to wait, consolidate his victories.

But it wouldn't take much to occupy Umung. Not if its natives were as docile as all reports had it. And then he could show some real progress to those fat money barons. Already the war would have begun to pay off, and they'd support him in further schemes, let him build up his own power and prestige until the day he turned on them and broke them.

Umung, yes. By all the hells, yes!

Imagine a creature somewhat like an ant—only in general outline, to be sure. It stands a meter tall on two horny legs whose cilia, rubbed together, are its voice organs. There is one pair of tentacles, ending in supple boneless fingers; above them are the true arms, and there is a small stalk on the wrist of each arm holding an eye with microscopic vision. The head is faceless, little more than a set of jaws and a pair of larger eye-stalks for normal seeing. The creature is utterly obedient to the mass-mind of its hivelike community, a patient, tireless, delicate worker. Apart from food and reproduction, its only need is work. Once you have persuaded the mass-mind—embodied in the queen—that it is to its advantage to do as you say, a hundred thousand little brown artisans are ready to slave to the death for you.

Umung is not a large planet. Its atmosphere is thin and dry, its landscape mostly dreary plains. The Ulugani soldiers stationed there grumbled about its dullness. But not many were needed, and soldiers have always complained; it is a healthy sign.

Technicians were required in large numbers, to educate the Umungi in the use of machine tools. But the hive dwellers learned fast. Goln of Aldebaran was invaluable, he knew the ins and outs of native ways. Before long, a good part of the entire planet was ready to start producing for Ulugan.

It produced!

"All right, colonel, don't just stand there! Give me your report."

"If it please you, lord, my scout squadron was investigating the Junnuzhik System as per orders—"

"I know! We have to watch every planet of this cluster now, we never know where the Patrol may sneak in next—

Well, what is it? Don't tell me they're trying to build another base!''

''No, lord. Our intelligence unit captured some leading natives of Ilwar for questioning—''

''Ilwar! What do you mean? I can't remember every stinking native name for every worthless little area of a thousand inhabited planets.''

''The world is Junnuzhik III, lord, the only inhabited one in the system. The natives are centauroids—big scaly fellows, beaked heads, crests—Oh, yes, I see that my lord remembers now. Well, Ilwar is the leading nation on the planet. They've attained a petroleum technology, are pretty good metallurgists, and so on. Under pressure, it was found out that the Patrol has been dickering with them. Wants them to supply several million troops, presumably for an invasion of our planet.''

''Patrol have any luck?''

''Well, lord, the natives are thoroughly anti-Ulugan. They assume that if we aren't stopped, we'll conquer them.''

''True enough. But . . . oh, blast and damn! We'll just have to take over the planet.''

''They're tough warriors, lord.''

''I know. And occupying a whole planet is a major operation. But we can't simply sterilize; we'll need it ourselves in the long run. And we must take over the entire world now, colonel. At the very least, we must garrison thousands of key points, or the Patrol ships can simply sneak in and pick up their recruits. At this time, too!''

''Lord—''

''Shut up! File a complete report. Now get out of here. Hello, hello, give me the General Staff building . . . Commander Tuac? Ready your planners, boy. We're going to invade still another world.''

''Tuac? Listen and obey.''

''Yes, lord.''

''You know the planet Yarnaz IV?''

"Hm-m-m . . . let me think, lord."

"Don't. You're not capable of it—you and your planning section!"

"Lord, how could we know the Ilwari would be such guerrilla fighters? Even under extreme difficulties, we're carrying on the conquest—it's just going more slowly than we had anticipated. If we could only have more troops, more supplies—"

"Shut up, I said! We haven't even finished with Tukatan itself, thanks to that Patrol. Junnuzhik will have to make do with what we can spare. Now listen, or I'll have your head. Yarnaz is a red dwarf sun about fifteen light-years from Tumu. Its fourth planet is trackless desert, poisonous air, venomous life. Nevertheless, our checkup reveals that the Patrol has been there. Not a base. They've been mining near the equator. *Why?*"

"Lord, I can't say. Unless they wanted supplies—fissionables, perhaps—"

"I checked up on that, idiot. Yarnaz IV is about as poor in natural resources as empty space itself."

"Could it be a camouflage, lord? A device to divert our attention from their real activities?"

"It may well be. But, we don't *know*! The Patrol seems to have studied the primitive planets of our cluster better than we have ourselves. Furthermore, they have the natives of a million worlds to choose from in making up their crews. Doubtless there is at least one race in the League to whom Yarnaz IV is just like home. We can't know where their real advantage lies."

"Well, lord, it . . . it looks as if we'll have to establish garrisons there."

"I'm glad you've seen that much. How soon can you send a force?"

"The planning—Lord, we're getting bogged down. There's just too much to handle. Even one world is a major problem in strategy, tactics, logistics—"

"Nevertheless, Yarnaz IV shall be occupied within one

month. Or do you want your head adorning a pole in Market Square?"

Fear was cold along the spine of Hurulta as he looked at the being in the cage.

It seemed harmless enough—a small kangaroolike mammal, with big ears on its round, blunt-muzzled head. The sensitive four-fingered hands spoke of intelligence, the basic tool-making ability. There was no menace in the soft brown eyes.

Nevertheless Hurulta was afraid. It took all the discipline he had to face that creature and hold his own visage expressionless.

"It was caught on the fringes of Dengavash City, lord, just after the riots there," said the police officer. "Obviously it was the thing responsible. It creates an aura of terror."

Hurulta forced his tongue to shape coherent words. "Where's it from?"

"We checked up, lord. It's from Gyreion, as the explorers have named it—a planet not unlike ours, on the fringes of our cluster. This is one of the natives. They haven't been studied much, but seem to be a timid paleolithic race. Telepaths, though."

"I . . . see. And when they're frightened, as must happen rather easily, they radiate the fear-impulse and our minds pick it up."

"Yes, lord. We think a Patrol sneak-boat must have taken a few and dropped them here on Ulugan. We'll soon round up the others and we'll be sure."

"Um-m-m." Hurulta's heavy blue face contracted in a scowl. It was hard to think clearly, when he had to keep fighting down the germ of panic that screamed far down within him. "Yes. A good idea. But quantitatively insufficient. The Patrol can't possibly smuggle enough of them here to make any significant trouble."

"No, lord. Just nuisance value. Like everything they've done so far, isn't it . . . if I may make bold to speak."

Hurulta turned and walked out of the room. Gyreion—hm-m-m. A tough nut to crack, that world—but worthwhile. If enough of those hoppers could be turned loose on an enemy planet—why, it was the ultimate in psychological warfare!

The League planets—a decadent bunch. They couldn't stand up long to such fear. They'd be ready to surrender to the first warship that came along.

Meanwhile, it was necessary to cut off the Patrol's access to Gyreion. Wouldn't take too big a force for an effective occupation; the natives weren't fighters. Once their fears had been calmed, they would be quite harmless—to Ulugan.

This time, my friend, he thought with a savage glee, *this time you've finally overreached yourself!*

Wing Alak was getting bored. He didn't have much to do now but sit in his flagship and read the reports of his scouts and radio monitors. He welcomed the newcomer who had arrived with the last courier ship from home, even if it did mean a struggle.

Jorel Meinz entered the vessel and followed Alak down a long corridor. His nose wrinkled a bit at the many odors that filled it. The crew of the battlewagon all came from terrestroid planets, but they had their characteristic smells and their own styles of cooking; no ventilation system could quite purify the air. But then, he reminded himself, a Terran probably didn't smell any better to them.

Alak's cabin was a spacious one, sybaritically furnished. One large view-port showed the eerie hugeness of space, the rest of the room seemed devoted to human comfort just to offset that chilling spectacle. The Patrolman waited till he was alone with his guest before pouring out drinks.

"Scotch," he said. "It may not mean much to you, but out here it's a real luxury."

"The Patrol seems to do itself well," observed Meinz.

"Quite," nodded Alak. "When you're out for months or years at a time, surrounded by total alienness, every comfort means a lot. It's pure superstition that the being with a low standard of living is hardier." He lifted his glass and sipped appreciatively.

"Are you sure you won't be found out here?" asked Meinz. "I imagine the enemy is ripping holes in space, hunting for you."

Alak grinned, which made him more than ever resemble a fox. "No doubt they are," he said. "The harder they search, the better I like it, since it means a useless waste of their time, men, and matériel. Several thousand cubic light-years makes a pretty effective concealment. Anyway, if by some freak they should blunder across us, we need only run for it."

Meinz scowled. "That's what I'm here about," he said brusquely.

"Aren't they satisfied at home with my conduct of the operation?"

"Frankly, no. Now I'm on your side, Alak. I was the one who pushed that approval through Parliament. But that was almost a year ago, and so far you've reported no results at all. Your dispatches have been so much meaningless verbiage. Finally certain political groups hired an investigating force of their own. They sent out observers—"

"A wonder they weren't nabbed. Hurulta has an efficient intelligence service and secret police."

"Well, they weren't. They saw enough to send them hightailing back home, and the stink it's raised on Terra—"

"Ah-hah! That explains it. Hurulta must have foreseen that result and let the observers do as they pleased. He's a canny lad, that old blueface."

"Well, you must admit there's some justification for the complaints," said Meinz with a hint of bitterness. "The authorization was of doubtful legality in the first place, and could only be justified at the next Council meeting if there were solid results to show. Instead, you've dawdled out here, skulking I might say. You haven't fought one battle, not so much as a skirmish. You've let Ulugan occupy no less than seven planets besides Tukatan—"

"At last reports, it was about twenty," said Alak blandly. "We've got them scared, you see. They're grabbing everything that might conceivably be of value to us."

"In other words," said Meinz, "you're pushing them in exactly the direction they want to go."

"Correct."

"Now look, Alak. I came out here myself, and it's a long troublesome journey, to get your side of it. I have to tell them something at home, or they'll pass a recall order in spite of everything I can do. Now I'm not even sure if I would resist such a move."

"Give me credit for some sense," urged Alak. "I can't tell you everything. The real reason why we operate this way is a Patrol secret. Let's just say, which is true enough, that outright war is cruel and expensive, and that I don't even think we could win one."

"But what *are* you doing then, man?"

"Just sitting here," laughed Alak. "Sitting here drinking Scotch, and letting nature take its course."

The medical officer halted at the entrance to the tent. The steady, endless rain dripped off his shoulders and made a puddle about his muddy feet. By the one glaring lamp inside, he noticed that the fungus had begun to devour this tent, too. It would be a rag before the eight-day was out. And you couldn't live in the metal barracks left by the Patrolmen—they were bake-ovens, and air-conditioning units rotted and rusted too fast to be of help.

He saluted wearily. The commandant of Garvish Base looked up from his game of galanzu solitaire. "What is it?" he asked listlessly.

"Fifteen more men down with fever, sir," said the medical officer. "And ten of the earlier cases are dead."

The command nodded. Light gleamed off his wet bald head. The blue face was haggard, unhealthily flushed, and the smart uniform was a sodden ruin. "The sanitators don't work, eh?" he asked.

"Not against this stuff, sir," said the doctor. "It seems to be a virus which isn't bothered by the vibrations, but I haven't been able to isolate it yet."

"We just aren't built for this climate." The commandant wagged his head, and one shaky hand reached for a bottle. "We're cold-world dwellers."

A beast screamed out in the jungle.

"Poison plants got several more this eight-day," said the doctor.

"I know. I've begged and pleaded with headquarters to send us air domes and space armor. But they claim it's needed elsewhere."

A faint hope flickered in the medical officer's eyes. "When that planet Umung really gets to producing—"

"Yes, yes. But we'll probably be dead then, you and I." The commandant shivered. "I feel cold." His voice was suddenly high and thin.

"Sir—" The doctor took a nervous step forward. "Sir, let me look at you—"

The commandant stood up. For a moment he leaned on the table, then something buckled within him and he went toppling to the floor.

There was forest, endless forest, and beyond it the plains and mountains and sea, and all of it was full of death.

The Ulugani patrol wound slowly through the woods. Every detector they had was straining itself—metal, mental pulses, the thermal radiation of living bodies. But still eyes were restless, shifting under the big square helmets, and hands strayed nervously toward guns.

In an armored car near the middle of the column, the Ulugani chief was sounding off to his aide. "It's no good," he said. "These Ilwari are just too tough for us."

"They can't stand up to us, sir," said the aide. "Not in open battle."

"And they don't try. What can you do with a people who're willing to scorch their earth and evacuate their own dwellings before we get there? What's the point of silly little actions like this one—going out, burning a city in reprisal, what does the enemy care? It's just a chance for him to harass us some more."

"We'll teach them manners, sir," said the aide.

"Oh, in time, of course. In time. When we get enough troops and supplies here. But curse it, I can't *get* enough!"

An explosion cracked before them. The chief saw three men fall screaming from the grenade. A heavy machine gun began to clatter.

"Guerrillas!" he roared.

He glimpsed the big green forms dashing in out of the brush. They could gallop like the wind, those devils, and they could carry as much armament on their backs as a small truck. The war whoop sent a brief tingle of fear along his nerves.

The tanks began to speak, throwing flame and thunder at the enemy. One of the machines was suddenly wrapped in red smoke—a fire bomb. The Ulugani infantry had thrown themselves to the ground and were shooting up at the trampling, yelling centauroids.

"Drive 'em back!" screamed the chief. "Drive 'em back!"

The patrol did, after a short interval of utter ferocity. But not before a bomb had struck the command car and incinerated its contents.

The colonel looked out of the thick plastic port and shivered. Beyond it, the landscape was one vast gloom. Poisonous mists curled between him and the unseen horizon, like a wall. He thought he could see the sudden red spouting of a volcano, somewhere in the fog. A moment later, the floor quivered under his feet.

"You fool!" he raged. "You utter imbecile!"

The base geologist stood his ground. "We did our best, sir," he answered. "As far as we could tell, the terrain here was stable."

"One whole base has already been destroyed in a quake. Isn't that enough for you?"

The wind slapped monstrously at the dome. They had never seen such gales as blew endlessly across Shang V. A blind whirl of sleet—solid ammonia—hid the outside view.

"Sir," said the geologist, "this planet is utterly crazy. The probes gave readings that on any normal world would mean safe, solid ground."

"Nevertheless, one of our domes has just been cracked open. Every man within it died instantly. You and your team are due for court-martial."

The geologist nodded.

"As the colonel says. But may I suggest that we find another site? This one is obviously dangerous after all."

"And do you realize what it means, in terms of effort and materials, to break camp on this planet?"

"I can't help that, sir. I am officially proposing that we move."

"Headquarters will have my skin, too," said the colonel gloomily. He looked out again at the sinister land. "How could we know? How could anyone have foretold it would be like this?"

The Patrol knew! laughed his mind. *They knew! Now all I can do is submit a recommendation that we evacuate. The other commanders here will back me up. But that's an invitation to the enemy to return.*

The floor trembled. He heard a paperweight jump on his desk. Outside, not five meters off, a hole opened in the ground—slowly, hugely, with all the time in the universe to do its work. Fire spumed from it, and magma crawled forth toward the dome.

The Elgash family had come up the hard way, from the peasant stock of a conquered land; it had been ennobled only fifty years ago. For that, and for its owning the Munitions Trust, Hurulta despised it. But he did not underestimate the being who sat across from his desk. The present Elgash was fat and wheezy and dandified, but there was a hard drive and a cold brain in him.

"I speak for several others, your excellency," he said. "I need not mention their names."

"The money barons," replied Hurulta sullenly. "The industrialists and financiers. What of it?"

"Shall I speak plainly?" asked Elgash.

"Go ahead. We're alone."

"The group I represent is not at all satisfied with the conduct of the war."

"Oh? And you have constituted yourselves the new General Staff?"

"Spare the sarcasm, your excellency. It was understood that Tukatan would be subjugated within six months. Now, after almost a year, we are still fighting there."

"They could be bombarded from space," said Hurulta, "but as you well know, that would destroy the whole value of the planet. We have to go slowly. Then the Patrol appeared to complicate matters."

"I realize all that." The insolence was more marked than ever. "And rather than concentrate on Tukatan and the Patrol, and get them safely out of the way, your ministry has tried to take on the whole star cluster. You have blundered disastrously into planets we hardly knew a thing about."

"To keep the Patrol from using them against us." Hurulta checked his temper. "All right, I admit we've had our troubles. But we're making progress. The overall timetable for the establishment of our hegemony has been accelerated enormously. In the long run, that will mean a saving."

"Will it now? Even your successes are dubious. Take that forsaken little pill of sand, Yarnaz IV. There's been no trouble in occupying it. But the expense of maintaining bases under such alien conditions is fantastic. The commoners are being taxed to the limit, and your new tax on the leading groups of society is outrageous."

"It has to be done. Or would you rather have the Patrol come in and run things?"

"Of course," said Elgash coldly, "your most inexcusable blunder was the occupation of Umung."

"What?" For a moment Hurulta could find no words. Slowly, then, he gulped down his rage, and when he spoke it was with thin precision. "That was the one operation which went off like clockwork. At a negligible cost in men and money, we have already doubled our war production. Inside another year, we can expect to quadruple it."

"I thought you were a realist, your excellency," said Elgash. "I thought you understood the economic foundation on which the empire rests. Or are you deliberately ruining my class?"

"Are you mad? First you complain about taxes, then when I find a way to increase production, a way that costs us hardly one crown, you—"

"Your excellency, we have only so many soldiers and there is a limit to the amount of war matériel they can use. When Umung is producing all of it, *what will become of Ulugan's factories*?"

Fear.

Shamuvaz, soldier of the empire, looked around him. He moved his head very slowly, lest he see something behind his back. There was only the landscape—distorted trees, murmuring reddish grass, a remote waterfall that echoed the furious clamor of his heart.

He felt ill. He wanted to vomit. Looking at the faces of his companions, he thought that they were impossibly alien. They were evil. They were made evil by the same horror that rode on him, and in their panic they might turn and tear him.

Shamuvaz whimpered, deep in his throat, and thought of his wife and children. They were so far away, so many centuries away, he would never see them again. He would rot on Gyreion, the wind would blow through his ribs and the small beasts of the field would nest in his empty, empty skull.

They said it was harmless. They said it was only that the natives—so thoroughly indoctrinated by the Patrol that there was no dealing with them . . . or was it that, being telepaths, they knew Ulugan meant them for pawns?—the natives were afraid, and you yourself heard their fear. Nothing to it. Ignore it. You are a soldier of the empire, and fear of nothingness is unworthy of you.

Only the generals didn't have to live with fear. They didn't have to torment themselves, night after night, to stay awake, for fear of the dreams; and when they finally did sleep, in spite of everything, they weren't brought up within minutes, screaming. They didn't see their comrades break, one by one, and be sent home muttering idiot words, and wonder when their turn would come.

Fear, panic, terror, blind howling horror. Shamuvaz groaned to himself.

When a hand touched his shoulder, he leaped up, cursing, and spun around. His pistol was out before he saw that it was only Armazan. Armazan had been his best friend once. But you couldn't trust anyone now. Shamuvaz held the gun leveled on Armazan's belly.

"Don't do that," he choked. "Don't ever do that again."

"Listen." Armazan spoke swiftly, a whisper that was blurred with his own trembling. "Listen, Sham, we're meeting after taps, down by the river. Sneak out of the barracks and join us."

"What, what, what? Go out after dark? You're crazy! This planet has driven you crazy."

"No, not that, not that. Listen, a lot of us have decided we aren't going to take any more of this. The empire can't ask it of us. It's too much. Can't trust those officers. Get them out of the way—a shot in the back, it's easy if we just stick together, and then we can grab the base spaceship—"

Hurulta had been sleeping poorly in the last month, and drugs no longer seemed to whip up his vitality. He clasped a ringing head in his hands and leaned on the desk.

"It's no use," he said aloud. "We'll have to pull out of

Gyreion. Every regiment there has been ruined for service. It'll take months to restore them to usefulness."

"But the Patrol, lord—" faltered Sevulan.

"Patrol! We'll maintain a base on the neighboring planet, and a few orbital scouts around Gyreion itself. Should have done that in the first place."

"But then a strong attack could come in, wipe out our forces, take over the whole system—"

"I know. What of it? A chance we'll have to take. If only the busybodies would come out of hiding and fight! It's like shadowboxing, this."

"Lord, I understand the General Staff plans to overrule you and order the evacuation of Garvish and Shang. They say it's too costly to hold them, they're just consuming men badly needed elsewhere—"

"Don't tell me that!" shouted Hurulta. "I know it, you idiot! I know all of it! The blind, bloody fools! Short-sighted—aaargh!" His fists clamped together. "But by all the hells, we're hanging on to Umung. Let the moneybags squawk. I'll lodge treason charges if they say much more."

The telescreen buzzed. Hurulta flicked a switch, and the excited voice gabbled out.

"Lord, a report just came in from space. Patrol activity around Ustuban VII. They seem to be rendezvousing—"

"Ustuban VII! They can't! It's a giant planet. It's surrounded by a meteor belt. It . . . no!"

"Lord, the report says—"

"*Shut up!* Send me the full report at once." Hurulta whirled on the general. His eyes were feverish.

"Action," he gasped. "I think we're going to see some action. The populace has been complaining about our retreats, have they? Their morale is bad, is it? All right, we'll give them something to talk about. We'll send the fleet and seize Ustuban VII, and just let the Patrol dare try to stop us!"

"Lord, it's impossible," whispered Sevulan. "We're

spread so thin already that we could never mount such an undertaking. It's just a trick of theirs to lure us out—"

"We'll turn the trick on them!" Hurulta's bellow rattled between the walls. "I'm still the supreme commander here!"

Slowly, as he regarded his chief, Sevulan's eyes narrowed.

"We have, of course, been propagandizing Ulugan," said Wing Alak. "Radio, message-scattering robombs, and so on—the usual techniques. I think we've gotten it across to them that, while League membership means a loss of imperial glories, it means a definite gain in material comfort and security."

"For the commoners," said Jorel Meinz. He was annoyed; three days aboard ship, with Alak engaged in directing some obscure maneuver and parrying every significant question when the two men did meet, had worn down his nerves. "But it's the aristocrats and the industrialists who run things."

"To be sure. However, they aren't stupid. They just need a hard lesson to convince them that imperialism doesn't pay."

"They were all set to make it pay."

"Of course, till we interfered. But as long as there is a Patrol, conquest will mean a money loss. We'll see to that! Once they're convinced that it's to their advantage too to come to terms with us, they'll do it."

"I see your general strategy, of course," said Meinz. "You've led them into taking over one unprofitable planet after another. Except this Umung, now . . . I can't see where that could fail to pay off."

"Oh, that was my proudest achievement," said Alak smugly. "I planned that years in advance. I had a cowardly little part-time agent who got to know Umung quite well. As far as he could tell, I meant to use it for the Patrol's benefit. Ulugan got hold of him, as I thought they would, and learned this. So naturally Ulugan had to grab it first.

"But don't you see, I've studied their economy for years. It's an archaic form of capitalism, like Terra's during the First Industrial Revolution. It depends on buying cheap and selling dear—and it must sell manufactured goods. In short, a colony which can manufacture better and cheaper than the mother country is, in the long run, impossible; it must be abandoned or ruined, or else the homeland's economic system must be changed. After a while, Ulugan's financiers realized that. And they're a powerful element."

He lit a cigarette and leaned back in his chair. "If I might generalize a bit," he said, "history shows pretty conclusively that an empire must form a natural socioeconomic unit if it is to be stable. Most empires of the past grew slowly, by accretion; or if they were conquered fast, they had to be reorganized swiftly. We forced the Ulugani into taking on more real estate than they could handle, most of it worse than useless; and we kept them off balance so that they couldn't get a chance to organize it properly. Result—an unstable situation which is now rapidly deteriorating."

"Do we *want* them with the League?" asked Meinz. "They look like a nest of troublemakers."

"They are. But in the long run, they can be integrated. Contact with other cultures will break down their paranoid attitude. Interstellar empires are economically unjustifiable anyway, more of a drain than a gain. If you've mastered faster-than-light travel, you are also able to produce just about everything you need at home, and trade for the rest. They'll come to see that too, eventually."

He glanced at the intercom. "I'm expecting a message hourly," he said. "My last scout ship brought some interesting political news from Ulugan."

"Eh?"

"Play me some chess, will you? I love dramatic revelations. You can allow me this one. It's been a rather dreary year."

It was only half an hour later that the ship's radioman announced a subspace broadcast, Ulugan calling the Patrol command. Alak made a leisurely way to the communications room, letting Meinz jitter behind him.

The blue face in the screen was trying hard to maintain its

old arrogance, but not succeeding very well. "Hello, Sevulan," said Alak. "What's new?"

"There has been a change of government in the empire," said the Ulugani stiffly.

"Violent, I'm sure. Did you shoot Hurulta or just jail him?"

"The Arkazhik is—very ill. Frankly, we suspected he was a mental case. His rashness brought on many actions of which the new cabinet never did approve."

"Well," said Alak genially, "if you want to negotiate, here are my terms."

When he had finished, and sent a representative off to meet the Ulugani delegation, he yawned mightily. "I think that's that," he said. "There'll be a lot of dickering, of course, and cleaning up the military forces there will take time. But we've got what we were after."

"You mean—" Meinz chuckled dryly. This success wasn't going to hurt his own career a bit. "You mean you let them give you what you wanted."

"Oh, no," said Wing Alak. "I was the donor all along. I gave Hurulta all the rope he needed."

The Live Coward

And here is another example of Wing Alak at his Machiavellian work. I could have written more stories in the series, but three were plenty. It was time to go on to something new.

The fugitive ship was pursued for ten light-years. Then, snapping in and out of subspace drive with a reckless disregard of nearby suns and tracer-blocking dust clouds, it shook the Patrol cruiser.

The search that followed was not so frantic as the danger might seem to warrant. Haste would have done no good; there are a million planetary systems affiliated with the League, and their territory includes several million more too backward for membership. Even a small planet is such a wilderness of mountains, valleys, plains, forests, oceans, icefields, cities, and loneliness—much of it often quite unexplored—that it was hopeless to ransack them meter by meter for a single man. The Patrol knew that Varris' boat had a range of three hundred parsecs, and in the course of months and man-years of investigation it was pretty well established that he had not refueled at any registered depot. But a sphere two thousand light-years across can hold a lot of stars.

The Patrol offered a substantial reward for information

leading to the arrest of Samel Varris, human, from the planet Caldon (Number so-and-so in the Pilots' Manual), wanted for the crime of inciting to war. It circulated its appeal as widely as possible. It warned all agents to keep an eye or a feeler or a telepathic organ out for a man potentially still capable of exploding a billion living entities into radioactive gas. Then it waited.

A year went by.

Captain Jakor Thymal of the trading ship *Ganash*, operating out of Sireen in the primitive Spiral Cluster area, brought the news. He had seen Varris, even spoken to the fellow. There was no doubt of it. Only one hitch: Varris had taken refuge with the king of Thunsba, a barbarous state in the southern hemisphere of a world known to the Galactics—such few as had ever heard of it—as Ryfin's Planet. He had gotten citizenship and taken the oath of service as a royal guardsman. Loyalty between master and man was a powerful element in Thunsban morality. The king would not give up Varris without a fight.

Of course, axes and arrows were of small use against flamers. Perhaps Varris could not be taken alive, but the Patrol could kill him without whiffing very many Thunsbans. Captain Thymal settled complacently back to wait for official confirmation of his report and the blood money. Nothing ever occurred to him but that the elimination of Varris would be the simplest of routine operations.

Like hell!

Wing Alak eased his flitter close to the planet. It hung in cloudy splendor against a curtain of hard, needle-sharp spatial stars, the Cluster sky. He sat gloomily listening to the click and mutter of instruments as Drogs checked surface conditions.

"Quite terrestroid," said the Galmathian. His antennae lifted in puzzlement above the round, snouted face and the small black eyes. "Why did you bother testing? It's listed in the Manual."

"I have a nasty suspicious mind," said Alak. "Also an unhappy one." He was a thin, medium-tall human with the very white skin that often goes with flaming red hair. His Patrol uniform was as dandified as regulations allowed.

Drogs hitched three meters of green, eight-legged body across the cabin. His burly arms reached out to pick up the maps in three-fingered hands. "Yes . . . here's the Thunsba kingdom and the capital city . . . what's it called? . . . Wainabog. I suppose our quarry is still there; Thymal swore he didn't alarm him." He sighed. "Now I have to spend an hour at the telescope and identify which place is what. And you can sit like my wife on an egg thinking beautiful thoughts!"

"The only beautiful concept I have right now is that all of a sudden the Prime Directive was repealed."

"No chance of that, I'm afraid . . . not till a less bloodthirsty race than yours gets the leadership of the League."

"Less? You mean more, don't you? 'Under no circumstances whatsoever may the Patrol or any unit thereof kill any intelligent being.' If you do—" Alak made a rather horrible gesture. "Is that bloodthirsty?"

"Quite. Only a race with as gory a past as the Terrans would go to such extremes of reaction. And only as naturally ferocious a species could think of making such a commandment the Patrol's great top secret . . . and bluffing with threats of planetwide slaughter, or using any kind of chicanery to achieve its ends. Now a Galmathian will run down a farstak in his native woods and jump on its back and make a nice lunch while it's still running . . . but he wouldn't be able to imagine cold-bloodedly sterilizing an entire world, so he doesn't have to ban himself from honest killing even in self-defense." Drogs' caterpillar body hunched itself over the telescope.

"Get thee behind me, Satan . . . and don't push!" Alak returned murkily to his thoughts. His brain was hypnotically stuffed with all the information three generations of traders had gathered about Thunsba. None of it looked hopeful.

The king was—well, if not an absolute monarch, pretty

close to being one, simply because the law had set him over the commons. Like many warlike barbarians, the Thunsbans had a quasi-religious reverence for the letter of the law, if not always for its spirit. The Patrol had run head-on into two items of the code: (a) the king would not yield up a loyal guardsman to an enemy, but would fight to the death instead; (b) if the king fought, so would the whole male population, unmoved by threats to themselves or their mates and cubs. Death before dishonor! Their religion, which they seemed quite fervent about, promised a roisterous heaven to all who fell in a good cause, and a suitably gruesome hell for oath-breakers.

Hm-m-m . . . there was a powerful ecclesiastical organization, and piety had not stopped a good deal of conflict between church and throne. Maybe he could work through the priesthood somehow.

The outworld traders who came to swap various manufactured articles for the furs and spices of Ryfin's Planet had not influenced the local cultures much. Perhaps they had inspired a few wars and heresies, but on the whole the autochthons were content to live in the ways of their fathers. The main effect of trading had been a loss of superstitious awe—the strangers were mighty, but they were known to be mortal. Alak doubted that even the whole Patrol fleet could bullyrag them into yielding on so touchy a point as Varris' surrender.

"What I can't understand," said Drogs, "is why we don't just swoop down and give the city a blanket of sleep-gas." This mission had been ordered in such tearing haste that he had been given only the most nominal briefing; and on the way here, he had followed his racial practice of somnolence—his body could actually "store" many days' worth of sleep.

His free hand gestured around the flitter. It was not a large boat, but it was well equipped, not only with weapons—for bluffing—but with its own machine shop and laboratory.

"Metabolic difference," said Alak. "Every anaesthetic

known to us is poisonous to them, and their own knockout chemicals would kill Varris. Stun beams are just as bad—supersonics will scramble a Ryfinnian's brain like an egg. I imagine Varris picked this world for a bolthole just on that account."

"But he didn't know we wouldn't simply come down and shoot up the den."

"He could make a pretty shrewd guess. It's a secret that we never kill, but no secret that we're reluctant to hurt innocent bystanders." Alak scowled. "There are still a hundred million people on Caldon who'd rise—bloodily—against the new government if he came back to them. Whether he succeeded or not, it'd be a genocidal affair and a big loss of face to the Patrol."

"Hm-m-m . . . he can't get far from this world without more fuel; his tanks must be nearly dry. So why don't we blockade this planet and make sure he never has a chance to buy fuel?"

"Blockades aren't that reliable," said Alak. Drogs had never been involved in naval operations, only in surface work. "We could destroy his own boat easily enough, but word that he's alive is bound to leak back to Caldon now. There'd be attempt after attempt to run the blockade and get him out. Sooner or later, one would succeed. We're badly handicapped by not being allowed to shoot to hit. No, damn it, we've got to lift him, and fast!"

His eyes traveled wistfully to the biochemical shelves. There was a potent drug included, a nembutal derivative, hypnite. A small intramuscular injection could knock Varris out; he would awaken into a confused, passive state and remain thus for hours, following any lead he was given. Much useful information about his conspiracy could be extracted. Later, this drug and other techniques would be used to rehabilitate his twisted psyche, but that was a job for the specialists at Main Base.

Alak felt more handcuffed than ever before in his pragmatist life. The blaster at his waist could incinerate a squad of

Thunsban knights—but their anachronistic weapons weren't so ridiculous when he wasn't allowed to use the blaster.

"Hurry it up," he said on a harsh note. "Let's get moving—and don't ask me where!"

A landing field had been made for the traders just outside the walls of Wainabog. Those bulked thick and gray, studded with turrets and men-at-arms, over a blue landscape of rolling fields and distant hills. Here and there Alak saw thatch-roofed hamlets; two kilometers from the town was a smaller community, also fortified, a single great tower in its middle crowned with a golden X. It must be the place mentioned in the trader narratives. Grimmoch Abbey, was that the name?

It was not too bad a mistranslation to speak of abbeys, monks, knights, and kings. Culturally and technologically, Thunsba was fairly close to medieval Europe.

Several peasants and townsfolk stood gaping at the flitter as Alak emerged. Others were on their way. He swept his gaze around the field and saw another spaceboat some distance off—must be Varris', yes, he remembered the description now. A dozen liveried halberdiers guarded it.

Carefully ignoring the drab-clad commons, Alak waited for the official greeters. Those came out in a rattle of plate armor, mounted on yellow-furred animals with horns and shoulder humps. A band of crossbowmen trotted in their wake and a herald wearing a scarlet robe blew his trumpet in their van. They pulled up with streaming banners and thunderous hoofs; lances dipped courteously, but eyes had a watchful stare behind the snouted visors of their helmets.

The herald rode forth and looked down at Alak, who was clad in his brightest dress uniform. "Greeting to you, stranger, from our lord Morlach, King of all Thunsba and Defender of the West. Our lord Morlach bids you come sup and sleep with him." The herald drew a sword and extended it hilt first. Alak ran hastily through his lessons and rubbed his forehead against the handle.

They were quite humanoid on Ryfin's Planet—disturbingly

so, if you hadn't seen as many species as Alak. It was not the pale-blue skin or the violet hair or the short tails which made the difference: always, in a case like this, the effect was of a subtler wrongness. Noses a shade too long, faces a trifle too square, knees and elbows held at a peculiar angle—they looked like cartoon figures brought to life. And they had a scent of their own, a sharp mustardy odor. Alak didn't mind, knowing full well that he looked and smelled as odd to them, but he had seen young recruits get weird neuroses after a few months on a planet of "humanoids to six points of classification."

He replied gravely in the Thunsban tongue: "My lord Morlach has my thanks and duty. I hight Wing Alak, and am not a trader but an envoy of the traders' king, sent hither on a mission most delicate. I pray the right to see my lord Morlach as soon as he grant."

There was more ceremony, and a number of slaves were fetched to carry Alak's impressive burden of gifts. Then he was offered a mount, but declined—the traders had warned him of this little joke, where you put an outworlder on a beast that goes frantic at alien smells. With proper haughtiness he demanded a sedan chair, which was an uncomfortable and seasick thing to ride but had more dignity. The knights of Wainabog enclosed him and he was borne through the gates and the cobbled avenues to the fortresslike palace.

Inside, he did not find the rude splendor he had expected, but a more subtle magnificence, really beautiful furnishings. Thunsba might throw its garbage out in the streets, but had excellent artistic taste. There were a hundred nobles in the royal audience chamber, a rainbow of robes, moving about and talking with boisterous gestures. Servants scurried around offering trays of food and liquor. A small orchestra was playing: the saw-toothed music hurt Alak's ears. A number of monks, in gray robes and with hoods across their faces, stood unspeaking along the walls, near the motionless men-at-arms.

Alak advanced under gleaming pikes and knelt before the

king. Morlach was burly, middle-aged, and long-bearded, wearing a coronet and holding a naked sword on his lap. At his left, the place of honor—most of this species were left-handed—sat an older "man," clean-shaven, hook-nosed, bleak-faced, in yellow robe and a tall bejeweled hat marked with a golden X.

"My duty to you, puissant lord Morlach. Far have I, unworthy Wing Alak of Terra, come to behold your majesty, before whom the nations tremble. From my king unto you, I bear a message and these poor gifts."

The poor gifts made quite a heap, all the way from clothes and ornaments of lustrous synthetic to flashlights and swords of manganese steel. Ryfin's Planet couldn't legally be given modern tools and weapons—not at their present social stage of war and feudalism—but there was no ban on lesser conveniences which they couldn't reproduce anyhow.

"Well met, Sir Wing Alak. Come, be seated at my right." Morlach's voice rose, and the buzzing voices, already lowered in curiosity, stopped at once. "Be it known to all men, Sir Wing Alak is in truth my guest, most holy and inviolable, and all injuries to him, save in lawful duel, are harms to me and my house which the Allshaper bids me avenge."

The nobles crowded closer. It was not a very formal court, as such things go. One of them came to the front as Alak mounted the high seat. The Patrolman felt a tingle along his back and a primitive stirring in his scalp.

Samel Varris.

The refugee war lord was dressed like the other aristocrats, a gaudy robe of puffed and slashed velvet, hung with ropes of jewels. Alak guessed correctly that a royal guardsman ranked very high indeed, possessing his own lands and retinue. Varris was a big dark man with arrogant features and shrewd eyes. Recognition kindled in him, and he strode forward and made an ironic bow.

"Ah, Sir Wing Alak," he said in Thunsban. "I had not awaited the honor of your calling on me yourself."

King Morlach huffed and laid a ringed hand on his sword. "I knew not you twain were acquainted."

Alak covered an empty feeling with his smoothest manner. "Yes, my lord, Varris and I have jousted erenow. Indeed, my mission hither concerns him."

"Came you to fetch him away?" It was a snarl, and the nobility of Wainabog reached for their daggers.

"I know not what he has told you, my lord—"

"He came hither because foemen had overwhelmed his own kingdom and sought his life. Noble gifts did he bring me, not least of them one of the flamer-weapons your folk are so niggardly with, and he gave wise redes by which we hurled back the armies of Rachanstog and wrung tribute out of their ruler." Morlach glared from lowered brows. "Know then, Sir Wing Alak, that though you are my guest and I may not harm you, Sir Varris has taken oaths as my guardsman and served right loyally. For this I have given him gold and a broad fief. The honor of my house is sacred . . . if you demand he be returned to his foes, I must ask that you leave at once and when next we meet it shall be the worse for you!"

Alak pursed his lips to whistle, but thought better of it. Handing out a blaster—! It was unimportant in itself, the firearm would be useless once its charge was spent, but as a measure of Varris' contempt for Galactic law—

"My lord," he said hastily, "I cannot deny I had such a request. But it was never the intent of my king or myself to insult your majesty. The request will not be made of you."

"Let there be peace," said the high priest on Morlach's left. His tone was not as unctuous as the words: here was a fighter, in his own way, more intelligent and more dangerous than the brawling warriors around him. "In the name of the Allshaper, we are met in fellowship. Let not black thoughts give to the Evil an entering wedge."

Morlach swore.

"In truth, my lord, I bear this envoy no ill will," smiled Varris. "I vouch that he is knightly, and wishes but to serve his king as well as I seek to serve yourself. If my holy lord abbot"—the title was nearly equivalent—"calls peace on this hall, then I for one will abide by it."

"Yes . . . a sniveling shavechin to whine peace when treachery rises," growled Morlach. "You have enough good lands which should be mine, Abbot Gulmanan—keep your greasy fingers off my soul, at least!"

"What my lord says to me is of no consequence," answered the cleric thinly. "But if he speaks against the Temple, he blasphemes the Allshaper."

"Hell freeze you, I'm a pious man!" roared Morlach. "I make the sacrifices—for the Allshaper, though not for his fat-gutted Temple that would push me off my own throne!"

Gulmanan flushed purple, but checked himself a bit, narrow lips together, and made a bridge of his bony fingers. "This is not the time or place to question where the ghostly and the worldly authorities have their proper bounds," he said. "I shall sacrifice for your soul, my lord, and pray you be led out of error."

Morlach snorted and called for a beaker of wine. Alak sat inconspicuously till the king's temper had abated. Then he began to speak of increased trade possibilities.

He had not the slightest power to make treaties, but he wanted to be sure he wasn't kicked out of Wainabog yet.

Heavily dosed with anti-allergen, Alak was able to eat enough of the king's food to cement his status as guest. But Drogs brought him a case of iron rations when the Galmathian came to attend his "master" in the assigned palace apartment.

The human sat moodily by the window, looking out at the glorious night sky of clotted stars and two moons. There was a fragrant garden beneath him, under the bleak castle walls. Somewhere a drunken band of nobles was singing—he had left the feast early and it was still carousing on. A few candles lit the tapestried dankness of the room; they were perfumed, but not being a Ryfinnian he did not enjoy the odor of mercaptan.

"If we got several thousand husky Patrolmen," he said, "and put them in armor, and equipped them with clubs, we might slug our way in and out of this place. Right now I can't think of anything else."

"Well, why don't we?" Drogs hunched over a burbling water pipe, cheerfully immune to worry.

"It lacks finesse. Nor is it guaranteed—these Thunsbans are pretty hefty too, they might overpower our men. If we used tanks or something to make ourselves invincible, it'd be just our luck to have some gallant fathead of a knight get squashed under the treads. Finally, with the trouble at Sannanton going on, the Patrol can't spare so large a force—and by the time they can, it might well be too late. Those unprintable traders must have told half the League that Varris has been found. We can look for a rescue attempt from Caldon within a week."

"Hm-m-m . . . according to your account, the local church is at loggerheads with the king. Maybe it can be persuaded to do our work for us. Nothing in the Prime Directive forbids letting entities murder each other."

"No—I'm afraid the Temple priests are only allowed to fight in self-defense, and these people never break a law." Alak rubbed his chin. "You may have the germ of an idea there, though. I'll have to—"

The gong outside the door was struck. Drogs humped across the floor and opened.

Varris came in, at the head of half a dozen warriors. Their drawn blades gleamed against flickering shadow.

Alak's blaster snaked out. Varris grinned and lifted his hand. "Don't be so impetuous," he advised. "These boys are only precautionary. I just wanted to talk."

Alak took out a cigarette and puffed it into lighting. "Go on, then," he invited tonelessly.

"I'd like to point out a few things, that's all." Varris was speaking Terran; the guards waited stolidly, not understanding, their eyes restless. "I wanted to say I'm a patient man, but there's a limit to how much persecution I'll stand for."

"Persecution! Who ordered the massacres at New Venus?"

Fanaticism smoldered in Varris' eyes, but he answered quietly: "I was the legitimately chosen dictator. Under Caldonian law, I was within my rights. It was the Patrol which engineered the revolution. It's the Patrol which now maintains a hated colonialism over my planet."

"Yes—until such time as those hellhounds you call people have had a little sense beaten into them. If you hadn't been stopped, there'd be more than one totally dead world by now." Alak's smile was wintry. "You'll comprehend that for yourself, once we've normalized your psyche."

"You can't cleanly execute a man." Varris paced tiger-fashion. "You have to take and twist him till everything that was holy to him has become evil and everything he despised is good. I'll not let that happen to me."

"You're stuck here," said Alak. "I know your boat is almost out of fuel. Incidentally, in case you get ideas, mine is quite thoroughly booby-trapped. All I need do is holler for reinforcements. Why not surrender now and save me the trouble?"

Varris grinned. "Nice try, friend, but I'm not that stupid. If the Patrol could have sent more than you to arrest me, it would have done so. I'm staying here and gambling that a rescue party from Caldon will arrive before your ships get around to it. The odds are in my favor."

His finger stabbed out. "Look here! By choice, I'd have my men cut you down where you stand—you and that slimy little monster. I can't, because I have to live up to the local code of honor; they'd throw me out if I broke the least of their silly laws. But I can maintain a large enough bodyguard to prevent you from kidnaping me, as you've doubtless thought of doing."

"I had given the matter some small consideration," nodded Alak.

"There's one other thing I can do, too. I can fight a duel with you. A duel to the death—they haven't any other kind."

"Well, I'm a pretty good shot."

"They won't allow modern weapons. The challenged party has the choice, but it's got to be swords or axes or bows or—something provided for in their law." Varris laughed. "I've spent a lot of time this past year, practicing with just such arms. And I went in for fencing at home. How much training have you had?"

Alak shrugged. Not being even faintly a romantic, he had never taken much interest in archaic sports.

"I'm good at thinking up nasty tricks," he said. "Suppose I chose to fight you with clubs, only I had a switchblade concealed in mine."

"I've seen that kind of thing pulled," said Varris calmly. "Poison is illegal, but gimmicks of the kind you mention are accepted. However, the weapons must be identical. You'd have to get me with your switchblade the first try—and I don't think you could—or I'd see what was going on and do the same. I assure you, the prospect doesn't frighten me at all.

"I'll give you a few days here to see how hopeless your problem is. If you turn your flitter's guns on the city, or on me . . . well, I have guns, too. If you aren't out of the kingdom in a week—or if you begin to act suspiciously before that time—I'll duel you."

"I'm a peaceable man," said Alak. "It takes two to make a duel."

"Not here, it doesn't. If I insult you before witnesses, and you don't challenge me, you lose knightly rank and are whipped out of the country. It's a long walk to the border, with a bull whip lashing you all the way. You wouldn't make it alive."

"All right," sighed Alak. "What do you want of me?"

"I want to be let alone."

"So do the people you were going to make war on last year."

"Good night." Varris turned and went out the door. His men followed him.

Alak stood for a while in silence. Beyond the walls, he could hear the night wind of Ryfin's Planet. Somehow, it was a foreign wind, it had another sound from the rushing air of Terra. Blowing through different trees, across an unearthly land—

"Have you any plan at all?" murmured Drogs.

"I had one." Alak clasped nervous hands behind his back. "He doesn't *know* I won't bushwhack him, or summon a force of gunners, or something lethal like that. I was figuring on a bluff—but it seems he has called me. He wants to be sure of taking at least one Patrolman to hell with him."

"You could study the local *code duello*," suggested Drogs. "You could let him kill you in a way which looked like a technical foul. Then the king would boot him out and I could arrest him with the help of a stun beam."

"Thanks," said Alak. "Your devotion to duty is really touching."

"I remember a Terran proverb," said Drogs. Galmathian humor can be quite heavy at times. " 'The craven dies a thousand deaths, the hero dies but once.' "

"Yeah. But you see, I'm a craven from way back. I much prefer a thousand synthetic deaths to one genuine case. As far as I'm concerned, the live coward has it all over the dead hero—" Alak stopped. His jaw fell down and then snapped up again. He flopped into a chair and cocked his feet up on the windowsill and ran a hand through his ruddy hair.

Drogs returned to the water pipe and smoked imperturbably. He knew the signs. If the Patrol may not kill, it is allowed to do anything else—and sublimated murder can be most fascinatingly fiendish.

In spite of his claims to ambassadorial rank, Alak found himself rating low—his only retinue was one ugly nonhumanoid. But that could be useful. With their faintly contemptuous indifference, the nobles of Wainabog didn't care where he was.

He went, the next afternoon, to Grimmoch Abbey.

An audience with Gulmanan was quickly granted. Alak crossed a paved courtyard, strolled by a temple where the hooded monks were holding an oddly impressive service, and entered a room in the great central tower. It was a large room, furnished with austere design but lavish materials, gold and silver and gems and brocades. One wall was covered by bookshelves, illuminated folios, many of them secular. The abbot sat stiffly on a carved throne of rare woods. Alak made the required prostration and was invited to sit down.

The old eyes were thoughtful, watching him. "What brought you here, my cub?"

"I am a stranger, holy one," said the human. "I understand little of your faith, and considered it shame that I did not know more."

"We have not yet brought any outworlder to the Way," said the abbot gravely. "Except, of course, Sir Varris, and I am afraid his devotions smack more of expediency than conviction."

"Let me at least hear what you believe," asked the Patrolman with all the earnestness he could summon in daylight.

Gulmanan smiled, creasing his gaunt blue face. "I have a suspicion that you are not merely seeking the Way," he replied. "Belike there is some more temporal question in your mind."

"Well—" They exchanged grins. You couldn't run a corporation as big as this abbey without considerable hardheadedness.

Nevertheless, Alak persisted in his queries. It took an hour to learn what he wanted to know.

Thunsba was monotheistic. The theology was subtle and complex, the ritual emotionally satisfying, the commandments flexible enough to accommodate ordinary fleshly weaknesses. Nobody doubted the essential truth of the religion; but its Temple was another matter.

As in medieval Europe, the church was a powerful organization, international, the guardian of learning and the gradual civilizer of a barbarous race. It had no secular clergy—every priest was a monk of some degree, inhabiting a large or small monastery. Each of these was ruled by one officer—Gulmanan in this case—responsible to the central Council in Augnachar city; but distances being great and communications slow, this supreme authority was mostly background.

The clergy were celibate and utterly divorced from the civil regime, with their own laws and courts and punishments. Each detail of their lives, down to dress and diet, was minutely prescribed by an unbreakable code—there were no special dispensations. Entering the church, if you were approved, was only a matter of taking vows; getting out was not so easy, requiring a Council decree. A monk owned nothing; any property he might have had before entering reverted to his heirs, any marriage he might have made was automatically annulled. Even Gulmanan could not call the clothes he wore or the lands he ruled his own: it all belonged to the corporation, the abbey. And the abbey was rich; for centuries, titled Thunsbans had given it land or money.

Naturally, there was conflict between church and king. Both sought power, both claimed overlapping prerogatives, both insisted that theirs was the final authority. Some kings had had abbots murdered or imprisoned, some had gone weakly to Canossa. Morlach was in-between, snarling at the Temple but not quite daring to lay violent hands on it.

". . . I see." Alak bowed his head. "Thank you, holy one."

"I trust your questions are all answered?" The voice was dry.

"Well, now . . . there are some matters of business—" Alak sat for a moment, weighing the other. Gulmanan seemed thoroughly honest; a direct bribe would only be an insult. But honesty is more malleable than one might think—

"Yes? Speak without fear, my cub. No words of yours shall pass these walls."

Alak plunged into it: "As you know, my task is to remove Sir Varris to his own realm for punishment of many evil deeds."

"He has claimed his cause was righteous," said Gulmanan noncommittally.

"And so he believes. But in the name of that cause, he was prepared to slay more folk than dwell on this entire world."

"I wondered about that—"

Alak drew a long breath and then spoke fast. "The Temple is eternal, is it not? Of course. Then it must look centuries ahead. It must not let one man, whose merits are doubtful at best, stand in the way of an advancement which could mean saving thousands of souls."

"I am old," said Gulmanan in a parched tone. "My life has not been as cloistered as I might have wished. If you are proposing that you and I could work together to mutual advantage, say so."

Alak made a sketchy explanation. "And the lands would be yours," he finished.

"Also the trouble, my cub," said the abbot. "We already have enough clashes with King Morlach."

"This would not be a serious one. The law would be on our side."

"Nevertheless, the honor of the Temple may not be compromised."

"In plain words, you want more than I've offered."

"Yes," said Gulmanan bluntly.

Alak waited. Sweat studded his body. What could he do if an impossible demand was made?

The seamed blue face grew wistful. "Your race knows much," said the abbot. "Our peasants wear out their lives, struggling against a miserly soil and seasonal insect hordes. Are there ways to better their lot?"

"Is that all? Certainly there are. Helping folk progress when they wish to is one of our chief policies. My . . . my king would be only too glad to lend you some technicians—farmwrights?—and show you how."

"Also . . . it is pure greed on my part. But sometimes at night, looking up at the stars, trying to understand what the traders have said—that this broad fair world of ours is but a mote spinning through vastness beyond comprehension—it has been an anguish in me that I do not know how that is." Now it was Gulmanan who leaned forward and shivered. "Would it be possible to . . . to translate a few of your books on this science astronomic into Thunsban?"

Alak regarded himself as a case-hardened cynic. In the line of duty, he had often and cheerfully broken the most solemn oaths with an audible snap. But this was one promise he meant to keep though the sky fell down.

On the way back, he stopped at his flitter, where Drogs was hiding from a gape-mouthed citizenry, and put the Galmathian to work in the machine shop.

A human simply could not eat very much of this planet's food; he would die in agony. Varris had taken care to have a food-synthesizer aboard his boat, and ate well that night of special dishes. He did not invite Alak to join him, and the Patrolman munched gloomily on what his service imagined to be an adequate, nutritious diet.

After supper, the nobles repaired to a central hall, with a fireplace at either end waging hopeless war on the evening chill, for serious drinking. Alak, ignored by most, sauntered through the crowd till he got to Varris. The fugitive was conversing with several barons; from his throne, King Morlach listened interestedly. Varris was increasing his prestige by explaining some principles of games theory which ought to guarantee success in the next war.

". . . And thus, my gentles, it is not that one must seek a

certain victory, for there is no certainty in battle, but must so distribute his forces as to have the greatest *likelihood* of winning—''

''Hogwash!'' snapped Alak. The Thunsban phrase he used was more pungent.

Varris raised his brows. ''Said you something?'' he asked.

''I did.'' Alak slouched forward, wearing his most insolent expression. ''I said it is nonsense you speak.''

''You disagree, then, sir?'' inquired a native.

''Not exactly,'' said the Patrolman. ''It is not worth disagreeing with so lunkheaded a swine as this baseborn Varris.''

His prey remained impassive. There was no tone in the voice: ''I trust you will retract your statement, sir.''

''Yes, perhaps I should,'' agreed Alak. ''It was too mild. Actually, of course, as is obvious from a single glance at his bloated face, Sir Varris is a muckeating sack of lip-wagging flatulence whose habits I will not even try to describe since they would make a barnyard blush.''

Silence hit the hall. The flames roared up the chimneys. King Morlach scowled and breathed heavily, but could not legally interfere. His warriors dropped hands to their knives.

''What's your purpose?'' muttered Varris in Terran.

''Naturally,'' said Alak in Thunsban, ''if Sir Varris does not dispute my assertions, there is no argument.''

The Caldonian sighed. ''I will dispute them on your body tomorrow morning,'' he answered.

Alak's foxy face broke into a delighted grin. ''Do I understand that I am being challenged?'' he asked.

''You do, sir. I invite you to a duel.''

''Very well.'' Alak looked around. Every eye in the place was welded to him. ''My lords, you bear witness that I have been summoned to fight Sir Varris. If I mistake me not, the choice of weapons and ground is mine.''

''Within the laws of single combat,'' rumbled Morlach venomously. ''None of your outworld sorceries.''

''Indeed not.'' Alak bowed. ''I choose to fight with my own swords, which are lighter than your claymores but, I assure you, quite deadly if one does not wear armor. Sir Varris may, of course, have first choice of the pair. The duel will take place just outside the main gate of Grimmoch Abbey."

There was nothing unusual about that. A badly wounded contestant could be taken into the monks, who were also the local surgeons. In such a case, he was allowed to recover after which a return engagement was fought. In the simple and logical belief that enmities should not be permitted to fester, the Thunsban law said that no duel was officially over till one party had been killed. It was the use of light swords that caused interest.

"Very good," said Varris in a frosty voice. He was taking it well; only Alak could guess what worries—*what trap is being set?*—lay behind those eyes. "At dawn tomorrow, then."

"Absolutely not," said Alak firmly. He never got up before noon if he could help it. "Am I to lose my good sleep on account of you? We will meet at the time of Third Sacrifice." He bowed grandly. "Good night, my lord and gentles."

Back in his apartment, he went through the window and, with the help of his small antigrav unit, over the wall and out to his boat. Varris might try to assassinate him as he slept.

Or would the Caldonian simply rely on being a better swordsman? Alak knew that was the case. This might be his last night alive.

A midafternoon sun threw long streamers of light across blue turf and the walls of Grimmoch Abbey. They fell on a hundred-meter square cleared before the gate; beyond that, a crowd of lords and ladies stood talking, drinking, and betting on the outcome. King Morlach watched ominously from a portable throne—he would not thank the man who did away with the useful Sir Varris. Just inside the gateway, Abbot Gulmanan and a dozen monks waited like stone saints.

Trumpets blew, and Alak and Varris stepped forth. Both

wore light shirts and trousers, nothing else. An official frisked them ceremoniously for concealed weapons and armor. The noble appointed Master of Death trod out and recited the code. Then he took a cushion on which the rapiers were laid, tested each, and extended them to Varris.

The outlaw smiled humorlessly and selected one. Alak got the other. The Master of Death directed them to opposite corners of the field.

Alak's blade felt light and supple in his fingers. His vision and hearing were unnaturally clear, it was as if every grass blade stood out sharp before him. Perhaps his brain was storing data while it still could. Varris, one hundred forty meters off, loomed like a giant.

"And now, let the Allshaper defend the right!"

Another trumpet flourish. The duel was on.

Varris walked out, not hurrying. Alak went to meet him. They crossed blades and stood for a moment, eyes thrusting at eyes.

"Why are you doing this?" asked the refugee in Terran. "If you have some idiotic hope of killing me, you might as well forget it. I was a fencing champion at home."

"These shivs are gimmicked," said Alak with a rather forced grin. "I'll let you figure out how."

"I suppose you know the penalty for using poison is burning at the stake—" For a moment, there was a querulous whine in the voice. "Why can't you leave me alone? What business was it ever of yours?"

"Keeping the peace is my business," said Alak. "That's what I get paid for, anyhow."

Varris snarled. His blade whipped out. Alak parried just in time. A thin steel ringing lay in the air.

Varris danced gracefully, aggressively, a cold intent on his face. Alak made wild slashes, handling his rapier like a broadsword. Contempt crossed Varris' mouth. He parried a blow, riposted, and Alak felt pain sting his shoulder. The crowd whooped.

Just one cut! Just one cut before he gets me through the

heart! Alak felt his chest grow warm and wet. A flesh wound, no more. He remembered that he'd forgotten to thumb the concealed button in his hilt, and did so with a curse.

Varris' weapon was a blur before his eyes. He felt another light stab. Varris was playing with him! Coldly, he retreated, to the jeers of the audience, while he rallied his wits.

The thing to do . . . what the devil did you call it, riposte, slash, *en avant*? Varris came close as Alak halted. The Patrolman thrust for his left arm. Varris blocked that one. Somehow, Alak slewed his blade around and pinked the outlaw in the chest.

Now—God help me, I have to survive the next few seconds! The enemy steel lunged for his throat. He slapped it down, clumsily, in bare time. His thigh was furrowed. Varris sprang back to get room. Alak did the same.

Watching, he saw the Caldonian's eyes begin helplessly rolling. The rapier wavered. Alak, deciding he had to make this look good, ran up and skewered Varris in the biceps—a harmless cut, but it bled with satisfactory enthusiasm. Varris dropped his sword and tottered. Alak got out of the way just as the big body fell.

The nobles were screaming. King Morlach roared. The Master of Death rushed out to shove Alak aside. "It is not lawful to smite a fallen man," he said.

"I . . . assure you . . . no such intention—" Alak sat down and let the planet revolve around him.

Abbot Gulmanan and the monks stooped over Varris, examining with skilled fingers. Presently the old priest looked up and said in a low voice that somehow cut through the noise: "He is not badly hurt. He should be quite well tomorrow. Perhaps he simply fainted."

"At a few scratches like that?" bawled Morlach. "Master, check that red-haired infidel's blade! I suspect poison!"

Alak pressed the retracting button and handed over his sword. While it was being inspected, Varris was borne inside the abbey and its gate closed on him. The Master of Death looked at both weapons, bowed to the king, and said puzzledly:

"There is no sign of poison, my lord. And after all, Sir Varris had first choice of glaives . . . and these two are identical, as far as I can see . . . and did not the holy one say he is not really injured?"

Alak swayed erect. "Jussa better man, tha's all," he mumbled. "I won fair an' square. Lemme go get m' hurts dressed—I'll see y' all in the morning—"

He made it to his boat, and Drogs had a bottle of Scotch ready.

It took willpower to be at the palace when the court convened—not that Alak was especially weakened, but the Thunsbans started their day at a hideous hour. In this case, early rising was necessary, because he didn't know when the climax of his plot would be on him.

He got a mixed welcome, on the one hand respect for having overcome the great Sir Varris—at least in the first round—on the other hand, a certain doubt as to whether he had done it fairly. King Morlach gave him a surly greeting, but not openly hostile; he must be waiting for the doctors' verdict.

Alak found a congenial earl and spent his time swapping dirty jokes. It is always astonishing how many of the classics are to be found among all mammalian species. This is less an argument for the prehistoric Galactic Empire than for the parallelism of great minds.

Shortly before noon, Abbot Gulmanan entered. Several hooded monks followed him, bearing weapons—most unusual—and surrounding one who was unarmed. The priest lifted his hand to the king, and the room grew very quiet.

"Well," snapped Morlach, "what brings you hither?"

"I thought it best to report personally on the outcome of the duel, my lord," said Gulmanan. "It was . . . surprising."

"Mean you Sir Varris is dead?" Morlach's eyes flared. He could not fight his own guest, but it would be easy enough to have one of his guardsmen insult Wing Alak.

"No, my lord. He is in good health, his wounds are negligible. But—somehow the grace of the Allshaper fell on him." The abbot made a pious gesture; as he saw Alak, one eyelid dropped.

"What mean you?" Morlach dithered and clutched his sword.

"Only this. As he regained consciousness, I offered him ghostly counsel, as I always do to hurt men. I spoke of the virtues of the Temple, of sanctity, of the dedicated life. Half in jest, I mentioned the possibility that he might wish to remounce this evil world and enter the Temple as a brother. My lord, you can imagine my astonishment when he agreed . . . nay, he insisted on deeding all his lands and treasure to the abbey and taking the vows at once." Gulmanan rolled his eyes heavenward. "Indeed, a miracle!"

"What?" It was a shriek from the king.

The monk who was under guard suddenly tore off his hood. Varris' face glared out. "Help!" he croaked. "Help, my lord! I've been betrayed—"

"There are a dozen brothers who witnessed your acts and will swear to them by the mightiest oaths," said the abbot sternly. "Be still, Brother Varris. If the Evil has reentered your soul, I shall have to set you heavy penances."

"Witchcraft!" It whispered terribly down the long hall.

"All men know that witchcraft has no power inside the walls of a sacred abbey," warned Gulmanan. "Speak no heresies."

Varris looked wildly about at the spears and axes that ringed him in. "I was drugged, my lord," he gasped. "I remember what I did, yes, but I had no will of my own—I followed this old devil's words—" He saw Alak and snarled. *"Hypnite!"*

The Patrolman stepped forth and bowed to the king. "Your

majesty,'' he said, ''Sir Varris-that-was had first choice of blades. But if you wish to inspect them again, I have them here.''

It had been easy enough, after all: two swords with retractable hypodermic needles, only they wouldn't do you any good unless you knew of them and knew where to press. The flitter's machine shop could turn one out in a couple of hours.

Alak handed them to the king from beneath his cloak. Morlach stared at the metal, called for a pair of gauntlets, and broke the blades in his hands. The mechanism lay blatant before him.

''Do you see?'' cried Varris. ''Do you see the poisoned darts? Burn that rogue alive!''

Morlach smiled grimly. ''It shall be done,'' he said.

Alak grinned, and inwardly his muscles tightened. This was the tricky point. If he couldn't carry it off, it meant a pretty agonizing death. ''My lord,'' he answered, ''that were unjust. The weapons are identical, and Sir Varris-that-was had first choice. It is permitted to use concealed extra parts, and not to warn of them.''

''Poison—'' began Morlach.

''But this was not poison. Does not Varris stand hale before you all?''

''Yes—'' Morlach scratched his head. ''But when the next engagement is fought, *I* shall provide the swords.''

''A monk,'' said Gulmanan, ''may not have private quarrels. This novice is to be returned to his cell for fasting and prayer.''

''A monk may be released from his vows under certain conditions,'' argued Morlach. ''I shall see to it that he is.''

''Now hold!'' shouted Wing Alak in his best Shakespearean manner. ''My lord, I have won the duel. It were unlawful to speak of renewing it—for who can fight a dead man?''

''*Won* it?'' Varris wrestled with the sturdy monks gripping his arms. ''Here I stand, alive, ready to take you on again any minute—''

"My lord king," said Alak, "I crave leave to state my case."

The royal brow knotted, but: "Do so," clipped Morlach.

"Very well." Alak cleared his throat. "First, then, I fought lawfully. Granted, there was a needle in each sword of which Sir Varris had not been warned, but that is allowable under the code. It might be said that I poisoned him, but that is a canard, for as you all see he stands here unharmed. The drug I used has only a temporary effect and thus is not, by definition, a poison. Therefore, it was a lawful and just combat."

Morlach nodded reluctantly. "But not a completed battle," he said.

"Oh, it was, my lord. What is the proper termination of a duel? Is it not that one party die as the direct result of the other's craft and skill?"

"Yes . . . of course—"

"Then I say that Varris, though not poisoned, died as an immediate consequence of my wounding him. *He is now dead!* For mark you, he has taken vows as a monk—he did this because of the drug I administered. Those oaths may not be wholly irrevocable, but they are binding on him until such time as the Council releases him from them. And . . . a monk owns no property. His wordly goods revert to his heirs. His wife becomes a widow. He is beyond all civil jurisdiction. He is, in short, *legally dead.*"

"But I stand here!" shouted Varris.

"The law is sacred," declared Alak blandly. "I insist that the law be obeyed. And by every legal definition, you are dead. You are no longer Sir Varris of Wainabog, but Brother Varris of Grimmoch—a quite different person. If this fact be not admitted, then the whole structure of Thunsban society must topple, for it rests on the total separation of civil and ecclesiastical law." Alak made a flourishing bow. "Accordingly, my lord, I am the winner of the duel."

Morlach sat for a long while. His mind must be writhing in his skull, hunting for a way out of the impasse, but there was none.

"I concede it," he said at last, thickly. "Sir Wing Alak, you are the victor. You are also my guest, and I may not harm you . . . but you have till sunset to be gone from Thunsba forever." His gaze shifted to Varris. "Be not afraid. I shall send to the Council and have you absolved of your vows."

"That you may do, lord," said Gulmanan. "Of course, until that decree is passed, Brother Varris must remain a monk, living as all monks do. The law does not allow of exceptions."

"True," grumbled the king. "A few weeks only . . . be patient."

"Monks," said Gulmanan, "are not permitted to pamper themselves with special food. You shall eat the good bread of Thunsba, Brother Varris, and meditate on—"

"I'll die!" gasped the outlaw.

"Quite probably you will depart erelong for a better world," smiled the abbot. "But I may not set the law aside— To be sure, I *could* send you on a special errand, if you are willing to go. An errand to the king of the Galactics, from whom I have requested certain books. Sir Wing Alak will gladly transport you."

Morlach sat unstirring. Nobody dared move in all the court. Then something slumped in Varris. Mutely, he nodded. The armed brethren escorted him out toward the spacefield.

Wing Alak bade the king polite thanks for hospitality and followed them. Otherwise he spoke no word until his prisoner was safely fettered and his boat safely space-borne, with Drogs at the control panel and himself puffing on a good cigar.

Then: "Cheer up, old fellow," he urged. "It won't be so bad. You'll feel a lot better once our psychiatrists have rubbed out those kill-compulsions."

Varris gave him a bloodshot glare. "I suppose you think you're a great hero," he said.

"Lord deliver me, no!" Alak opened a cupboard and took forth the bottle of Scotch. "I'm quite willing to let you have that title. It was your big mistake, you realize. A hero should never tangle with an intelligent coward."